Ticket to Ride

...a musician's journey through the sixties...

Graham Sclater

Cover artwork Anna Turchan

Graham Sclater - Hamburg 1965

Graham Sclater, today working as a music publisher in England, has spent several years of his active career as a musician during the "Hamburg Sound" era in the clubs of the Hanse city.

As organist of "The Wave" "The Birds & Bees" as well as the "Manchester Playboys," he has gained first-hand experience of what he describes so vividly in his debut novel of "Ticket to Ride." Five inexperienced juvenile English beat musicians maturing in a merciless world of prostitution, alcohol, uppers and criminality like on some alien planet.

There are numerous books documenting the iridescent careers of those who have made it to the very top in the world of rock'n'roll. Sclater's novel, however, describes - with an unusual sense of reality - the fate of all those groups who were not quite fortunate enough to have their dreams fulfilled.

"Ticket to Ride" is a monument to those who almost might have succeeded, if their Commer or Bedford van had not decided to take its final breath in the backyard of some obscure German beat club. A highly recommended book which is currently only available in English from Tabitha Books.

Ulf Krüger - K&K oHG *****
Center of Beat Hamburg

This is a gritty and in some places extremely harrowing story about a group of musicians who want to make it big and decide Germany is the best place to go. Their names are Dave Simpson, the driving force and the instigator of the group. Tony Tucker, Jimmy Harris, Adrian Palmer and Gerry Simms more commonly known as Reg because sitting behind the big organ he looked more like Reginald Dixon who played the organ in Blackpool Tower. But put them all together and they became the Cheetahs. They have very little in the way of equipment and even less money, but they have determination, drive and the biting need to be up there on the stage doing what they love to do best. Their journey takes them from England to Germany, from one life style to another totally alien to them, and a life changing experience they will never forget. They played in night clubs, hotels and American Army Bases, in fact those were the nicest places they did play, at least there they received decent food and a habitable place to stay. They started off with a contract to play in a club, but as we see through the book in many cases these contracts are not worth the paper they are written on. Once in Germany they are at the mercy of the venue owners who can decide to get rid of them after one or two nights, which means no money and nowhere to stay.

The Cheetahs have to make themselves available for long hours and little pay and still pander to the owners to keep their slots. The group live together, eat together, sleep together and often do drugs and women together. They are forced to live in close proximity until such times as they find someone else, usually prostitutes, to let them live with them. Drugs are rife, as is alcohol and prostitutes. It is a common occurrence for a prostitute to take a fancy to a musician and bed them when they feel like it. Sex is easily available and the combination of sex, drugs and music is a heady lethal combination. Sexually transmitted diseases are common as is hunger and violence. Ticket to Ride shows us the seamier side of life in Germany in the 60's and how it is easy to fall into the dangers of this kind of living.

The music scene in Germany was in those days fascinating and very unhealthy both physically and mentally. Not everyone was able to cut the mustard. Tony Tucker went back to England because he could no longer cope with the way they lived and he knew if he didn't leave that he might die. Jimmy in particular fell deeply in love with a prostitute and was very willing to share her life, including the child she was having to someone else. The free love and peace of the 1960's was very evident as was the constant drug use and abuse, there were often violent clashes with others, including pimps and gangs etc. There were beatings, and wrecked venues, but eventually they made it reasonably big, although they had also a name change and a change of line up during the time they spent in Germany. They achieved what they had wanted, but at what cost to them both physically and mentally. Was it all really worth it in the end, I will let you decide that when you have read the book.

Graham Sclater has written an exciting, mind blowing graphic detailed novel, which I found extremely entertaining. Quite frankly I had to be dragged away to do other things when I was reading it. I lived those highs and lows with the group, often crying when things were going bad and shouting out for joy when the news was good. I felt every moment of their trip, and in many ways it was like I was there watching them as they lived the story. When asked if that was anything like what he had experienced during his own time in Germany, Graham said that he had been gentle on the readers because what he saw and experienced in Germany was so much more and he felt the readers wouldn't believe it. If that's the case, then I'm glad I was never in Germany then, but I am also very glad that Graham wrote this story. The ending of the story left me wanting more and I hope that Graham will be writing more books in this vein soon.

Yorkie - Airradio *****

Graham Sclater spent much of the sixties playing in beat groups in and around Britain, and more importantly, in Beat Central, Hamburg. Of course, we all know that The Beatles set the beat boom off over in Deutschland, and literally hundreds of English groups went over chasing the same dream. "Ticket to Ride" Sclater's first novel, sees him charting the insane rock & roll life of The Cheetahs, a group of young lads finding their feet (both in music and in their life) slap bang in the middle of the Reeperbahn, the infamous red light district made so famous by the Fab Four.

The book is a cracking little kitchen sink drama, littered with all the hopes and dreams that any young kid with an interest in music has. As opposed to being a wordy effort, that many books of this ilk suffer from, Sclater has kept it simple and straight forward, which allows Sclater to show the reader that he's still a fan, and the enthusiasm he has is shared quickly. From the tales of uppers, backroom sex and teenage fumblings, to name checking vintage gear and records, the whole tone of the book is one shot through Super 8. Obviously, with any book dealing with The Dream, it occasionally gets a little dewy eyed, but this again underlines how much the subject means to Sclater, rather than being someone writing about something from borrowed nostalgia. As Sclater lived it, the devil of the book is in the detail. Ticket to Ride perfectly captures that youthful optimism that was prevalent during the mid sixties, and that feeling that any young Englishman with a guitar or a Vox Continental, could take over the world. Thankfully, Sclater has kept the warts in, with the lads getting 'a dose' and the constant shivering that seems to prevail through the tour.

The innocence that is now lost in teens is alive and well with The Cheetahs. The post war fall out has not given birth to a Cosmopolitan bunch; if we now have backpackers and worldly teens, Ticket to Ride shows a bunch of lads almost unable to look after themselves in what might as well be an alien planet. A lot of music books have the 'us against the world' attitude in the band featured, but Sclater is smart enough to sidestep it. The fractions that appear throughout the shifting hierarchy expertly show how bands operated back then, when rock music was in its infancy, and without a five year plan, and thankfully, an absence of spin and PR.

The book itself is a breeze to read, and difficult to put down. Just about anyone with an interest in music (and not just sixties music) will be able to buy into the ride detailed by Sclater. Ticket to Ride has it all. Prostitution, deceit, drugs, alienation, violence, camaraderie, and most of all, good time rock and roll.

Mof Gimmers **

The Reeperbahn, the notorious red light district of Hamburg, Germany in the 1960s became the veritable porch light drawing bands from England in droves with the promise of becoming the next Fab Four. Ticket to Ride (Tabitha Books), by Graham Sclater, tells the tale of The Cheetahs, a band put together on the promise of a gig in Hamburg. This story is not about the Beatles, this is a story about a band that didn't make it.

The Cheetahs immediately find themselves awash in the sea of all that the 60s mod scene had to offer - prostitution, drugs, booze, venereal disease and even underground abortion. The band finds their sound and loses themselves in the neon lights of the various towns in Germany where they find gigs. At one point, one of the characters perfectly sums the Hamburg experience up as not being about the music, it's about the vices of the Deutschland.

Ticket to Ride has a great pace to it and difficult to put down. I had read another review of the book prior to writing this and they had used the phrase "kitchen sink drama" - this is spot on. The book is not high brow grammatical acrobatics, it is just a story seemingly told from the perspective of a barfly observing this band falling apart and getting chewed up by the scene. All in all, the book exudes the optimism and "damn the torpedoes" attitude of any young rock and roller from any era - definitely recommended!

Van **

Ticket to Ride by Graham Sclater is a gritty and in-depth look at the German music scene in the early to mid 60's - the same ticket to ride the Beatles took. In this case it's the Cheetahs. They get a gig in Hamburg and without a manager they travel to Germany and begin to learn what the music scene there is all about.

It wasn't all glamour and fun times, but those are in this book as well. Musicians and music lovers alike will want to take this ticket and ride and make the journey with the Cheetahs.

Hillorie Rudolph - Music Connection Magazine **

Graham Sclater, today a music publisher in England, was active as a musician in the "Hamburg Sound" era when Germany was fertile ground for English "beat groups" plying their trade and crafting their sound and style. Sclater was there as organist of The Wave, The Birds & Bees and Manchester Playboys. With this "ticket to ride," he gained the experiences translated into fiction form in this, his debut novel.

However, I think this rich trove of experiences would be more entertaining in a work of non-fiction, as anecdotes to add colour to the lives of working musicians, perhaps easily integrated into the largely known history of Brit rock with some occasionally recognized names, albums, etc. This, I think, would add a depth to the story that is currently lacking.

Ticket to Ride is full of wild tales and outlandish incidents as the musicians become prisoners in a foreign land to tiring and harsh transitions from desperation to decadence. Through this, the characters are remarkably flat, lacking in dimension and emerging at the end of their tribulations lacking in real transformation. Sclater fails to give the characters in his work real emotional depth and believable motivations.

However, do not let my arguments against the book detract from its joys. I myself have walked the streets of Hamburg's St. Pauli district and eventually met Erin Ross, who designed posters for Rory Storm and Hurricane, The Beatles, and more. I was hoping for just such an encounter to somehow find my own link to this era and place.

So it is quite fun to muse upon Sclater's book as to what facts and real events are behind the elements of his story. Do we think that we recognize anyone in these scenes, composite and representative characters and dialogue? The chapter titles have lyrical references like the book title, do you recognize them? Also, as a former indie rocker myself I feel a connection to the characters in this book. I have gone through and experienced and seen much of what they have and I think any current or former amateur gigging musician will also make that connection.

Link: Ink19.com***

Titles by Graham Sclater

We're gonna be famous

Hatred is the key

Ticket to ride

Ticket to Ride

...a musician's journey through the sixties...

Graham Sclater

Published by Tabitha Books 2012
First published by Flame Books Ltd in 2006

Tabitha Books is a division of Tabitha Music Limited
Exeter EX2 9DJ England

TabithaBooks@tabithamusic.com

www.tabithabooks.webs.com

Tabitha Books

'Dedicated to the many musicians who followed their impossible dream and the late Tony Ashton, a very special keyboard player and friend.'

Graham Sclater, the author of this book, spent much of the sixties living and working as a musician in Hamburg. *Ticket to Ride* is an account of some of the events that many English groups experienced and wished to forget. It is dedicated to the many musicians who failed to survive the trauma and returned to England.

During the mid-sixties, at the peak of the English group scene in Germany, dozens of groups made the short trip across the English Channel to northern Europe in search of fame and fortune. This novel follows the exploits of a naïve under-age five-piece group from the South West of England as they make the futile search for success in Germany.

Although they set out to follow the path of the Beatles, they soon fall deep into the world that their contemporaries were fortunate enough to escape.

Based predominantly on the Reeperbahn, the Red Light district of Hamburg, the group is soon dragged down, their lives affected forever by the everyday world of prostitution, sex, drugs and violence, resulting in a total breakdown of the values that they once believed in. Realising too late that they have no way out, the story charts their desperation and untimely failure.

'Given the opportunity, I would do it all over again.'

Reg Simms - Organist - The Cheetahs 1967

Acknowledgements

Denise who spent many weeks editing my words, Fedia Lavrov - my Russian buddy, Malcolm Littler for returning to Hamburg with me to photograph my old haunts and relive my memories, Annie Samuels for the wonderful massages after a long day at my PC, Chris Bailey for her encouragement and belief, Juan Artes for his support, Steve Osborne for his ongoing help and support with interviews, Ulf Kruger @ K & K Hamburg, Andrea Lownes, Anna Turchan, Antje Voit for the "original" Star Club badge and all those who reviewed the book.

Contents

Foreword

The mid to late sixties was a magical period, never to be repeated. Everyone had hope, none more than the young people did.

The new generation - my generation.

Everything was possible. If you had a dream, you could achieve it. Conscription had been abolished, there was little or no unemployment, and whilst some of the jobs were no more than a way to earn enough to buy the latest fashionable clothes, or an LP or 45 by your favourite group, there was a feeling of optimism as things began to happen so fast, especially in the world of fashion, music and drugs.

The Mods tried to rule, egged on by groups like the Who, Small Faces and the Kinks, whilst the Rockers tried to hold on to their old Rock and Roll heroes of the late fifties and early sixties, such as Gene Vincent, Eddie Cochran, Billy Fury and, of course, Elvis Presley. Although they tried to ignore the new sounds, they would soon become very aware of the new styles of music played by groups like the Rolling Stones, the Troggs, Status Quo, and the numerous American groups and artists who suddenly appeared, and just as rapidly disappeared back across the Atlantic. Exceptions were Bob Dylan, Jimi Hendrix and a stream of black artists producing record after record of the inspirational, rootsy soul music.

The Sixties was the era of Flower Power: massive outdoor Pop concerts, beginning with Woodstock; Super groups; all nighters at clubs and parties; drug experimentation; Radio Luxembourg; James Bond; and Brian Matthew's Saturday Club. The numerous floating Pirate radio stations triggered the launch of Radio One, and television shows such as Ready Steady Go and Top of the Pops.

Anyone who wanted to play a musical instrument, providing that they could find the deposit and a sucker to sign as a guarantor, could get H.P. - a hire-purchase loan, for whatever instrument they wanted. Whether they could play it, or would ever strike it rich, was another matter.

The more proficient, confident, but often foolhardy musicians travelled to Germany, following in the path of the Beatles, to try their luck in the larger cities such as Hamburg, Hanover, Munich and

Frankfurt, where the clubs and German girls had an almost insatiable appetite for English groups.

Some of these musicians made it, most didn't - this is the story of one of them.

Ticket to Ride

a musician's journey through the sixties

Graham Sclater

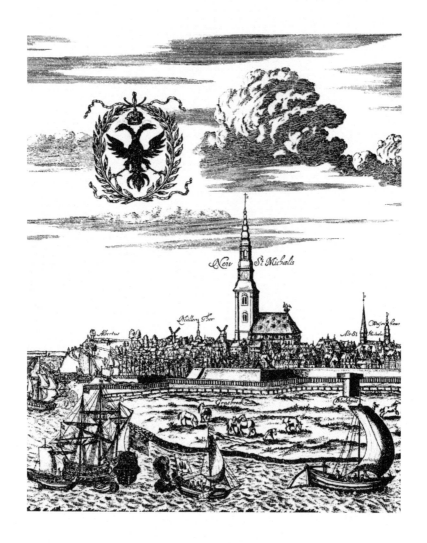

Hamburg

Chapter one

Hello Goodbye

March 1967

The rusty, mud-splattered van made its way uncertainly between rows of identical brick terraced houses. The acrid smoke from the coal fires created a blue haze that hung above the frost covered rooftops, partially obscuring the clear blue morning sky.

The van pulled into the kerb and came to a standstill at the corner of the street. The driver's door slid open noisily and Barry, a tall young man, climbed out. With a sigh he leaned against the van, tilted his head back towards the weak wintry sun and smiled. For a split second he seemed to enjoy the morning until he coughed and, shaking with the cold, thrust his hand deep into his army surplus overcoat pocket and pulled out a soft packet of Lord cigarettes and a shiny Zippo lighter.

The passenger door opened, grinding against the distorted bodywork and Ronnie, a petite young girl jumped out, pulled her collar around her bare neck and straightened her creased coat.

Without a word she snatched a cigarette from Barry, walked to the rear of the van and threw open the doors.

The driver watched impatiently and kicked at the pavement with his worn Cuban heeled boots as he tried to warm his feet..

Ronnie climbed onto the rear bumper and, reaching into the darkness, poked blindly at a pile of torn and frayed blankets on top of the neatly stacked equipment.

There was movement beneath the blankets and she helped the passenger to slide down onto the pavement. He stood, shaking and coughing, while she tugged at the tangled mass pulling one of them down and smelling it before wrapping it around him. He turned his head from side to side and, blinded by the weak sun, squinted until he recognised the house in front of him.

Although the van had been stationary for only a few minutes, the remaining passengers bawled out at her. 'Come on Ronnie. What's the sodding hold up?'

'We wanna get home as well you know!'

'Yeah, we're freezing our balls off in here.'

She shouted back at them. 'Shut up you bastards! Just give us another minute will yer?'

Ronnie walked towards the passenger door but before reaching it hammered repetitively against the side of the van with her tiny hands.

She screamed again, 'You'll just have to bloody well wait until I'm ready. What difference do you think another few minutes is going to make to you idle sods? If you want to get home, get your lazy arses out here and help us.'

Their response was total silence.

While Barry wrestled with some of the van's contents, piling it against the wall of the house, their deathly pale passenger stumbled across the road dragging the blanket along the ground behind him.

Ronnie, her age belying her girlie looks, ran over and propped him up against the door while Barry, now satisfied with his handiwork, walked back towards the van and slid open the door. He shivered, lit another cigarette and watched in amazement as she wrapped the blanket even more tightly around her patient.

'Come on Ronnie, we gotta go now,' he said impatiently.

She threw him a fierce look and he continued softly. 'Oh, come on Ron, we've done all we can for him. Let's go.'

Ignoring Barry, she concentrated her efforts on gently patting her patient several times on the back and shoulder. 'Good luck Reg, you should be all right now.'

He acknowledged her with the slightest movement of his head.

Ronnie glanced back once more as she walked towards the van, before climbing inside. As it pulled away in a cloud of smoke, she gently rubbed her cold hands and concentrated on giving directions to an impatient Barry. 'I hope the poor sod's going to be alright,' she said, shaking her head. 'He's such a great player.'

Barry ignored her as he cleared the windscreen and lit yet another cigarette. A few minutes later he turned and gave her a long hard look of indifference. 'He was once... who really gives a toss? We should have left him in Hamburg.'

He took a deep drag of his cigarette, changed gear and feigned concentration as he accelerated on to the dual carriageway.

Reg summoned every ounce of strength, pressed the doorbell, then slumped awkwardly down onto one knee, coughing and retching.

An attractive woman answered the door. Although still relatively young, she looked tired and drawn. Her long grey hair aged her dramatically. At first she saw no one but, on looking down, noticed the stranger slumped on the top step draped in the filthy blankets. She stepped back. 'Can I help you?'

Reg mumbled to her but she had difficulty making out what he was saying. She hesitated before nervously repeating her question. 'I'm sorry, but can I help you?'

'Mum... it's me... I've come home,' he whispered, and slid down onto the bottom step, fighting for breath.

A young teenage girl, wearing a dressing gown and matching slippers, joined the woman at the door. 'Who is it mum?' she asked inquisitively.

'I don't know!' screamed the woman. Nervously she lifted the filthy scarf from the stranger's face and pulled her head back in disgust. She screwed up her face and staring closely at the contorted lifeless face, she cried out, 'It can't be... My God, it's Gerald. Come on Jenny, help me get him inside.'

'Gerald?' repeated the young girl.

They struggled to lift him into the nearest room and laid him gently on the settee. They propped his head with the hand embroidered cushions and gently covered him with the coats which were hanging on the back of the door.

Shaking uncontrollably, his mother reached into her apron pocket, opened her purse and blindly passed her daughter a handful of coins. 'Jenny, go and telephone Doctor Hutchings.'

'But mum, I'm not dressed,' she pleaded.

'Go on... don't worry about that... just hurry up!'

Jenny tightened her dressing gown around her and ran across the road to the nearby telephone box.

Gerald coughed heavily and started to fight for breath. His mother rushed into the kitchen and returned with a small bottle, carefully shook out a yellow tablet, pushed it into his mouth and forced it under his tongue.

'Gerald, why didn't you tell me you were in trouble? We could have done something to help,' she whispered, glancing across at the box containing the letters she had read and re-read every night before crying herself to sleep.

Gerald lay staring at the room.

Nothing had changed since the day he'd left. The wallpaper complemented by brightly coloured curtains and carpet, two large cut glass fruit bowls on the polished rosewood sideboard, and in front of the window, the radiogram which had stood silent for more than a year. In pride of place on the mantelpiece was a photograph of his mother flanked by a very different Gerald and his sister.

Jenny returned, pleased with her efforts and speaking as she exhaled. Short of breath, her sentence ended in a whisper. 'The doctor will be here as soon as he's finished his surgery.'

Gerald's mother took her eyes off him for a split second, smiled, and silently thanked her daughter.

'Mum, he looks so old, but he's only… seventeen.'

His mother knelt beside him and stroked his matted hair. 'I know, but he's home now, and it's up to us to help him the best we can.' She tried not to cry but the tears continued to build up until she could no longer contain them. Through her tears she could see only blurred images. The deep shadows around his sunken eyes, the yellow poisonous lumps that covered much of his pale face. Open sores covered his mouth and nose, and beneath his long greasy hair, spots festered on his neck and ears.

Gerald's skeletal frame shook violently as he continued to cough loudly.

Jenny attempted to comfort her mother; something that had become second nature to her since Gerald left them a little over a year earlier. 'Shall we try and get him upstairs Mum?'

Gerald moaned in pain.

'No, just leave him where he is. The doctor will be here in a few minutes, let's wait and see what he suggests before we do anything,' said his mother.

The doorbell finally rang and Jenny rushed to the open door and led the doctor into the dimly lit room. Doctor Hutchings knelt down beside Gerald and stared at him for a moment, as he became accustomed to the poor light. He opened his worn bag and meticulously checked his patient before giving him an injection. Still holding Gerald's wrist, he continued to subconsciously take his pulse before finally returning his stethoscope to his case.

'Mrs Simms, could I speak to you alone?' he said.

She didn't hear him. He turned to look at Jenny and continued to stare at her until, reluctantly, she left the room.

'I've given Gerald an injection of cortisone that should help his chest.' He turned awkwardly to look down at his patient. 'I... I... must be blunt. I've seen starving animals in better condition. How on earth did he get like this?' He pushed the coats tightly around Gerald's shrunken body while he waited for an answer.

Unable to take her eyes off her prematurely aged son, Mrs Simms replied slowly. 'Gerald's been in Germany.'

He gave her a concerned look. 'The Forces?'

She couldn't look directly at him. 'No...' she replied nervously, 'he played in a group.' She coughed and whispered, '...a musician.'

Doctor Hutchings suddenly lost much of his concern and nodded knowingly. 'Maybe that explains it.'

He looked at Gerald and then sternly at his mother. 'He is extremely poorly Mrs Simms. He's emaciated, he has pneumonia and a serious chest infection, and... I can't be sure... we will need to carry out tests, but I think that Gerald....' He paused before finishing his diagnosis and slowly shook his head, 'your son... well... he may have also contracted Syphilis.'

'Syphil....' She couldn't repeat it.

The Doctor spoke gently. 'Perhaps I'm wrong, but I'll arrange for an ambulance. We'll get him into hospital and in a few days we'll know one way or another.

Chapter two

The Times they are a Changing

October 1965

The Cheetahs came together by chance.

Never failing to seize any opportunity, Dave Simpson was in the right place, and the mid sixties was certainly the right time.

He was a little overweight and not particularly good looking but he was already the singer of a successful local dance band and at 21, having gained the experience from his crippled mother, Freda, a local agent, had already learnt how to take care of business.

Dave's parents, Jim and Freda, met at the local dance hall at the beginning of the war. Jim, a printer by trade and considered to be vital to the war effort, was not conscripted. Being available and with the enforced shortage of suitable musicians he became the drummer in a local dance band. Freda was the glamorous singer and within a few short weeks they became inseparable. However, their world changed dramatically when Freda badly damaged her leg fooling about on a bombsite. Her reluctance and stubbornness to accept treatment allowed gangrene to set in and her right leg was amputated within three weeks of an injury that ironically could have been treated without any long-term effects.

Jim and Freda were married soon after the accident in 1943. Dave arrived in early 1945 and, due to Freda's disability and the baby; soon after the war they were given a new council house and a telephone.

Freda hated to be seen in a wheelchair and within a few months became a recluse. With the addition of a dark green wartime blackout roller blind which was permanently pulled down, obscuring all natural light from the outside world, she based herself on a chaise longue and lived, worked and slept in the sitting room. With the wireless and telephone being her only contact with the fast changing outside world, she turned the disability to her advantage and in less than two years had sole agency with numerous concert halls, social and youth clubs. In the mid 50's she booked dance bands and trios but as the interest in Rock and Roll grew she engaged bigger names from out of town, making her a powerful woman. Her love affair with the telephone and never knowing or caring if it was day or night ensured she was available at any time. Consequently she soon built up an enviable reputation for reliability by putting in another act or band if a club was let down.

After leaving school Dave took a job as a sales assistant in Horne Brothers, where he was able to buy all his clothes at a discount, or if he was lucky, damaged or soiled stock for next to nothing. He loved his suits and built up a passion to show them off on stage.

He was not slow in realising that with his mother's contacts he could pick all the best venues to play so he used his inside information to poach the better players. Freda did a deal with Bill Hitchins, the saxophonist from her old band and owner of the town's biggest music shop, to supply him with a pair of Selmer column speakers and amp. And with Bill's contacts, Dave put together a mixed band of musicians of all ages.

Within three weeks, he was the proud singer of a new dance band Music Box that soon became the envy of many of the new groups springing up in every street.

The times they were a changing.

In the late fifties and early sixties most groups played instrumentals and there was therefore no need for a microphone or public address system. Whenever anyone needed to make an announcement, it was made through a microphone plugged into the nearest guitarist's amplifier. Business for every music shop was booming. There were so many groups, many who practised for a few days and then, realising that they had no chance, split up before the end of the week.

The demand following the success of the Beatles and other vocal groups had caused a tremendous shortage of amplification, especially portable P.A. systems. Vox, Selmer and Marshall were all competing with each other to supply bigger, better and more efficient column speakers.

Music Box was a new type of band, playing all styles of music including early Rock and Roll, some of the newer hit songs, and instrumentals. Consequently, they were booked to play all over Devon, Cornwall, and Somerset, sometimes supporting name recording groups from as far away as London.

The instrumental tunes gave Dave time to chat up the most likely but unsuspecting young swooning girl who made the mistake of standing in front of the stage. He had the knack of slipping away during the interval or after a show with any girl he found would accommodate him; in the van, against the nearest wall, or on the grass in the summer, he didn't care. Perhaps his fans liked it that way?

Whenever Music Box returned to a dance hall, Dave's conquest from the previous visit would always be waiting at the front of the stage panting in anticipation. Being the singer, he was the most successful - the girls always fancied the singer - but if he was otherwise engaged they would look further afield at the musicians standing impatiently behind him.

Dave became frustrated singing in what was a glorified dance band. He wanted to play the new music with his own group of young musicians, not the hotch potch of young and the much older ex-army musicians, who of course could play. Compared to the new generation of groups and musicians, they were brilliant, but they lacked the edge. The fact was they played too well.

Music Box was exactly what their name suggested. They played everything, from a waltz and quickstep to the number one record of the week. Unfortunately for Dave the audience seldom reacted to the music. Perhaps there would be a small round of appreciation after the latest Beatles tune but certainly not for Pat Boone, Eddie Calvert, Russ Conway or the odd Ruby Murray and Doris Day songs featuring Harry, the trumpet player, who regularly sang his heart out centre stage while Dave was in the van or backstage satisfying his adoring female fans.

Following repossession of his drummer's 'skins,' Dave was desperate for a replacement.

Once again, he was fortunate. Anthony Tucker, or Tony as he wanted to be known, was less than five foot three, bespectacled and well overweight. Despite his size and looks he did have a shiny new Sonor drum kit.

The turning point came when Tony joined the band.

New to the scene, he needed constant reassurance of his abilities and this always came at the end of the first half with his drum solo in *Diamonds*, a song recorded by Jet Harris and Tony Meehan. In the second half, as he thrashed around the kit playing the whole of the drum solo of Sandy Nelson's hit, *Let There Be Drums*, his inhibitions faded away and for a few minutes he looked and played like a true musician.

Dave saw Tony as the first step in fulfilling his dream. He had his own drums, no ties and knew many of the latest tunes.

Freda's highlight of the day was opening the post. She had perfected her daily ritual and loved to open every envelope herself and count her commission, it was always short and she would spend much of the morning telephoning the offending groups for payment in full.

On the morning of her quarterly hospital check-up the ambulance arrived early but, because the postman hadn't arrived, she kept it waiting. After twenty minutes, and trying various delaying tactics, she had no choice but to give in and allow the two ambulance men to hoist her unceremoniously into the ambulance. Her inactivity over the years meant she had gained a great deal of weight and volunteers to fetch her for her check-up had become very scarce.

As the ambulance drove away and turned the corner, the post arrived.

The opportunity to go and play in Germany came about by chance. Dave's first daily chore was to pick up and deliver the post to his mother in her office, but today was different. It was his only day off and, still feeling the effects of the previous night, he shuffled down the stairs, climbed over the mountain of envelopes, bent down and collected them together. He flicked methodically through the post until a pale blue envelope grabbed his attention. Printed on the back was the name of the sender... *Sidney Goldstone, International Agent, London.*

Freda had already received a call from the notorious Sidney Goldstone asking if there were any local groups keen to play in

Germany. She didn't follow it up, knowing she would lose her commission if any of her groups travelled abroad and out of her control.

Although Dave knew his mother wasn't in the house, he still had the feeling she was watching his every move. Nervously, he looked around before slowly slipping the letter into his pyjama jacket pocket.

Finding it difficult to control his excitement and hardly allowing time for the kettle to boil, he made himself a cup of tea and toast and, after checking the letter was still in his pocket; he carried his breakfast upstairs to the privacy of his bedroom. Dave took great care not to tear the envelope knowing that at some point he might have to reseal it and give it to his mother. He sat on the edge of his bed and began to read.

14th October, 1965

Sidney Goldstone Entertainments,
International Agents,
Wardour Street,
LONDON.

Dear Mrs Simpson,
Following our recent telephone conversation, I would confirm that we are looking for suitable groups to play in various German clubs.

This is an excellent opportunity for a number of select acts to audition for us in London at the end of this month. When you have had the opportunity of reviewing your acts please call me in order that we can discuss the specific type of groups we are seeking.

Yours sincerely
Sidney Goldstone

Dave read the letter again and again, each time getting more excited, wondering how he could get an audition to go to Germany. The more he thought about it the more he became confused. He didn't have a group and he needed to get to London.

He reached out and sipped his tea; it was cold, and he spat it out in disgust. He shook his pillow and settled back on the bed.

Within a few minutes he started to talk to himself. 'Surely it can't be that difficult to find a name? Mind you if I am going to pull it off and get to Germany....'

His eyes locked on to the ripped and faded posters of the Rocking Cats, the Snakes, the Cougars; publicity photographs; and the black and white photographs of his idols that filled every inch of wall.

Suddenly he jumped off the bed. 'The Cheetahs... why not?'

He stood and let out a huge sigh of relief before smiling and congratulating himself.

Once he had carefully chosen his suit he dressed in record time, neatly folded the letter and went downstairs. After checking that his mother hadn't come back, he locked the front door, walked into her office, switched on the light and, still shaking, he dialled London.

'Sidney Goldstone's office' said the woman with a smile in her voice.

Dave paused nervously and then replied. 'Could I speak to Mr Goldstone please?'

'Who's calling?' questioned the woman with an air of authority.

For a split second he hesitated. 'It's... no, it's David Simpson from the... from the Simpson Agency, I'm phoning regarding Mr Goldstone's letter.'

There was a long pause. Dave was becoming more and more nervous. He thought he heard the ambulance pull up outside and slammed the phone down so hard that the bell was still resonating a whole minute later.

'What do I do now?' he asked himself.

Nervously he glided across to the window, peeled back the edge of the blind, checked it was clear, walked back to the telephone and, after taking a deep breath, he dialled again.

But without giving the respondent a chance to speak he gushed forth. 'Good morning, this is Mr Simpson from the Simpson Agency in Devon, we received your letter this morning regarding suitable acts for Germany.'

To his amazement the great Sidney Goldstone spoke. 'What have you got for me?' he asked assertively.

Dave swallowed hard. 'Well...um... we have just one group, the... the Cheetahs.'

'Girl singer or organist?' asked Sidney Goldstone.

Without allowing Dave any time to think of an answer he continued, 'It has to be one or the other.'

Dave didn't really understand why he had been asked that question and hesitated before blurting out, 'Organist.'

'That's fine. Monday week at Charlie Chester's club in Soho, be there about nine, you'll get confirmation in a few days. Oh, and by the way, give my regards to your mother.'

'What?' said Dave, as he replaced the receiver. 'If she finds out what I've done, she'll kill me.'

He had no time to think, the ambulance pulled up outside and the doors opened noisily.

He jumped up from the desk, wiped his forehead, repositioned the telephone several times, straightened the envelopes which he had piled precariously high in the usual place, turned off the light, walked out of the room and closed the door behind him.

Freda couldn't get in quick enough. Hardly acknowledging Dave, she wheeled past him, into her office and the neatly stacked piles of unopened post.

Dave checked himself in the mirror and let himself out of the front door. He couldn't wait to tell Tony the good news.

He walked around to the rear of the brewery and into the yard unnoticed. Tony, in faded blue overalls that were several sizes too big, even for him, was struggling to wheel a fully loaded sack-truck towards the waiting lorry. Dave crept up behind him and dug him hard in the ribs, forcing him to lose his balance and tilt the sack-truck. The crates and bottles slid off and crashed across the cobbled yard.

'You'll be paying for any breakages, an' get a move on will ya!' yelled the Irish foreman angrily.

It went strangely quiet before he continued in an even louder voice. '*Tony*, will yer be getting that lorry loaded now?'

Tony turned and scowled at Dave.

Ignoring Tony's reaction, Dave leaned towards the drummer and whispered. 'Wait till you hear my news.'

'I'm not bloody interested,' replied Tony as he continued to refill the crates with the full bottles, inspecting each one as he put it into the crate.

'I'll help you,' said Dave. Almost immediately he snagged his suit trousers, swearing under his breath as he stretched the material and carefully pulled the extended threads back into the fabric.

After loading the lorry, Tony climbed awkwardly onto a tower made up of empty crates and began to eat the first of five rounds of sandwiches while Dave stood and preened himself in front of the imaginary mirror.

'Sit down,' said Tony, 'you're making me nervous.'

'No way! I'm not doing any more damage to this suit,' he replied harshly.

He had already lost some of his enthusiasm, but as soon as he noticed Tony starting to relax, it returned. 'Guess what?'

'What?' asked Tony.

'Guess who phoned me this morning?' asked Dave, a smile spreading across his face.

'What is this? Twenty bloody questions?' garbled Tony as he bit into yet another sandwich.

'Sidney Goldstone wants me to put a group together to go to Germany. What do you reckon?'

Tony showed a little more interest but only long enough to nod his luke-warm interest before the yard foreman started bellowing at him again.

Dave slipped out of the yard, looking back briefly at the seemingly disorganised mountains of empty beer crates and wooden kegs. Surely Tony wanted to get away from there and do something more meaningful with his life? Did he really have a passion to be a professional musician?

At 8.10am precisely every morning, the post cascaded through the enlarged letterbox onto the lino covered hall floor and Dave immediately rushed to pick it up. If he didn't, his mother would scream out until it was collected and delivered to her. For the last few days he had not given her the chance. He had become deliberately clumsy, dropping the letters, and as he picked them up again and again he was able to sort his way through the envelopes.

On Saturday morning it arrived. His eyes darted in the direction of the blue envelope. He picked it up, nervously slid it into his suit jacket pocket and carried the remainder into his ever-impatient mother who sat waiting like a bird of prey. She would always snatch them from him and tear the envelopes open, often ripping the cheques or pound notes inside, but sadly, as soon as Dave had performed his task, she no longer noticed him.

He smiled to himself as he slipped out of the front door, walked quickly to the bus stop and waited for the 8.25am bus into town. Once safely installed upstairs on the back seat he carefully opened the letter, looking around furtively at the other passengers before finally reading it.

His face couldn't hide the extreme disappointment at the contents. It was a standard pre-printed letter confirming the audition date, with the time filled in by hand... not such a big deal, after all.

Dave sat watching the world outside, wondering what Germany was going to be like when he was a professional singer with his own group. He decided that no one else needed to see this letter; it was only the first one that mattered.

Dave had worked in the same men's outfitters in the High Street since leaving school, and now, regarded as the assistant manager, his weekly wage had risen slowly to £11/15/6 before deductions. He knew he was underpaid but he wasn't worried; he knew his dreams of becoming the first person from the area to have a hit record would eventually change his financial situation.

As soon as it was time for lunch he raced to Bill Hitchin's shop to prolong the realisation of that dream. Saturday was the day every musician made their weekly pilgrimage to the music shop to try out the latest guitar or amplifier; repeatedly playing their favourite, most well-practised licks.

Bill was making a fortune selling cheap guitars to beginners for less than eight pounds and buying them back, a few weeks later for three, often reselling them the same day for another eight pounds. Guitars changed hands weekly and he never complained even when the weekly hire purchase repayments were not kept up and the odd instrument was repossessed because he knew that he could sell the instrument again and again.

Dave listened patiently to the would-be guitarists all playing similar tunes at different volumes until he heard a note-perfect instrumental being played by a young curly haired rocker hidden in the corner. He pushed his way through the crowded shop until he was standing almost directly above the guitarist, sneaked a look at his wristwatch and waited until the guitarist had finished playing.

He acknowledged the guitarist with a nod. 'Who do you play with?' he asked casually.

The guitarist looked up. 'No one at the moment,' he replied shyly. 'I've only been in town a few days.'

Dave couldn't believe his luck. 'Listen, I'm forming a new group to go to Germany. Are you interested?'

The guitarist responded with frenzied nodding.

Dave looked at his watch for the third time. 'I have to rush but can you meet me in the coffee bar next door at half five tonight?'

The guitarist gave a wide smile and continued to nod excitedly and Dave smirked to himself as he pushed his way through the massed musicians and rushed back to work.

Most of the working groups would visit Bill's late on a Saturday afternoon to buy anything they needed that night; to keep up to date with any news; or occasionally, if they had a very special engagement, to rent an amplifier or P.A. system. Dave was no exception and, after finishing work, would meet the rest of Music Box at the coffee bar or in the music shop.

Having reached an understanding with his shop manager, Dave changed into his travelling suit just before a quarter past five. As soon as the shop was locked, he left by the back door and drove the group van to the coffee bar. He straightened his suit and walked into the coffee bar, bought himself a coffee and two chocolate biscuits, looked around until he spotted the guitarist, and motioned to him to ask if he wanted a coffee. The guitarist shook his head. Dave paid and, trying hard to hide his desperation, walked over to join him.

'My name's Dave Simpson.'

The guitarist reached out and shook Dave's hand. 'Jimmy Harris.'

'Pleased to meet you Jimmy,' said Dave smiling from ear to ear.

Dave sipped at his coffee. 'I haven't got long, we're playing tonight but I'm putting a new group together... with an organist, and I've been asked by a London agent to go over to Germany.'

Jimmy nodded enthusiastically.

Dave pulled the letter out of his pocket and slid it to Jimmy under the table.

As Jimmy began to read it his face couldn't hide the excitement. 'Great. But I don't know you. In fact I don't know anybody here,' he paused and sipped nervously at his coffee. 'Listen, I can't lie to you but I moved here to find a group, I'm only living in a bed sit.'

Without stopping to take a breath he continued, 'I can go whenever you want me to.'

Before Dave could explain anything else the rest of Music Box arrived. He reached across the table, grabbed the letter, folded it carefully and slid it into his pocket. He took Jimmy's address, shook his hand and left.

Jimmy sat enviously watching as the spotless Commer van pulled effortlessly away and, after carefully counting the change in his pocket, treated himself to a celebratory coffee. Although the café was buzzing he was oblivious to the noise around him and the music blasting out from the jukebox. He sat alone at the table and dreamt of joining a group while he subconsciously sipped his coffee.

Throughout the evening, on and off stage, Dave had his mind on other things. Could he put a new group together in time? Which songs should they learn for the audition? Would they be good enough? Time was running out. He still needed a bass player and an organist. He guessed they would only need to play two or three songs at the audition - not a problem.

Monday lunchtime couldn't come quick enough. Dave returned to Bill's shop where he began to mentally shortlist contenders from amongst dozens of hand-written advertisements placed by budding musicians or groups, trying to find his new band members.

He finally decided to contact the bass player of the only typed advertisement on the board.

> *Ex-professional bass player, with own equipment,*
> *seeks professional group. Available immediately.*
> *Contact Adrian Palmer, 43 Addison Street.*

Dave had seen Adrian play many times but had never spoken to him. Adrian was cool and had moulded his statuesque stage presence on Bill Wyman of the Rolling Stones. He had already tasted success as a professional musician and unusually had already paid for his equipment. His group, the Snakes, played in the finals of the Oxfam competition in London in 1963, judged by two of the Beatles. They didn't win. The group split up the following year and Adrian returned to work in an office and wait for the next opportunity.

Dave knocked at Adrian Palmer's door and stepped back awkwardly. The door opened and the young musician, in his early twenties, stood looking down at him. Almost unrecognisable, with extremely long, brown hair and a tiny well-sculptured moustache and beard, Adrian looked more like a beatnik than a musician.

Dave stood in the shadows while Adrian remained on the doorstep, three steps above him. 'Evening, I'm Dave Simpson, singer with Music Box.'

Adrian didn't try to hide his mocking smile. 'Yeah, I know.'

'No, don't worry; it's got nothing to do with them. I'm putting a group together to go out to Germany.' He paused and looked up. 'Interested?' he mumbled.

'Might be... when you going?' teased the bass player.

Dave proudly passed him the letter but, with the front door pulled closely behind him, Adrian struggled to read it. He pushed the door open a little more and studied every word.

While he read it, Dave took a closer look at his chosen bass player. The very long matted greasy hair masked his good looks but Dave could see that beneath it, his unmarked, olive skin, gave him the look of a very handsome Italian.

Adrian finished reading the letter, folded it neatly, put it back into the envelope, and passed it back to the singer. Dave carefully slid the letter into his inside pocket and waited apprehensively while Adrian looked out into the darkness.

He hesitated for a moment, nodded and then smiled. 'Yeah man, I'll give it a whirl, but if the other players aren't up to it, we *will* change them, won't we?'

Dave was shocked at the response but Adrian, having already been a pro, had something, and he needed him desperately. He paused before responding to the request; his lips tightened but, knowing he had no option, nodded his agreement.

'That shouldn't be a problem, but let's get over the audition before we even think about that.' Adrian seemed happy with Dave's response and agreed to be at the first practise. As Dave walked down the garden path Adrian shouted after him. 'Man, that's one hell of a van.'

Chapter Three

Let It Be Me

Gerry Simms had loved music for as long as he could remember and, at the age of seven, he was given the chance to learn the piano accordion. He had always been a sickly child, suffering from asthma, and unable to take part in any of the normal sports or play activities with his friends. His widowed mother, realising he was unlikely to ever be able to do anything that required strength or stamina, decided that Gerry should learn to play the piano. He never really warmed to the idea but, by luck, a distant aunt on holiday in England from America played and taught the accordion. Gerry liked the idea of being able to carry an accordion rather than rely on someone else's piano whose owners hardly ever had them tuned, and consequently always made even the best player sound bad. Gerry's aunt gave him his first lessons; he seemed to have a gift for playing the accordion, so much so that his mother bought him a 140 bass Hohner.

Gerry practised every day, often under duress, but his weekly lessons with a very proficient player and teacher paid off and within two years he regularly played at school assembly and at the family Christmas parties.

Unable to carry the accordion himself, his mother continued to carry it to and from school or to the nearest bus stop and on to the various venues whenever he played.

Groups played at the youth club every Saturday and when Gerry saw the overnight metamorphosis of instrumental groups to groups with vocalists, copying the Beatles and the numerous Liverpool recording groups, he knew he wanted to join them.

Now fourteen, many of his friends were either playing in groups or aiming to in the not too distant future. Unfortunately no one wanted an accordionist so Gerry spent the next eighteen months buying sheet music and learning the latest hits in the hope that someone might. He did attempt to play the guitar, swapping his treasured stamp collection for an electric guitar, but without an amplifier he had no option but to plug the guitar into the back of the radio in the sitting room. This was totally unacceptable to his mother and sister and, after spending endless hours trying to play a basic three chord twelve bar, he gave up and swapped the guitar for a bicycle for his sister.

Worried by Gerry's frequent asthma attacks, Mrs Simms made numerous visits to his doctor who finally suggested neo-epinine, a yellow tablet that could be placed under the tongue at the first hint of an attack. It seemed to be the ideal solution and Gerry carried a tablet in almost every pocket. At the first sign of breathlessness he would break off a small piece and put it under his tongue. Unless he was very ill, he would begin to recover within a few minutes.

There were however side effects; after taking even the smallest piece his whole body would pound uncontrollably until the drug had the required effect.

Just before Gerry's fifteenth birthday, Terry Rawlings, leader of the Blue Tones, asked him to join them. All Gerry needed was an organ.

Although he loved the look of the stylish Vox Continental, with the reversed colouring of the keys, which was used by most groups including the Mike Smith of Dave Clark Five and Alan Price of the Animals, on their latest hit *House Of The Rising Sun*, his mother could not afford the deposit for it.

The equally popular Farfisa organ, played on Del Shannon's *Runaway*, was also outside of her price range.

All was not lost however and, not wanting to lose a sale, Bill showed him a reed organ. It was nowhere near the same league as the Vox or Farfisa and worked on the same principle as the piano accordion. But with the addition of a microphone strategically placed inside the casing, and also a volume pedal, Gerry had his organ for a mere £25.

He joined the Blue Tones and adapted well to playing with the other musicians.... too well sometimes, often taking days off school to practice. Gerry had often seen Julie, who was a few months older than him, dancing with her girlfriends at the youth club. She wasn't particularly pretty but her blonde hair, shapely figure and confidence made her stand out from other girls of the same age.

She didn't really pay much attention to him until he performed with the Blue Tones but from that first night they were inseparable.

Julie seemed genuinely pleased to be seen with Gerry who, after only a few performances in town, was frequently recognised as being the Blue Tones' organist. They weren't the best group in town but they were the most controversial, playing early R and B music and some of the more obscure Rolling Stones songs.

As well as taking time off from grammar school to practise with the group, Gerry spent several afternoons a week at Julies while her parents were at work and although they regularly had sex, it soon became boring; it was all they knew.

Missing school meant his studying began to suffer, especially his 'O' Levels. Within two months of meeting Julie, he was summoned to the Headmaster's office and expelled. He never told his mother, instead he convinced her he wanted to learn a trade and play music in his spare time. Although disappointed, she quietly went along with Gerry's wishes and while his working life as a trainee surveyor, started immediately, Julie stayed on at school until the end of the summer term before starting an apprenticeship as a hairdresser.

Jimmy Harris, now 17, had lived in the heart of Somerset with his ageing and partially deaf grandmother since he was eight. His parents split up as a direct result of his father's bouts of drunkenness and violence, a well-known period that was still talked about in the small close-knit village community.

Jimmy's mother moved to Watchet where she took a job as housekeeper for a wealthy gentleman. Soon after she left, the villagers turned against Bob, her husband, and it wasn't long before he moved away to work as a gardener at a hotel in Torquay. It suited him because he could spend his evenings after work in the local pub, where he was happy to entertain the tourists with his never-ending stories about village life. They kept him well supplied with cider and beer before he drunkenly staggered back to his room to round off the evening with a few more bottles of brown ale. The unfortunate break up of Jimmy's parents left him to his own devices and after school he would go to his cramped bedroom and play records on his Dansette record player. Later in the evening, when the reception was good enough, he would tune his transistor radio into Radio Luxembourg.

At the age of twelve, he started to teach himself guitar using Bert Weedon's Play in a Day books. They had become incredibly popular with all his guitar-playing school friends and proved to be a great help to Jimmy who, once outside of school, had very little contact with other would-be musicians or anyone his own age. He continued to practise and gradually improved, well enough to play along with most of the instrumental songs recorded by the Shadows, although they didn't sound quite the same played on an acoustic guitar.

Jimmy left school at fifteen and worked in the village, carrying out odd jobs for anyone who needed a spare pair of hands, unless the work was likely to risk damage to his fingers. He saved every penny for an electric guitar.

His seventeenth birthday was to be the turning point in his life. Jimmy's Nan surprised him by giving him enough money to make up the deficit. Initially, Jimmy was reluctant to accept the money, until she convinced him that she had enough to last her for the rest of her days. 'What else did she have to spend her money on?'

Jimmy took the bus into Taunton and after a great deal of deliberation, bought a white Fender Stratocaster and a second hand Vox AC30 amplifier.

Over the next few months he spent every spare minute playing his guitar, combing his curly greasy hair into the almost identical style of Gene Vincent and posing in front of the mirror.

By the end of the summer he became more and more frustrated and, after reading an article in the regional newspaper about the music scene in Torbay, he decided that he should leave the isolation of the country and join a group.

It wasn't easy leaving his Nan because she had come to rely on his help but she knew his heart was set on playing music although she didn't understand how anyone could make a living playing music, especially the new tuneless pop songs.

As the bus passed the cottage that had been his home for the last eight years he saw his Nan standing at the gate waving her arms off. His eyes filled with tears as he suddenly felt frightened and very alone.

It was late into the afternoon when he arrived at Torquay. He waited nervously on the deserted station for nearly two hours before he gained his nerve and took a taxi to the Sheldon Hall Hotel.

The taxi drove along the sea front before winding its way up the long impressive drive until it reached the main entrance.

Jimmy climbed out of the taxi and stood looking up at the intimidating building, carelessly slinging his check duffel bag around his neck.

With his guitar in one hand and amplifier in the other he struggled clumsily up the wide granite steps, arriving in the foyer breathless and exhausted. Still grappling with his worldly belongings he staggered towards the pretty young female receptionist.

'I've come to visit Mr Harris,' he whispered.

She looked directly at him, shrugged her shoulders, and walked off to answer the ringing telephone.

While he waited for her to return he looked nervously around at the antique furniture, marble rug covered floors, and the failing Victorian splendour.

The receptionist returned to the desk. 'Who is it you want?' she asked impatiently.

'I've come to visit Mr Harris,' he blurted out.

'Who?' she asked for a second time.

'Mr Harris... my father,' he stuttered. 'He works here.'

'Will you take a seat? I'll be back in a moment.' She screwed up her face and stormed off, muttering under her breath.

He waited nervously while she disappeared into a back room.

The silence left him feeling uncomfortable and self-conscious but he thought to himself that one day, when he 'made it,' the welcome would be totally different.

The receptionist eventually strolled out of the office followed by an elderly man in uniform who walked across to Jimmy.

'You've come to visit Mr Harris?' he thought for a moment, 'You mean Bob... Bob Harris?'

'Yes, that's right... Bob Harris, he's my father,' replied a much relieved Jimmy.

'Fine. Go down the steps, turn left, go past the stable block and you'll find the cottage at the end of the drive.'

Jimmy started to walk towards the door before the man could finish.

He shouted after him. 'You can't miss it, it doesn't go any further.'

Before Jimmy could ask anything else the man turned and walked off in the direction of the opening lift door and the well-dressed, heavily made-up, elderly lady who appeared carrying a miniature white poodle.

Jimmy struggled down the steps and off through the exotic grounds.

By the time he reached the old gatekeeper's cottage, it was dark. Totally exhausted, he took a deep breath and knocked on the door. There was no reply. He took a deep breath and continued to knock until a light came on and a man appeared at the first floor open window.

'What the hell do you want? Sod off will yer,' shouted the man.

Jimmy stood on the gravel path and stared towards the silhouette.

Bob Harris screwed up his face and looked again and again until he finally recognised his grown-up son. 'What the hell are you doing here?' his father slurred.

Jimmy was so tired he could hardly speak.

'Wait a minute, I'll come down,' continued his father. He disappeared from the window and eventually staggered out through the door and stood uneasily looking at Jimmy. 'Your Nan's alright isn't she?'

Jimmy nodded.

'Well then, what the bloody hell are you doing here?'

'I've come to see you,' said Jimmy nervously.

'What... why now?' asked his father.

'I want to join a group,' mumbled Jimmy.

'A group? What sort of group?' he thought for a second. 'Doing what?'

'I just want to play my guitar; I don't care what sort of group it is.'

He continued to stare at him in disbelief.

'You need your bloody head testing, why don't you get a proper job?' Shivering in the cold night air, he cursed under his breath. 'I suppose you'd better come in.'

He bent down and, as though it weighed nothing, lifted the heavy amplifier high up into the air.

Jimmy appreciated his help but was quietly concerned that his treasured equipment would become damaged as his drunken father carried it up the narrow creaking stairs.

The door opened to reveal a room bursting with rubbish. Empty beer bottles, old newspapers lay strewn all over the floor; greasy fish and chip papers piled in the corner beside the stinking cardboard box used as an excuse for rubbish bin, overflowing ashtrays and bottles stuffed with cigarette ends.

Jimmy was too tired to care about anything except sleeping and literally fell asleep in the filthy armchair.

Bob pulled on his jacket, muttered curses in the direction of Jimmy and now suddenly feeling sober and wide-awake left for the pub.

The next morning Bob shook Jimmy awake and handed him a disgustingly strong cup of tea.

'So what are you really here for? You can't stay you know,' he paused, 'we're not allowed guests.'

Jimmy, although still partially asleep, couldn't believe it. Surely his father had some feelings?

He pushed himself up onto one elbow and, still feeling extremely tired, he lied by giving the only answer that he knew that his father would accept.

'That's no problem, I'll be moving out in a few days... only my train was late last night.' He coughed, 'but I am here to join a group.' Pointing in the direction of the guitar case and mysteriously covered amplifier. 'That's what that is.'

'Are you any good?' his father asked, although it was evident he had no interest.

Jimmy shrugged his shoulders confidently. 'I think I am.'

Bob had now run out of conversation. 'Fine. Some of us have work to do.'

With that he grabbed his one and only jacket and walked down the creaking stairs, disappearing into his vast green world of shrubs, trees and flowers.

Fortunately gardening was one thing that he was very good at otherwise he couldn't have kept his job. He had been told by the general manager, in no uncertain terms, that as long as he kept his distance from the hotel guests, he would keep it.

Jimmy was beginning to feel hungry but, after looking around at the mess, was strangely glad there was nothing for him to even consider eating. He washed his face and walked out into his strange new world. Everything looked so much better in the sunshine as he picked his way between the shrubs and trees and, after leaving the hotel grounds, he continued walking until he found a shop. He bought two pints of milk and completely emptied the first bottle in one large gulp before standing on the edge of the pavement to catch his breath. No longer feeling hungry he strolled along the cliff tops.

It was a perfect autumn day, the clear blue sky with only a few clouds on the horizon. The calm sea was such a contrast to the cottage and uninteresting countryside that he had left behind only the day before. He kicked at the piles of crisp dry leaves whenever the opportunity arose as he walked far around the headland to Hope's Nose and back.

When the second milk bottle was empty he recklessly threw it high into the air towards Thatcher's Rock and watched it fall slowly and silently into the sea below.

As he walked, he reflected on his childhood and remembered how his father had changed soon after Jimmy started at primary school.

Bob Harris had taken a very active role in the Second World War, spending much of wartime undercover in Europe, and immediately at the end of the War, assisting in the repatriation of the pathetic survivors from the Jewish concentration camps. Although badly affected by those years, in 1951, because of his vast experience, he was selected to go with a handful of Special Forces to Korea, where he stayed until the end of the war in 1953. When he returned he was a changed man and, finding it hard to come to terms with normal everyday life, was discharged within a few months on the grounds of ill health.

His return to the idyllic country life in Somerset was short-lived. Following regular mood swings and bouts of silence, he took to drinking heavily, and the family problems started. No one knew what really happened during those years, how much he was mentally scarred and tortured by the events that he had witnessed on two continents, in what were two very different wars.

Jimmy's attention was drawn to an old newspaper lying under one of the cliff top seats, which were carefully positioned to allow everyone to take in the fantastic views. He sat down, searched for and found the entertainment page and read it thoroughly, paying special attention to the list of groups that would be playing in Torbay that weekend.

He stared at the distant horizon and tried to imagine what really lay across the channel. He felt confident that he had made the right decision. He would get a job, any job, find a bed-sit, and then look for a group.

Dave discovered him a few days later and Jimmy couldn't believe his luck.

Dave lived in the same street as Gerry's aunt. The musicians had known each other for some time, having met when Gerry, along with his mother and sister, went to stay for one weekend that soon turned into a weekly ritual.

Bored with the adult company Gerry and his sister would spend as much time as possible out of the house and, intrigued by the only vehicle in the street, the group van, they spent hours watching and waiting for anyone connected with it. Their patience resulted in meeting Dave and after that almost every Sunday was spent helping him to wash and clean the van.

Gerry also met Dave's mother and father, but only once.

It was a glorious summer Sunday afternoon and Dave proudly invited them both in for some raspberries that he had picked in his garden. Although all the houses in the street were identical, once inside the difference between Mr and Mrs Simpson's house and Gerry's aunt's was incomparable. The darkness, the smell of stale cigarette smoke, and the fact that there was no natural light, was extremely unpleasant and very scary, especially considering that even on the sunniest of days the family relied totally on electricity to give any light.

While Gerry and his sister gulped the foul tasting raspberries Mrs Simpson spent the whole time on the telephone and failed to even acknowledge them.

It didn't matter. Gerry was extremely impressed with the nicotine stained posters and numerous signed group photographs displayed haphazardly all over the walls.

Gerry and his sister made their excuses and left.

The next time Dave spoke to Gerry was almost a year later. Now desperate for an organist to complete his line-up, seeing Gerry at the burger stand jogged his memory.

The next morning Dave was knocking at Gerry's house, waving the now well-read letter at him. He read it and, showing more than a little interest, agreed to go to the practise the following week.

Dave now had his group; the Cheetahs were about to be born.

Chapter Four

Shaking all Over

The Salvation Army hall was cold and extremely draughty throughout the year but this time of year it was almost unbearable when the desperate musicians occupied the vast cavernous building. There was no stage so Dave, too preoccupied to notice the cold, began to secretly set up the Music Box equipment at the back of the hall. He had decided to use the equipment without the owners' permission. It would save time and, more importantly for him as unelected manager, create a professional impression with the Cheetahs.

Jimmy was the first to arrive. Dave smirked to himself as the guitarist watched in stunned silence while he set up the immaculate Selmer P.A., followed by the amplification for the bass and guitar. Lastly, with Jimmy's help, he set up the shiny Vox Continental.

Gerry and Tony arrived at almost the same time. Tony made for his drum cases, carefully unpacking and setting up the shiny contents, then placing the empty cases neatly in one corner. Gerry walked towards the organ, stood and stared at it, much too nervous to touch his dream instrument. He soon got the better of his nerves and faultlessly played his party piece, the solo from Del Shannon's *Runaway.*

Everything was set up by the time Adrian arrived. He looked every bit the professional, his hair tied back in a ponytail, carrying his bass guitar in one hand and an unmistakable foul smelling Galloise in the other.

Dave introduced everyone and explained that as the audition had now been confirmed for the following Monday in London, they need only learn three or four songs. He asked for suggestions. There were none. Instead they sat in silence fidgeting with their instruments; except Adrian who sat on his amplifier and lit another cigarette until Dave finally broke the ice, suggesting that they should play at least one instrumental.

Jimmy could play the entire Shadows catalogue blindfold. He started to play *Wonderful Land* but, after a few bars, realising he had started in the wrong key, stopped and nervously sat back on the amplifier.

'Why not *Blue Moon*?' suggested Adrian. He pushed the part smoked cigarette between the machine heads and effortlessly tuned his bass. Without another word he started to play, quickly followed by Tony. Gerry picked up the chords and, before the end of the first chorus, Jimmy regained his confidence and was playing the melody.

The Cheetahs were playing together for the first time.

Dave walked to the other end of the hall to watch and listen. He carefully studied the collection of musicians that he had assembled in less than a week. No one except Adrian, and of course himself, looked the part. He knew that if they could pull the audition off then he could work on the image.

At the rather ragged ending of the song he clapped enthusiastically. Everyone was relieved and it showed.

The next three songs came from the set played by Music Box, *Shaking All Over* by Johnny Kidd and the Pirates; *All I Have To Do Is Dream* by the Everly Brothers. For this song Dave was joined by Tony, and then Jimmy who surprised himself by harmonising all the way through. Their final choice was *Sixteen Tons* by Tennessee Ernie Ford.

All the songs were played over and over in every conceivable sequence until they were almost perfect, with everyone congratulating each other on the success of the evening.

The group had one more practice before the audition in London and, wanting to be on the road before midnight, Dave arranged the order in which he would pick everyone up on Sunday evening.

The next weekend, after arriving home late from the show in the depths of Cornwall, Tony reluctantly spent the night at Dave's house. Despite the late night they were up early, spending most of

Sunday rearranging the equipment and cleaning, checking and fuelling the van for the long journey. By early Sunday evening everything was going to plan. All the members were in the van except Gerry. Dave drove to Gerry's house and Mrs Simms answered the door.

'Gerry's not well,' she said. 'He's had an asthma attack. He... can't come with you.'

Dave couldn't believe it. Without a word he walked back to the van and broke the news. 'The bastard's not coming!'

They all sat in complete silence until Adrian spoke up. 'Well what are we waiting for? We'll have to go without him.' Reluctantly everyone agreed.

The van pulled away, making its way towards the A30, London, and the Charlie Chester Club.

Mrs Simms closed the front door and walked back into the sitting room where she found Gerry sitting in the armchair looking pale and tired, and wheezing uncontrollably. 'You'll feel better in the morning,' she reassured him. 'Get some sleep, and call me if you need anything.'

He got up slowly from the chair and with a great deal of effort climbed the stairs and went to bed.

The next morning Gerry was up much earlier than usual and, showing no ill effects from the previous night, went to work. But at eleven o'clock, the time of the audition, his heart began to race. He spent the whole day wondering how it had gone, one minute glad he was working, and the next wishing he was in London with the group. But why should he? He was the one who had lost his nerve; it was crazy, stage fright the day before an audition. Perhaps he would marry Julie and settle down. Was he really cut out to be a professional musician?

After work, instead of seeing Julie, he took the bus home.

She was no longer happy with him playing in a group. At first she had been ecstatic but when he had the opportunity to join the Cheetahs, she changed her mind.

Gerry sat at the table pushing the vegetables around his dinner plate, when the doorbell rang. He made his way out to the front door and opened it apprehensively.

Dave stood in front of him the heavy rain running down his face.

'How did it go?' Gerry asked nervously.

'It didn't,' replied Dave, now joined by Jimmy. 'We've got to go back tomorrow with *you*, they won't audition us without an organist.'

Adrian climbed out of the van and ran towards the door. 'You look better, come on bring your things and we can get started.'

They all stood in the rain waiting for the only answer they were prepared to accept.

Adrian continued. 'Come on, if you don't hurry up we'll all be too ill to play anyway.' He disappeared back into the shelter of the dry van and waited.

'Who's at the door at this time of night?' called out Gerry's mother.

'They've come back for me,' he replied.

'Who have?'

Although still very unsure, Gerry knew he had no option.

'The group; I've got to go to London with them,' he replied.

'What?'

'I've got no choice have I? I've got to go with them.'

'Surely you're not going this time of night?' pleaded his mother. 'You're just getting over your asthma attack; you know what will happen if you don't rest.'

'I'll be all right. I can sleep in the van and we'll be back tomorrow.'

Dave walked into the kitchen. 'It's all right Mrs Simms; I'll take care of him. Honestly, there's no need to worry.'

She turned to Dave. 'Just make sure you do.'

Dave smiled and nodded enthusiastically. 'Don't worry, of course I will.'

Gerry raced up to his room, grabbed a handful of warm clothes and the bag he'd prepared the day before, and returned downstairs. In the meantime Mrs Simms made him several luncheon meat and cheese sandwiches.

Gerry kissed her on the cheek, turned and ran through the heavy rain towards the van. She stood in the doorway, shivering in the cold wet night, watching as he struggled to get past Adrian who had returned to sit regally in his front seat. But before the van had turned the corner Gerry's mother had already began to worry.

The journey to London was uneventful except that each member of the group took it in turns to talk to Dave to keep him awake. The van arrived outside Paddington station at four o'clock in the morning. Dave parked in a side street and, although desperately tired, everyone found it hard to get to sleep. As soon as it was light they trooped along the platform looking more like young tramps than musicians, the early morning commuters paying little attention to them as they wound their way down the stairs into the public washrooms. For sixpence each, they all had a bath, washed their hair and changed for the audition, with the exception of Adrian who only shaved and changed.

Dave, having been there less than twenty-four hours earlier, drove directly to the Soho club. As it was still closed, he treated them all to breakfast in the tiny Italian café next door. Looking out of the window onto the hustle and bustle of the Soho streets, they were a little overawed at the difference between London and their hometown. Although Adrian, as always, tried to hide his feelings, one thing was agreed by all of them, at last they all felt like professional musicians, even it might only last for the next few hours.

At twenty to ten, an elderly man in a cloth cap unlocked the club door.

'Do you reckon that's Charlie Chester?' joked Adrian.

'Come on, let's get the equipment in,' said Dave, getting up.

They walked across to the van and Dave unlocked the rear doors. 'Tony, you stay here until we get it all downstairs, then I'll come and lock it up.'

Tony smiled; he was pleased that he didn't have to carry anything down the long winding staircase to the basement club.

The remaining group members followed the caretaker down into the darkness, all wanting to satisfy their curiosity and have their first look inside a Soho nightclub. Everyone was disappointed, including Adrian, who soon appeared in the daylight at the top of the stairs, shaking his head in disgust. 'What a filthy hole, wait till you see it,' he paused, 'Nothing more than a flea pit.'

It didn't take them long to carry the equipment down into the basement, everyone was keen to get set up before the Sidney Goldstone entourage arrived. The caretaker wouldn't let them use the stage so they set up on the floor - probably a good move.

Tony was making the final adjustments to his cymbals and hi-hat, when the door opened and in walked a tall, dark, imposing Jewish man in his early thirties. He was smoking a massive cigar and had a dark knee length overcoat hanging around his shoulders.

'Look at that p....' spouted Adrian.

Dave grabbed at him before he could complete his offensive sentence.

'Morning boys' said Sidney Goldstone, as he counted the number of musicians. 'I see we've got a full complement this morning.'

Dave walked over to him, at the same time looking towards the blushing organist.

'Good morning.' He smiled nervously. 'I did tell you Gerry was ill, but he's here this morning.'

Gerry kept his head down and fiddled nervously with the pull bars which ran along the top the keyboard.

Sidney Goldstone glanced at the shiny equipment, took a long hard drag on his cigar and spoke through the smoke as he exhaled. 'When you're ready boys,' he said impatiently.

Dave motioned to Tony to hurry up and, after quickly tuning their guitars; they started with *Shaking all Over*, immediately followed by the instrumental *Blue Moon*, *Sixteen Tons* and *All I Have to Do is Dream*.

With the music still vibrating around the empty club they looked towards the agent and waited for his response.

There was nothing but a silence that seemed to last forever. They nervously looked around and waited but, as the silence continued, they began to doubt their performance.

The agent took yet another massive drag on his cigar and as he exhaled he spoke. 'That's fine.' He paused, and then, with an almost couldn't care less voice, 'When can you go?' Before anyone could take it in, the agent continued, 'Mind you, there's a lot of work to do on your presentation and image.'

Dave regained his confidence and walked across the dance floor. 'Stage suits are being made and we'll have a new P.A. system before we go out to Germany.'

Sidney Goldstone looked back towards the group. 'I'd like you out there next month.'

Dave thought for a moment. 'That's not possible,' he said.

The musicians found it hard to hide the shock.

'We're booked right through December,' Dave continued, and smiled broadly. 'But...we could go out in January.'

Sidney Goldstone took yet another huge drag on his cigar, becoming almost invisible through the smoke.

'That's fine, January the second. Hamburg, for a month, and if you go well there'll be a second month.'

The musicians tried hard to control themselves but, as the smoking shadow walked towards the stairs, he shouted back at them. 'I'll send your agency the contracts tomorrow. Good luck.'

Before they could even attempt to thank him, he was gone.

They sat down on the amplifiers, numb and elated. But their euphoria was short-lived when the caretaker appeared from the toilets. 'Come on you lot, get this stuff out of 'ere. I'm not paid for this ya know.' He lit a cigarette and continued. 'As quick as ya can. Now get a move on.'

They didn't hear him.

'Come on, let's go and celebrate,' said Dave.

The equipment was packed without anyone remembering doing it and they left Soho without looking back.

Their celebrations continued throughout the long journey home until Jimmy asked a question he had been desperate to bring up with Dave before leaving London. 'What's that about us being booked for December?' he asked.

'Listen, we've got dates for December… well paid at that,' replied Dave.

'Have we?' asked Adrian.

'Well not exactly but when I get back I'm leaving Music Box and we can cover their dates,' said Dave.

'There is the small matter of a van and equipment,' said Adrian trying not to put a damper on the euphoria.

'No problem, leave that to me,' said Dave, brimming with confidence.

'Well if that's the case, for seven pound five shillings a week, I'm not going back to that poxy job,' chipped in Adrian. 'Why do any of us need to work? If we're going to be pro in a few weeks, why not start now?'

Dave pulled in at the next transport café and, after buying drinks, they all sat down together. Adrian looked out of the window, disinterested with the formalities. After all, they knew he had already made his decision. Tony was still apprehensive; Jimmy couldn't hold back his enthusiasm, while Gerry was more concerned with getting his hands on a decent organ.

Reassured by Dave's confidence and Tony's eventual decision to join them, they all agreed they were ready for stardom and the money.

It was surprisingly easy for everyone except Dave. His mother went berserk when he told her that he was leaving Music Box but, as soon as he explained that the Cheetahs would be able to take on their dates, she calmed down. She wasted no time and spent hours calling in favours and filling the date sheet with engagements all over southern England.

Jimmy's father, keen to patch up the differences with Mike and now used to having him around, hassled the head chef continually. Eventually he gave in and agreed that Jimmy could work in the kitchen whenever he was available and, providing he worked over the busy Christmas period, Jimmy could legitimately stay with his father in the cottage.

At first Jimmy didn't like the idea but saw sense when he realised that if he did move in he would be able to save the cost of a bed-sit and perhaps earn a little much needed cash.

The next day was spent cleaning up the cottage. It wasn't easy but, after an inordinate number of hours, buckets of disinfectant and water, and use of the commercial cleaner from housekeeping, the place was at last habitable.

While he was clearing away a pile of screwed up fish and chip newspapers, a short piece in the Entertainments section grabbed his attention. It was an article about the Silhouettes, a Plymouth group who had been to Germany several times. Carefully avoiding the dried chips and batter stuck to the newspaper; he ripped out the article and put it in his pocket

Chapter five

Shapes of Things

The next week was spent back in the freezing inhospitable Salvation Army hall, learning as many songs as possible. Dave became more confident as he watched the way the musicians worked together and, although he expected it, Adrian never mentioned his wish to ditch any of the players.

The failure of the contracts to arrive gave Dave some concern but no one bothered to bring it up. Dave, having seen the constant problems his mother had with promoters and other agents, knew that if they didn't arrive he would have a real problem holding things together.

Jimmy's mutilated newspaper article put a whole new complexion on their future repertoire. It had given all the members of the Cheetahs the opportunity to dig out their particular favourites and, much to Jimmy's relief, gave Dave the opportunity to trawl through the Chuck Berry classics. In no time at all, they had two forty-five minute sets and the makings of a third.

Dave, for obvious reasons, delayed telling the members of Music Box he was disbanding the group, consequently every time he and Tony travelled with them they found it hard not to let slip that they would soon be leaving the group.

The Cheetahs continued to use the equipment although it did mean that sometimes they had to break all the equipment down and reload the van, but that was a small price to pay.

Dave needed every penny he could get to subsidise his new group and because he had the set of duplicate keys to the shop, was able to slip back in and steal new suits for each member.

Much to everyone's relief, the Cheetahs first paid gig was at a grammar school in deepest North Devon. As they carried the equipment towards the makeshift stage in the gymnasium the trailing line of musicians came to a sudden stop when they saw row upon row of huge black and white posters of the Cheetahs, with the caption *Direct from Germany* written across them.

Adrian was the first to comment. 'Nice one. You didn't waste any time did you Dave? When did you have those printed?'

'Last week,' replied Dave as he struggled on with the speakers.

'I'm having one of them before I leave tonight,' said Jimmy.

They talked excitedly about the posters while they changed into their new suits for the first time, and fought to look at themselves in the only full-length mirror.

They looked good, very good.

Much better than any of them had ever imagined; even better than the Beatles.

They were more than a group, they were unmistakably… the Cheetahs.

With tears in his eyes Jimmy stuttered. 'Dave you've done a great job.' He looked around for agreement. 'Hasn't he guys?'

Gerry nodded, Tony smiled, and for once even Adrian acknowledged Dave's achievements.

Jimmy lifted his plastic beaker of tea. 'We won't let you down.' He toasted Dave and swallowed the last few drops.

'Come on let's prove we're worth it,' said Dave trying not to show how much Jimmy's appreciation had affected him.

Following the rather pathetic performance of the head teacher playing records on an antiquated record player, not a hard act to follow; the Cheetahs took to the stage.

From Jimmy's first chord, and looking every bit the professional group that Dave's posters had promised, the teenage kids crowded around the stage, pushing and shoving each other to get to the front and watch the group that had just returned from Germany. Although the first two numbers were not played particularly well, the more than enthusiastic response from their audience gave the group a new found confidence.

During the break, while the rest of the group took time out in the boys toilets, Adrian disappeared, only to reappear smirking a few minutes before they were due to play again.

Everyone was extremely pleased with the evening, no one more than Jimmy who had played his first real gig. Following two encores, the tired but relieved band of musicians left the makeshift stage.

Most of the pupils had already left except for a few young, hopeful musicians who played in the school band. They had stayed behind to watch in awe as the 'Stars' packed their equipment.

Suddenly a pretty young girl ran towards the stage followed by the record-spinning teacher. When she saw Adrian she became hysterical, pointing and shouting at him.

'That's him, he's the one!'

Without a word of warning the teacher jumped onto Adrian and punched him around the head several times in quick succession. The rest of the group tried to hold him back before Adrian had been the recipient of several well aimed blows to the nose, eyes and lips.

The teacher continued to stare at the wounded bass player as he lay on the floor bleeding. Shaking with anger, and still clenching his fists, he screamed at Adrian. 'You dirty bastard, taking advantage of a young girl, you lot are all the same!' He paused, and looked at the equipment lying around on the floor. 'Get that lot out, before I... I... smash it up.' The teacher's intense eyes turned angrily towards the rest of the stunned musicians and as they desperately tried to understand what was happening, he screamed at them. *'Making a noise, that's about all you layabouts are fit for!'*

Dave moved slowly towards the head teacher while at the same time motioning to the rest of the group to pack up the equipment. 'I'm sure we can sort this out.'

The young girl ran towards Adrian; he ignored her and immediately she became hysterical again.

'Look, we'll be away in a few minutes,' pleaded Dave.

The teacher looked him in the eye and pushed his finger hard into Dave's chest. 'Don't push your luck sonny... you've not heard the last of this.'

He turned his attention to the young school girl. 'All right Janice come on, let's get you home.'

While the Cheetahs loaded the van, the few remaining pupils looked on and silently wished that they were in the group.

The musicians climbed into the van and after slamming his door Dave accelerated towards the school gates. Adrian, sitting upright in the passenger seat, smirked defiantly and poked two fingers at the head teacher as the van drove past. The bewildered occupants remained silent until Tony managed to say what everyone was thinking. 'She wasn't under age was she Adrian?'

Adrian sucked his bleeding lips.

'Who cares, under age or not, she wasn't worth it.' He gasped as he felt the pain for the first time. 'I don't know why I bothered,' he slurred.

'Nor do we,' mumbled Jimmy from the depths of the van.

Adrian wouldn't let it rest; 'But she was a pretty young thing.'

Dave chose to remain silent as he drove through the dark country lanes hoping they could get out of the country before the police took any action against Adrian.

By the time they arrived home, Adrian had a very black swollen eye, split lip and a badly bruised face. Unable to hide the obvious discomfort and bruised ego he climbed out of the van and, without saying a word, shuffled towards his front door.

The next morning Dave waited for the letters to pour through the box. He sifted and sorted them before they hit the mat and to his great relief he noticed the long awaited large blue envelope from Sidney Goldstone. He kissed it, expertly rearranged the other post and took it into his mother, who grabbed it without saying a word.

He shook with anticipation as he ripped the large envelope open, read the short letter and then proceeded to read the contract. He let out a sigh of relief and a smile broke out across his face as he read the contents a second time.

The contract stipulated the Cheetahs were a five piece group, including an organist and would play at The Funny Crow in Hamburg for one month, commencing 2nd January 1966 for a fee of £700, less 10% commission payable to the Sidney Goldstone Agency. The group was expected to pay its own travelling expenses - in the region of £25, which Sidney Goldstone would pay to them as an advance.

Dave quickly calculated that each member would earn about £35 a week, a great deal more than anyone was currently earning. He, as manager, would then deduct 10% to cover administration costs, and further deductions for any running costs which would include fuel, insurance and the commission to Sidney Goldstone.

Dave could hardly contain his excitement. He rushed out of the front door into the street and stood on the deserted pavement looking first one way then the other and back again.

If the van was there he couldn't miss it as it was the only vehicle in the street. Dave was absolutely stunned, unusual for him because he always had an answer in any situation. He closed his eyes, rubbed them hard, opened them and looked both ways one more time. Still unable to believe it, he slowly turned and walked back up the path and into the house.

Mrs Simpson, having already opened and sorted her post and placed it in neat piles around her, was quick to notice the look on Dave's face. 'What's happened to you?' She asked sharply, 'Seen a ghost?'

'I wish I had,' he paused, still in shock. 'The van's not outside, it's disappeared.'

His mother lit a cigarette and sat in silence blowing the smoke around the room, creating a thick heavy cloud. 'I wondered when they would get wind of something; you should have told them what was going on.' Not stopping for breath, she continued, 'I don't blame them, do you? You would have done the same,' she said.

'Of course I would have, but that's not the point. What do I do now?' replied Dave.

After many years of negotiating, his mother didn't need any time to think. 'If they'll agree, reach a compromise. Let them take some dates with you and Anthony' - she would never change his name. 'When they're not booked, I can fill in other dates for you.' She hesitated, 'And get yourself another van.'

Dave thought about what she had just said; it all seemed so easy. He began to relax and smiled at her, the first time for months.

The smile worked, she answered his prayers. 'Go and see Ronnie and the Roosters, they're about to split.' The telephone rang and before she could answer it Dave was gone.

The results of Adrian's requested meeting with the news reporter was not just an article in the local evening paper but a front-page story with a large, close up photograph of his swollen and distorted face below the headline... *Musician attacked by school teacher.*

By the time Adrian arrived in the coffee bar the Cheetahs were big news. The rest of the group sat tightly clutching their copy of the paper and couldn't wait to see Adrian's reaction. He had two, one for his scrapbook and the other to show to anyone who hadn't already seen it.

'How the hell did that get in there?' asked Jimmy angrily.

'Contacts… you gotta know who to talk to,' replied Adrian, sucking his swollen lip.

'Fucking embarrassing if you ask me,' said Tony.

'Who asked you,' snorted Adrian. 'It's publicity… right Dave?'

'Yeah right.' Dave coughed loudly to gain everyone's attention. 'Now just listen. The contracts have arrived.'

They all clapped and cheered excitedly.

'It's confirmed, 2nd January next year, that's six weeks from now. If you haven't got a passport get one.' Without taking a breath Dave dropped the bombshell and, looking directly at Gerry with a voice lacking all emotion he spoke. 'If you want to come with us, you need to get hold of something half decent. You can't take that crappy excuse for an organ you've got.'

Adrian nodded before lifting his head from the front page of the newspaper.

They all turned to face Gerry knowing that if he couldn't find someone to stand as guarantor, and buy an organ on HP, then that would be the end of it. Unless, of course, they could find someone else, but having already discussed it amongst themselves, they all knew that there was no one else.

Gerry fidgeted nervously replying with the answer he prepared the first day he met them. 'It won't be a problem… It won't.'

The tension eased a little and Adrian returned to his newspaper.

'But there's no way that I can afford a Vox,' continued Gerry.

Jimmy interrupted him, 'I'm sure there are loads of second-hand instruments at Hitchins. I'll come in with you tomorrow if you want me to.'

Gerry smiled half-heartedly; 'Thanks.' He continued, his voice quivering nervously, 'Yeah, I suppose we can at least see what they've got?'

Adrian managed to pull himself away from his newspaper, now it was his turn to drop a bombshell. 'How are we supposed to get to Germany? We haven't even got our own van.'

Dave was quick to reply.

'No problem. I've been dealing with that today. Ronnie and the Roosters are splitting at Christmas and I've agreed to buy their van. And to help you Gerry, we will be playing several nights a week until we go to Germany so we will be earning money.' He smiled broadly, 'Tell that to your guarantor.' He raised his voice, 'Oh, and Tony, we will be finishing the Music Box dates.'

While Dave collected yet another free tray of coffee, the contract passed from one to the other; no one understood or wanted to understand it. That was Dave's job.

There was surprisingly little discussion; instead, they all began to secretly imagine what playing in Germany would be like.

By the time Jimmy arrived at the music shop the next morning, Gerry had already spent more than half an hour trying to narrow his options. There were no other customers in the shop so Gerry felt a little conspicuous as he played his way through the assorted organs. Bill Hitchins recognised Jimmy and immediately approached the pair and tried to establish how much the organist had to put down as a deposit. Gerry had a little more than he wanted to let on, having saved nearly every penny he earnt playing his accordion in the pubs.

After nearly an hour, Bill realised that Gerry couldn't afford any of the organs in the showroom. Not wanting to lose a sale, he took them upstairs to the storeroom where he kept the cheaper and more unusual instruments.

In the corner were two second-hand Bird organs. They were much bigger than the Vox and Farfisa organs, although still portable, with speakers built into the detachable side panels. The sound was smoother and with two manuals they were very adaptable. The choice was either a grey or cream vinyl finish.

Bill could see that Gerry preferred the grey organ and, when Jimmy agreed with him, he was hooked. He agreed to buy back the original reed organ for five pounds plus a cash deposit of eighty pounds for the Bird organ and a second hand Vox AC30. Bill threw in a drum stool to complete Gerry's set-up. The organist told him he would return later that afternoon, or the following morning, with the deposit and a guarantor to sign the hire purchase agreement.

As he left the shop he began to panic. His only option was to ask Julie's parents to sign the agreement for him.

Much to Gerry's surprise, Julie's mother and father both wanted to sign the forms when they heard that he had saved enough for the deposit, and by the following afternoon he was the proud owner of both an organ and amplifier.

Julie and her mother made quilted covers to protect the organ and speakers and by the beginning of December Gerry had completed his part of the deal with the group.

Dave still needed a replacement P.A. and microphones but his father had no qualms in signing as guarantor for him. Rather than buy a Selmer or Vox, Dave bought a new Marshall system. The speakers were much smaller and more efficient; he felt they would be more suitable for the sort of clubs that they would be playing in Germany.

At the next practise, Jimmy helped Gerry set up his new organ while Dave and Adrian set up the new P.A.

The overall sound was a tremendous improvement but Adrian was far from happy with the look of Gerry's newly acquired Bird organ and couldn't resist the opportunity to tease him.

'Sat behind that monstrosity, you look more like Reginald Dixon at the Blackpool Tower than a member of a group. Come on Reg, give us a tune then,' he teased.

Pleased that at last he had a decent organ of his own, Gerry let Adrian's joke wash over him, but Adrian wouldn't let it rest and his continual use of the nickname resulted in everyone in the group calling him Reg.

To explain his change of name to Julie, his family and friends, he told everyone that he needed to change it because anyone called Gerry wouldn't go down too well in Germany. They all believed him and he never used his real name again except on official documents.

The following evening the group met in the coffee bar and, after delaying drinking the last dregs of their coffee for as long as they dared, they all left and made their way to the shop where Dave had spent all his working life. He glanced over his shoulder, unlocked the front door, pushed them all inside, locked the door and disappeared into the rear of the shop, returning a few minutes later struggling with another set of stage suits.

Each member nervously tried on their particular size, and Dave then wrapped and handed them over. While Dave wrapped the last suit, Adrian lit a cigarette. The flare from the match created a large flash in the darkness. At that moment the local police constable checking the shops saw the flash and immediately shone his torch into the property.

Everyone froze.

Adrian put out his cigarette and they shuffled backwards into the shadows. Dave walked towards the front door, smiling, and waving his arm to hold the constables attention. 'Evening constable,' he said.

'Oh, good evening sir, everything all right?' asked the policeman.

'Sure it is. We're fitting up the lads before they go off on tour to Germany,' he replied confidently as he motioned to everyone to leave the shop.

Tony forgot his suit and had to be reminded by Gerry with a sharp dig in the ribs. 'Don't forget why we're here?' he whispered.

Tony looked at him blankly until he finally got the message, shuffled inside, picked up his suit and joined the others on the pavement.

The police constable, still not convinced, shone his torch from one to the other. When it fell on Adrian, he left the light shining directly into his swollen face. 'Don't I know you?' he asked.

Adrian didn't flinch. 'You might do.'

'You're the one in the paper tonight. What a disgrace?'

Adrian's whole body tensed as he saw the police constable reach into his top pocket and take out his notebook.

'Ought to be locked up,' continued the policeman.

'Of course he should,' said Dave as he pulled at Adrian's jacket.

The policeman smiled. 'Jealousy, that's what it is, that teacher should know better. What sort of example is he setting?'

Adrian forced a painful smile and the rest of the group joined in with him.

The police constable was now in full flow. 'Musicians eh? Off to Germany.' He smiled proudly. 'Course I play a bit of guitar myself, probably not as well as you.' He passed his book to Adrian. 'Come on then let's have your autographs.'

They each signed his book, except Dave, who nearly fell into the innocent trap.

Pleased with his trophy the police constable walked off up the street whistling.

Adrian laughed loudly, ignoring the pain. 'I don't believe it, our first autograph to Dixon of sodding Dock Green.'

Dave shot back into the shop to tidy up and as he was about to leave he reached up to the top rail, precisely targeted a thick, black, fur effect overcoat and put it on. He then pulled out an armful of pink shirts, stuffing them inside the new coat.

Quite obviously pleased with his evening's work, he locked the front door and followed the rest of the group up the street.

Chapter six

Promised Land

The pressure of driving all over the south of England, collecting and then dropping off the rest of the group before and at the end of every rehearsal or date, was beginning to take its toll on Dave. He was also beginning to worry about the long distances he would be driving across Europe.

The Cheetahs had played in Pontypridd, the home of Tom Jones, and as they approached the outskirts of Bristol, Dave fell asleep.

Adrian noticed that something was wrong and grabbed the steering wheel.

Dave woke up and immediately realised they were driving headlong towards a lorry coming the other way. He braked hard, at the same time pulling at the steering wheel, not an easy task considering the weight of the gear in the back, managing to closely avoid colliding head on with a lorry.

The guitars, which were always laid ritually on top of the equipment, shot forward, landing heavily on the three sleeping musicians in the back.

The van careered and skidded to a halt, embedding itself in a grassy bank at the side of the road. Dave turned off the engine and sat staring at the muddy hedge.

Adrian and Dave both climbed out and stood in the moonlight imagining what might have been until they heard Tony, Jimmy and Gerry's moaning and screaming reaching a crescendo.

They ran to the back of the van and unlocked the doors to reveal that the equipment had moved forward by nearly two feet squashing the now shocked and confused passengers against the back of the two front seats.

Blindly they grabbed at the amplifiers and drum cases, laying them unceremoniously on the muddy road before releasing those trapped in the back who were terribly shaken but miraculously unhurt.

Jimmy, fearing for his future safety, blurted out. 'I can drive!'

'Can you?' asked Dave.

'Yeah, I've driven since I was able to reach the pedals. I used to tear through the orchards.'

'Driving what?' asked Adrian.

'Tractors' replied Jimmy proudly.

'Poxy tractors... call that driving,' said Adrian sniggering to himself. 'What the hell has that got to do with driving?'

'Can we just get this sorted out now? The gear's getting wrecked,' screamed Dave, finding it hard to disguise his anger and embarrassment.

On his seventeenth birthday, Jimmy had bought himself a provisional licence, intending to learn to drive properly and perhaps join a group in Taunton. But all that changed once he had made his decision to move away from the country. Anyway, he knew that he would never earn enough money to buy even the cheapest car if he stayed in Somerset. He hadn't driven since, but the much-relieved Dave acted immediately.

The next morning Dave went out and bought a pair of L-plates and, before driving round to pick everyone up, he carefully tied them to the front and back of the van. However, Adrian tore them off as soon as he saw them, adamant he would not be seen dead inside a group van with them on. What impression would L-plates give? He thought. What sort of set-up had he joined? Was he a professional, or expected to be a clown in Dave's Rock and Roll circus? Adrian felt he would become a laughing stock overnight and he was not prepared to let other musicians have that opportunity.

The L-plates were never replaced.

Jimmy initially drove the van to Torquay after practise or local dates. This taught him his basic skills and gradually Dave would let him drive back from some of the dates outside of Devon.

Adrian didn't like the new arrangement because he was forced to squeeze into the cramped darkness in the back with Tony and Gerry while Dave sat in his front seat.

On Christmas Eve, after dropping off the rest of the group, Dave took a nap in the back while Jimmy drove the van to Torquay. Now, in the early hours of Christmas morning, Jimmy was desperately trying to extend Christmas Eve, driving slowly through the clear moonlit night, hoping to make the magical moment last as long as he could. He drove over the top of Haldon, the highest and coldest part of his journey. The forest and woodland trees on both sides of the road, laden with the microscopic white ice crystals from the night's frost, and Dartmoor now clearly visible in the distance, completed the almost perfect Christmas landscape.

Arriving at the hotel, he was pleased to find that the frost was just as heavy, a little unusual for an area so near to the sea. He drove the van carefully between the huge wrought iron gates, which hadn't been closed for years and probably would never be closed again, into the hotel grounds and along the gravel road. The hotel was still brightly lit and he could see the guests dancing to the resident band. Although everyone seemed to be enjoying themselves in their luxurious surroundings, he felt greater satisfaction as he reflected on the evening in Uffculme village hall where the Cheetahs had played their hearts out to an adoring audience. He knew nothing could have been better than that.

Turning away from the main building, he drove slowly past the stables, now used as garaging for some of the richer guests' cars, until he arrived at the cottage, bringing the van to an almost silent controlled halt on the gravel. He tapped Dave on the shoulder, quickly jumped out and unlocked the back door; at the same time glancing upstairs. He could see that the light was still on in the flat.

Jimmy took out his guitar, amplifier, and suit, and closed the doors as quietly as he could. By the time, he walked around to the front of the van Dave was sitting wide-awake in the driving seat.

'Fancy a cup of tea?' invited Jimmy.

Dave smiled as he started the engine. 'Not tonight Jimmy, but thanks for the offer.'

'I understand,' replied Jimmy, trying hard to hide his disappointment.

'Maybe next time eh? Happy Christmas,' said Dave as he wound up the window and accelerated away.

Jimmy stood watching the van drive back through the frosty grounds, the heat from the exhaust creating huge white clouds in the cold night air.

He picked up his equipment and stage suit and struggled through the unlocked front door, up the stairs and into the flat.

He opened the front door to find his father slumped uncomfortably in the armchair next to the fireplace, surrounded by nearly two dozen, empty, brown ale bottles. The remains of a log fire still bright in the hearth. In one corner of the room was a large pine branch, carefully selected from one of the many trees in the grounds, draped with ribbons and assorted brightly coloured decorations. Sprigs of holly hung randomly from the picture rail and around the mantelpiece. Carefully positioned in the centre of the table was an old cracked casserole dish filled to the brim with mixed nuts, a bowl of oranges and packets of assorted biscuits. But in pride of place, resting against a box of Dairy Milk Tray, was a large white envelope.

Jimmy desperately wanted to complement his father on his handiwork but realising that it would be impossible for him to comprehend or hear anything, he reluctantly gave up. He took off his overcoat and hung it behind the door before carefully removing the only bottle with any visible liquid left in it from his father's tight grip. Somehow he manhandled his semi-conscious father into his own room and carefully lowered him onto the bed.

As soon as his head hit the pillow, he began to snore. Jimmy pulled the washed out, faded, and ripped blankets over his father, and stood looking down at him, praying that he would wake up. After all, it was Christmas Eve.

Realising that that was too much to hope for, he bent down and for the first time in his life, quietly whispered into his father's ear.

'Happy Christmas, Dad.'

Bob muttered a few incomprehensible drunken words in response and fell soundly asleep.

Jimmy hovered for a few seconds more and, with a tear in his eye, turned out the light and walked back into the warm festive sitting room. He made himself a cup of tea, placed a few small logs strategically onto the dying embers, and sat staring into the flames, occasionally pulling himself away from the hypnotic fire to gaze in disbelief at the transformation of the room.

As the logs began to burn away, Jimmy remembered the envelope on the table. He reached over and picked it up. He couldn't open it. He didn't want to open it. Finally, after carefully peeling back the flap, he removed a card from the envelope and read it.

Jimmy

Happy Christmas, son. What a wonderful gift it is to have you with me this Christmas.

Love Dad XXXXX

Jimmy had never felt so odd, he was extremely happy and yet tears filled his eyes.

Christmas Day for each of the group was very different.

Tony always spent Christmas with his mother and father, his older sister and her beautiful three-year-old twin daughters. His sister Sylvie was taller than and not as plump as Tony. Her husband Rupert, a tall well-educated, city stockbroker always drove the family Jaguar down from Reading, arriving as late into Christmas Eve as the youngsters could bear. He hated to leave his spacious suburban home to spend the two special days in the small cramped council house. Each year it became more and more obvious to everyone that he only came down to Devon to visit Sylvie's family under sufferance. On the surface, he appeared to be a perfect family man, but he only adored his two small daughters.

He often travelled to Europe on business and never failed to bring the girls back irrelevant but expensive presents, while at the same time bringing the freebies he collected in the expensive hotels for Sylvie. She strangely didn't appear to mind as she also doted on the twins.

By late Christmas morning, the growing strain between the families was visibly evident. As soon as the twins had opened their presents, and reluctantly finished their breakfast, Uncle Tony only needed to be asked once to take the duo out on their brand new tricycles while Mummy and Nanny prepared the lunch.

The Council estate was exceptionally busy and the pavement, as if in a time warp, was the stage for a never-ending procession of cowboys, Indians, soldiers, the occasional Zorro, mini Beatles with plastic guitars and the obligatory wig, boys on stilts or metal roller skates. The group was completed by girls of all ages pushing their prams and pushchairs containing their newborn dolls.

Uncle Tony, along with many other adults, were all doing their best to help the kids try and maintain their sense of balance on their shiny new presents, without coming to grief before lunch.

Adrian appeared from around the corner, carrying his bass guitar. When he got close to the drummer, he upended his case and rested his elbows on it. 'Morning.' He looked down at the little girls, smiled and then looked at Tony. 'Yours?'

Tony ignored his remark. 'You're not playing today are you?'

'Yeah, Ronnie and the Roosters are playing a special farewell date at the Swan. Probably be packed with other groups. Ronnie's desperate for a decent bass player, so she asked me. It's only for an hour, free drinks and then back for lunch.' He smirked. 'Mind you, I didn't say lunch at home.'

'Do they need a drummer?' Tony waited and hoped.

'No way, but I tell you what...' he said, laughing loudly, 'they'd kill for a piano player.'

With the disappointment still showing on Tony's face, Adrian wished him a Merry Christmas, picked up his bass and walked off down the road, looking more like a hunter than a musician.

The twins started to fight with each other and, for a split second as Adrian was about to disappear around the corner, Tony really envied him. And for the first time, he began to look forward to the coming New Year in Germany.

Gerry's father died when his son was five years old and since then Christmas had been the same for as long as he could remember. Two of the closest sets of aunties and uncles came to stay and helped his mother to cook the lunch.

But this year was different. Julie came as well.

On Christmas night the whole family gathered in the front room, normally reserved for special occasions, and Gerry played the old sing-along tunes that he had played so often in the pubs.

His family continued with the annual ritual, singing until they were too drunk to sing any more. But this year he was determined to make this, what was probably the last family Christmas for some time, a Christmas to remember, although he was finding it more and more difficult to stop his mind continually wandering to his imminent journey across the channel to Germany.

Christmas in the Simpson household was almost the same as any other day, except that early Christmas morning Freda painstakingly worked her way down the long list of telephone numbers that she'd been preparing all year. She would not rest until she had wished everyone on it a Happy Christmas.

While his father worked away in the kitchen, preparing and cooking the Christmas meal, Dave locked himself away in his room and worried about the huge weight that he had now placed upon his own shoulders; the cost of not only getting to Hamburg, but also how much he might need in case of emergencies,

The blinds in the lounge were raised for the one and only time in the year. Natural light burst into the room and the whole family sat and ate together.

After lunch Jim and Freda proudly presented Dave with a large de-luxe road map of Europe and together the three of them spent the rest of the afternoon plotting the Cheetahs route to Hamburg.

Jimmy woke up early on Christmas morning, a little afraid to open his eyes in case the previous night had been a dream, but sure enough everything was still the same. He lay for a few minutes, tucked up under the warm covers on the settee, staring across at the mantelpiece and the large Christmas card from his father and the smaller card from his Nan. Suddenly he stopped daydreaming and, remembering he was due in the kitchen, dressed in double quick time.

He hurriedly threw a large log onto the fire but for some inexplicable reason dawdled as he made his way through the grounds towards the rear of the hotel.

By the time he arrived at the hotel kitchen he was several minutes late. For once it didn't matter, the kitchen was buzzing with everyone in a good mood, even the head chef who was busy overseeing the preparation of the rows of duck, pheasants, and a huge turkey.

The highlight of the gourmet Christmas lunch was the walk through the dining room by the head chef, holding the huge turkey high in the air, his team resplendent in freshly starched whites, followed by the sous and commis chef, each carrying a smaller bird. A never ending procession of clapping waiters and waitresses filed through, prompting the now well-oiled guests to join in the festivities.

Two hours later, as the carefully prepared trays of cheeses made their way out towards the dining room, leaving behind the chaotic scenes in the kitchen; everyone let out a loud cheer and heaved a sigh of relief. The lunch was pronounced a success and at three thirty precisely Jimmy finally hung up his steaming apron and, after sharing a crate of beer supplied by the hotel management, he left.

He walked back to the cottage feeling pleased with himself and hoped that his father wouldn't be too drunk. He bit his lip and stopped, feeling bad at having lost the newfound confidence in his father within the short space of just a few hours.

Much to his surprise his father had already laid up the table for two and was in the kitchen putting the finishing touches to the lunch, while the record player pumped out endless 45's of Shadows and Chuck Berry tunes.

As the sun went down, the pair tucked into the delicious Christmas meal, occasionally stopping to play imaginary drums with their knives and forks before downing another couple of brown ales.

When they had finished and the table was cleared, Bob disappeared into his bedroom, reappearing proudly carrying a brightly wrapped rectangular present. 'Happy Christmas son, at least I'm awake today.' He smiled. 'You know you've got to catch me early don't you?'

Jimmy nodded in agreement as he unwrapped his most precious gift. 'A Copycat... a Watkins Copycat... It's brilliant, what a fantastic surprise.' His voice faded, 'Can I try it?'

'Course you can, you silly sod, get playing.'

'I've always wanted one of these, you know.'

''course you have. What chance have you got of sounding like Hank Marvin if you don't use one of them?'

Jimmy was about to start to play when he looked across at his father. 'But I didn't give you anything, it's not right.' He thought for a moment, 'I'll get you something after the holiday.'

'You don't need to do that; being here and watching you play is enough.' His father turned his head to hide his tears. 'Come on, are you going to play that thing or not?' he said softly.

Jimmy played along with the records for hours, fine tuning the effects while Bob sang along.

The brown ale flowed and by a quarter to ten, Jimmy couldn't stand. Now it was Bob's turn to put his son to bed. Effortlessly he picked him up and, taking care not to wake him, laid him on his own bed.

He dragged over a new crate of brown ale placing it next to him, rested one foot on it, and finely adjusted its position before he sat back in his chair in front of the blazing fire. He still had to finish his celebrations and, for the first time in years, he could remember Christmas day. It really was a day worth remembering.

The impending trip to Germany became the topic of conversation for all members of the Cheetahs during the family celebrations. In turn, everyone gave their cash donation, expert advice and encouragement. But the only adult not consulted, who really had any experience of Germany and the German disposition, was Bob, Jimmy's dad, and his experiences had not been good.

The few days immediately after Christmas were frantic. Julie had a session cutting and styling everyone's hair. Gerry lost his greasy slicked back hair, his Tony Curtis tubular quiff and Boston, for the latest mod style, along with his real name,

Jimmy had his meticulously groomed rocker hair chopped. Gone were the waves and grease, transforming him into a younger version of Eric Burdon.

Dave had the most daring makeover, having his hair restyled and dyed blond.

Tony settled for a tidy up, nothing as drastic as the other four, but he did lose his pronounced parting for the more popular Beatle cut.

Adrian was the last to fall reluctantly under Julie's scissors; slowly his hair dropped in clumps onto the floor until he was transformed and almost unrecognisable with collar length hair. 'I hope it's going to be worth it,' he joked as he finally looked at himself in the mirror. He needn't have worried; he looked more like a professional musician than any of the others.

The transformation affected them all and at last they felt as though they really were on their way to the big time. Tony still did not look like a musician let alone a member of a professional group on its way to fame and fortune in Germany. He always quoted

Roy Orbison, Buddy Holly and John Lennon as successful musicians, who all wore glasses, although he knew it was only occasionally that John Lennon, the most successful of the trio, was seen wearing them.

On New Years Eve, Dave, having finally acquired the old, battered Bedford J4 van from the now defunct Roosters, visited each house in turn to pick everyone up for the last time. He had painted out the Roosters name, fixed posters to the inside of the rear door windows and managed to force a three-seater settee into the van behind the two front seats. As the rather pathetic excuse for a heater didn't work, he'd bought five sleeping bags from the army surplus store.

Dave repeated his rehearsed reassurances to all the parents and friends that he would look after everyone and they need not worry, except when he collected Adrian, who looked a little embarrassed as Dave spoke to his parents.

Reg was the last member to be collected, Dave had deliberately planned his pickup in that way to enable him to have the weight of numbers and give him moral support if necessary. It wasn't needed though, although Julie did break down as Reg squeezed into the van behind Adrian.

Their last date in England was a high-class bash at Killerton House, a listed stately home set in its own extensive grounds on the outskirts of the city. It was to be an easy night because they were only booked to play one set. As they started the second number Jimmy looked out into the audience to see his father dressed smartly in a three piece suit, and wearing a tie for the first time since he could remember.

That night Jimmy played his heart out and, before they started the last number, Dave wished the audience a Happy New Year and announced that this was to be their last show in England, and after this song they would be travelling over to Hamburg.

The audience didn't believe him; none of them cared. Nevertheless, the fact was that in less than an hour the Cheetahs would be on their way. As soon as they finished the last song the audience turned their backs and walked away from the stage to dance to the headlining Bristol group.

Bob walked proudly up to the stage. 'I couldn't miss the opportunity of seeing you play at least once could I?' He paused.

'You all look the business, and anyway I wanted to hear if you've mastered your Christmas present.'

'Well, have I?' asked Jimmy.

'I reckon you have,' he smiled.

Jimmy stepped back and looked his father up and down. 'I like the suit.' Bob looked a little embarrassed. 'I do? You look really smart.'

'Well it's a New Year and I thought I'd waited long enough to get a grip of myself,' said his father.

'That's good,' smiled Jimmy, as he guided him over towards the stage and proudly introduced him to the rest of the group.

As soon as the equipment was very carefully stowed away, Gerry, Tony, Jimmy and his father went into the bar for a last drink, while Dave and Adrian went to collect the fee for the night.

Bob bought the drinks and as he passed them across his mood suddenly changed. 'I suppose you know what you're letting yourselves in for with those Gerry bastards?'

He paused, looking at them for their reaction. They all looked at each other. 'What do you mean Dad?' asked Jimmy.

'Don't trust them, they really are a cruel lot of bastards. If you'd seen what I've seen....' Bob began to remember his experiences, shuddered, and shook himself out of it. 'I'm sure you'd think twice about going to live amongst them bastards.'

Dave and Adrian came back to hear the end of the conversation and without a second thought Dave joined in. 'I'm sure you're right, but they've learnt their lesson by now. We're going over to entertain them, not fight with them.'

'You all seem to be sensible enough... just be careful and watch your backs.'

They finished their drinks and Bob walked out to the van with them.

While the others checked the doors Bob hugged Jimmy tight as tears filled his eyes, 'Take care son, and don't forget to write to your Nan and me.'

Bob bent down and picked up his beat-up blue and white Dansette record player and an armful of L.P's and 45's that he'd struggled with all evening. 'I reckon this will come in handy when you get over there and I've put in a few new LP's for you.'

'Don't you want it?' asked a concerned Jimmy.

'No, I think you'll find more use for it than me, and perhaps you will think of me when you play your records.'

Jimmy nodded and, as Bob reluctantly pulled away, he pressed a neatly folded five-pound note into Jimmy's hand.

'Dad, are you sure?'

'Course I am son, what's money for if you can't help your kids?'

Jimmy smiled as he acknowledged the gift and again felt very proud of his father as he walked away to join the others.

They all climbed into the van.

Bob closed the doors and stood waving, alone in the large empty car park as the noise of the revellers inside the building attempted to invade his most precious moment.

Chapter seven

Rescue Me

For the first few hours the journey was spent in almost complete silence, although Dave would occasionally ask Adrian for a light or directions. As they pulled in to Dover docks everyone started to become agitated.

Apart from three other vans in a similar condition, a spotless Volkswagen van, two cars and half a dozen lorries, the icy tarmac was almost desolate. The freezing easterly wind blew directly off the sea and in the bright moonlit night everything that it illuminated looked sharp and fresh.

Dave leaned over the steering wheel and looked across at Reg hunched next to him. He had changed places with Adrian when he became too uncomfortable.

They both looked dazed, apprehensive, tired and deep in thought as they stared out onto the eerie landscape. There was movement in the back of the van as Tony's head appeared from under the coat he had draped over himself to try and keep warm. His clumsy movements woke Adrian, who fumbled in his jacket for his cigarettes and lighter. He lit a cigarette and blew the smoke deliberately in Tony's direction.

'What's the time?' asked Tony, coughing violently.

Adrian struggled to look at his Christmas present, a new Timex with a luminous dial. 'Six o'clock. I'm freezing my cock off sitting here? Can't we get on the boat now?'

Dave forced himself out of the van and walked across to the booking office where he bought a one-way ticket to Ostende.

For the first time on the journey, Adrian had stopped smoking and there was an unnatural silence in the van. They all watched Dave walk back to the van, perhaps hoping that they were unable to get onto the ship. As he climbed into the van he could sense that they were all as frightened as he was, and he now began to realise that if things didn't work out he would undoubtedly be the one to get the blame. He tried desperately to break the ice. 'It's sailing on time; we'll be boarding in about quarter of an hour.'

There was deadly silence as each of them finally realised that at last it was for real.

Dave turned the ignition key and, to his relief, the van started first time. He moved a few yards forward and then stopped while he waited for instructions to board.

'Are you sure we're doing the right thing? We're soon going to be a long way from home?' stuttered Tony.

'This is our job now; it's not just a one night stand,' spurted Adrian. 'There's no turning back is there? I'm going to be all right.' He paused, 'And one more thing; professional musicians don't practise; they rehearse.' He gave a defiant shrug and fell back into his seat.

Tony looked at Jimmy for reassurance, there was none; instead he nodded in agreement with Adrian, and then looked nervously back to Gerry and Dave. They all knew what Adrian said was true. Could they really make a living as professional musicians? Were they good enough?

The other vans and lorries started their engines and began to edge towards the huge ship now swathed in moonlight.

Within a few minutes, and much to Dave's relief, he was signalled to follow them onto the ship and into the cavernous metal belly. As he parked up inside the ship he held his breath expecting someone to change their mind and confirm his fear; that the whole thing would be over before it started. But when other musicians clamoured out of their vans, the atmosphere suddenly changed as the Cheetahs realised they were not the only group on board.

At last it felt as though the link with their previous world had finally been cut.

They rushed up on deck and, as they stood in awe of the white cliffs and watched the sun begin to rise, they all had different thoughts and expectations of what the next stage of their short musical lives would bring.

It was nearly an hour before the ship finally pulled out of Dover; they stood on deck and watched for as long as they dared as the biting wind blew directly into their faces.

Tony, now blue with the cold, was the first to walk away, and before he reached the doors the others were close behind him.

Dave seized the moment, 'Come on, I'll buy us all breakfast.'

Breakfast together seemed to bring out a newfound camaraderie between them and they all talked openly about their own expectations and what they felt Hamburg would really be like.

Adrian soon became bored and moved off into the bar, in search of the other groups on the ship. He wasn't disappointed and he was soon drinking with a dozen seasoned musicians on their latest of many trips to Germany. They all looked like professionals, wearing modern expensive clothes, with long, well-styled hair and a certain air of confidence about them.

He was very conscious that the Cheetahs looked a poor naive bunch compared with his newfound drinking partners. They were in a different league and it showed.

Dave changed his money but no one else would change theirs, preferring to keep secret how much they had in their pockets. And, by the time Adrian found what he thought was a secretive moment to change his, the desk had closed and he had a nervous wait until it reopened shortly before docking at Ostende.

As the ship glided into Ostende, everyone excitedly filed out on deck to take their first look at Belgium, but they were disappointed, agreeing that it wasn't much different than England.

The ship docked effortlessly and, within fifteen minutes, they were sat in the van waiting to disembark. Dave drove the van slowly down the ramp but within a few yards he was directed to pull into an area off the main carriageway by a uniformed man who asked to see their papers.

Dave showed him the passports and tickets, but he shook his head.

'Carte and items list?' asked the uniformed man.

Looking totally confused, Dave turned towards the rest of the group.

Reg leaned forward. 'He wants our green card.'

'What green card? I don't know anything about a green card,' muttered Dave.

Reg squeezed out of the van and the three of them walked off into the office, returning a few minutes later.

Dave drove the van away from the other traffic and explained to his passengers that they had to prepare a full list of all the equipment with the make, model and serial numbers before they could leave the dockside.

He was met with a stream of abuse and disbelief from everyone and, for the first time, he raised his voice and snapped at them. 'Come on, the quicker we do it, the sooner we can get on the road,' he roared.

Without waiting for any sort of response he walked around to the back of the van and unlocked the doors. Reluctantly, they joined him and unloaded everything onto the tarmac in the freezing afternoon.

Tony started to fill in sheet after sheet of paper until every item had been listed, then while the van was repacked Dave and Reg were at last able to return to the customs office with the forms, and pay the relevant taxes.

Dave jumped into the driver's seat while Reg pushed uncomfortably past Adrian. Much to their relief, they were waved through the barrier by another customs officer and out onto the roads of Belgium for the first time.

It was now freezing inside the van and they climbed into the welcome sleeping bags. The novelty of travelling had already begun to wear a little thin and, except for the odd directions from Adrian, no one spoke.

It was early evening by the time they reached the outskirts of Brussels, passing the Atomium, a futuristic metallic spacelike monstrosity built for the recent Expo, which jutted out into the skyline of the dusky evening. While the passengers in the back pushed forward to get a better look, Adrian spoke out. 'It doesn't look anything like the pictures I've seen, it's plain bloody ugly.'

The others had already lost interest; they were too cold and hungry to care about architecture or foreign landmarks.

Dave drove around the surprisingly quiet streets in the centre of Brussels looking for somewhere to eat. A neon sign above a dimly lit café attracted his attention and he pulled up outside. He hesitated for a few minutes until the impatience of the occupants forced him to let them out.

They piled out onto the pavement and were soon sat in the warm restaurant at a table near the window, looking at a menu that may as well have been written in Chinese. It was then that they realised how difficult it was going to be. Reg was the only person who could understand anything at all. Even he had great difficulty reading the menu but, after staring at it for several minutes, he realised that his French was not that good after all and that the only thing he was sure he could translate was steak and chips.

Dave finally agreed they could all order steak and chips and begrudgingly paid what seemed to be an incredible amount of his money.

An hour later they trooped out of the café. Noticing a small tobacconist across the road they raced over, bought a few postcards, excitedly wrote and posted them.

Their exit from Brussels was swift and they were soon on their way to Aachen and the German border.

At the border, Dave was asked to stop by a rather large and authoritative German in uniform, who asked for his papers. Dave confidently handed over the passports and inventory of the equipment, but it was not acceptable, and he was told firmly to make another payment of import duty to allow entry into Germany. Knowing that he had no option, he reached into his fast emptying wallet and handed over more money.

Once inside Germany, Dave stopped at a service station to refuel the van; Adrian disappeared inside and came out with armfuls of chocolate and assorted snacks.

'What the hell have you bought that lot for? Do you know what's in those bags?' asked Jimmy.

'No idea, and I don't care,' replied Adrian with a smirk. 'Don't you realise that things are less than half price if you use shillings?'

'Shillings? What the hell are you talking about?'

'They're almost the same size, everybody does it,' replied Adrian cockily.

Jimmy shook his head in disbelief. 'Why didn't you tell us?'

'Why should I? You would have emptied the machines.'

Tony stirred inside his sleeping bag. 'If the police find out, it's quite obvious that it had to be an English person and there aren't many of them around here are there?'

'Can you lot shut up? I can hardly keep my eyes open and all you want to talk about is sweets,' screamed Dave.

'Do you want me to take over for a while? I don't mind... you do look like shit,' said Jimmy nervously.

'Yeah go on,' replied Dave.

'Get on Reg, give Jimmy a hand,' said Adrian as he pulled himself out of his sleeping bag and followed Dave in to the back of the van.

Reg struggled out of his sleeping bag and dragged it into the front before he slipped inside and sat proudly holding the map.

They drove along the almost deserted autobahn for several hours, he and Jimmy both wide-awake chatting to each other, overawed at the fact that they were in control and that they had actually made it to Germany.

Suddenly their peace was shattered. 'Jimmy we should have turned off then,' shouted Reg.

'Sod it. You told me you could read one of those!'

'Well I can, but it's so bloody dark.' He paused, 'I'm sorry Jimmy.'

'It's not your fault; just get us back on the right road. All right?'

Jimmy pulled in at the side of the autobahn; they both checked the map and, not seeing any other vehicles, he reversed along the autobahn until he reached the slip road, and continued their journey.

'That wasn't so bad was it, seeing as this is right hand drive? Just make sure you give me plenty of warning next time or we'll end up in Berlin,' laughed Jimmy.

'Of course... I...' Reg stopped abruptly. 'I think we're being followed.'

A police car, light flashing, overtook the van and signalled to them to pull in. Two towering policemen got out of the white Volkswagen beetle and, with the light on the roof still flashing, walked towards the van shining their powerful torches through the windscreen of the van.

Reg whispered through his teeth. 'It looks like they've come for Adrian.'

Jimmy shook his head in agreement. 'He's such a stupid bastard.'

As the two policemen came closer, Reg and Jimmy could see that they were both wearing guns, and as they approached the van they removed them from their leather cases. Not realising that the van was right hand drive the largest of the policemen walked around to Reg's side of the van, while his slightly smaller companion walked towards Jimmy. Both policemen alternated the beams from their torches between the musicians' faces in the front and Adrian and Dave who were sleeping soundly in the back.

'Your papers?' demanded the policeman.

'Papers?' stuttered Reg.

Now absolutely terrified, he totally lost control and, as he shook with fear, he felt the warm urine running down his leg and into the sleeping bag.

The policeman, realising that Jimmy was the driver, spoke to his colleague who approached Jimmy's window.

'Your papers? Where are your papers?'

Jimmy reached down and handed the policeman the assorted customs sheets.

'Your licence? Schnell,' he demanded.

Jimmy reached nervously into his pocket and handed over his driving licence.

The tallest policeman looked at it then passed it to his partner for close scrutiny, before both walking round to the driver's side.

Without warning they opened the door and dragged Jimmy from the van, propelling him backwards towards their car and forcing the struggling guitarist into the back seat.

Reg sat in silence while the car drove up the autobahn, lights flashing, until it disappeared into the night.

Suddenly, for some unknown reason, he jumped out of the van and ran screaming in the direction of the police car. Realising that it was pointless, he ran back along the autobahn screaming louder and louder until he reached the van. Out of breath and shivering with the cold, he ran uncontrollably around the van beating repeatedly on the sides.

Although Tony remained dead to the world, Dave and Adrian immediately woke up.

'The police took Jimmy… they pulled us in and… we thought they wanted Adrian…but,' there was a long pause, 'they just took him!' screamed Reg.

'Who did what?' asked Dave calmly.

'We took the wrong turn… Jimmy reversed back and before we

knew it this police car came after us and pulled us in.' He sobbed loudly. 'They took Jimmy. What are you going to do about it?'

'Well, I'm going to have a cigarette,' said Adrian. 'And you'd better get yourself dried out Reg, you stink.'

Dave and Adrian climbed out of the van and took up their usual seats.

'Sod you Adrian,' screamed Reg. He leaned across to Dave. 'What *are* we going to do?'

'Easy, there's only one way to go and we'll keep driving until we get to the police station. There must be one on the autobahn... what option have we got?'

He tried to start the van. It refused.

'Bollocks!' Dave hit out at the steering wheel and door at the same time.

It still wouldn't start.

A few minutes later, out of the night, an ADAC breakdown vehicle came to their assistance Within a few minutes and after parting with yet more money, they were on their way in search of their guitarist.

Dave drove along the empty road until he saw the light of a rastatte ahead of them. He pulled in and drove slowly around the large car park until he saw the illuminated Politzei sign at the edge of the picnic area.

'Come on Adrian, just you and me. Let's see if Jimmy's here.'

Reg tried to get out of the van.

'I reckon you'd upset 'em Reg. Stay here,' said Adrian firmly.

'All right, but can I have the keys to get some clean clothes while you're gone?' he pleaded.

Dave passed him the keys and walked off with Adrian.

They had no problems in finding Jimmy. He was sitting sombrely in the corner behind the desk, bewildered by what was going on, and unable to understand a word that his captors were saying. 'Bloody hell, am I glad to see you,' he mouthed.

'Hang on a minute, don't get too excited,' said Dave.

He nervously moved nearer to the desk. 'Excuse me officer, Jimmy is our friend.'

'Und?' replied the policeman.

'We are musicians and we need him to travel with us to Hamburg.'

'Und?' he repeated. 'The papers are not good... the date is bad. Yes?'

He reached out, grabbed Jimmy's driving licence and pointed at the date. 'December 1965... today it is 1966, yes?'

While Adrian lit a cigarette and walked off pretending to read the posters, Dave stood rooted to the spot unable to speak.

The policeman continued, 'He cannot drive the vehicle with this.'

'Fine, that's OK isn't it Jimmy?' He nodded to Jimmy, 'You can't drive the van all right?'

'Course,' stuttered Jimmy as he stood up.

'You must sign this paper, and you can go.'

Jimmy signed several pages and Dave reached for Jimmy's licence.

'No sir, I will take this and send it to England, yes?'

Dave motioned to Jimmy and Adrian to shake hands with the policemen and they left.

'That was so bloody lucky, it's a good job that they couldn't see it was a provisional licence or that would have been the end of it,' said Dave. 'Now let's get on the road before they do find out.'

'I need a piss,' said Adrian.

'You'll have to wait. I've got no intention of setting foot in there, and there's no way you're hammering the machines with your shillings now,' said Dave firmly.

It began to snow as they drove out of the services, onto the autobahn and off on the next stage of their journey towards Hamburg.

The next rastatte was more than a hundred and thirty kilometres away but none of them could go back to sleep. Dave wrestled with the steering wheel on the snowy autobahn while they all hypothesised at what might have been had Jimmy been arrested and either sent to prison or deported back to England.

When they eventually stopped, with Adrian under strict instructions not to use any more shillings, Dave once again delved into his wallet and bought the cheapest item on the menu, pea and ham soup, for all of them. It still cost almost 40 Deutsche marks, the equivalent of nearly a week of Reg's wages back in England.

After their meal they felt a lot happier and even had time to attack Tony in the deserted car park with a relentless bombardment of snowballs, but as soon as they realised that they had to get back into the freezing van their fun stopped abruptly.

They rushed back to the van and slid into their sleeping bags.

As they slowly made their way along kilometre after kilometre of the never ending autobahn, Dave thought hard, and making sure they were all still awake he spoke. 'You're going to have to start paying your own way from now on.' His speech faltered. 'If you don't, at this rate, we'll be broke before we get to play a note in Hamburg.'

His remarks shook all of them and, although they all had money of their own, Dave's words still came as a severe shock, frightening even Adrian.

Dave continued, 'What do you think we're going to do when we run out of money?' Before anyone could reply, he answered his own question. 'We'll be finished.'

He sensed that quietly they were all blaming him for their financial predicament and he knew that things wouldn't get any easier until they reached Hamburg.

Chapter eight

Rock Around the Clock

As every hour of the journey passed and Dave found it increasingly difficult to keep awake, the group members took it in turns to talk to him and coax him on. The snow gradually eased and stopped and, by late afternoon as darkness approached, they arrived on the outskirts of Hamburg.

For the first time Dave began to find that the right hand drive set-up of the van, combined with the single wing mirror, made driving extremely difficult. He tried to negotiate the busy rush hour traffic and the numerous trams silently bearing down on them in the centre of the wide cobbled and worn tarmac streets. That, combined with the tramlines, made it an almost impossible task to maintain total control of the heavy and overloaded vehicle. Despite the problems, the passenger's realised that thankfully they were nearing the end of their exhausting journey.

Adrian navigated across Hamburg using the map and directions provided by Sidney Goldstone's office and finally the overheated van approached their final destination. They limped through the suburb of Eppendorf, down Lehmweg into Grindelberg, and pulled up outside the club that was to be their musical home until the end of the month.

The Funny Crow was effectively two shops converted into a club that had retained its front windows, which were decorated with huge cardboard cut-outs of Crows advertising Old Crow Whiskey.

They were thankful to have finally reached their destination but somehow it was not what they had imagined. Dave parked the van outside the entrance and, before he could turn off the engine, Adrian was gone, closely followed by the others.

They looked terrible but as they were so tired they didn't care. After all, they had just arrived from England.

'Look at that,' shrieked Reg pointing at the windows.

'Yeah, just look at it,' shouted Adrian.

Several of their English posters were displayed in the window and written diagonally across them in large letters were the words *Englischer Beat Gruppe*.

'We made it... thanks Dave, great,' said Jimmy slapping him hard on the back.

Adrian rushed eagerly into the club, followed closely by Jimmy and the rest of the group. They all looked at each other in disbelief at what they saw. The club was small and very dark and, as their eyes became adjusted to the light, they could see that it was deserted with the exception of a few people sitting at the bar. The non-descript German group was crammed onto the tiny stage, playing songs that were unrecognisable.

Dave made his way to the bar and passed the contract to the young barmaid who, after briefly looking at it, called out in the direction of the office. The door opened and an overweight middle aged man came out of the office, snatched the contract and glanced at it as he walked along the bar towards Dave.

When he reached the singer, he smiled and quickly cast his eye over each member of the group, reached out, and shook Dave's hand. 'Good evening, my name is Herr Langstein, welcome to the Funny Crow. I am pleased that you arrive safely.'

Dave smiled, relieved that the owner could at least speak some English.

'Would you like to drink something?' he asked.

Dave looked at the others, who all nodded at the same time. 'Yes please,' replied Dave nervously.

As if by magic, five huge, litre glasses of frothy bier were placed on the bar in front of them. They sipped shyly at the bier without saying a word as they tried to take in their surroundings, until gradually one after the other they all emptied their glasses.

When the German group stopped for their break and it was a little easier to speak, Herr Langstein approached Dave. 'You come early, I expect you to arrive in the morning.' He corrected himself, 'Sorry, I mean tomorrow in the evening.'

Dave was taken aback, not realising that that was the case.

'I can arrange a hotel for you tonight, but you must pay,' continued Herr Langstein.

The group members were becoming impatient and too tired to think or care about anything else. Dave knew that he had no option but to accept.

He smiled and, after agreeing to accept the offer, Herr Langstein leaned over and spoke to a young, overweight man sitting at the bar, who then acknowledged Dave.

'Hello, my name is Bruno. I will take you to your hotel.'

He stood up and waited for them to finish their second glass of bier before walking with them to the van.

It began to snow as Bruno at first tried to get into the wrong side of the van. Eventually, after squeezing himself into the passenger seat, he guided Dave to the Park Hotel, checked them in, wished them all goodnight, and left.

They climbed the stairs to the first floor room, revealing one double bed and a settee under the window. Adrian raced towards the settee, jumped onto it, completely covering himself with a blanket. 'Goodnight,' he mumbled through the blanket.

Before anyone bothered to answer, he was asleep.

The remaining four musicians looked at each other, took off their shoes and jackets, threw them onto the floor and climbed onto the same bed. They tried various positions to make enough room, but eventually realised that they had no alternative but to all lie lengthways across the bed.

It didn't matter because within minutes they were also asleep.

Adrian was the first to wake up as the winter sun burnt through the glass, and beneath the curtains directly onto his partially covered face. Feeling very hungry, he rolled off the settee and woke the others by shaking them as hard as he dared without upsetting them too much. Gradually they came around, except Dave who took much longer to revive.

They were stiff, tired and aching after their long journey, but the realisation that they were really in Hamburg soon woke them up. They took it in turns to wash in the basin in the corner of the room, put on their shoes and jackets, and before they knew it they were walking on the streets of Hamburg for the first time in search of something to eat.

As they stood and tried to take in their adopted home, trams heading down the centre of the wide roads, stopped at the pedestrian islands between the Mercedes taxis, cars, vans and lorries.

The traffic raced in every direction and, taking their lives in their hands, they crossed the road into the sunshine on the other side. It helped momentarily, but as the clouds built up and the wind began to strengthen the euphoria of walking on the streets of Hamburg soon wore off as the ice cold wind began to bite through their thin coats and jackets. Dave however, wrapped snugly inside his black fur overcoat, didn't have that problem.

Once inside the nearest imbiss they took it in turns to stare with confusion at the many different types of sausage and the other available hot food they didn't recognise. After deliberating for several minutes and determined to choose something they at least liked, all chose the same, a large fried sausage and chips.

After each handing over a foreign note, having absolutely no idea of the value and receiving only a few coins in change, they joined the other customers standing around the pedestal tables.

'Can't they afford chairs?' joked Adrian, looking around at the other customers as they stood eating in silence. 'I can't believe this, standing to eat at the table.'

Tony and Jimmy weren't interested, they were both extremely hungry and it showed. They were the only ones to remotely enjoy the food. The fried sausages were served on white cardboard plates and they were all handed a small piece of cardboard to hold the hot sausage while they dipped it into the mustard and tomato sauce.

Adrian fought hard to swallow the first and only piece of his long, greasy sausage. 'This is shit,' he said. 'I can't live on this.'

The others took a few more bites before following suit, pushing their plates away in disgust.

Standing in the warmth of the imbiss, they were at last in a position to take stock of things and watch the outside world go by. They came to the conclusion that, on the face of it, Germany didn't look much different to England, although they accepted that they couldn't read the signs or understand anything going on around them.

Having eaten their own food and argued over Dave and Adrian's leftovers, Tony and Jimmy felt good and both wanted to explore some more. Convincing everyone else to follow suit, they went off walking along the busy streets expecting everyone that passed to notice they were different, and realise they were an English beat gruppe.

It didn't happen, in fact it became quite embarrassing as Adrian and Dave began to approach any half-decent looking young girl within shouting distance of them. Realising that their efforts were futile, they tried a different approach. As a suitable candidate came within a few feet of them, they would stop and ask if they spoke English. It worked, and the five musicians were soon surrounding two unsuspecting frauleins in a bar, drinking bier and schnapps.

The remainder of the afternoon was spent asking each other questions, the girls about the Cheetahs, and the group about rude words and easy to learn German phrases.

Several hours into the afternoon, and an incalculable number of drinks later, for no reason at all they found themselves in the large office block next to the bar watching what looked like a lift, but it had no doors and never stopped. It appeared to be a continuous loop and, because it didn't stop at any floor, anyone wishing to go up or down had to time it to the second and leap on. For the next hour they had a great time, getting on and off at different floors, each attempt getting more difficult as the alcohol began to take effect.

By chance Jimmy looked at his watch, tapping it twice. 'Do you know it's a quarter past five?' he blurted out.

'It can't be?' said Dave.

He checked his watch, while Adrian followed suit, rolling back his sleeve and checking his reliable Timex.

Leaving the girls standing speechless in front of the lift they ran out of the office block, down the street to the hotel and van where Bruno, now joined by his friend Pieter, was waiting for them.

'You know the time? I think so,' he growled.

'We're very sorry,' slurred Dave.

'Come on, we must leave now,' pleaded Bruno.

He looked at Dave. 'I can drive... yes?'

Dave nodded, knowing he was in no fit state to drive.

They piled into the back seat and fell asleep, only to be woken by a very aggressive Bruno nearly an hour later. They didn't want to wake up and would have been content to sleep for hours if they could have had their way. Bruno persevered and shook them vigorously until they were aware of where they were and the fact that they had less than half an hour to unload the van, set up the equipment and play.

While they all set about unloading the van, Bruno checked inside the club. Returning a few minutes later and, for the first time since meeting him, his fat round face almost broke into a smile. 'We are very lucky, yes? Herr Langstein has not yet arrived, but you must be quickly, you will begin at seven o' clock.'

They all rushed around the stage without anyone saying a word and within twenty minutes the equipment was set up, the empty drum cases were back in the now empty van, and they were ready to play, although none of them wanted to do much more than sleep.

There was however a major problem. The English plugs would not fit into the German sockets. Jimmy scrambled around in his bag for a pair of wire cutters and snapped through the cable, cut back the plastic sheathing until he had exposed the shiny wires, jammed the wire into the wall sockets, and miraculously the power came on.

They all looked rough as hell but, faced with no alternative, started their first set.

Five minutes later Herr Langstein walked into the empty club with the remaining waiters and bar staff and, after briefly glancing towards the stage, much to the group's surprise he walked directly into his office.

Twenty minutes later he came out and walked over to the stage, stood right in front of Dave, and waited for them to finish the song. He paused and smiled before his face changed to a frown, then motioned to them all to join him at the bar. 'Come. I will buy you a drink and tell you how you will spend your time at The Funny Crow.'

'I can't touch another drink,' Tony whispered to Reg.

They followed Herr Langstein to the bar and joined Bruno on the row of stools. Herr Langstein passed a bier to each of them in turn, including Bruno, and when they all had a glass, he raised his high in the air. 'Prost.'

He waited for them to do the same and, when they realised what they were expected to do, they slowly raised their glasses and sipped at the bier, before placing the nearly full glasses awkwardly back onto the bar.

'I feel that you will be good for the Funny Crow but you must not play so loud or I will lose all my business. And you all look limp; maybe you are all a little tired from your journey.'

Not needing an excuse to confirm that, they all forced a smile.

'Tonight is not so very busy, so I think… perhaps you will play only until one o'clock, but…' He sipped at his bier and continued, 'I must ask you one more time, not so loud bitte.'

They couldn't believe it. Jimmy and Adrian simultaneously looked at their watches confirming that it was still only seven thirty.

Herr Langstein coughed loudly to regain their attention. 'You will be expected to play for twenty minutes… take a ten minute pause, and this will allow the guests to drink.' A smile filled his large face, 'They don't drink when they are dancing and, when there is not so much people to pay for the electricity, you will stop. You can buy drinks for half of the price, but *not* for the customer, it is verboten.'

They sat in silence, tired and stunned, but before they could reflect any longer Herr Langstein pointed to the large clock behind the bar. 'That is your master.' He looked sternly at Dave. 'Can you watch it from the stage?'

Dave grasped what he meant and nodded.

'You will play now? Yes?' He turned and pointed at the clock again and smiled. 'And be sure that you don't forget my friend on the wall.'

Dave slowly nodded and forced a smile. While the rest of them nodded unconvincingly, Dave gently pulled them away from the bar and onto the stage. They all had one thought. How would they be able to play for at least six hours a night when they only knew enough songs to play for an hour and a half?

As Jimmy started to fumble the intro of *Shakin' All Over*, they all felt totally disillusioned and despondent with the prospect of playing continuously at this club for the next twenty-nine evenings.

Although the club was far from busy, young people came and went all evening. By carefully repeating songs in a different order throughout the evening, they survived.

At five to one Bruno approached the stage. No one noticed him. Playing the last set by autopilot they had lost all track of time and were now too tired to even care.

As Adrian packed away their guitars, storing them behind the drums, Jimmy turned off the amplifiers. Johnny, the head waiter, approached him and asked if he wouldn't mind turning the jukebox on at the end of each set, and off again before they started to play. Jimmy looked at him blankly and nodded.

Bruno once again dutifully drove them to the Park Hotel, arranging to pick them up the next evening at six o'clock prompt.

When they eventually woke up, they were still confused and upset but, their hunger getting the better of them, dressed and made their way to the same imbiss for a belated breakfast. This time, with the exception of Tony who chose fried sausage and chips, they became a little more adventurous. By pointing, they each ordered a Frigadella - a large ball of fried mince and onion, served with a spicy tomato sauce, and a portion of potato salat. It was a much better decision but, with the thoughts that they had on their minds, anything would have tasted good.

'Listen guys,' said Dave, 'I know what you're thinking, and it's a bit of a bastard, but we can take it easy until there's an audience, and as you saw last night it kept changing so we can repeat songs for the next few nights while we learn some new ones.'

'I think we should sod the bloody Funny Crow and go home,' said Adrian. He paused and brought his fist down heavily on the table. 'Right now,' he shouted.

The other customers looked around and gave a collective look of disgust.

'We don't have enough money for the petrol, let alone the ferry,' replied Dave beginning to lose his temper.

Reg stood quietly, secretly terrified, and while Jimmy prayed that they wouldn't have to go home, Tony continued to eat his sausage, tomato sauce dripping from his chin, disinterested in the discussion for the moment.

Tony finally finished his food and wiped the tomato sauce from around his mouth. Unable to hide his fear, he fiddled with his plastic knife and fork.

'There's no way we can go back until at least the end of the month,' said Dave.

Jimmy smiled and looked across at Reg, who was beginning to feel a little more comfortable with the way things were progressing.

'Even if we could, we would be a laughing stock,' said Reg.

Adrian turned back from the window. 'I suppose we could give it a bit of time, but if things don't improve I'm not hanging around for another month.'

'If we don't think it's working by the end of January, then we'll go back,' said Dave. He looked around the table, 'Agreed?'

He stood up and, not wanting to give anyone another opportunity, walked towards the door and out onto the freezing street.

That night, now sober and having agreed to stay in Hamburg, they were at last able to begin to enjoy their new life as a group.

At twelve thirty Herr Langstein motioned to them to finish. Dave walked over to him and together they went into his office. He was surprised how small it was and wondered how Herr Langstein could spend so much time closed away in such a claustrophobic space. The walls were covered with the pictures of their predecessors; groups of all types and ages, photographed huddled around the club owner. They all seemed happy enough; perhaps Dave had not got to know him well enough.

Dave smiled. 'Herr Langstein, could you tell us where our hotel is and would it be possible... for us to have an advance?'

'Of course my friend, I will give to you five hundred Deutsche marks each week and the remainder at the end of the month. It's all right with you?'

He started to count out the money and stopped, picked up the contract and waved it at Dave and smiled. 'Your contract is brutto, you must pay tax and your own accommodation, and you must of course repay some money that you were given by Herr Goldstone.'

Dave spoke as his face broke into a forced smile. 'Of course, that's fine, thank you.'

He reached out, took the money from Herr Langstein, and counted it.

As he did so, Herr Langstein finished off with a broad smile. 'Don't forget to pay for your hotel.'

Dave stared at him in disbelief.

Herr Langstein continued, 'For yesterday evening, you will pay for the Park Hotel. Yes?'

Dave nodded in agreement.

He had already calculated that each member would not receive the fortune that they had imagined, instead an amount much less than £35 a week, less the costs of getting to Hamburg, and repaying the advance to Sidney Goldstone. Although it was still a great deal more than some of them earned at home, he quickly calculated that they would each earn less than £15 a week.

Herr Langstein reached out and shook his hand. 'Thank you my friend. I will ask for Bruno to take you to your accommodation tonight, it is already arranged. Oh, and it would also be a good idea if you played a very little piece of music before you finish each time and then my guests will know that you have finished for a short pause. And when you play the slow songs, I think that you should play two songs together. It is better yes?'

Dave divided the money five ways and left the office, deciding to wait for the right moment to break the news.

Chapter nine

She's a Woman

While Bruno drove them to their accommodation, Dave passed the money to everyone.

'Listen, I've spoken to Herr Langstein and he's going to pay us the same every Saturday and he'll pay the balance at the end of the month.'

There were smiles all round.

Bruno turned into Hein Hoyer Strasse, an unlit street made up of five and six storey buildings, unlike anything anyone had previously noticed in Hamburg.

He drove to the far end of the street and stopped. 'Here we are my friends,' he said with a smile.

They each pulled out their own suitcases and hand luggage while Bruno, noticing that Dave was struggling with his three cases, begrudgingly gave him a hand.

The entourage blindly followed Bruno up one flight of stairs after another until he stopped out of breath at the fourth floor. They waited on the landing while he knocked several times until a middle-aged lady partially opened the door.

Recognising Bruno, she opened it fully allowing them to troop inside.

Dave and Reg were placed jointly in one room with a double bed; Jimmy and Tony in a room with a double and single bed; and

Adrian not surprisingly had a room to himself with a double bed.

The rooms had no heating, carpets, curtains, over sheets or blankets, only what appeared to be an eiderdown on the bed, linoleum on the floor, and a small wardrobe.

The tiny bathroom was situated at the end of a long corridor; the bath was pointless as there was no hot water anyway, a stark change from home.

Too tired to care, they began to unpack and hang up their few clothes, except Dave who was soon rushing into every room trying to grab any additional coat hangers for his huge collection of shirts, trousers and suits.

This was going to be their home for almost a month; an adventure - the Beatles didn't have it easy either.

'David. Could I take the van and I will collect you tomorrow? Yes?' asked Bruno.

'Um... I'm not sure about that,' replied Dave. 'You will be here for us won't you?'

'Yes. I will be here tomorrow at six... of course. Good night.' He attempted to straighten his back, shook Dave's hand and left.

Good to his word, Bruno arrived at six o'clock the next evening. He borrowed the van again that night and once again failed to arrive the following night, forcing them to take two taxis to the club.

Late into the evening Bruno arrived at the club with Pieter and as soon as the group took their break he sidled over to Dave. 'David, I am very sorry that I did not come to you this evening but I was working and I could not come in the time.'

'That's not an excuse! Do you know we had to pay for two taxis? No more van. Forget it, that's the last time. OK!'

Dave stormed off into the snowy night.

But later that night when they were packing away their guitars Bruno walked across to Dave carrying two large biers. He handed one to Dave. 'There you are my friend, I apologise, you were correct to be angry, yes?'

'Fine, but do you realise what it costs for taxis?' said Dave sharply.

'Um... I understand my friend but I know you find it difficult to know our wonderful city and I can help you... save much time if I drive you to your lodgings and,' he paused, 'bring you here.'

After dropping them at Hein Hoyer Strasse, Bruno and Pieter drove off into the night.

In the morning the musicians made their way to the nearest imbiss but the mood had changed. Reg and Jimmy stood at a separate table and ate in silence.

'What's up with you two?' asked Dave.

'Why do you let that fat bastard drive the van?' asked Jimmy. 'Without it we're going to be stuck here.'

'I don't see that as a problem,' said Adrian from the other side of the imbiss.

'Listen, as long as Bruno comes for us, I don't see it as much of a problem,' said Dave, shrugging off their concerns.

The next evening they decided to take the underground and found it to be the easiest and cheapest way to get to the club. Bruno and Pieter arrived for the last song of the night and suggested that they and a small group of their friends go to the Reeperbahn and the Star Club.

They all piled into the van but this time Bruno drove like a man possessed, weaving from one side of the road to the other. Without the heavy equipment, the van bounced around on the cobbled roads, throwing the passengers around in the back. After a thankfully short journey, Bruno drove down a wide brightly lit street.

They recognised it as the street they had all walked down their first morning but somehow it was different, transformed into a very different world.

'This is St Pauli, the Red Light district, similar to Soho but with a reputation so much worse,' explained Bruno smiling, and licking his fat lips.

He parked the van in a side street and they pushed their way through the crowds, the majority of whom were drunken men.

The main thoroughfare was made up almost entirely of bars and clubs, and in the windows were life-sized photographs of naked girls. Reg had to look at least twice at every photograph, he had never seen anything like it; and Jimmy, having been brought up amongst animals in the country, made rude remarks to Tony. Adrian, however, pretended to have seen it all before.

Outside of each club stood a man wearing a navy blue hat edged with gold braid, their vocation to persuade or lure any man, drunk or sober, inside. They approached the huge group but Bruno muttered something that seemed to have the desired effect.

They turned the corner and, after walking past even more clubs and strip joints, they were soon standing outside the world famous Star Club. While Adrian and Jimmy gazed admiringly at photographs of many of the famous groups that had played there, Dave followed tightly on Bruno's footsteps, and within a few short minutes everyone was inside.

The Star Club was a converted cinema and, like many other German clubs, had been converted as cinema declined. The buildings although not perfect had a large stage, and with a minimum of alterations were ready to open. Owned by Manfred Weissleder and rumoured to be part owned by Don Arden, the prominent English promoter and coincidentally the manager of the Small Faces, The Star Club in Hamburg was the forerunner of many pseudo Star Clubs which sprouted up throughout Germany during the sixties. The stalls and rows of seats had been removed to be replaced with tables, chairs and occasional larger circular tables for parties from out of town, or the many groups of tourists, eager to visit the adopted, German home of the Beatles. The walls and ceilings had been painted black, and a few coloured lights had been positioned along the walls. The aisles down each side had been retained for easy access to the tables, and a bar had been built part way up the auditorium.

The stage was huge; it needed to be to accommodate the three resident groups and the additional name artists who appeared at weekends. Each group's equipment had already been set up on the raised section at the rear of the stage, and between sets the curtains would close for a few minutes while the female stage hands carefully repositioned the house microphones and the next group arranged their equipment. Groups booked for the month would play one set on and two off during the week but, as the club opened before any other club on the Reeperbahn and closed last, they were expected to play at least six sets finishing at six o'clock in the morning.

A waiter in a waistcoat and bow tie appeared from nowhere and showed them to one of the many vacant tables in the centre of the club. For a few minutes they sat in silence trying to get over the disappointment; the club was dark and almost totally deserted. In front of the stage, middle aged businessmen attempted to dance with a few pretty girls who appeared to have no interest in them whatsoever.

Bruno ordered bier for everyone and the waiter returned almost immediately with a tray, skilfully balanced on one hand, crammed with bottles of bier.

The German group on stage was appalling. Thankfully, as they finished playing an unrecognisable song, the curtains closed and a record by the Animals brought the place to life. The drunks staggered back to their seats while the girls walked over and started talking to the waiter.

A girl with cropped hair, wearing flared velvet trousers and a t-shirt, pushed her way between the curtains and repositioned the microphones across the stage, and as the record finished the curtain opened to reveal a different group who were worse than the last.

Adrian and Jimmy were now deep in conversation, picking the individual musicians in the group to pieces; while Dave, with the help of Pieter, was trying to have a conversation with two girls that had come with them from the Funny Crow. Tony was busy trying to have a conversation with Ria, the barmaid from the club, and her friend Helga. Reg sat next to Helga feeling left out, but tried awkwardly in pidgin English to ask her to dance. Much to his embarrassment, she refused.

Bruno leant over and whispered into his ear. 'She,' he nodded his head in the direction of Helga, 'is upset with every musician because she is loaded from the singer of the last group that played at the Funny Crow.'

'What?'

'Sorry,' he laughed. 'Helga is having a baby.'

Undeterred, Reg persevered; he took to the dance floor with her and danced for the first time in the Star Club with the rest of the girls. While Adrian hated to dance and was left sitting with Bruno, someone he had begun to dislike immensely.

By the time they sat down the club was full, transformed into the exciting place they had imagined it to be. They danced until the club closed at which point Pieter suggested that they all go to the bar where the majority of groups congregated after playing.

For some reason Reg had lost touch with Helga after their first dance, but by the time they left the Star Club Jimmy had attached himself to her. The rest of them staggered blindly along the brightly lit streets until the column stopped below a sign; Mambo Schankey's.

Pieter shepherded them into the small, smoke filled bar, a jukebox pounded out the latest English records, and for the first time since leaving England it felt a little like home, but much, much better. They could have been in Liverpool.

The place was alive, filled to capacity with English musicians and wall-to-wall German girls, who all spoke English with the twang of the Liverpool accent, and the foul language to go with it.

After one drink, Helga and Ria asked Tony and Jimmy to take them to a taxi, and they slipped out unnoticed.

Adrian was soon deep in conversation with the group he met on the ferry and drinking glass after glass of rum and coke. Dave was having an intense discussion with a group from the Top Ten Club, and Reg with a well-built, busty girl called Babs.

Bruno soon had enough and was again plaguing Dave to let him borrow the van. By now Dave was well drunk and the request was simply a formality, which was again granted. Adrian tried to go to the toilet but couldn't stand, so at that point they all decided to leave. Babs agreed to guide the remaining musicians home but, as they attempted to hail a taxi, she laughingly informed them that their flat was less than a hundred metres away in the next street.

Although it was only a short distance, it seemed like several miles as they all took it in turns to support Adrian, eventually arriving at the flat at half past six in the morning. Babs didn't hang around, wisely refusing to go into the building.

Now the real struggle began as the three of them tried to negotiate the many stairs and landings until, bruised and tired, they fell onto their respective beds.

It was four o'clock in the afternoon when they woke up. Dave and Reg hurriedly dressed and went to wake the others but they could only find Adrian who, although still dressed, lay shivering in the freezing room. He wanted to die but he didn't have the time; after washing his face in the sink, he tidied himself up, and they all rushed downstairs, walked out to the already busy Reeperbahn and took a taxi to the Funny Crow.

Dave kept repeating over and over, 'Where the hell are Tony and Jimmy? If they've been arrested, Herr Langstein will throw us out on our ear.'

'Who cares?' replied Adrian. 'They probably slept it off in some bar.' He laughed loudly, 'Neither of them knows the address of the flat.'

'I'm sure they're all right Dave. Let's just wait and see eh?' said Reg,

When they arrived at the Funny Crow, Dave climbed out of the back seat and rushed into the club, followed some yards behind by Adrian. Reg, having sat in the front of the taxi, was left to pay the driver.

As they walked into the club they saw Tony sitting at the bar smiling and extremely pleased with himself, although looking a little tired. Jimmy sat beside him but he didn't seem to have the same glow as Tony.

Dave didn't waste any time. 'Where the hell have you been?' he asked.

Tony couldn't reply quickly enough. 'Ria's place,' he gushed excitedly.

They all looked at him, feeling jealous, annoyed and envious at the same time, as he took great pleasure in graphically describing his night of pleasure with Ria.

Dave couldn't help but wonder to himself how and why it was that probably the most unlikely member of the group should be the first to conquer a German fraulien?

Reg moved closer to the bar and sat next to Jimmy. 'What did you get up to then?'

'I went back with Tony and Ria, and slept with Helga. *And* before any of you ask, Ria was more than satisfied with him.'

Jimmy nodded in Tony's direction, causing him to blush once more with pride.

At seven o'clock prompt they started and, during the next few hours, there was a strange atmosphere on stage as Ria continued to crane her neck to look across at Tony.

Adrian sensed that Tony was acting differently and towards the end of the evening, as the overweight drummer climbed down from the rostrum, he whispered in his ear. 'That was your first time wasn't it?'

Tony coloured up, then nodded to confirm Adrian's hunch. 'Yes,' he whispered, 'it was.'

Later that evening, while Tony sat at the bar laughing and talking to Ria, Dave whispered to Reg with a jealous and determined tone in his voice. 'I'm going to have a go at her. If he can do it, so can I.'

He did… the next night. And, for the first time since arriving in Hamburg, and much to Bruno's disgust, Dave took the van and drove Ria home. It didn't drive very well and he realised that Bruno had damaged the suspension by thrashing it around the cobbled streets and across the tramlines.

Dave woke the next morning to find that, following a blizzard, the van was totally engulfed in deep snow. He left the van buried beneath the frozen drifts and travelled back to the flat on the underground.

As he walked towards the flat, Dave's mind was preoccupied, trying to remember the German phrase that he had been taught so painstakingly by Herr Langstein.

Since their first evening, at precisely ten o'clock, Herr Langstein had taken to the stage and, after reciting a few words, the majority of the audience left, to be replaced by a more mature crowd. He told Dave that in Germany there was a curfew at ten o'clock, young people under the age of eighteen were not allowed in clubs or bars after that time and had to be travelling to their homes. The Police regularly visited clubs and bars, and would arrest anyone under age. After cautioning them and their parents, they would be released, but if they were caught a second time then they would be sent to a borstal.

Dave shook uncontrollably when he remembered that Reg was still only sixteen and Jimmy seventeen. How could they possibly hide that from the police? To make things worse, Herr Langstein told Dave that the group had to register at the police station within a week of arriving in Germany. It made it very difficult to concentrate on his German lesson, when he had a potentially catastrophic situation on his hands.

Why hadn't Sidney bloody Goldstone told him about it?

Dave decided to take a chance; he would register the group as a trio, and hope that the police would not check up.

When he broke the news to them, Reg found the situation almost impossible to bear, bringing on a serious asthma attack, whereas Jimmy took it philosophically, knowing that if they were caught and deported, he could come back in a few months when he was eighteen.

The first Saturday was a terrific evening, the club was full and the audience seemed to enjoy the music. As ten o'clock approached, Dave understandably began to get nervous. Precisely on the hour they finished their last number, Herr Langstein appeared from his office.

Dave stood awkwardly and began. 'Alle Jugendlichen unter achtzehn Jahren, müssen jetzt das Lokal verlassen.' He paused for a split second, 'Danke schön.'

The place erupted with cheers, claps and whistles. Herr Langstein raised his hands and clapped, simultaneously the waiters and bar staff did the same.

As the group left the stage for the brief but well-earned rest, Dave's efforts had paid off; the whole atmosphere between the group and the audience had changed. The young girls and boys in the crowd reached out smiling, wanting to shake their hands as they pushed their way towards the bar where a row of free drinks had mysteriously appeared.

That evening their worries were forgotten as they played their hearts out until, at one forty five, Herr Langstein gave them the signal to finish.

By two o'clock they were on their way to the Reeperbahn, the Star Club, and on to Mambo Schankey's, where they drank, talked excitedly of the future, and sang along with the jukebox until dawn.

They staggered and slipped on the icy pavements as they made their way back to their flat. But who cared. They finally realised how lucky they were and relished the thought of the many evenings that they would have, living on the Reeperbahn. They were on their way.

Chapter ten

Anyone Who Had a Heart

Sunday afternoon came too soon as the alarm clocks that no one wanted to hear began to ring in each room, signalling the beginning of their new day. They gradually stirred in their warm beds and then rolled over; wanting desperately to go back to sleep, but Tony wisely persevered, eventually shaking them all awake. The euphoria of the night before was now only a distant memory as they tried desperately to pull themselves together. They made the effort, hurriedly put on their suits, brushed their hair and forced their feet into boots still wet and cold from the night before.

It was even colder than in the early morning and even Dave felt the biting wind as it whipped between the buildings and penetrated his thick overcoat.

After making their ritualistic visit to the schnell imbiss for breakfast, it began to get dark as they made the short walk up the Reeperbahn to the St Pauli station.

Deep underground they felt safe from the elements, albeit short lived, as their train burst out of the tunnel onto the elevated Landungsbrücken station to reveal the dark threatening snow clouds building up out over the docks. From the warmth of the carriage, they watched the ferries and tugs darting between the huge container ships and tankers as they vied for their own precious piece of the congested waterway. The train stopped to allow a few passengers to alight, while a group of cold and tired dockers climbed aboard still eating Rollmops and swilling bottled Astra bier. They gave the musicians a cursory glance, made a remark to each other, laughed and carried on eating.

As they sat looking out at what must have been the busiest dock in Europe, for the first time the musicians felt different, special. They were changing, becoming more confident; after all, they now felt like professional musicians.

The train took them from St Pauli to Hoheluftbrücke, five stops along the line, stopping at the top end of Gründelberg.

When they arrived at the club, they were surprised to find that there was already a small crowd waiting outside for the doors to open. They were in demand, and that helped to relieve the hangover they were all trying hard to fight off.

Reg noticed a pretty young girl continuously watching him as she danced directly in front of him. She smiled every time he looked at her and at the end of the second set she walked up to him as he left the stage.

'Hello.' She smiled. 'My name is Angelique.'

Reg smiled back at her.

Shyly, she continued. 'What is yours?'

'Reg,' he replied, finding it difficult to hide his excitement.

'I am sorry. My English is not so good. It will get better, I think so.'

Reg was flattered and, wasting no time, sat down next to her and her two girl friends.

Herr Langstein encouraged the group members to sit with the audience but on no account would he condone them buying cut price drinks. It was as if he had radar in his office. Every time a member of the group sat at a table with anyone, he appeared from his office and watched them like a hawk until they got up to play again.

Reg and Angelique immediately hit it off with each other, so much so that she agreed to come again the following Wednesday. The ten o'clock ritual soon came around and with it saw the departure of Angelique, but not before waving several times to Reg on stage until she was reluctantly dragged away by her two friends.

At the end of the evening Dave collected the first real payment and this time gave everyone 150 Deutsche marks, which was gratefully received. At last earning a wage, they felt as if they were professional musicians with some real money in their pockets.

After another raucous night at Mambo Schankey's they all wandered off; Adrian went in one direction with Anita, an attractive blonde prostitute with cold penetrating eyes; Jimmy took a taxi with Helga; Dave climbed into another taxi with Ria; while Tony, Reg and Babs staggered off in the direction of Hein Hoyer Strasse. Once again Babs failed to go in but this time she pleased Reg by kissing him on the cheek, then just as quickly disappointed him by also kissing Tony.

It was too cold to stand around and talk so they wished each other goodnight and made their way up the long staircase and into their respective bedrooms.

When they woke up the next afternoon to the strains of the alarm clocks, they were surprised to find that they were still on their own. Undaunted, they got dressed and made their pilgrimage to the schnell imbiss for a late breakfast, and then up to the postampt to collect the first letters from home.

Much to their surprise there was post for everyone and, as they made their way to the club on the underground, they read their letters over and over.

Tony was far from happy with the contents of his first letter. He opened the second, read it and folded it up again, then re-read the first letter, shaking his head as he did so

'The bastard!' He shouted angrily. 'That's why he didn't give a damn about lending that fat pig the van. Do you know what he's done?'

'Who?' enquired Reg, still not particularly interested.

'Dave. He didn't buy the van; he only borrowed it for the weekend.'

Reg thought for a moment and then a smile began to break out across his face.

'Are you telling me that Dave borrowed the van from the Roosters for the *weekend* and then drove it over here?'

'Yeah, that's exactly what I'm saying. He's a sly bastard… a thief. How are we ever going to live that down?'

'Ask him,' replied Reg, desperately wanting to finish his first letter.

'I bloody well will.'

When they arrived at the club Dave was sitting at the bar with Adrian and Jimmy. The bar was lined with brightly coloured expensive cocktails which Ria had obviously concocted for them, and even this early in the evening they appeared to be drunk. Jimmy sorted through the pile of letters, passed them over, climbed onto the stage, turned on his amplifier and began to tune his guitar.

Tony said nothing. He waited until nearly midnight and, as they finished the penultimate set, he questioned Dave. 'You told us you bought the van.'

Dave looked directly at him. 'That's right… I did.'

Tony's confidence was at an all time high and he was enjoying being the centre of attraction as he challenged Dave. 'Well, I know different.' He folded his arms across his large stomach and waited. Instead, an unruffled Dave climbed down from the bar stool, walked across to the stage, turned on the P.A. and adjusted the microphone stands.

Tony shouted across the club. 'Ronnie said that you asked her if you could borrow the van for the weekend. And what did you do?' He faltered and began to stutter. 'You, you, you, you bloody stole it and drove it over here.' He ran short of breath and swallowed before continuing. 'What do you think they'll do to us when we go back?'

They all waited to hear Dave's response, and on this occasion even Reg stopped fiddling with the lead between his organ and amplifier and stood looking at him.

'Going back? Who's going back?' Dave slowly looked at each member in turn. 'I'm never going back.'

The reaction was a mixture of excitement, fear, and then panic.

Reg was as shocked as the others but he finally broke the silence. 'Never going back?'

'That's what I said. What have I got to go back to?' Dave continued to look from one to the other. 'If I do go back, they'll have me for the suits, the P.A. and that poxy, rusty heap of shit.'

He jumped off the stage, walked over to Ria, took the full glass she held out for him, and walked off to attempt to talk to the group of drunken men sitting at the corner table.

The remaining group members said nothing for the rest of the evening, instead they silently thought about the possible consequences, their own situation, and how everything would affect them.

They finished the evening, drifted separately towards the door and out into the night. It began to snow as they walked to the underground, took the train that arrived almost immediately, and sat in silence looking into space.

Adrian broke the silence. 'Don't take it so hard. You know he's been under a lot of pressure since he set this whole thing up.' He looked across at Dave who sat alone on the other side of the carriage staring out into the dark tunnel. 'He's done it all on his own... I mean... have any of you helped him?' He paused for a moment. 'I know I haven't.'

Adrian looked around for any hint of disagreement but there was none. 'Who knows what we'll be doing in a few months, we've got to enjoy it while we can. Don't forget where we are... Hamburg, where every group dreams of playing.'

'Yeah, I suppose you're right,' replied Jimmy.

For the first time since reading the letter, a smile gradually began to break out across Tony's face. 'Maybe you're right. Lets' see what happens, eh?'

They piled out of the train at St Pauli, ran up the stairs to be blasted by a blizzard.

Walking directly into the full force of the snow, they struggled down the Reeperbahn feeling a strange sensation of being released and able to take on anything. After a quick cheap meal of chicken livers and bread in the Weinerwald restaurant, they decided to go and spend the rest of the evening at Mambo Schankey's.

Reg was disillusioned and incredibly disappointed that Dave had lied to them. He held such respect for Dave and expected him, as the group leader, to always be honest with him and the rest of the group. Because Mambo's was overflowing, he decided to go a bar near the bier shop in Gros Freiheit. Unfortunately, it was almost as busy as Mambo's and he was left with no choice but to sit at one of the two remaining empty stools at the bar. He ordered a bier and sat silently questioning why Dave had lied to them, but before he had time to finish his bier a woman walked in and immediately made for the seat next to him. She smiled when she saw him and, after ordering two schnapps, passed him a fifty Deutsche mark note. 'Go and buy some flowers for me. Yes?'

'Me?' Reg looked at her blankly.

'Just go and buy me a bunch of fucking flowers will you.' The Liverpool twang strangely intertwined with her German accent.

Reg was in no doubt that she was serious. He swallowed the Schnapps, took a large mouthful of bier, and walked out.

Several minutes later he returned with a huge bunch of flowers and, in a matter of fact manner, handed them to the woman.

She snatched them from him with one hand, grabbed at him with the other, pulled him towards her and kissed him hard on the lips. Raising her voice to attract everyone's attention, she feigned surprise. 'You've remembered my birthday, thank you darlink.'

While the customers clapped and sang Happy Birthday, Reg shook his head in disbelief. Now gasping for breath, he slipped a whole neo-epinine under his tongue.

The blonde was ecstatic; she ordered a bottle of champagne and two glasses and pulled her bar stool close to Reg. She repositioned herself until she directly faced him and proceeded to wrap her arms around his neck, smothering him.

Reg had never had this sort of attention from a woman before, he was intimidated by the sheer size of her breasts and how she was treating him. The Champagne soon had an effect on him but, unable to escape, he sat at the bar until they had finished not only the first bottle but also a second, followed by round after round of Schnapps.

Reg made his excuses to leave and eventually found his way home. For what was left of the night and following morning continued to be extremely sick.

They all made the daily ritual to the postampt to collect their letters and in Reg's case a further supply of neo-epinine which was kindly forwarded by his mother. They took time out in the imbiss, to read and re-read their letters and to swap news, before walking up the Reeperbahn to the tube.

The contents of the letters initially set the mood for the evening, but once on stage the adoration of their new found fans affected all the musicians dramatically, giving them much more confidence and causing them to perform and play like they had never played before. Adrian received no letters and consequently drank rum and coke throughout the evening, followed by heavy drinking at Mambo Schankey's, and then away with Anita for hours of rampant sex. By Monday night he could hardly stand, he had severe stomach pains and stood doubled over as he played. It was easy. He stopped drinking coke and the pains suddenly disappeared.

Dave spent almost every night with Ria and started to drink much, much more, and chain smoke, even on stage. This caused his throat to become extremely sore and painful, so much that he had no alternative but to visit the doctor, where he was given an injection and tablets at a cost of fifty Deutsche marks.

Jimmy took over lead vocals on many of the up-tempo songs and, to give Dave a rest, the group played more instrumental tunes. At the first opportunity they jammed and played twelve-bar blues to pad out the evening and, by Dave carefully weighing up each audience, were able to get away with it.

Jimmy spent every night with Helga while Dave, in spite of his painful throat, and Adrian visited one club after the other, drinking and experimenting with various substances at every opportunity.

Despite the problems, they knew it was imperative they had a club for the next month, and surprisingly it was remarkably easy. Herr Langstein took Dave to meet an agent friend of his, and with his help, Dave was able to negotiate the following month, for the same fee as the Funny Crow, at a small club in Coburg, eight hundred kilometres away.

When the contracts arrived, Dave signed and sent them back.

The pressure was off and they could now get back to enjoying themselves. With a guarantee of another month of work and money, they went shopping, buying lots of things they didn't really need, except Jimmy, who appeared reluctant to buy anything except a pair of socks. Tony noticed there was a problem and Jimmy reluctantly admitted he was handing over most of his money to Helga to save until the baby was born. Although he didn't agree with it, Tony swore that he wouldn't tell the rest of the group.

After an enjoyable night at the Funny Crow and with the next month's contract signed and sealed, it was agreed they would all go for a celebratory drink at Mambo's. When they arrived it was incredibly busy. Reg and Dave squeezed into one of the three semi-circular fixed seats that at a push would seat six people.

They felt pleased with themselves and Dave ordered a round of drinks for their table, while Adrian and Jimmy were more than happy to stand at one end of the bar.

The remaining people squeezed rather uncomfortably around the table were two Scottish musicians playing at the Kaiser Keller; Margot, a young prostitute with bobbed blonde hair who sat between Reg and Dave; and Babs who perched herself at the end.

Initially, no one noticed the blonde woman walk in and sit at the bar. Reg finally saw her and recognised her as the birthday woman. Realising she was staring at him, he became very nervous.

Although she was sitting on a bar stool, he could see that she was getting very drunk as she swallowed one korn after another, followed by several large biers. She then began to fill a coke bottle with mustard from a pot on the bar. It was proving very difficult for her as every time she successfully pushed a full spoon of mustard into the bottle, she swallowed another korn. Having eventually filled the bottle she climbed down from the stool and disappeared into the kitchen, returning a few minutes later with a large chef's knife. After several attempts she managed to climb onto her stool, laid the knife in front of her, drank another korn and took another large swig from the bier glass.

Without warning, she swung round and threw the mustard filled bottle at the laughing and noisy table. It smashed against the wall directly above Reg, Dave and Margot; glass and mustard sprayed all over them. Not satisfied with the damage she had caused, she made a lunge towards Margot with the knife. Her victim, now absolutely terrified, pushed Reg to the floor, jumped over him and ran screaming through the open door out into the deep snow. She ran for her life, precariously picking her way through the deep icy taxi tracks, pursued closely by the taller blonde woman, who staggered behind her letting out menacing high pitched screams as she waved the knife threateningly above her head.

Bernd, the owner, cleaned up his customers as well as he could and the free drinks that continued to flow for the next few hours more than compensated for the discomfort.

When the excitement had died down, Babs told Reg that the mystery woman was Trude, a prostitute who at one time had been a girlfriend of one of the Beatles. Although pressed by him, Babs could give no reason as to what might have caused the problem between the two prostitutes other than jealousy over Reg.

That night they drank more than ever before and, at dawn, too drunk to be of interest to any of the girls, finally crawled out of the bar.

Tony was so drunk he slipped on the ice and rolled along the pavement in the very deep snow, picking up layers of snow as he rolled along; eventually coming to a standstill against the wall on the other side of the street. As he tried to stand, he was almost unrecognisable, looking more like an incredibly plump abominable snowman.

For the first time in weeks they all helped each other to get home and, covered in ice and melting snow, finally made their way up the stairs to their rooms.

They were absolutely frozen and, after removing their soaking wet shoes, socks, and wet clothes, gingerly walked across the freezing linoleum and climbed into bed. It took a long time to get anywhere near warm, feet and legs tingling with the cold, until the alcohol finally took over, forcing them all to sleep.

The next day, although seriously hung over, they decided to learn new songs from the records that Jimmy's father had sent them. Their material had been a problem from the beginning. The article that Jimmy found in his father's flat turned out to be several years old. Rock and Roll was now no longer acceptable to the younger audiences, except in small doses. Fortunately for the group, Herr Langstein loved it and for some reason did not notice the lack of enthusiasm from the crowd.

The next few nights went very well, they improved almost daily and the audience continued to grow, pleasing Heir Langstein.

With the following month now confirmed, Dave decided that he should turn his attention to digging out the van which had remained buried beneath the snow and ice for nearly two weeks. He borrowed a shovel from Herr Langstein and he and Tony set off to Ria's flat to retrieve it.

When they arrived, they were both taken aback to find that it was almost totally engulfed in solid ice and frozen snow. The sheer weight of the accumulation pushed onto it by the snow ploughs as they made the daily run to keep the road open, had caused the van to tilt towards the pavement.

They dug for nearly an hour in the freezing wind, eventually freeing the ice from around the passenger door. Dave climbed inside, slid across the seats and turned over the engine. Much to his surprise it started first time. He inched the van backwards and forwards trying to force a way through the remaining mounds of frozen slush.

Tony noticed smoke appear from under the bonnet and, although he tried desperately to attract Dave's attention, he was too engrossed in trying to control the wheel spin. Suddenly, flames shot high into the air. Dave turned off the engine, raised the bonnet, and in sheer desperation grabbed handfuls of ice and snow and threw it over the engine. Tony followed suit and the flames died back to be replaced by masses of smoke and eerie sizzling beneath the melting ice.

On seeing the smoke Ria panicked. She rushed back inside and telephoned the fire brigade, but by the time they arrived the smoke had dispersed and Dave was busy trying to assess the damage.

It was not as bad as it had first looked and, with the help of another of Ria's male friends, the wiring was fixed and the following day Dave drove the van back to Hein Hoyer Strasse, parking it in relative safety outside the flat.

Although Jimmy moved out of his room, preferring Helga's company and her flat in Altona, a suburb at the other end of the Reeperbahn, Dave continued to deduct his share of the rent.

During the week while Helga worked at her office, Jimmy would return to the flat and wake the remaining members of the group before spending the rest of the day with them. At the end of each night, after the obligatory drink with Herr Langstein, he would often leave with Helga, much preferring his new German plaything to the other group members.

Adrian was the next to leave the flat. He dumped Anita and moved in to the Park Hotel with Hazelle, her friend and fellow prostitute. Anita then immediately turned her attentions to Reg but Babs was strangely protective of her young friend and always seemed to be around when Anita tried to swoop onto her young prey.

At the weekend, Reg finally got over his nerves and went to tea with Angelique in Alsterdorf. Her parents were very polite but somewhat reserved at meeting Reg. It transpired during the conversation that it was the first time they had ever met an English person and, although they could both speak a little English, they were both too embarrassed to try. Nevertheless, the afternoon was a success and Reg could see that Angelique was becoming fond of him, touching him at every opportunity and holding his hand whenever she could. Although she was still a virgin, Reg had every intention of changing that before leaving Hamburg.

The next time she came to the club he borrowed the van keys from Dave and sneaked off with her. They were both extremely nervous and, after spending only a few minutes in the van, Adrian and Jimmy hammered on the side of it, frightening Angelique so much that she refused to go outside with him again. Reg was extremely angry they had spoiled his first opportunity but said nothing, deciding to wait until the time was right.

Over the next few days the Cheetahs tried to learn more songs but, despite a number of attempts to arrange an afternoon in the club, Adrian failed to turn up; he was either drunk or too busy with Hazelle. Instead, the remaining members learnt two German songs, which more than pleased Herr Langstein.

Playing those songs gave the group a greater rapport with the audience, so much so that it was difficult to remember the names of their many new found friends. To get over it, they collectively decided to call all the girls they met by the name of John. It confused the girls, who never failed to question it and immediately tell them who they really were.

It solved the problem overnight.

Chapter eleven

Let's Spend the Night Together

The German clubs had a very important rule, not to allow anyone into the club unless there was a seat for them. This prevented the problem that never failed to cause an argument or fight in English clubs; when someone went to dance they would inevitably return to find they had lost their seat and probably their drink.

Johnny, the head waiter at the Funny Crow, had become very friendly with Dave and for some strange reason continually boasted to him about his ability to fight and beat anyone, although he didn't seem to have the physique to carry it off.

On Friday night the club was full and for once Herr Langstein was outside working behind the bar, mentally counting his takings. He motioned to Johnny to find a table for a group of drunken, middle-aged businessmen, accompanied by two even drunker prostitutes, who collectively staggered and laughed their way into the club.

Johnny obligingly found them a table in front of the lively group of people on the dance floor. After ordering drinks, two of the men got up and started dancing with the two prostitutes. The remaining men, not wanting to be left out of the party, stood up and staggered towards the dance floor and forced themselves onto two girls who were already dancing with their boyfriends. Their uncontrollable drunken actions soon got out of hand and began to annoy the other dancers.

Johnny collected payment for the drinks from a man who could barely sit upright on his seat, before wading through the dancing mass towards his victims. He checked to make sure that Dave was watching and without a word grabbed two of the men, marched them out into the street and returned to collect their colleagues.

It was not so easy the second time and they attacked him. But before they had the opportunity to land a punch, he head-butted one, then the other, and punched the third man so hard that he fell into the dancers, landing in a heap.

Looking a pathetic sight, they helped each other up and staggered, bleeding, towards the exit, muttering as they went.

The two prostitutes immediately joined their last drunken client who was still sitting at the table unaware of what had happened. Not wanting to lose him they took it in turns to ply him with even more drink, until eventually he had to be carried out of the club by Johnny and another waiter.

At the end of the evening, Johnny proudly pushed out his chest and approached Dave, and for some inexplicable reason took the whole group out for supper.

The following evening they forced their way through the surging Saturday crowds and made their way up the Reeperbahn to the tube station.

Jimmy was the only one to notice the heavily lacquered tubular quiffs projecting nearly six inches in front of each of the group of flamboyant, teenage, Teddy boys in leather trousers and luminous jackets.

While the guitarist was preoccupied with outright jealousy at seeing who were without doubt the epitomy of his previous existence, the rest of the group were more than a little preoccupied with what were the most beautiful, large breasted women they had ever seen.

With the freezing wind cutting through them they turned their attentions to the U bahn, arriving at the club earlier than usual.

After playing their hearts out at what was without any doubt the best night since arriving at the Funny Crow, they rushed back to the Reeperbahn to enjoy the rest of the evening.

It was now early Sunday morning and, although feeling tired, after drinking round after round of Schnapps, bier chasers, and devouring an instantly forgettable snack at the nearby imbiss, the exhilarating atmosphere at the Funny Crow and the raucous people now milling around, had somehow given them a new burst of energy.

Saturday night into Sunday morning was undoubtedly the busiest night in St Pauli. The crowds changed almost hourly as new people found their way onto the Reeperbahn for their fix of sex, drugs, music, entertainment and fun.

Tony, Reg and Dave crossed the road, dodging the taxis, buses and trams and walked up Gros Freiheit and into the Kaiser Keller situated directly opposite the Star Club.

The Silhouettes, from Plymouth, was one of the two resident groups at the club. This was their third trip to Hamburg in the last twelve months and it showed. The polished harmonies, distinctive sound, stage presence, and handling of the audience, showed the long hours of continually playing to an appreciative audience was paying off, although for some reason best known to themselves, they only played in Hamburg, never venturing outside of St Pauli.

The Silhouettes had relied on Freda to book them in England for several years so in turn they made it their business to look after Dave whenever they could. If they only knew, it was really the other way round because Dave was more than aware his mother never had a problem filling their date sheet.

When they finished their set, Jeff, the drummer, made a bee-line for him and shook his hand enthusiastically before buying them all a drink. 'Do you fancy coming to the fischmarkt?' he asked.

They all nodded despite having absolutely no idea what it was.

'Great.' He finished his bier and ordered another round. He smiled excitedly. 'We don't need to leave until six o' clock. Finish your drinks while I get changed and then we'll get over to the Star Club and have a bit of fun.'

The curtains opened to the sound of The Remo Four.

They were fantastic and Reg sat spellbound for the whole set as Tony Ashton's arms flailed madly and the sound of his Vox organ swirled around the club.

By five o'clock, and several rounds later, Tony was asleep and Dave and Reg were beginning to find the going hard whereas Jeff continued to dance as though there was no tomorrow. When he returned to the table, he fumbled in his waistcoat, pulled out two small white tablets and passed them across. 'You both look shagged. Try these,' he said with a smile.

Dave swallowed his with a mouthful of bier but Reg sat rolling the tablet between his thumb and forefinger.

Jeff stood over him, watching and waiting. 'Come on, it won't kill you. Look, Dave's all right,' he laughed loudly.

Dave managed an unconvincing smile, took another mouthful of bier, placed his bottle heavily onto the table and walked towards the dance floor.

Reg sheepishly put the tablet up to his mouth and with a little more coaxing from Jeff washed it down with a massive swig of bier, emptying the bottle and almost choking himself in the process.

As Jeff walked off to join Dave, Reg sat waiting in anticipation. He ordered himself another bier and within ten minutes began to feel alert and acutely aware of everyone and everything around him. The tiredness had suddenly gone and he joined Dave and Jeff on the dance floor.

Tony woke up, sat in silence, every few minutes taking the obligatory sip of his bier. Jeff slipped a tablet into the bottle, shook it and handed it to the unsuspecting drummer. Minutes later, an exceedingly happy Tony wandered off alone into the night.

At exactly six o'clock the German group finished their set and Jeff led Reg and Dave out of the club. The three of them made their way down Gros Freiheit.

Standing back to allow the continual stream of police cars with sirens screaming rush up and down both sides of the Reeperbahn to the police station which was situated inconspicuously half way up on the quieter side of the Reeperbahn, a few hundred metres from David Strasse.

Having crossed the Reeperbahn and wound their way through the side streets, Jeff stopped abruptly and pointed in the direction of a busier and brighter mysterious side street and, with his eyes bulging, promised to take Dave and Reg there some other time.

As they walked down Silbersacktweite, through Langstrasse Square towards the fischmarkt, they stopped at several bars and once again saw the gorgeous women that they had passed earlier in the evening who were now, hours later, extremely drunk and under the influence of a variety of drugs. They were slumped awkwardly at a table in the corner of the bar. The low cut, figure hugging dresses that earlier in the evening had attracted the attention of every hot blooded male, raising eyebrows and arousing feelings, now exposed flat hairless chests. Stubble had sprouted on their chins and their wigs were perched awkwardly on their heads.

Jeff explained to a confused Reg that they had injected themselves in the chest to temporarily form the breasts. Unable to get out of St Pauli, the injections had worn off leaving them looking a sad and pathetic sight, while the metamorphosis speedily continued and nature took its course.

Jeff handed Dave and Reg another tablet before leaving to mingle with the masses of people all moving in the same direction in what seemed like a never-ending journey up and down steps and along dark narrow side streets.

Reg and Dave found it impossible to stop talking about any subject as the pills really took hold; the three of them continued to burst with new found energy as they pushed their way towards the fischmarkt.

What they saw seemed so out of place early in the morning. There were stalls selling everything from Chinese and Indian silks, linen and other fabrics, intricately carved hardwood, to cage after cage of rabbits, pigeons, puppies and kittens. Live fish of all types and sizes struggled to survive in tin baths, constantly prodded and poked by prospective buyers and sellers alike. Drunken men carrying huge parlour palms, which obscured their faces and view, picked their way unsteadily between stall after stall of Nordseekrabber - North Sea crab, raucheraal - smoked eel, Rollmops, sizzling wurst, frigadella, and reisenpfanne - huge frying pans in which chefs were cooking prawns and mixed seafood.

They pushed their way to the first of many packed bars where they had to virtually fight for a drink as people continued where they had left off the previous night.

Every bar had entertainment, whether it was a fireater, accordionist, magician or a mundane trio playing traditional German music.

The three musicians were on another planet and every time they began to flag Jeff handed out more pills. There was no stopping Reg, who danced with anyone standing. Dave tried his luck at speaking to the locals and, although they didn't understand him, they pretended to for as long as he bought them drinks.

At nine o'clock the crowd began to thin but Reg and Dave were ready to start again and the three of them found their way back to the Reeperbahn, and the bier shop, until it was time for them to take the U bahn to the Funny Crow.

Towards the end of the month Reg had an amazing stroke of luck. Dave made his ten o'clock announcement and Reg walked off to buy a bier. While he stood leaning against the bar talking to Tony, a slim, dark haired girl approached him. 'Hello. My name is Carola.'

Reg acknowledged her and carried on talking to Tony.

She interrupted him again. 'I am sorry but my friend would like for you to have a drink with us.'

Reg looked towards the table and a young lady in her mid twenties smiled and waved to him. 'All right, I'll come over in a minute,' he mouthed.

Carola smiled and walked back to the table. She spoke to her friend who, upon hearing Reg's response, gave him a wide smile.

Reg finished his conversation with Tony, walked over, and sat down. Immediately Johnny approached and stood staring at Carola until she ordered three biers and three korn. Johnny winked at Reg before rushing to the next table.

'This is Astrid and I'm sorry but we don't know your name,' said Carola.

Reg smiled at Astrid and, as he told them his name, Johnny arrived with the drinks; he placed them on the table and winked again at Reg while Carola paid him.

'Well Reg, Astrid does not speak any English but,' she lowered her voice. 'She likes you very much.'

Reg blushed not knowing what to say.

'Listen Reg, we know that you leave Hamburg in two days and Astrid would like you to come with her tonight… to her home.'

Before Reg could answer, Dave called them to the stage. 'I'll come back in the next break.' He smiled nervously and left.

After the first song he whispered to Jimmy. 'Guess what mate?'

'No idea.'

'I've been invited back to her place. What do you reckon?'

As soon as Jimmy started to play the introduction to *Walking the Dog*, Carola and Astrid were up and dancing.

He glanced at them and shouted across to Reg. 'Why not?'

When the dance floor filled, Astrid forced her way towards the stage and spent the whole set smiling at Reg. He returned a nervous smile and recalled his only previous sexual experience had been with Julie. As Astrid danced, he took the opportunity to look her over. She was shorter than Carola, with dark brown shoulder length hair; not as pretty as Angelique, but she had a fantastic figure.

During the next break, Reg sat with them and Carola arranged the seats so that he could sit next to Astrid. She continually tried to hold his hand but Reg resisted, feeling extremely embarrassed. 'When you finish this evening we will take a taxi to Astrid's apartment, a short distance away, yes?'

For the first time his small travel bag had a use; it contained a toothbrush, a spare pair of underpants, a pair of socks and his faithful hairbrush. Every musician carried a bag except Tony, who had never expected to spend a night away from the group flat.

The three of them stood outside the club sheltering from the heavy rain, squeezed under one umbrella while they waited for a taxi. Reg and Astrid sat together in the back and throughout the short journey she pushed herself close to Reg, and this time he had no reason not to hold her hand.

They arrived at a new six-storey tenement block. Carola paid the driver and the three of them took the lift to the top floor. Astrid opened the door and as they filed into the large hall a middle-aged lady came out of the sitting room, spoke a few words, put on her coat, and left. Carola showed Reg into the sitting room that was so different to the apartment where Angelique lived. The window cills were crammed with dried out pot plants while framed photographs filled every inch of wall. She poured him an Asbach and left the room.

He sat alone looking at the many photographs trying to work out who was who. It didn't take him long to determine that there were four children; three girls and a boy. The girls were pretty and the boy good looking; they all seemed to be happy, giving what looked like natural smiles at the camera. Because Astrid featured in most of the pictures, it was obvious they were her children.

The greatest concern to Reg was a very large photograph, which took pride of place in the centre of the main wall, of Astrid with a smart well dressed businessman and almost certainly her husband.

Reg had so many questions he wanted answered but didn't dare to ask; Astrid couldn't understand or answer him anyway.

Where was he? Who are these women? Did Dave have any idea that he'd gone?

Astrid went into the bathroom and methodically removed the rows of baby clothes hanging above the bath on makeshift lines. After cleaning the bath she ran the water, adding pine scented bath foam which wafted into the lounge.

Carola topped up Reg's glass and Astrid gave an expectant smile before both proceeded into the bedroom. They stripped the bed, put on clean white sheets and pillowcases, and removed the light bulb.

Astrid showed Reg into the bathroom, smiled at him and left.

He attempted to secure the door but there was no lock. Unable to resist the inviting bath and the smell of pine that filled his nostrils, he stripped off, and for the first time since leaving England he stood totally naked. Reg took the opportunity to look at himself in the mirror. His hair had lost the style that Julie had so painstakingly cut, it was greasy and much too long. His thin pale body, hairless concave chest, a sign of the permanent attacks of asthma, seemed exaggerated in the light.

He took one more look around the bathroom and cautiously climbed into the bath. It was heaven. He lay for several minutes enjoying the sheer pleasure and then began to soap himself thoroughly before washing his hair. Temporarily blinded by the soap, he did not see Astrid enter with another glass of Asbach.

She spoke quietly to him but he was too shy to try to understand. So in silence she carefully guided the full glass up to his mouth and after he had taken several large gulps she placed it to the side of the bath and left.

He dried himself with the large towels that had been warming on the cast iron radiator, took another large swig of the Asbach, and at last he felt ready. Wrapped in a huge towel he walked nervously into the lounge. Before he could sit down, Carola whisked him into the bedroom and directed him to the bed. 'Reg I am leaving now. Astrid is a very nice girl, have a good time and enjoy yourself. Believe me, she is a very special girl... oh,' she paused, 'and don't worry, she will take you back to the Reeperbahn in the morning.'

Carola gave a reassuring smile and left.

Reg lay in silence while Astrid ran herself a bath before joining Reg in the bedroom.

That night he realised what sex should really be like. It was dawn before Astrid forced herself out of bed, returning a few minutes later with a tray of coffee and assorted cheeses.

The language barrier had not been a problem; there had been no need for them to speak to understand each other.

Astrid ran Reg another bath, the second in a month. He then dressed and waited in the sitting room. The middle-aged lady returned and was already busy in the kitchen. Although he could hear children's voices, he didn't see any of them.

Astrid returned with his jacket and helped him to put it on. It was then that she realised that he did not have an overcoat. She rushed out of the room to return with a long brightly coloured woollen scarf and a pair of black leather gloves. Carefully, she wound the scarf around his neck before she forced it in under his jacket and pushed his hands into the gloves. Reg realised they were several sizes too large but, not wanting to lose them, he stretched and wiggled his fingers to show that they did actually fit him.

Astrid put on her long coat, smiled, and led him out of the apartment into the lift, and out into the freezing morning.

They took a bus, then the U bahn, and throughout the journey, unable to converse, they took it in turns to smile at each other. At St Pauli they walked along the platform until they reached the bottom of the steps leading up to the Reeperbahn. She put her arms around him and kissed him several times. Gradually and reluctantly, she released her grip on him, allowing him to climb the twenty or so stairs up to the Reeperbahn. 'Goodbye Astrid, Danke schön,' he said, as he squeezed her hand.

'Auf weidersehen Reg.'

He pulled his hand free and walked slowly up the stairs, turning at the top to discover that she was standing in the same spot gazing up at him.

Reg gave a half-hearted wave and a smile. She smiled back, turned, and walked down into the warmth of the station.

As he walked slowly along the almost deserted Reeperbahn, he had mixed emotions; proud of himself, but also feeling guilty because, although he had tried so many positions he had no idea were possible or comfortable, he knew he held no deep feelings for

Astrid and that she had been no more than a sexual object for him to experiment with.

Chapter twelve

It's too Late

The final set at the Funny Crow, on the last day of January 1966, was more like a family gathering hundreds of miles from home than a German rock club. So many familiar faces filled the dance floor as the Cheetahs unanimously agreed that they had finally conquered the big beat metropolis of Hamburg.

Anita and Hazelle arrived early and bought several rounds of whiskey for the group, before they triumphantly took to the stage. The two girls danced directly in front of Adrian, while Ria and Helga danced as near to Dave and Jimmy as they could without actually standing on the stage.

Following Dave's ten o'clock announcement, Angelique left crying, promising that she would write to Reg every day until she saw him again. He wasn't particularly bothered whether she did or not, but felt it was important not to cut all his links, just in case he needed somewhere to stay in Hamburg in the future.

Astrid arrived later in the evening and, after downing several shots of Weinbrand, stood in one spot and gazed up at Reg, while Carola, still sober, was happy just to dance and enjoy the music.

As they finished with a rousing version of *Johnny B. Goode,* the crowd went wild; Adrian joined Jimmy at his microphone, reminiscent of Paul and George, while Reg screamed at the top of his voice and Tony tried desperately to harmonise. Dave jumped off the stage and onto the nearest table as the crowd built themselves into a frenzied whistling, singing and clapping mass.

Before they knew it the group were packing up the equipment for the first time in a month and loading it into the van. Dave had been firm, telling them in no uncertain terms that loading the van was the first priority and they shouldn't waste time having more drinks, or talking to the girls.

Despite the now unfamiliar job of stripping down the equipment and packing it into the van, within half an hour, and with the help of the crowd, it was loaded.

With the task complete, the rest of the group joined Dave in the cramped office with Herr Langstein, who up until now had only paid them two thirds of the contract figure. 'Well boys, the month has been great. I thank you all. Now we must finish the business and we can all have a farewell drink, yes?' They all nodded in agreement. 'Now I will deduct ten procent of the contract fee for the German agent and a furser ten procent for tax.' He then proceeded to count out eleven hundred Deutsche marks – approximately one hundred pounds. 'Oh, and I will pay the advance to Herr Goldstone on your behalf, yes?'

Dave was speechless.

Herr Langstein had the money and Dave had no option but to sign the previously prepared receipt. As he did so, Herr Langstein smartly handed over the cash.

As soon as the receipt was signed, as if it had been rehearsed, Johnny walked into the tiny office carrying six glasses of weinbrand.

Herr Langstein raised his glass and proposed a toast. 'I hope that all you have a safe journey and you one day come and work one more time at the Funny Crow.' Still on a high, they forgot the problems, and as they held their glasses high ready to drink, Herr Langstein's expression changed to a look of sadness. 'I'm not so sure if I will still be here the next time that you come because I have a sick heart.'

They falsely reassured him that he would live for many more years, but their minds were one thing; to get to Mambo's.

After all shaking his hand, they were ready for the short drive to the Reeperbahn for yet another round of farewell drinks before the long journey south.

As well as the group members, the van was filled with another nine people, jammed into every spare inch of space, making the last trip together. Dave struggled to control the overloaded van as it slipped, swayed and skidded over the tramlines and icy cobbled roads, finally pulling up outside Mambo Schankey's.

The place was incredible; it could have been New Years Eve as the jukebox pumped out distorted indistinguishable songs at maximum volume. The groups and girls partied, sang along with the music, drank heavily, and through the noise they said their goodbyes to their new found friends, before dispersing, and driving out of town to start all over again at the next club somewhere in Germany.

The lucky ones were much quieter, they didn't need to travel out of town, and having already moved their equipment to the next club, were able to slowly celebrate and drink the night away with their female companions.

After several more drinks and a meal, Dave reluctantly assembled his now drunk and unhappy band outside, shepherding everyone in the direction of the uninviting van.

Jimmy was firmly locked by the lips to Helga, while Dave and Ria kissed non-stop as they walked. Adrian found a shop doorway to upstage everyone else with Anita and Hazelle; and Astrid tried to cling to Reg, but unfortunately for her his embarrassment was beginning to show.

It was left to Tony to coax the musicians and, following lengthy kisses and more drunken promises to the girls, they climbed into the van. Once again, as the doors closed, Adrian managed to grab the much-prized navigator's seat. He sat waving as the van pulled away in the direction of the dawn sky and continued his regal gestures until they were totally out of sight.

They had less than twelve hours to reach Coburg which by all accounts was a very long way away.

Although drunk, the whole group felt sad to leave their new found friends and what had almost certainly been a fantastic beginning to their professional career.

As the van neared the autobahn, and the sun began to rise in the grey sky, they climbed into their sleeping bags. Tony found his usual place on the floor and they settled back to dream about the last few weeks and wonder when, or if, they would ever return to Hamburg.

Reg wasn't able to sleep; his mind kept wandering back to the previous night at Astrid's flat. Although she wasn't pretty, he couldn't stop thinking about her. There was so much excitement and freedom with her, she was experienced and was different. Although it had only been one night, he could remember it all so clearly. Perhaps there was a lot more to learn, maybe he was naive, but then he was still only sixteen.

When Adrian began to snore, Dave nudged him awake, and without a word he climbed blindly into the back of the van. Reg seized the opportunity and jumped into the front, only too pleased to be able to sit in the treasured passenger seat. He and Dave spent the next four hours discussing anything and everything to keep awake, during which time they travelled almost three hundred kilometres.

The van suddenly lost power; coming to a standstill with smoke bellowing out from beneath the bonnet. Dave jumped out and raised the bonnet to reveal a cloud of steam spiralling from the radiator. The sudden panic woke everyone and within a few seconds they were all standing on the side of the autobahn wondering what to do next. They realised that they could do nothing until the engine cooled, so they all climbed back into their sleeping bags and waited.

After what seemed like hours, but what in reality was no more than fifteen minutes, Jimmy carefully removed the radiator cap and refilled the radiator. 'It looks like the thermostats had it,' he told them. 'I can't see how we can make it to Coburg with that sort of problem.'

Dave started the van and began to drive. 'We'll have to try, we don't have any alternative do we?'

'Maybe we could part exchange the van,' suggested Tony.

Dave thought it was a good idea and worth a try so he took the next exit off the autobahn. He drove through several small villages stopping at every garage that had anything suitable for sale on the forecourt, and tried to part exchange the van without success.

Jimmy refilled the radiator and Dave drove for another thirty minutes before it overheated again. They knew that something more permanent had to be done if they were to have any chance of reaching Coburg.

While Dave and Reg walked to a garage, bought a plastic five-gallon drum and filled it with water; Jimmy, despite the difficulty of using makeshift tools, was eventually able to remove the thermostat. However, the first aid repairs would mean regular stops for the rest of the journey and they were still only half way.

Several forced stops later they pulled into a café on the outskirts of Fulda, to buy sandwiches and coffee, while the radiator cooled down and Dave refuelled the van for the fourth time. When they walked in, the few customers stared at them in silence; perhaps with good reason as the long haired musicians were dirty, tired, and looked very different to anything the villagers had ever seen before.

Dave swallowed three Captagon and without thinking threw the empty packet onto the floor; he had taken a whole packet of ten tablets to keep him awake since leaving Hamburg. As he drank his coffee he started to twitch and shake uncontrollably.

It was becoming increasingly obvious they would not get to the club on time, and Jimmy was having grave doubts as to whether they would get there at all. He took to the passenger seat once more and did his best to coax Dave ever nearer to their journey's end.

It started to get dark and became more and more difficult to read the road signs and the demands on the two of them were incredible. By nine o'clock the roads began to deteriorate and, as Dave drove down the narrow lanes, they had a number of near misses with oncoming vehicles when the drivers frequently dazzled Dave. The increasing risks and danger kept all the passengers alert and made everyone feel so nervous that, at the first opportunity, they stopped.

Revived, but still feeling incredibly tired, they grudgingly climbed back into what was fast becoming hell on wheels, and certain punishment for the last four weeks of gratification.

Dave heroically drove on into the darkness, down even narrower and darker roads. Adrian, now back in his seat, noticed watchtowers strategically placed on the skyline, housing searchlights that continually scanned the high fence and the overgrown landscape. Soldiers carrying machine guns and torches patrolled the area, while other silhouettes restrained large Alsatians as they pushed their way between the trees and undergrowth. Not believing what he saw, he leaned over and nudged Reg who in turn scrutinised the map. 'Bloody hell...we're almost in East Germany.'

'What the fuck are you talking about,' screamed Jimmy.

'Look, you can see over there,' stuttered Reg.

They were terrified and this time even Adrian was too frightened to snatch a glance in the direction of the border and, disregarding his hairstyle, covered his head with a scarf.

'Be bloody careful Dave or we'll all end up?' screamed Tony.

'End up what?' interrupted Adrian.

'Well… you know what I mean,' sighed Tony.

'If we stick to the road we'll be alright,' blurted out Adrian, the fear evident in his quivering voice.

'Just take it easy Dave,' pleaded Reg.

Dave grunted a response and continued to drive blindly along the uneven and potholed road. His senses, disorientated by the cocktail of drugs, were mesmerised with the combination of darkness and random flashes from the searchlights as they penetrated the bare trees and bushes, illuminating the high barbed wire fences and night sky. The van bounced along the track shaking and rattling the equipment while the exhausted and tired musicians minds, twisted and confused, conjured up imaginary situations of being captured and taken prisoner by the East Germans.

A few miles later, the roads dramatically improved and, just before midnight, they arrived in the small border town of Coburg.

For the next twenty minutes they drove around the town searching the deserted streets for someone to ask directions to the club. An American jeep appeared from nowhere and Adrian waved like a maniac to attract the driver's attention. The army vehicle screeched to a halt in front of them; the occupants at first wary, until Adrian spoke, and realising he was English, obliged by escorting them to the club.

A small crowd had gathered outside and as the exhausted musicians climbed out of the van they were met with catcalls, whistles and boos.

Too tired to care they stretched their legs and walked through the front doors and down a short flight of stairs into a foyer that opened directly onto the side of the stage. A six-foot high section of trellis fence, decorated with plastic ivy and flowers, formed the token division between the small foyer at the entrance and the stage. The tables were placed in rows with chairs unevenly spaced along each of them and the extremely bright lights made the club clinical and cold. The paintwork on the high walls was cracked and peeling, and in serious need of redecoration. With the exception of a few large outdated coloured posters of unknown German recording groups, that had come unstuck and now hung precariously high above the tables, the walls were bare.

A small group of people sat drinking at one end of the full-length bar while two shabby waiters played cards. The remaining customers consisted of three elderly men sat together, as if on an island, at a table in the centre of the club.

As Dave walked slowly towards the bar, the place fell silent. It looked and felt like a Wild West saloon, when the bad guys hit town.

An agitated elderly Jewish man stood carelessly polishing glasses while a much younger, and unusually short haired man, filled the shelves. An antiquated Bel Ami jukebox played the former hit songs, transformed into unrecognisable tunes by the appalling acoustics.

After a few minutes of irate conversation and frantic arm waving by the Jewish man, who repeatedly pointed at the large clock above his head, Dave, slouching and his face showing intense anger, shook his head in disbelief. The group looked at him expectantly, perhaps hoping that he was going to tell them that they were in the wrong club.

Instead Dave grimaced and spoke through his gritted teeth. 'He wants us to play.'

Adrian walked towards the bar for a drink.

Dave pulled him back. 'Adrian, he wants us to play *now*, tonight.'

Adrian turned and simultaneously they all asked the same thing. 'Now?'

'If we don't, then he…' Dave stopped, and without directly pointing at the man behind the bar but at the same time making it quite clear who had given him the ultimatum, continued. 'If we don't set up and play within half an hour, he's going to tear up the contract.'

Without a word they walked up the stairs, pushed through the small group of sneering and abusive people, and out to the van.

As they stood in the middle of the road, unloading their suitcases, yet another American jeep roared around the corner narrowly missing Adrian. '*Bastards,*' he screamed as he grabbed a microphone stand and holding it menacingly above his head pointed it in the direction of the jeep until it disappeared into the darkness.

The group set up, beating the deadline by ten minutes, and at five to one, still in a state of shock and feeling incredibly tired, they jammed twelve-bar instrumentals and a series of R and B tunes.

They couldn't believe this was really happening to them.

As they played, the eldest man behind the bar eyed them menacingly, while a stream of drunken people appeared around the entrance and stood staring at them from the side of the stage, making them feel more and more angry at the thought of four weeks in this hell-hole.

They had only one thought, to sleep, preferably in a bed.

At two o'clock, the Jewish man gestured to Dave to finish. He limped towards the stage followed close behind by one of the waiters holding a set of keys. 'In case you do not know who I am, I will tell you. My name is Herr Mankovitch, and yes, I am the owner. My manager Herr Fischer will deal with you when I am not here.' He raised his arm in the direction of one of the waiters and pointed. 'He will show you to your accommodation but there are some rules, no girls and not so much noise, and tomorrow.' He gave a false smile, almost a sneer. 'You will play much better, and one more thing,' he paused, 'and not so loud, yes?'

They didn't care much about tomorrow, only to sleep.

The waiter climbed into the front of the van and being unable to speak any English whatsoever directed them to what was going to be their home for the next month. Eager to get home, he led them up three flights of stairs, climbing two and sometimes three stairs at a time, while they struggled with their bags and cases. When he reached the top floor, he unlocked the door, turned on the light and left.

Dave was still in the van searching amongst the drum cases and amplifier covers when the waiter appeared in the street. Somehow the singer managed to get him to understand and they drove back to the club. He returned a few minutes later. 'Bastards, sodding bastards, they've stolen my case, all my suits... gone!' The others just looked on.

What else could go wrong?

As well as having three bedrooms, the flat had a kitchen and a bathroom, with hot running water. Adrian, although very tired, rushed around like shot from a gun looking for the best room, and once again struck lucky. Reg and Jimmy shared a room with two single beds. They all quietly agreed the room with a double bed should go to Dave, while Tony ended up with no choice but to sleep on one of the two settees in the sitting room.

They all fell into bed except Dave, who sat in an armchair close to tears as the effects of the Captagon, and the last twenty-four hours, finally took its toll. Waking late the next afternoon, and feeling terribly hungry, they found it hard to believe that yesterday was real, and as they drank their first cup of tea, made by Tony, it gradually became clear that it was; they would soon have to get ready and play in that awful club.

With the exception of Adrian, who had had the benefit of a hotel room with either Anita or Hazelle for most of the last month, one by one, they had a bath and washed their hair, for only the second or third time since leaving England.

It seemed like a million years ago and, as they all sat around the lounge drinking their second cup of tea, they once again felt like a group, bonded by the problems at hand, except Adrian who stood looking out of the window onto the almost deserted town square. 'How could there be such a difference between the Funny Crow and this excuse for a club in such a God forsaken place?' he said.

He shook his head and went back to bed.

Dave only had the clothes he'd been wearing throughout the journey and, fortunately, an old suit and shirt which had been moved from van to van since his days with Music Box. Despite the problems, he was philosophical. 'If we can get through this month, we'll be alright. I can slowly replace my clothes and stage suits, and we can sort out the poxy van while we're here,' he said.

The next evening they played the best they could under the circumstances, then returned to the flat in silence. Tony made a tray of tea and they sat staring at each other until he broke the deadly silence. 'What do you reckon Dave?' he asked.

'We're not going anywhere until we get that poxy van fixed, replied Dave.

"Assuming it can be fixed, there's no option but to see out the month, is there? That is, if we want to stay in Germany,' said Jimmy.

'We won't be spending much money in this sodding place and I don't think there's much life here, so there's no fear of any late nights,' said Adrian. 'Ah fuck it. I'm off to bed.'

Tony waited for the others to follow Adrian and half an hour later he was snoring on the settee.

The following morning they went out to explore and find a cheap imbiss for breakfast. They were in for a shock. They were able to find only one and it was closed for the day. 'That's lucky, 'said Dave. 'We'll put five marks each in a kitty and share the cost of the food and we can eat here in the flat.'

'And we can save money,' chipped in Tony.

After walking street after street they eventually found a little shop immediately behind their flat. What at first seemed a good idea soon turned into a major problem as it became difficult to decide what they should buy with the money collected. Everyone liked different things, especially Adrian who seemed to have developed expensive tastes overnight.

It was difficult for them because the items were packaged differently to those at home. Unable to understand the labels it took many minutes deliberating over what was actually inside the packets. Nevertheless they agreed on two baskets of basic items, including bread, rolls, eggs, bacon, butter, ham, cheese, fruit juice, jam, cornflakes, milk, tea, coffee, bottles of Coca-Cola, bier and chocolate. This was to last for the first four days.

Jimmy prepared what was probably the most delicious breakfast they'd had since leaving England. Things didn't seem so bad after all; at least they had a civilised start to the day, and a base for the rest of the month.

Two days later nearly all the food had gone and Dave asked for a further five Deutsche marks from everyone. They were all happy to pass money over to Dave, except Adrian who refused. He preferred to eat in the nearby bar, but when the rest of them were asleep would secretly raid their food.

Herr Mankovitch was a difficult man to understand and, despite Dave's diplomatic manner, things were not going well. Fortunately he had the following night off and this gave Dave the opportunity to talk to the much younger Herr Fischer. He was much more understanding and preferred the group to play louder.

After that, every night became a battle of wits between the

owner, his manager and the group, who tried to please both of them.

Despite the apparent harmony at the club, the problems at their flat were going from bad to worse. Every time of the day or night, whenever any of them opened the ground floor entrance door, it seemed to trigger an invisible alarm. By the time they reached the first floor landing an elderly lady was waiting for them, peering around the door of her flat.

One evening when a very drunk Dave and Adrian returned from the club she appeared at her door; at first they ignored her, but then suddenly turned and blew the loudest raspberry in her face. She cursed them under her breath and tried to hide her anger as they staggered on up the stairs laughing loudly. Undeterred, she continued to spy on them every time they entered the building, irrespective of the time of day or night.

During the week the club wasn't busy but at weekends the place was full and the Cheetahs went down very well, especially with the Americans from the nearby base.

One evening when Herr Mankovitch was not at the club, two English lads and a girl came in and sat in the front of the stage. They were dirty and looked as though they had been sleeping rough. Taking care not to be seen from the bar, the waiters slipped them all a drink.

In the interval, Dave and Tony joined them. 'You're English?' asked Dave.

'Yeah,' replied the girl. 'We played here last month.'

'It's a bit grim ain't it?' said Dave.

Her boyfriend continued. 'Yeah, you can say that again. We'd only been here two and a half weeks when Tony our bass player....'

'That's my name,'interrupted Tony.

'Ah right... well he was so homesick he left, just disappeared overnight... left all his gear.'

'Bloody hell, where is he then?' asked Dave.

'If he's got any sense he's home by now, probably trying to forget it,' said the girl.

'The thing is, I can play bass but that bastard, Mankovitch, said we broke our contract and kicked us out. Said he booked five and only had four.'

The girl interrupted. 'He threw all our gear out in the street and locked the doors.'

'And he refused to pay us. So here we are. No money, sleeping in the van and waiting to get the hell out of this place.'

The girl whispered in Dave's ear. 'Just be careful, don't let either of 'em catch you out or you'll end up like us.'

In the next break Dave bought them all a drink and promised to meet the next day and buy them breakfast. It was enlightening to listen to the problems they had encountered; almost a mirror of the Cheetahs experiences since arriving in Germany.

Richard, the drummer, was also a mechanic and Dave, not wanting to miss an opportunity, offered to pay him to sort out the van. For the next few days Richard, pleased to have been able to help and at the same time earn some money, worked hard to repair the water pump gasket, replace the thermostat and a few other minor parts that were defective.

The two groups spent a lot of time together. Richard and his fellow musicians showed them around the area and, using his expensive camera, took three films of new publicity photographs.

Fortunate to have a free day, which coincided with the completion of the repair of the van, they were up early to test it out. The two groups made the journey to a concentration camp. It was sunny when they arrived at the entrance. Dave parked the van and, as they walked under the metal arch, they were struck by the eerie silence. As they continued past the ghostly grey buildings, they noticed that there wasn't a flower on the site, or a bird in the sky. It was as if the birds instinctively knew what had happened and deliberately avoided the area.

Dave shivered. 'Come on let's get the hell out of this spooky place.' No one disagreed and they left for the nearest bar.

Coburg had been relatively unaffected by the allied bombing and therefore the local people still remembered the propaganda, and harboured hatred for the English and more recently the Americans who now lived nearby and patrolled the border.

Living within the shadow of the lookout towers, a short distance from the East German border, and the constant reminder of the division of their country kept those appalling feelings alive. It was quite obvious that the Coburg residents hated the intrusion and given the opportunity showed their feelings.

Adrian and Dave were bored and one afternoon found a tiny shop that sold replica guns. They bought one each and then spent most of the afternoon drinking in a bar; the alcohol made them tired so they each took several Captagon.

Now on a high, they chased each other through the streets shooting at each other and scattering the local residents. Adrian ran upstairs into the flat and started shooting out of the window at Dave who was standing in the street. Dave faked being shot and fell onto the pavement.

Within minutes, both the American military and German police arrived. They were furious when they realised what had happened and argued who should arrest them. The Americans won the day and, much to the disgust of the German police, Dave and Adrian were released after a serious reprimand.

That was how Dave and Adrian met and became friendly with Walrond Weislinger, the American GI, or Wally as he was instantly nicknamed by Adrian.

The evening immediately after the fracas, Wally visited the club and wasted no time in buying the group drinks and joining them at their table. 'You's guys are crazy man. Are all English men the same?' he said on more than one occasion.

Wally and his buddy George spent the evening buying the group drinks and, as they left, invited the group to join them the next day at the Sunday afternoon concert at the newly refurbished community centre. Preferring to stay in bed but feeling obliged to accept their offer they agreed to join them.

The hall was packed with teenagers, mostly young girls who looked fresh and innocent. The two local amateur German groups were extremely bad and Adrian found it hard to keep a straight face. Had it not been for Wally buying the drinks and the looks and smiles from the giggling girls, he would have left.

Wally secretly persuaded the supporting German group to let Dave and his group use their equipment and play a couple of songs.

Standing centre stage, Wally built up the atmosphere until the Cheetahs were ready. When they burst into life everyone surged towards the stage, the young girls crowded around the front while the boys hung back until they too were drawn into the excitement.

The atmosphere in the hall continued to rise as the group built up to a crescendo finishing with *Johnny B. Goode*, sending everyone into an animated frenzy.

As the Cheetahs left the stage, it could have been a Beatles concert. They were mobbed, and the bier, schnapps and weinbrand flowed. Wally paid, he was so proud; it had suddenly cheered him up after the boring and mundane months since leaving America.

He boasted to the young swooning girls and the massed jealous male would-be musicians, who were now as anxious to talk to the group as the girls, that he was their American manager. As long as he bought the drinks no one minded, least of all Dave and Adrian.

Tony drank too much and consequently had to be carried back to the flat. It wasn't easy to find any volunteers to carry him up the stairs until George and Wally manhandled him to the top floor.

They had less than an hour to get ready but, after a wash and copious cups of black coffee, they were all ready except Tony. Dave couldn't wake him.

Wally drove them to the van, where Richard and the remnants of his group had made their temporary home, and persuaded him to play with them for the evening.

Fortunately for them Herr Mankovitch had that night off and, despite it having been much busier than usual, the following night he called Dave to the bar.

'I understand what was happening last night. I missed nothing, yes?' He faked a smile and continued. 'If there is one more situation you will be fired.'

Dave told the rest of the group what he'd been told and they all went back to the flat, swallowed a couple of Captagon each and drank until they could drink no more.

The following morning Dave heard someone come into his room. Thinking it was one of the group, he ignored it and closed his eyes. A few minutes later, still semi conscious, he felt a warm naked body pushing against his and fingers groping his penis. He thought he was in heaven and sleeping with an angel with tits.

Dave wasn't dreaming. It was Tania.

After that first morning, Tania visited him every day on her way to school.

Because Dave enjoyed her visits so much, she invited her school friends for Adrian, Reg and Jimmy. Apologetically, she told Dave that she couldn't find a friend for Tony.

Dave didn't care.

Somehow Tania had managed to get hold of a key and, despite the problem with the old woman downstairs, she was never seen or heard, and came again after school most afternoons to clean and cook for them, or do anything else that was needed.

It was bliss; it was how they imagined a musician's life in Germany should be.

Chapter thirteen

I Think I'm Going Back

Tony received half of his expected wages at the end of the week, it had cost him fifty Deutsche marks for the privilege of getting drunk and missing Sunday evening, but he accepted that it was his own fault and took it in good heart.

It was soon forgotten because Saturday 16th February, as well as being pay day, was a very special day; it was Jimmy's eighteenth birthday and, although the rest of the group knew it, Jimmy received no cards.

Up early, he walked to the postampt hoping for at least one letter and cards from England, and a card from Helga in Hamburg. Two hours later he returned empty handed in an awful mood, miserable and short-tempered. The rest of his day was uneventful; everyone kept their distance and, when possible, avoided him completely. Jimmy disappeared off to the bar next to the flat and spent most of the afternoon drinking and feeling extremely sorry for himself.

The evening started badly. Although already drunk, Jimmy continued to drink heavily and consequently Herr Mankovitch refused to sell him any more biers. Rather than help, it further compounded the problem and in every break Jimmy left the club and walked to the nearby bar for even more drinks.

At nine o'clock Tania and three of her friends arrived at the club and sat at the front table. Always enthusiastic and even more so tonight, they began to get through to Jimmy till at last he pulled himself together. The group started to build up the atmosphere and enjoy themselves and at a quarter to ten they took an early break. Jimmy took off his guitar and when Tania and her friends produced a large birthday cake the whole club erupted into a rousing chorus of Happy Birthday.

'You bastards!' screamed Jimmy, smiling.

He jumped off the stage and squeezed himself between the young girls, who in turn showed their feelings by wrestling with each other to kiss him.

The musicians each handed him a birthday card and Dave passed him two more cards from England. Jimmy tried without success to open them as all the young girls struggled to wish him a happy birthday for the second time. In the mêlée, Jimmy felt a pair of soft arms around his neck and a warm tongue in his left ear; he tried to look around but the adoring clutches of the young girls were too tight. Seeing Helga over his shoulder, he pulled himself free and almost crushed her in his arms.

Reg walked back from the bar carrying a tray of bier and noticed Astrid standing near the stage. She smiled adoringly at him and moved closer. He tried to ignore her but she was determined and, after following him around for several minutes, he gave in, grasped her hand tightly and then almost immediately released it. She was happy at last.

Dave climbed back onto the stage, made his ten o'clock announcement to the audience, and summoned the rest of group to join him.

Jimmy, now elated and no longer interested in drinking, rushed back from the bar where he had been thanking Herr Fischer, and buying drinks for Helga and Astrid.

The young fans reluctantly left the club. For the next few hours, and while Astrid sat sipping her bier and trying to attract Reg's attention, Jimmy, now almost sober, couldn't take his eyes off of Helga.

During the next interval, Reg prised Helga away from Jimmy. He had so many questions and he desperately wanted to know the answers. 'Who was the man in the photograph at Astrid's flat?' he asked his face unusually serious for such a young man. 'And where are her children?' he continued.

Helga already knew the answers. She glanced briefly at Astrid, and replied in perfect English. 'Helmut, Astrid's husband, was a very successful businessman in Hamburg, but during the terrible storm and flood in 1962, he was drowned with many other people. I think maybe three hundred people died and more than twenty thousand others were evacuated. It was a very serious and sad time for her and the people of Hamburg.' She stopped and smiled at Jimmy, then reached over and gave him a kiss on the cheek before continuing. 'Today, the sixteenth of February, the same as Jimmy's birthday.' She turned to the guitarist and smiled. 'It is the third anniversary of the catastrophe; it has been very difficult for Astrid, alone with four small children. But she loves you Reg and so she make a decision to leave her children for you.'

Helga turned to look and smile at Astrid, paused, and took a long look at Reg. 'Now you know how much she cares about you. You are very lucky Reg.'

'What do you mean, she's left her children for me? I only spent one night with her,' he said angrily. Reg found it hard to speak, let alone understand what Helga had just told him. 'I don't believe it,' he screamed.

Helga replied in a different tone of voice. 'Reg, it is true, very true, you *must* believe me,' pleaded Helga.

Reg shook his head erratically. 'I'm sorry, but I don't believe I'm hearing this. Jimmy did you hear what she's done?'

Jimmy couldn't care less, Helga was with him to celebrate his birthday and that was all that mattered.

Dave called them all back to the stage and for the remainder of the evening Reg had great difficulty in even looking at Astrid.

As soon as Dave received the signal from Herr Fischer, they finished the last song and left the stage. Helga, already waiting at the door, stood impatiently holding a large brightly wrapped package, tempting Jimmy to hurry and follow her. Reg rushed over to Helga, and much to Jimmy's annoyance pushed him to one side. 'Helga, are you telling me that *she*,' he pointed across at Astrid, 'has put her family in a home for me?'

'Yes Reg, she has done that, only for you.'

'Bloody hell, the silly cow,' he screamed.

Jimmy was fast running out of patience, he pulled Helga away from Reg and out towards the exit, preventing her from answering any more questions.

Helga gave a parting shot as she left. 'Reg, I think you have a stone cold heart, I feel sorry for you.'

Reg stormed off in the direction of the bar, shaking his head in disbelief while Astrid stood alone waiting patiently near the exit. She didn't seem to mind.

An hour later, worn down by her smile and sexy posturing, Reg got up from the bar and left with her.

The short walk to the flat seemed to take forever, while Astrid desperately tried to make him understand she was *so very* pleased to see him again. Reg made no attempt to try and communicate with her. As they entered the building Reg signalled to Astrid not to make a sound and, taking care not to be heard, they tiptoed up the stairs past the old lady's front door. The rest of the group followed close behind talking loudly, laughing and joking as they staggered up the never-ending stairs.

Once inside the flat, Astrid seemed almost by instinct to know which was Reg's room. She walked in pulling him behind her, passing Helga and Jimmy who were already squeezed into the single bed nearest the door, pulled back the cover on the empty bed, turned towards Reg and gave him an incredibly sexy smile stripped off and jumped under the covers. Reg smiled for the first time of the evening stripped and joined her under the covers.

Almost immediately he heard horrendous banging followed by loud shouts. 'Politzei…Politzei.'

Adrian nervously opened the door to be met by three huge policemen, accompanied by the old lady from the first floor. One of them held a gun, while his colleagues held their truncheons menacingly in front of them.

The first policeman burst past Adrian, 'Wo sind den madchens?' screeched the policeman.

Tony fell from his chair hitting his head against the kitchen door. Dave sat arrogantly but motionless, slowing drawing on his cigarette.

Adrian couldn't understand the question, which made the policemen even angrier.

Eventually the leading policeman spoke in English. 'Ze girls, where are ze girls?' he asked.

Tony, still on the floor, started to shake, and now absolutely terrified pissed himself.

Dave, realising that the police meant business, carefully pulled a handful of Captagon from his trouser pocket and squeezed them unnoticed into his half-finished bottle of bier. Relieved, he sipped thankfully at the lethal concoction.

A fourth policeman, egged on by the old woman, stormed into the flat. He immediately released the flap of his leather holster and rested his hand on his gun, while he menacingly waved his long black truncheon with the other.

The first policeman, watched over by his colleagues, began waving his truncheon in the air and pointing at the kitchen. Rather than turn the handle, he proceeded to kick down the door, causing Tony to fall back for the second time and hit his head on the floor.

When the policeman found no one, he stormed towards the bedrooms.

He broke into Dave's room; it was empty.

Then into Adrian's, which was also empty.

When the two policemen eventually reached the room shared by Jimmy and Reg, they both screamed at the top of their voices. *'Rouse - get out.'*

The four occupants attempted to hide under the covers but the quilts were too small to adequately cover even one person.

When the policeman guarding the door to the flat heard that his colleagues had been successful he tightened the grip on his gun, while the old lady sneered and slowly nodded at the English musicians.

Jimmy slowly crawled out from under the cover. He was naked; terrified, his whole body covered in goose pimples. The largest policeman walked towards the bed and pulled off the cover exposing a naked Helga. He made her get off the bed and stand in front of them. Jimmy tried to pass her the cover but was pushed aside as the policeman struck out at him with his truncheon, causing the mat to slide and Jimmy to fall heavily. The two policemen stared at her, their eyes leering over every inch of her naked body and her enlarged pregnant stomach. They muttered something to her, faked a laugh, spat onto the floor and motioned for her and Jimmy to leave. The nearest policeman noticed the wrapped birthday present on the floor; lifted his foot and brought his heavy boot mercilessly down onto it, smashing the contents to pieces.

As their naked victims scrambled around the floor trying to find their clothes, the policemen lashed out mercilessly at Jimmy before allowing them to scurry into the adjoining room and get dressed.

The two policemen smirked at each other, turned to the next bed, pulled off the cover and stood menacingly over Reg and Astrid. The first policemen held his gun a few inches from Reg's hands, which tightly clutched his penis. The other poked his truncheon into Astrid's firm stomach, despite having borne four children. The moment was intense.

As they both lay shaking, it was obvious that the policemen were now enjoying their game, and began to taunt them. They motioned to Reg and then Astrid to stand beside the bed.

Their initial attention was directed at Reg who, still wearing his socks, looked a pathetic sight. Sneering at him and leering at each of them in turn, they began to make crude remarks that only Astrid could understand. She blushed with embarrassment but could do nothing.

Before finally permitting him to get dressed, Reg was subjected to further humiliation in front of Astrid, as the thugs took it in turn to rain blow after blow with their truncheons onto his back, legs and arms,

Helga and Jimmy were already dressed and waited in the sitting room when Reg and Astrid shuffled apprehensively out of the bedroom. No one dared to speak as Reg and Jimmy were grabbed and handcuffed.

The two couples were led out of the flat, down the stairs, and pushed forcibly into two police cars.

As she reluctantly moved her tiny frame away from the door, the old lady could not resist her last jibe and unexpectedly spoke in English. And, as if savouring the moment, she dragged out every syllable. 'Englischer pigs...' She spat at them. 'Go home.'

Adrian, Dave and Tony ignored her. Instead, drained of all strength, they sat open-mouthed, staring at the smashed doors.

At the police station, the group was separated. The girls were locked in a cell near reception while Reg and Jimmy were pushed and beaten as they made a hellish journey to a cell in another part of the station. The door slammed heavily behind them and they stood in silence, in almost total darkness, squinting at the closed metal door, unable to believe this was really happening to them. Reg could feel pain throughout his bruised and battered body and, while he tried desperately not to break down, Jimmy suddenly cracked and ran screaming towards the metal door. Unable to cope any longer, Reg followed suit and the two of them kicked and hammered at the door until they slid to the floor totally exhausted.

The realisation and seriousness of the situation finally caught up with Reg as he began to gasp for breath. He frantically searched his waistcoat for a neo-epinine and, finding a small piece, slid it under his tongue. 'What's going to happen to us?' he asked, his heart racing uncontrollably.

'I haven't got a clue, I only wish I had. My worry is what they're doing to my Helga.' He paused. 'The bastards, if they hurt her I'll... I'll kill 'em.'

'They can both look after themselves, don't you worry about that. I'm wondering what they'll do with me, you seem to forget that I'm still only sixteen. I shouldn't even be here, let alone playing in a club.'

Jimmy started to twitch and clench his fists. 'They're more interested in the girls than us, they better not hurt my Helga or I swear I'll...' he said.

Not wanting Jimmy to blow again, Reg quickly interrupted him. 'Try to relax, we should know something soon.'

Ignoring the two beds, they remained on the cold concrete floor and waited nervously, their whole bodies tensing at even the slightest sound until any footsteps faded.

When daylight eventually filtered through the cell bars, they heard people walking down the corridor. They knew instinctively they were coming to their cell and jumped to their feet, not realising how weak they were and how the cold floor had affected them as they struggled to stand upright. The key turned and the door slowly opened. There were four uniformed policemen and a civilian standing in front of them.

Unaccustomed to the half-light, they squinted until they noticed the civilian was Herr Mankovitch. He moved forward and spoke authoritatively, a smile of satisfaction and power crept across his pained face. 'You are free to go,' he said.

But before they had the opportunity to savour the euphoria, the look on his face changed dramatically. He tilted his head backwards allowing his pointed chin to jut out threateningly towards them, straightened his body, screwed up his face, his piercing grey eyes cutting through the tired expectant musicians. 'You will be pleased to know that the cause of your problem has been dealt with,' he said.

Jimmy suddenly lost all control. 'What do you mean... dealt with? You bastards, you're all as bad as each other, bloody Nazis.'

His whole body shook with rage as he continued to spit his venomous anger at his captors. 'You'll never change... I should have listened to my father.'

Reg struggled to hold him back, fortunately only one of the uniformed policemen understood Jimmy's outburst and he appeared to disregard it.

Jimmy, jammed between Reg and the partially open door, continued to struggle.

Herr Mankovitch, unaffected by the outburst, replied. 'They will be leaving Coburg in a few moments.' Jimmy pushed and struggled to get at him but Reg managed to wedge him against the door. 'You may of course say auf weidersehen,' said Herr Mankovitch. Pausing, as he relished the moment. 'But of course...' He sneered at Jimmy. 'Not in private.'

'Where are they? You'd better not have hurt my Helga,' screamed Jimmy.

Unruffled by the continuing outburst, Herr Mankovitch motioned to the police to let Reg and Jimmy out of the cell.

With a policeman standing on each side of them they were marched down a number of identical long brick corridors until they finally reached the cramped interview room. Helga and Astrid were sitting behind a table flanked by two hard-faced policewomen. The girls burst into tears when they saw Reg and Jimmy.

Jimmy and Helga desperately wanted to hug each other but, despite their violent attempts to do so, were held as far apart as the room would allow.

Reg could not fake any feelings for Astrid and, lacking all emotion, stood looking blankly at her. For the first time in his life he thought only of himself, all the while expecting the police to grab him and take him back to the cell before deporting him.

Helga spoke very slowly. 'Jimmy, I am very sorry to cause this problem for you and for Reg.'

She tried desperately to hold back from bursting in to tears again. 'We will leave now and perhaps we will meet again soon in Hamburg.'

It was the last time that anyone except Jimmy was to hear Helga speak in English.

Astrid, unable to communicate verbally with Reg, blew him a kiss and then burst into tears, followed immediately by Helga and Jimmy. Reg felt a lump in his throat and forced back his tears.

Astrid and Helga were dragged screaming out of the door at the rear of the building and, under express instructions not to return, were driven in a police car to the city boundary and left at the side of the road to make their own way back to Hamburg.

Herr Mankovitch led Jimmy and Reg to the street outside and, as he climbed into his Mercedes, wound down the window. 'I expect to see you all on stage tonight, and please try to make it special for me. Yes?' he said slowly.

He closed the window and drove off.

The relief was unbelievable as they savoured the freedom and were reunited with their fellow musicians. It was as though Dave, Tony and even Adrian had been glued to the floor; sitting in exactly the same positions as when Reg and Jimmy were arrested. Dave opened several bottles of bier and they spent the next hour relating their story, showing their cuts and bruises, and continually repeating how lucky they had been at having received no damage to their fingers or hands.

As Jimmy told them how Herr Mankovitch had rescued them he temporarily forgot Helga; then unexpectedly he flew into a rage. 'Do you realise that Helga and Astrid were treated like criminals? Driven out of town and then left to walk back to Hamburg...' he screamed. He got up and punched at the air. 'And bloody hell, don't forget that she's soddin' well pregnant.'

Adrian listened intently as he took yet another bier. 'I don't know why you all say such terrible things about Herr Mankovitch? He must have something good about him to get you two out,' said Adrian. He raised his bottle and the others followed.

No one was watching the clock and, before they knew it, it was almost time for them to be on stage at the club. Without changing their clothes, they brushed their hair and made the short journey down the road to the club. It was then they realised how much they had consumed and how drunk they all were.

They arrived at the club with only five minutes to spare. Herr Mankovitch and Herr Fischer were waiting for them at the door. News had travelled fast and crowds of people were waiting to get into the club to see whether the whole group would take to the stage that night. The club was packed.

A nod of gratitude to Herr Mankovitch was all Reg and Jimmy had time for as they climbed unsteadily on to the stage, switched on the amplifiers and waited for them to warm up. They all knew how lucky they had been, no one more than Reg who could well have been on his way back to England instead of playing with the group.

Despite the effects of the alcohol, and the pressure of being continuously under the watchful eye of Herr Mankovitch, they played like never before. And much to the pleasure of the crowd, relying on sheer adrenaline they completed the night.

As they put away the guitars and microphones Herr Fischer and Herr Mankovitch slowly approached the stage. Adrian saw them out of the corner of his eye and, seeing their expressions, raised the alarm to Dave. It was too late; Herr Mankovitch stood in front of the stage. 'I suppose you think that your show this evening has made everything alright?' He paused. 'Do you really think that this is so, yes?'

Dave gave them a cocky smile. 'It was a good night wasn't it?'

The rest of the group smiled and nodded, pleased with themselves and relieved that the evening was over and that they could at last get some well-deserved sleep.

The expression on the face of Herr Mankovitch changed to a look of outrage. 'You have made me look a fool to this town. I will deduct three days pay from you all and if I have some more trouble from you…' He spat with rage. 'You, you crazy Englishmen, you will be fired from the club.'

Herr Mankovitch shook his head wildly as he limped towards his office, closely followed by Herr Fischer who turned every few paces to stare back at the musicians.

They all thought it, but only Tony spoke. 'Shit, we really have upset him.'

He looked across to Adrian. 'But *you* said he had a good side.'

Adrian was too angry to say any more, he closed his guitar case and cursing under his breath stormed out of the club.

That night Jimmy and Reg both had nightmares, but they were totally different. Reg could see Astrid's husband drowning in the muddy water of the great Hamburg storm, while the four children screamed at Astrid to help him. But she took no notice; instead she preferred to be fucked by Reg in a luxurious hotel room overlooking the Alster. When Reg saw Astrid's dead husband float past the fifth floor hotel window in the turbulent raging water he leapt out of bed screaming, his scrawny, pale body soaked in sweat.

Jimmy could see Helga and Astrid struggling to walk along the never-ending dark and deserted autobahn towards Hamburg. Exhausted she fell to the roadside bleeding profusely with a miscarriage, but as he drove the van past her was unable to stop and no matter how hard he pressed the brakes the van raced on down the road.

Jimmy and Reg woke at almost the same time but the events of the previous night had finally got to them and wouldn't go away.

The bad feeling between the management and the group continued and the following Monday, with a five hundred Deutsche mark pay off, they were thrown out of the club.

Chapter fourteen

Keep on Running

In the evening rush hour, the drivers began to get more and more impatient as the traffic queued for several hundred metres behind the unlikely sight on the Hamburg streets.

It wasn't long before they started to sound their horns uncontrollably as the tractor towing the broken-down van struggled up the hill in the direction of St Pauli.

Dave fought hard to steer the van while the remaining musicians sat silently waiting for the inevitable. Hans, the tractor driver, was nervous and uneasy; the final insult came when an adventurous and impatient driver, swearing at them loudly, overtook the struggling vehicles. Now totally embarrassed, pulled into a tram stop at the top of the Reeperbahn.

As he climbed down from the tractor he was met by a stream of extended abuse from the respective drivers of the ever-growing stream of cars, as they at last were able to pass the cause of the delay. Hurriedly he untied the rope linking the van and tractor while the group nervously climbed out of the van and stood in the middle of the road. The farmer shook each of the exhausted musicians' hands in turn before wishing them good luck and jumping back onto the tractor. Under cover of the dark misty evening, he disappeared in the opposite direction to the long queue of traffic.

The group stood in silence, incredibly relieved at making it back to the welcoming and brightly lit oasis. They were excited to be home but that was short lived as a fully laden tram headed in their direction, wishing to discharge its passengers at the island stop. Without a second thought, Dave climbed into the driver's seat while the others gave one spontaneous huge and desperate push to move the offending van out of the way and send it down the hill. As it began to build up speed they were left behind, with the exception of Adrian who had somehow managed to get into the passenger seat before he and Dave sped down the Reeperbahn, threading silently between the other traffic, and coming to a halt in the lay-by outside the Park Hotel.

It was several minutes before Jimmy, Reg and Tony arrived. Tony, absolutely exhausted, slid unceremoniously to the floor and sat resting against the shop window.

Reg, fighting for breath, reached into his pocket for a large piece of neo-epinine, hurriedly placed it under his tongue, and leaned against the van and waited for the drug to take effect.

It started to snow heavily and Tony slid again as he tried to stand.

Cold, wet and out of breath, he shouted to Dave from the pavement. 'So what do we do now?'

'Go into the imbiss and get yourselves something to eat, we'll be back soon,' said Dave.

Adrian and Dave walked off into the warmth of the Park Hotel, while the others sat impatiently in the imbiss for almost two hours watching the cars and taxis skidding and sliding all over the road, miraculously dodging the buses and trams.

Dave eventually came out of the hotel, followed by Adrian with Anita and Hazelle each clinging tightly to an arm. He kissed them both goodbye and crossed the road with Dave. Ignoring the fact that the others had been waiting patiently for almost two hours in the imbiss, they walked calmly in, ordered, and then sat down at a nearby table to eat their food.

Reg, Tony and Jimmy sat staring expectantly at Dave and, finally running out of patience, Tony stood up and walked across to their table. 'So what's the plan?' he asked.

'We're going over to the Funny Crow tonight to see Herr Langstein,' said Adrian.

'Now?' asked Tony.

'Yeah, why not? We can all go over, Herr Langstein's bound to help us, he's got loads of contacts not only here in Hamburg but all over Germany,' said Dave. He looked around at each of them in turn and, while he took a large gulp of his coffee, they knew there was no option.

'OK, I suppose it is a good idea,' agreed Tony.

Too cold to walk to the underground they took two taxis to the Funny Crow, arriving in style just before the club opened. They felt good as they walked into the club, pleased to be back in the old surroundings and amongst friends. The club was empty except for the new German group sitting at the bar and the waiters preparing the tables for the evening. Ria was busy with the German singer, holding and kissing his hand, while Lotte, the other barmaid, was well and truly wrapped up with the drummer. Helga sat at the end of the bar talking to an overweight long haired and very ugly guitarist.

Although they had been noticed, no one bothered to acknowledge them except the now blushing Helga who, upon seeing Jimmy, jumped awkwardly off the bar stool and walked over to him. At the same time, she attempted to introduce him to the German guitarist. Jimmy was devastated. Dave tried desperately to calm him down but he stomped angrily out of the club into the freezing snow followed closely by Helga.

Adrian made a snide remark, grabbed Reg's arm, walked up to the bar and ordered a round of drinks. Ria opened five bottles and, after lining them up on the bar, asked Adrian to pay the full price. Disguising his surprise and anger, he reached into his jacket pocket and slowly passed over a hundred Deutsche mark note, a present from Anita earlier that evening. He maintained his cool and, while Ria desperately tried to find enough change for Adrian, he calmly asked her if he could see Herr Langstein.

She didn't try to hide her indifference towards him. 'He is not here tonight, I think so, you must come back tomorrow if you really want to speak with him.'

Adrian passed Dave a bottle of bier and took a sip as the German group started to play - desperately trying to master *Boom, Boom, Boom, Boom* by John Lee Hooker. The staff immediately burst into life becoming animated as the music reverberated around the empty club.

Dave faked choking and, unable to resist, shouted as loud as he could. 'They're shit, come on let's get out of here.'

As though it had been rehearsed, they all slammed the unfinished bottles on the bar and walked out.

Outside the club Jimmy stood shivering, becoming more and more upset as Helga tried her best to convince him that she had no feelings for the German guitarist.

Adrian burst out of the club and, embarrassed at Jimmy's apparent show of weakness, hailed two taxis, bundled him and Helga into the back, opened the front door and jumped into the first car himself. The remaining members climbed into the second car.

The deep snow could be felt trying to push its way up under the floor of the taxis as the drivers, following the now well-worn tracks in the road, skidded and swayed.

Over the course of the evening the taxis had designed and formed their own one-way system allowing only themselves and their fellow taxi drivers exclusive and uninterrupted movement around the paralysed city.

When the taxis arrived at the deserted Reeperbahn, Adrian and Jimmy got out leaving Helga to travel home alone. The musicians trudged blindly along the Reeperbahn behind Dave, picking their way through the deep snow until their leader realised he had no option but to spend more of the fast dwindling cash that he had set aside.

Aware that he could not walk much further, he stopped in a doorway and struggled to speak. 'For tonight we'll book into the Park and then tomorrow we'll decide what we do next.'

It was just what they wanted to hear, they quickly unloaded their cases and bags from the lifeless vehicle and trooped into the hotel.

Dave held the key tight in his hand and looked at each of them in turn. 'We all need to meet in the morning, ten o'clock sharp, at the imbiss across the road. Don't be late, *no* one.'

Adrian took his chance and disappeared, spending the next few hours with Anita and Hazelle doing what they all did so well, followed by a celebration dinner and a visit to the Star Club.

Dave opened the door to reveal a double bed where, within twenty minutes, three of them were asleep.

Jimmy, still fully dressed, lay wide-awake, twitching and sweating on the settee. Distraught and very confused, he found it hard to come to terms not only with Helga, but the fading dream of stardom that he had held for such a long time. Unable to sleep and trying hard not to wake anyone, he walked out into the freezing night.

The usually hectic and noisy Reeperbahn for once was eerily quiet; there was absolutely no one around, and for the first time the whole area looked clean and pure with the blanket of virgin snow.

Jimmy hesitated, his face illuminated by the flashing neon lights, looking in the direction of Altona, until he finally gave into his feelings and, with the need to move to keep warm, started to walk slowly away from the Reeperbahn. He persevered, struggling through the deep snow. As the biting raw wind whipped the snow around his face, the tears on his cheeks began to freeze.

It took him nearly an hour to get within sight of Helga's flat; suddenly he broke into a run, covering the last few yards with very little effort. He reached for the door bell with his frozen fingers.

It was several minutes before a sad, tired and swollen-faced Helga opened the door. When she saw him standing in front of her she burst into tears, sobbed loudly, threw her arms around him and then rubbed his frozen face tenderly trying to melt the ice that had built up on his eyebrows and eyelashes.

The next day Jimmy, looking fresh, happy and very pleased to be back with Helga, arrived at the hotel a few minutes before nine. He woke the remaining group members who reluctantly packed their things while Dave paid the bill.

Outside, the fierce wind whipped the snow into deep drifts completely engulfing the van, creating a most inhospitable landscape. The deep snowdrifts made it extremely difficult to open the back doors of the van and stow their meagre belongings inside but when a snowplough towed the car in front of the van away Dave was able to let the van roll forward.

Tony, suddenly realising that he was such a long way from home, fought hard to hold back his tears. 'W.... w... what are we going to do this time?' he asked.

'Let's get something to eat and discuss it,' said Dave.

Dave stumbled off through the snow towards the imbiss.

With one look at the worsening conditions outside, Tony, unable to control his feelings any longer, suddenly snapped. 'It's all right for you Jimmy, it suits you to be here in Hamburg, and you've got somewhere to stay... for as long as you want.'

Jimmy knew that Tony was probably correct having seen how she had behaved with the German guitarist at the Funny Crow.

Adrian ignored everything going on around him; he was hungry and it showed. Already on his second breakfast, he continued to eat ferociously, hardly allowing time to chew his food.

The argument between Jimmy and Tony had given Dave time to think. He slammed the table hard, causing the Germans who were quietly enjoying their snacks to jump with fright. 'Come on, what the hell are you arguing about, we've still got loads of options left,' he screamed.

That seemed to calm the situation but before they had time to ask him what those options were, he walked back up to the counter and came back with another tray of food and drinks. 'We all know how desperate the whole situation is, and whatever happens, we must get some work to tide us over until the end of the month. In the meantime, I'm going to circulate the agents and clubs around Hamburg to try and book next month. It won't be easy, but if we all put in some effort....'

Dave paused and looked directly at Adrian. '...then maybe, if we're lucky, we just might get through it,' he said.

For the first time in several days they all felt in a more positive frame of mind, but he hadn't finished. 'If we don't, then we're fucked, we'll have to split up and there isn't enough money left for any of you to get home.'

Dave pulled his notebook from his pocket and his face took on a sterner look. 'From now on I'm going to keep a record of any money that I spend on food or drinks and I'm gonna deduct it from each of you before I pay anything out,' he said.

It was clear no one liked what he said but they had no choice. His words struck exactly where he wanted and unanimously they agreed to make an effort.

Dave and Reg went to the post office and telephoned Sidney Goldstone and a few other agents in England. Their attempts were futile, for some strange reason no one was prepared to help them; in fact, Sidney Goldstone refused to even talk to Dave.

Jimmy asked Helga to help him and she telephoned agents based in and around Hamburg. By late afternoon they had the promise of five dates over the next twelve days and, thanks to Hazelle, the possibility of a month at the Crazy Horse, a relatively new club in the centre of Hamburg.

The following night Tony, knowing that Jimmy had gone to stay with Helga, slept on the settee and was woken by the sun burning his face beneath the curtains.

The thaw well underway since dawn had caused the snow and ice to start melting. They dressed and made their way to the imbiss where surprisingly Adrian was already waiting for them.

Things did look brighter although no one knew why that should be; the promises still had to be turned into reality. Dave once again dug into his pocket, bought breakfast and noted the cost in his book.

Hazelle negotiated a special low rate for a three-bedded room at the Park for Dave, Reg and Tony and, while Jimmy moved in with Helga, Adrian alternated between the two girls.

Dave arranged for the van to be towed to a nearby garage where they agreed to look at the possibility of locating a second hand engine. Unable to store anything in their hotel room they had no option but to leave the equipment and most of their belongings in the van and make the daily walk up to the garage and change in the back of the van.

As soon as the Cheetahs started playing the one-off dates, the girls, other musicians and their friends on the Reeperbahn began to take notice of them again. It was just like old times, only this time they conned drinks rather than buying them, and it worked.

Adrian began to have problems with Hazelle and Anita, who took it in turn to vie exclusively for his favours. Following a heavy drinking session in Mambo's it came to a head. With the women having had too much to drink it resulted in a major fight. Hazelle came out of it worst, falling down the narrow stairs into the basement toilets, badly damaging her legs and bruising her arms.

The mostly cosmetic injuries would prevent her from working for at least a week; customers didn't want to pay for damaged goods. Still able to walk she beat a hasty retreat, threatening to get even with Adrian, who by now stood nonchalantly at the bar, having relished the spectacle of two, albeit drunk and prostitutes fighting over him in front of other musicians.

During the day, Reg, Dave and Tony took the opportunity to explore the rest of Hamburg, and much to their surprise St Pauli was only a small part of what was a beautiful city. They spent much of the afternoon in the centre around Alsterarkaden, fondly referred to by Hamburg residents as their touch of Venice, drinking coffee and schnapps until dusk.

In the evening Dave went off in search of more bier and perhaps an innocent fraulien. Reg and Tony returned to have a meal in Mambo's and an evening of pills, pot and alcohol. For an early Wednesday evening, the place was buzzing. Two giggling German girls sat at the bar while Tony and Reg, a few of the Silhouettes and three Scottish musicians all talked excitedly. The mixed accents, noisy laughter and the jukebox, as always pumping out the musicians' favourites, created a party atmosphere.

The front door swung open and Jeff rushed in; he jumped over the table, squeezed between Reg and Tony, grabbed his bottle and took a massive gulp of bier. Tony's bottle was still in his mouth when the door burst open and two huge traffic policemen rushed in, their guns drawn, and looking extremely angry. One of them stood at the door with his legs apart, preventing anyone from leaving. The second policeman marched across and spoke to Bernd, who was polishing a litre mug. He listened intently, looked across the bar and then responded by shaking his head.

The record finished and, in the silence, the jukebox clicked loudly as it took its time to choose another record, creating a deathly silence. The policeman, already angry, began to lose his temper and stormed away from the bar towards the occupied tables, looking everyone in the eye as he reached their respective table.

No one dared to speak.

Jeff was sweating profusely, the perspiration running down his neck onto his pale blue shirt and creating random dark patterns. As the policeman moved nearer to Tony's table, he stiffened, looked at Reg, who by now was on the verge of a major asthma attack. The policeman still holding his gun spoke directly at him. 'Fuhrershine?' he said.

Reg, struggling for breath, shook his head.

Immediately the police concentrated his efforts on Jeff, asking him the same question. Jeff moved his hand towards his inside jacket pocket, the policeman's grip tightened on his gun and he pointed it threateningly at the musician. The musician slowly withdrew his driving licence and passport from his pocket and shaking nervously passed them to the policeman. He scrutinised them, at the same time taking care not to relax his fixed gaze from Jeff. Without a word, the policeman lunged forward, grabbed at Jeff's shirt and pulled him across the table, knocking the part filled glasses and bottles onto the floor.

Jeff protested loudly as the policeman handcuffed and dragged him out of the bar and into the police car. 'Help me somebody, please help me,' he screamed.

No one dared move. After they had gone there was an unusual silence as everyone sat looking at each other, until the juke box burst into life and started to play *Off the Hook* by the Rolling Stones and the bar erupted into frenzied and intense discussion.

Reg was in a very bad way but now he was able to reach into his pocket and grab at his lifesaver. The whole neo-epinine worked and twenty minutes later, although badly shaken, he could at last speak.

The rest of the Silhouettes were shell shocked and for a while they just sat and thought. After finishing their drinks they left, walking off up the Reeperbahn in the direction of the police station.

The next morning Dave and Adrian were walking past the Top Ten Club and saw that the Silhouettes loading their equipment into the van. 'What are you doing?' asked Dave.

'Haven't you heard?' replied the guitarist.

Dave and Adrian shook their heads and waited to be told. 'Jeff's been arrested for a hit and run,' said the guitarist.

Dave and Adrian looked on in disbelief.

The bass player joined in. 'The police reckon that, last night...' He shook his head in disbelief. 'Jeff killed a young girl and drove off,' he said.

'What?' asked Adrian, almost speechless. 'Have you spoken to him? Surely that can't be right?'

'Yeah, we have.... he did it. He was stoned and drove one of the waiter's cars down by the Alster... Why?'

He slowly shook his head and continued. 'The bastard's such a great drummer and now we've been all been booted out, I doubt if we'll ever get to work in Germany again.'

For a moment Dave was genuinely concerned, he also knew that his mother liked Jeff and she would be devastated. 'You're surely not going to leave him here on his own?' asked Dave.

'They've taken his passport, it's going to be months before it gets to court' replied the guitarist. 'And, he won't get bail in case he does a runner.' He coughed loudly to clear his throat. 'Anyway he's bound to be put away.'

They were all too upset to continue the conversation and threw Jeff's drums into the van.

Dave and Adrian stood on the pavement and watched as the van drove up the Reeperbahn, and the incomplete group faced what was going to be a very sad, long and difficult journey back to England.

'Poor sods,' muttered Adrian.

The two of them went for a coffee and they sat staring out onto the rain soaked pavements.

Dave left, returning several minutes later, his face beaming.

'We've got an audition at the Top Ten this afternoon; you'd better get hold of Jimmy,' said Dave.

They took three taxis to the garage in Altona, collected the organ, drums and guitars while Dave walked to Helga's flat to fetch Jimmy. In less than an hour they walked onto the hallowed stage of the Top Ten Club.

They were fortunate; the club supplied all the amplification, P.A. and microphones; the reason for that was quite simple. The club wanted to control the sound level and consequently the volume of all the amplifiers was governed. The owner, a Yugoslav, came down from his office, listened to two songs, smiled and left.

Dave jumped down from the stage and followed him up to his office where he agreed that they would play Monday, Tuesday and Wednesday. There was another group already booked and they would alternate with them playing an hour on and an hour off each night, starting at six o'clock.

They trooped triumphantly out of the club and walked next door to celebrate in the Paprika, a Hungarian restaurant and bar. At last, they were actually playing on the Reeperbahn and at the same club where the Beatles had played a few short years earlier.

The manager allowed them to stay in the accommodation above the club on the nights they played. Although it was rough and the misshapen bedsprings dug into their ribs, at least it was free, and they spent hours reading the graffiti, which had taken their predecessors hours or possibly days to write.

Chapter fifteen

Wishing and Hoping

At the end of February it became a little warmer and spring seemed to have arrived early. The wind changed direction and, with the warm sunshine, the mood of the whole group began to pick up as they looked forward to a month of regular work and money.

Dave and Adrian visited the Crazy Horse before the start of the month to make sure there were no last minute hitches with the contract.

The group for February was a five-piece from Indonesia.

Although they played most of the songs well, and they were at least recognisable, they followed the same path as the German groups and copied the record as closely as possible, even fading out the endings of the songs. There was no feel, edge or expression in the music; perhaps that's what was expected in most clubs.

At lunchtime on the first of March the Cheetahs, having managed to borrow a VW van from yet another German group that Helga had introduced to them, finally arrived at the Crazy Horse.

Jimmy was reluctant to even consider getting into the van but the rest of the group told him in no uncertain terms that if it meant saving money, they would do it.

The Crazy Horse was different because the musicians were caged inside a timber coral that rose high around the stage. Steps on the left-hand side gave them access to the stage between a forest of branches. To complete the effect, all the tables around the dance floor were made of rough sawn timber whilst larger tables constructed of thick chunks of wood were set back under a canopy of large overhanging branches.

After suspending the P.A. speakers from the timber beams above the dance floor and loading their equipment on to the stage, they drove to the accommodation. They pulled up outside a delicatessen on the ground floor of a four-storey building. Adrian shot out of the van, through the door and up the long winding staircase to the rooms.

While the rest of them made their way towards the front door, Adrian was already making his way down the stairs. He pushed past them, both hands covering his mouth as he rushed out into the street. 'Don't go in there,' he pleaded.

They thought it was a joke until a large rat shot down the stairs and out through the partially open door. On seeing it, Adrian couldn't hold himself any longer and was violently sick along the side of the borrowed van. Dave and Tony stepped over him and into the flat but almost immediately rushed back out, unable to hide their disgust. 'Bastards!'

'Pigs!'

'What a mess!'

'How could anybody live in that shit hole?' said Dave.

The Indonesian group had completely trashed the bedrooms, pissing on the mattresses and defecating on the bed covers and spreading it all over the walls. The smell was horrendous. Rotting food littered the floor and row after row of filthy plates and dishes covered every available surface. Mouldy and partially eaten tins of corned beef, and remnants of baked beans and pilchard tins, had been stacked on the wardrobe shelves.

Adrian had now begun to recover. 'There's no way I'm staying in that,' he said.

Thinking that it was all a joke, Reg and Jimmy took an inquisitive look inside, only to exit vomiting.

They all climbed back into the van, returned to the club, and surrounded the manager, barely giving him room to breathe. 'Have you seen the place?' questioned Dave.

The owner looked at him blankly, so Dave explained the situation. He eventually agreed to take a look for himself while they finished setting up the equipment.

Although still upset, they were pleased to have a new home, somewhere to play and an opportunity to get back into the world they now knew best.

The club owner returned while Dave was retying the P.A. speakers to the beams even higher above the stage, walked as near to the stage as he could and apologised profusely.

'You are of course correct. No one can sleep in this mess, I am sorry,' he said.

Adrian shook his head firmly and smirked to Reg, the owner continued. 'Can you please wait with me? And I will arrange some place else,' he said.

The alternative accommodation couldn't have been better; the rooms were in a small hotel close to the Top Ten Club.

Dave unpacked his few remaining belongings. When he opened the wardrobe drawers he found a strange looking latex penis and straps which he sat playing with before putting it away.

Adrian fondly called the Crazy Horse the OK Corral and the audiences were very different to any club they had played at before. They were friendly, more mature, and seemed to appreciate the music. Even the manager appeared to be on their side, offering them free drinks whenever the club was full or the crowd enjoyed themselves. They were at last happy and started to get back into the swing of things; even Jimmy, labouring his echo chamber to celebrate the fact that they had survived the difficulties of the last few weeks.

By the end of the first week the letters started to arrive again from England and all seemed well. Jimmy received probably the best present he could have hoped for; his father sent him a fuzz box and he could now effortlessly copy the guitar sound used by Steve Winwood, the Spencer Davis group, on the record *Keep on Running*.

There was a non-stop supply of young girls and, with the exception of Jimmy, and unfortunately Tony, sex was almost too regular.

The Crazy Horse had three different types of people; teenagers until the witching hour of ten o'clock, when it changed to young women in their mid-twenties who seemed more mature and hell bent on enjoying themselves. When they left, prostitutes, strippers and staff from the other bars and clubs would arrive to begin their night. All of these were fair game for the Cheetahs, often kissing one girl good night as the next was arriving at the club.

It was fantastic.

Reg was beginning to learn what Germany was all about and why so many musicians wanted to play there and, after what was a particular rowdy night at the club, he escorted two young girls to the Star Club and then back to his hotel room.

The three of them were engrossed in a contorted sexual act when Tony pushed open the unlocked door. Before he had chance to pull the door closed, Julie and her hairdresser friend, Kathy, burst into the room. Her euphoria turned to rage when she saw the grotesque sight of Reg and the girls on the bed in front of her. She screamed and threw a bouquet of flowers at Reg, then took her full anger out on Tony.

Reg's female companions weren't particularly interested in the intruders and continued to claw at him trying to gain his attention. He pushed them aside and scurried around the floor for his clothes. A few minutes later, after checking his appearance in the mirror, he ran down the stairs to look for Julie.

Tony, realising that he had made an awful mistake, rushed after Julie trying to make a good enough excuse to salvage the situation for Reg. He was too late and, as Julie stormed onto the crowded street, she bumped into Dave who was gobsmacked to see her. Realising that she was extremely upset, and not one to pass up an opportunity, he invited her and Kathy for a drink in the Paprika.

Seeing Dave with Julie, Reg turned and walked back up to his room and the waiting girls.

Dave chose a quiet corner and sat strategically between Julie and Kathy. 'He knew that I was coming over to see him. I wrote to him more than a week ago. Has he been with many other girls? I bet he does it all the time. What a bastard,' sobbed Julie, hardly stopping for breath. She paused for a second to take a gulp of air and catch her breath but when she saw Jimmy walk in arm in arm with Helga she became hysterical. 'I don't know why I bothered to spend my hard earned money to come over here and see him; I knew he never cared about me.' She sobbed and thought deeply for a second. 'I saved every penny to get over here, I thought that he cared, why did I bother? The bastard!'

Dave carefully stroked her long hair, pulled a clean white handkerchief from his pocket and wiped her face. He ordered drinks and a meal for the three of them, and for the next two hours he continued to ply Julie and Kathy with a potent mixture of schnapps, bier, korn and the occasional pill.

'Did you know I was his first girlfriend?' said Julie.

Dave shook his head.

'And he was my first boyfriend,' continued Julie.

Dave spoke to her quietly while simultaneously smiling at Kathy. 'Well you said it... he is only a boy... now you're a young woman.'

'I suppose you're right, but he is lovely,' she sobbed

As the alcohol and drugs began to take effect she became tearful and Dave fanned her trauma. He listened intently, pretending to sympathise and understand her predicament, until the three of them were sufficiently drunk. Carefully choosing his moment, when neither Julie nor Kathy cared any longer about the earlier events, except to make the long journey worthwhile, he helped them to their feet and shepherded the inebriated girls in the direction of the door. They all stood hovering in the street amongst the drunken pushing crowds. The girls found it hard to stand on their own but Dave held them firmly in each arm as they staggered the short distance to the hotel. The girls hesitated on the pavement, standing at the entrance, unsure where they were. The front door opened and Reg walked through. As soon as Julie saw him, she let out a drunken laugh, threw her arms around Dave, stroked his hair, giggled, and called over his shoulder as loud as she could. 'Come on Dave let's go.'

Julie looked at Reg and waited for his reaction. Maintaining a look of indifference he smiled falsely and, with hunger getting the better of him, walked off in the direction of the nearest imbiss.

Dave took a firm hold of the two drunken girls, helped them to climb the stairs to his room and closed the door behind him.

After a short setback, when Kathy was violently sick, he spent the rest of the night entertaining them in as many positions as he could and leaving them just short of begging him to stop. When the girls thought that it was over he pushed a handful of pills between their lips and, as the drugs took effect, produced the latex penis he had carefully guarded. He strapped the dildo onto Julie and gradually persuaded her to enter Kathy as she lay hallucinating on the bed.

Although incredibly tired, he found it hard to sleep that night.

Dave treated them well, spending most of the afternoon showing them round the city. He took them down to the docks for a boat trip on the Alster, and for a short ride on the underground. In the evening they joined him on the group's table at the Crazy Horse.

Reg was surprised to see that Dave had the bravado to parade them in front of him but he knew he had no choice. He had mixed feelings; he was jealous because he still fancied Julie and this was coupled with anger when he knew that Dave had spent the night with his girlfriend.

During the evening Reg occasionally looked at Julie from the stage and, although he believed that she would still prefer to be with him, made the decision to continue with his never ending supply of German girls.

Dave was a faultless escort, spending every break with Julie and Kathy, knowing that he would have another night with them before they returned to England.

Despite another energetic and sleepless night they were still up before noon. Dave took them to the 'bahnhof and waited faithfully on the platform until they boarded the train back to England.

Reg woke up unusually early and, as he tried to move, an excruciating pain shot through his body. Cautiously, he pushed back the cover to find that his penis was stuck to the quilt cover. He gritted his teeth firmly as he removed the material from his hard penis. When he squeezed it, green fluid oozed from the end of it and the foul smell hit him. He lay back, petrified and disgusted, afraid to cover himself again, not wanting to endure the pain a second time.

What was it? He had never experienced anything like this before.

He lay awake on the bed and waited for what seemed like hours until he saw Adrian, for once in his own bed, begin to move. He whispered until Adrian acknowledged him. 'Adrian. You've got to help me, I've been poisoned,' he said.

Adrian, still half asleep, wasn't interested and promptly fell back to sleep. Reg raised his voice. 'Adrian, did you hear me? I've been bloody well poisoned.'

Adrian pushed himself up onto one elbow and looked over at his room mate, his eyes barely open. 'What do you mean... poisoned?' he asked.

Reg rather embarrassingly explained his predicament.

A smile spread across Adrian's tired face. 'You silly sod... I suppose you have been poisoned in a way, you've got a dose.'

Reg stared across at the bass player with a glazed look, finding it hard to come to terms with what he'd just been told.

Adrian reluctantly pulled himself out of bed. 'Come on I'll take you to a doctor, but it's gonna cost you.'

He couldn't resist teasing Reg as he saw him begin to blush and try to hide his face. 'You're disgusting you are, you should be more careful,' said Adrian.

'Who could have given that to me?' asked Reg.

'You've got more chance of playing with the Beatles than finding out who it was,' replied Adrian.

Adrian seemed to know instinctively where to go and, after spending a few brief minutes with the understanding doctor on the Reeperbahn, an injection in the right buttock, and fifty Deutsche marks poorer, they were both on their way to find something to eat.

As they stood eating breakfast, Reg explained why he was not as careful as he perhaps should have been. 'I hate using a Durex. I had a terrible experience the first time I did. My mother always went to Bingo on a Thursday so Julie and I decided to arrange our first encounter on one of those nights. I saved my money from my paper round and bought a Durex from Freddie, a boy in my class whose father was a barber. He would steal them from his father's shop for anybody who had the money,' he said.

He took a sip of his Fanta and continued. 'As soon as my mother left we went up to my bedroom but we were too nervous to take any of our clothes off.' He could feel himself blushing and shook his head.

'Come on,' said Adrian. 'Get on with it; just get it off your chest.'

'All right,' said Reg. 'I'll never forget it. Julie wore a thick petticoat, layer on layer of net wrapped round her legs. I had only just put on the Durex and started to get down to it when the doorbell rang. We both panicked and I jumped up and ran down to answer the door. It was Basil wanting to copy my homework. I remember throwing my books at him but by the time I got back up stairs, Julie was sitting in front of the mirror brushing her hair.'

Adrian smirked and forced ridiculous faces but Reg continued unamused. 'We both tried to find the bloody thing but it had disappeared. I walked her to the bus stop, waited for her to get on, and after she waved to me from the top of the double decker bus, I ran all the way home. I searched everywhere but I couldn't find it. Every day I dreaded coming home from school, half expecting my mother to have found it.' Reg paused, and Adrian looked at him expectantly. 'But she never did, and it was several months before Julie's mother found it... in her bedroom, amongst her books. The Durex had got caught in Julie's petticoat; she had gone home on the bus with it hanging under her dress. After all that hassle I swore that I would never use one again.'

Adrian dropped his tea as he rolled with laughter, clutching at his chest.

Following the injection Reg was under strict instructions not to drink any alcohol for at least a week, and to drink only soft drinks, tea or coffee. This was to prove not only difficult but also extremely embarrassing for him, as everyone seemed to know he had a dose by the change in his drinking habits. But what surprised him most was the number of other musicians with the same problem and under the same strict treatment. He found an old accordion at the club and with the manager's permission took it back to his room. Unable to drink, with time on his hands, and rather than go to Mambo's, he spent most nights practising the old songs and occasionally some of the newer hit tunes he heard on the jukeboxes.

Dave was finding it difficult to get any interest in the group for the following month and by the end of the third week he was becoming more and more desperate, and it showed. As well as drinking heavily between sets, he began to drink on stage. The ill feeling between Reg and himself didn't help matters and watching them on stage it was quite obvious.

Dave's drinking was causing them all problems, often starting without telling the rest of the group which song he was singing and causing confusion until they recognised it and were able to join in.

A few days later there was a strange irony as Dave had great difficulty in going to the toilet, experiencing the same ill effect and painful symptoms of the pox. He reduced his intake, not only of alcohol but liquid of any sort, and attempted in vain to cut the need to go to the toilet and stand in agony at the urinal.

Unable to cope any longer with the discomfort, he walked in to Reg's room looking frightened and bewildered. 'Bloody hell Reg, I've really done it this time,' he said. He walked across to Reg and struggled to sit down on the end of the bed but as he bent down his screams reverberated around the room and could be heard across the Reeperbahn. 'What can I do Reg? I'm in agony.'

Reg burst out laughing.

'You don't give a toss do you? I might have expected that,' said Dave.

'No it's not that. I was just thinking you've probably passed it on to Julie and her mate. How's she going to explain that to her fucking mother?' said Reg.

'Who cares?' replied Dave.

'Come on, I'll take you to the doctor but it's going cost you.'

For the first time since meeting Dave, Reg felt that he was in control and he liked it. From then on things changed, the old camaraderie returned to the group and for the rest of the week, instead of drinking any alcohol, Dave joined Reg and the other unfortunate musicians by drinking orange juice, tea or coffee in a quiet bar out of sight of the girls and other musicians.

By the start of the final week it was evident that they would not have any work at all for the next month and Dave prepared them for the worst.

The last night came and, whilst the audience showed their appreciation and the usual high energy finish to the month took place, this time it was different, much different. They packed the equipment in silence; Dave unravelled the P.A. cables, cleaning off the dirt and grease caused by spilt bier, packing them meticulously in their cases.

At two o'clock the taxis arrived and took the equipment back to the van in the garage, where they stowed it carefully as if making it ready for a journey that they knew they would not be making.

With the exception of Jimmy they all walked down to the Reeperbahn and sat in Mambo's in silence, as they watched many of the groups say their goodbyes before travelling on to the next town. Dave had been able to negotiate an extra night at the hotel, but as for tomorrow, he had no idea. They all got drunk.

When they finally stepped out of the bar the bright morning sunlight hurt their tired eyes, and as they staggered back to their rooms for the last time they all secretly hoped that something would turn up.

Chapter sixteen

I Should Have Known Better

The musicians slept until well into the afternoon and it was two o'clock when the hotel manager, the cleaner and Jimmy collectively woke them up with thunderous hammering on the door. Not knowing what was happening, the alcohol and drugs having numbed their senses, they dressed in a hurry, picked up the few things they had and left.

They set off for the imbiss where, after an uninteresting and tasteless meal, they sat depressed, waiting for inspiration. Dave paid everyone, less the advances already handed out, but this time he decided to hold on to a larger amount than usual in case there was no way out. He kept the actual amount tightly under wraps having not decided what he would do with the money if and when the situation did become desperate.

After a less than positive discussion, it was agreed that they should do whatever they could to save money. For Jimmy that was no problem. Adrian was also set up until Hazelle probably became bored with him. Dave had made good friends with a waitress from the Crazy Horse and would be fine for a few weeks providing he could perform again soon and presupposing that it was not her that had given him the dose.

It was nearly an hour before Tony realised that he had lost his glasses and, although he could still see reasonably well, his eyes were becoming bloodshot. At first he thought he had left them at the Crazy Horse but Dave soon reminded him that he was able to see until they struggled into bed. Nevertheless Dave gave him the benefit of the doubt and the two of them retraced their steps back over the places they could remember visiting the previous night, but there was no sign of Tony's glasses.

Reg had a number of admirers keen to ensure that he had a bed for the night. He chose Klara, who lived near the Funny Crow. She was different to the girls he had previously slept with; petite, with very short stylish dark brown hair and a face that was stunning even without make-up. Like many of the girls in Hamburg she lived with her parents, had her own self-contained bed sitting room, and was never bothered by them. Her best girlfriend, Gabriel, was a model who appeared regularly in teenage magazines published in Hamburg, and was the girlfriend of Franz, Klara's brother.

Whenever Reg stayed with Klara, the four of them would spend most of the night smoking pot, popping pills, listening to records by the Who and the Small Faces, speaking in English and teaching Reg the odd German phrase. They got on so well it wasn't uncommon for Franz or Gabriel to bring Reg and Klara breakfast in bed before they left for work.

Following a late night session, Reg left the confines of Klara's bedsit and now under the influence of the potent mixture, found himself in her father's dental surgery adjoining the flat. The street light shone through the partially open Venetian blinds, shedding an eerie light on the stainless steel equipment and white tiled walls. For some reason Reg panicked and, instead of making his way back to the bedsit, found himself in total darkness. His fingers fumbled along the wall for the light switch and as it illuminated the room he came face to face with a life sized dummy wearing full German SS uniform. On the back wall a huge swastika took pride of place beside an SS flag. The whole room was a shrine to Nazi Germany and the fact that Klara's father had continued to maintain his obsession with his past shocked him. That, combined with the dental surgery and possibility of torture and pain, absolutely terrified him. Did Klara's father know that an Englishman was having sex in his home with his daughter?

Reg was not prepared to take the chance and, although he continued to sleep with Klara, he never returned to her home.

Tony tried his best to rekindle the earlier interest from Ria but after two nights at her flat he was back at the Reeperbahn. For the next week he used his money to rent a room at the Park Hotel and ate just one meal a day; the rest of the time eating baked beans or rice directly from the tin. As the money ran out he could no longer afford to eat, let alone stay at the Park. His eyes became sore and swollen and bright red veins gradually began to criss cross his enlarged eyeballs.

As the days went by Tony became more and more embarrassed and when he saw anyone that knew him, his frightening eyes were the first thing they noticed. Although they tried to hide the shock, they cruelly made any excuse they could to get away from him as quickly as possible

He was used to spending his nights in the quietest bars and would spend the days wandering aimlessly around the Reeperbahn feeling depressed and exhausted. During the occasional afternoon meetings with the group they would buy him something to eat and drink and, providing they were with him, the girls and English musicians would at least talk to him. But when he was alone he was ignored. It was as though he didn't exist.

A cold and desperate Tony finally retreated to his temporary home, an abandoned VW beetle on a bomb site at the end of Grosse Freiheit, where he would sleep at night. Occasionally the police would try to move him on but, unable to hold a conversation or understand each other, they eventually left him alone.

The effects of being without glasses were making his life a nightmare and in a final attempt to help him Dave persuaded the rest of the group to buy him a new pair. They visited an optician but, after trying to test Tony's eyes, he made it clear that he was unable to help the drummer until he had several nights of real sleep and rest.

By now they were getting short of money and there was no way they would waste what little they had on the luxury of a hotel room for a drummer in a group that had nowhere to go, let alone play.

Tony continued to struggle, a sorry sight wandering around the Reeperbahn alone but too tired to walk any longer, he retired early to his rusting home. Later that night a group of drunken servicemen noticed him huddled inside the metallic shell. They shook and rocked the wreck, finally setting it alight, leaving Tony with no option but to leave his last bizarre refuge. Coughing and blinded by the smoke he was unable to get out of the burning vehicle until they grabbed his arms and dragged him onto the wet pavement. When they realised that he was English the kicks and blows began with a vengeance, raining thick and fast over every part of his body. They continued to beat him until he was no more than a pathetic heap, bleeding, and crying in the gutter. But as the rain became heavier, uninterested in their prey, they staggered off to the shelter of a nearby bar.

Tony lay perfectly still beside the blazing car until he could hear the fire engines and police sirens approaching. He picked himself up and, although in great pain, limped off into the darkness and the relative safety of a nearby alley. He slumped to the floor and that night, unable to sleep, fought for his very existence, trembling at the slightest sound, fearing any second he would have to take yet another beating.

Feeling and looking more like the monster in a Hammer horror film, he fumbled inside his overcoat pocket. When he felt his passport he smiled painfully through his distorted face and, holding his most treasured possession, his ticket to ride, between his bruised and swollen hands, he pulled it firmly against his chest.

Early the next morning he stood by the roadside hailing one taxi after another until thankfully one stopped and drove him to the garage where he carefully removed his drums from the van and loaded them into the taxi.

For the last time he climbed into the rear of the van, removed his putrid blood stained clothes, changed into his black polo neck, creased stage suit and boots, and grabbed the holdall which contained his few remaining belongings. Then, having second thoughts, he threw it back into the van.

In the quiet sunny morning the taxi drove him majestically up the Reeperbahn to Music City, where he reluctantly but thankfully sold his pride and joy for one hundred and twenty Deutsche marks. The train fare to England and on to Devon was exactly one hundred Deutsche marks.

Tony bought himself a cheap pair of sunglasses to hide his grotesque eyes and left on the afternoon train. As it pulled out of the 'bahnhof, he didn't look back. He was pleased to be going home to the real world he knew and preferred, and wondered why he had been weak enough to believe everything Dave had promised him. Surely, he should have known better?

With Tony gone and no immediate chance of any dates, Reg spent many of his evenings sitting in the all night café at number 1 Gross Freiheit, situated at the junction with the Reeperbahn. Any money he had was used to buy the cheapest item on the menu - pea and ham soup with a few complimentary slices of bread. It enabled him to get through the day until he could afford the next meal or he was treated by one of his lady escorts. He would sit for hours waiting to be picked up. Sometimes it was daylight before he struck lucky but at least he would have a bed for what was left of the night and, after performing, would eventually get a few hours sleep and perhaps a few Deutsche marks for his efforts. It wasn't easy to function on an empty stomach night after night, but he gradually began to improve his technique.

While he waited he would write to his mother asking her to send him the money to buy a ticket home, but every morning he tore it up, never having the money to buy even a stamp.

Ever the optimist, and after only a few hours sleep, he believed that something would soon turn up. After talking to an experienced busker in the café, he remembered that he still had the old accordion in the van and decided to try his luck playing in the many small bars around St Pauli. He collected the ancient, heavy instrument, and struggled back to the Reeperbahn.

The first three bars were not interested in him but in the next bar, after playing a few songs that even he didn't recognise, his luck changed. A group of drunken English sailors recognised a cockney medley and immediately began to sing along, followed by their even drunker shipmates.

Reg played for the rest of the evening and at three o'clock in the morning he was paid twenty Deutsche marks and passed the hat amongst the sailors. That collection gave him another hundred and fifty Deutsche marks and, for the first time in days, he felt good. He agreed to play at the bar a few nights a week and, with his increased confidence, soon built up regular bars for the remaining nights of the week, and the marathon all night session down at the fischmarkt.

He rented himself a room in David Strasse and life was good.

Now that he was playing regularly and had an income, he was accepted back into the circle at Mambo's and a new bar that was becoming popular.

The Blockhütte at the end of Grosse Freiheit seemed to take off overnight. It had a fantastic atmosphere, it was smoky and noisy; everyone always had a good time. The seasoned musicians mixed with the regular influx of new groups keen to learn from them what Germany was really like. The place was packed with musicians of all ages, some who had stayed behind to be with what they felt was a permanent girlfriend, and the more successful groups, who played only at weekends, at the larger clubs and stadiums all over Germany, for a fee that a group like the Cheetahs would earn in a month.

Reg's female friends were very different to those he attracted when he played with the Cheetahs; all ages, all sizes and all comers were welcomed with open arms, and for once he didn't care. But his most special guest was Klara who visited him at the oddest times, often in the middle of the night.

He was fast turning into a loner and, as well as becoming streetwise, learning more and more German phrases in the unique Hamburg dialect. He was growing up and beginning to enjoy his freedom. Although part of him wanted desperately to be back on stage with the group, without a drummer the Cheetahs really had no chance.

The mail continued to arrive from England and surprisingly two letters arrived from Julie at the same time. Reg sat quietly in his flat, made himself a coffee and opened them. He laughed out loud when he read the letter he should have received before her visit. The second letter was more recent and as he read it his expression changed. She told him that she was now pregnant and couldn't possibly tell her parents she had slept with Dave. She had also contracted Gonorrhoea but had been able to keep it a secret from her parents and now, after three embarrassing visits to the clinic, she was clear. She begged forgiveness and pleaded for him to go along with the idea that she was pregnant by him and not Dave. Losing his temper he tore them up and threw them angrily onto the floor. 'Sod you Dave!' he fumed.

He never opened any of her letters or wrote to her again.

Playing at the Sunday morning fischmarkt was fantastic and he soon became a welcome player in the majority of bars. During the early morning he would make a round trip of as many as he could before the drunken audiences made it futile for him to continue.

At ten in the morning, he felt that he had milked the crowd for as much as he could and decided to get off to bed. He nursed his precious instrument into its case and, after acknowledging the barman and some of the regulars, finished his bier and left.

After walking a few yards up the gradual cobble stone slope he stopped to catch his breath on the seat beneath the carved stone mermaid and water fountain overlooking the hafen. As he reflected on the long night, he smiled to himself with satisfaction. He knew that his mother's persistence in cajoling him into practising every day had finally paid off.

Looking down onto the harbour he noticed the middle aged lady he danced with earlier in the evening had also stopped and was peering into one of the many tiny cages crammed with kittens. Unexpectedly, she turned and smiled at him. He politely smiled back and thinking no more of it got up and started to walk again. After a few paces the weight of the accordion made him short of breath preventing him from walking at any speed. He searched in his pocket, found a small piece of neo-epinine and sucked at it impatiently.

As he looked back over his shoulder, it was obvious that the woman was following him. That was not too much of a problem, but for the first time he could see that she was dragging one leg behind her and it was then he noticed she had a wooden leg. It reminded him of Dave's intimidating mother and her dark and depressing house. He began to panic and started to walk as fast as he could, only to find that even with her handicap, she was gaining on him. He reached for yet another piece of tablet and, with his heart racing out of control, took a deep breath and put on a final spurt until he reached the front door of his block.

Reg dropped his accordion onto the pavement but while he fumbled through his pockets for the key, she reached him. Suddenly sober, he now felt alone and strangely threatened.

She smiled and began speaking in such a slurred voice that he couldn't understand anything she was saying. She moved even closer and stroked his hair and whispered in his ear.

The extreme amount of neo-epinine caused his whole body to throb wildly and as he tried repeatedly to force his key into the lock he broke into a sweat. The lock had never been easy, but at that moment the key engaged and the door unexpectedly opened under their weight. She fell onto him and, while he struggled to push her off, she tried desperately to kiss him. Reg managed to roll her to one side and, now without the burden of her weight, was able to break away. She tried to get up but had great difficulty in keeping her balance. He grabbed the accordion and, using his last ounce of strength, picked it up and started to climb the stairs. Not even wasting energy on looking back, he reached the fourth floor, opened the door at the first attempt, pulled the accordion inside, slammed the door shut, bolted and locked it.

He slid his accordion against the door, stretched his neck and rested the back of his head on the door, while he caught his breath. Slowly he began to relax, but then remembered she was still in the building. It wasn't long before she was banging on his door and screaming at him. 'Mein chatze, mein chatze, ich leiber dich.' Her shrill voice reverberated in the stairwell as she repeated it over and over.

Reg climbed into bed and covered his head with the pillow. Although he dozed periodically, he woke with a start at even the slightest sound. It was late afternoon before he felt safe enough to sleep, and Monday afternoon before he dared to venture out of the flat.

Because Hazelle and Anita spent most of their spare time with Adrian, he became bored and began to act like so many of the pimps that lived in St Pauli. He would spend most of his time in the clubs and bars drinking heavily and experimenting with drugs until he met them at Mambo's or the Blockhütte. That was until his new found friend at the Star Club died from the same concoction of pills and korn.

Adrian had no intention of finishing his musical career that way, if he could help it.

Chapter seventeen

What Kind of Fool am I?

The depleted Cheetahs sat alone in Mambo's late on a May afternoon. It was very unusual for them to visit the bar much before midnight but they were there for a special reason.

While Bernd stood polishing and re-polishing row upon row of glasses, and with only the jukebox breaking the silence, the musicians sat quietly waiting for the telephone to ring. It seemed strange to have the music playing so loudly when the place was empty, but it did bring in the occasional punter who was lost or already drunk.

The telephone rang; they all looked across apprehensively at Bernd and waited. He talked for what seemed like an eternity but eventually looked across at Dave and held the receiver out in front of him. Dave grabbed the phone and listened intently, looked across at the rest of the group, nodding and animated as he spoke. He handed the phone back to Bernd and casually walked back and sat at the table.

After contemplating his recent telephone conversation for a few moments, he suddenly leapt into the air. 'Yeeees… we've got it.' He couldn't hold back the combination of excitement and relief. 'They're sending four cars for us tomorrow. We start on Friday at the Star Club in Bochum.'

They looked at Dave in total bewilderment. Adrian cleared his throat and spoke slowly. 'That's bloody great news but haven't you forgotten something? We don't have a drummer and we can't get Tony to play with us, he's probably back at the poxy sodding brewery by now.'

Dave didn't seem concerned. 'I reckon we can find a drummer easy, they're ten a penny, there are dozens looking for a group.'

'Let's hope you're right,' replied Jimmy.

Although pleased, he found it difficult to decide if it was good news or not as he knew that he would have to leave Helga again. He slowly pushed himself up from the table and left to break the bad news to her. 'I'll be back tonight,' he said.

Reg, Adrian and Dave sat celebrating with round after round of biers and schnapps, and patiently waited.

As it began to get dark a longhaired, trendy teenager walked into the bar. They'd seen him around and, after buying him a drink, Dave called him over to their table. 'Are you a musician?' asked Dave.

The young man struggled to reply in broken English. 'Yes, I do play music.'

'What do you play?' asked Dave enthusiastically.

'I play the drums, but not at the moment, I don't have me a group,' he replied.

Dave asked him to join them by explaining in pidgin English and flaying arms that they had been booked to play in Bochum and they needed a drummer to go with them the next morning.

The drummer looked around at the musicians. 'But I don't have me the drums,' he said.

Dave returned to the telephone, handed Bernd a piece of paper and asked him to call the number. After what seemed like a difficult conversation, he walked back towards the table smiling from ear to ear. 'It's all right, we can use the other group's drums, perhaps we will have to make a small donation towards their bier but leave that to me.'

The German musician didn't really understand, but smiled.

'What's your name?' asked Reg.

'Fritz,' replied the musician.

Dave patted him on the back. 'Well Fritz, welcome to the Cheetahs.'

They took it in turns to shake his hand and the bier flowed well into the evening.

When Jimmy returned, Dave excitedly told him the good news.

The guitarist was not easily convinced. 'Have you heard him play? He doesn't even have any drums; he may be a load of shit,' said Jimmy, wildly shaking his head. His doubts were ignored in the euphoria of the moment and for the rest of the evening Jimmy found it hard to take his eyes off Fritz, who had become a member of the group without playing a single note.

There was one thing that Fritz had going for him, he certainly looked the part. He wore tight chequered trousers, a black roll neck jumper and had shoulder length hair which fell over the collar of his striped jacket.

After arranging to meet the next morning at eleven o'clock, they drifted off in different directions to enjoy their last night in Hamburg.

The next morning, at eleven o'clock precisely, the line of Mercedes taxis pulled up outside of Mambo's. The musicians with the exception of Jimmy were waiting for them; they each climbed into separate cars and Dave, sitting in the first car, directed them to the garage in Altona. When the taxis drew up outside the garage, Jimmy was already standing proudly with his arms wrapped around the now very large Helga. She didn't acknowledge any of the English musicians but spoke to Fritz, who briefly responded while he helped to load the equipment into the respective taxis.

Adrian travelled alone in front while Dave had to physically prise Jimmy away from Helga and push him into the second taxi with him, leaving Reg and Fritz to squeeze uncomfortably into the last taxi.

The journey to Bochum took six hours of unusual luxury for the musicians, who were used to the discomfort of the inhospitable van. At each stop the drivers paid for the food and drinks and, for the first time, the musicians seemed to be travelling in the way in which they had always imagined they would.

As the entourage wove its way through the industrial town and out into the suburbs, it turned into the car park of the Star Club. Above the entrance printed in large letters were the names, 'The CHEATERS' and 'The CONTOURS. '

The cars glided up to the side door but before any of the drivers could pull on the handbrake the musicians had jumped out and run around to the front of the club, craning their necks and laughing. They looked up, excited at seeing their name displayed in such large letters for the first time. Adrian was the first to scrutinise the large sign. 'Fucking hell, look at that, they've spelt our name wrong,' he said.

'No problem, I'll get them to change it later,' said Dave.

Before they could discuss it the drivers started shouting. Reluctantly they unloaded the equipment and carried it through the door directly onto the stage.

While Dave set up the P.A. next to the other group's speakers, the remaining musicians set up the amplifiers, pleased at last to be playing again, and feeling on a high. Jimmy and Adrian tuned their guitars in excited anticipation while Dave methodically tested the microphones. The atmosphere inside the converted cinema seemed unusual with the mixture of the houselights and the sunlight from the double doors at the side of the stage. The heavy full width curtains were pulled back to reveal the interior.

The layout was similar to the Hamburg club but the décor was fresh and bright with large framed posters of the latest German and English chart groups on each wall.

Fritz carefully adjusted the drum stool, snare, cymbals and hi-hat, and then sat waiting for instructions. Jimmy started the riff for *Walking the Dog*; Adrian and Reg followed and waited for the drums to accompany them, but there was nothing. They stopped playing and turned to look at Fritz. He frowned and once again fiddled with the kit, then his seat, followed by a whole range of adjustments.

Finally he smiled and Jimmy started to play. When Adrian and Reg joined in, Fritz started to hit the snare drum and cymbal without playing the bass drum. Jimmy grabbed his guitar lead, walked across to the raised drum rostrum, pushed Fritz off his stool, took off his guitar and proceeded to play the drum pattern for the song.

Fritz gave a knowing nod, smiled, re-took his seat and on cue started to play again. There was no improvement. Jimmy went wild. 'You bloody German bastard, you're not a drummer, you're a...' He stuttered with anger. 'You've never touched the drums before have you? You've got no fucking idea. Do you know what you've done?' He looked straight into the terrified face of the German and then at the rest of the group. Despondent and almost in tears, he continued. 'I thought at last things were getting better, and we're fucked again, by that bastard.'

Still wearing his guitar, he stormed towards Fritz raising his clenched fist but at the last minute changed his mind and direction, walked through the open doors and out into the sunshine.

He sat on the wall in front of the club and gazed unbelievably at the hoarding and picked up a handful of stones and threw them angrily at the sign, the dust dispersing in the light afternoon breeze. 'Bastard... the bastard, who does he think he is? What right has he got to fuck up our lives?' screamed Jimmy.

He continued to gaze up at the name. 'Perhaps it is spelt right after all,' he muttered.

While the hot sun burnt the back of his neck, he sat reflecting on the events since leaving England. Were they ever going to get a break? Were they wasting their time? Or were they just unlucky?

As the sun moved behind the building, he thought he heard music inside the club. He did; it was the unmistakable sound of the Bird organ and Reg playing *Woolly Bully*. The sound blasted through the open door and across the car park, followed by the other instruments, until finally he heard Dave's distinctive gritty voice.

Jimmy stood up and, still wearing his guitar, walked towards the club. As he got nearer he broke into a run, finally sprinting onto the stage. He stopped and looked in the direction of the drums, not knowing what to expect. Perhaps Fritz had been playing a joke, unusual for a German, but instead he saw a total stranger playing them.

They played for nearly an hour until they were forced to stop by the smiling and satisfied club manager who wanted to show them to their accommodation behind the stage.

Jimmy had so many questions but surprisingly he didn't need any answers, only to suggest that it might be a good thing to change the name of the group. They did.

The drummer was a member of the German group the Contours and he agreed with Dave to play with both groups providing they also paid him.

In less than an hour Axel was a bone fide member of the renamed Cheetahs, and the Contours, and he liked the idea.

Axel was a real life Hamburger having been born and brought up in the roughest part of the city, close to the docks. At twenty-seven he was by far the oldest musician on stage but his experience was second to none. His parents loved music and his father, a docker, continually quenched Axel's insatiable thirst for more and more music, regularly bringing home records from the American and British seamen. There were however two drawbacks, he spoke very little English, looked like the Neanderthal man with huge gaps between his teeth and, contrary to the current trend, had long thinning blond hair which he brushed across the top of his head. His physique, built up over several years of amateur wrestling when he represented Germany, prevented anyone from arguing with him, but beggars couldn't be choosers and he played the drums better than any drummer the Cheetahs had ever played with before.

Later that night, in the bar near the club, Adrian reflected. 'He is sitting at the back and no one ever looks at the drummer. I mean look at Ringo and Dave Clark, they're both ugly bastards, perhaps that's what we've been missing.' He nodded and smiled. 'Axe man will be fine.'

The Contours played the same traditional music as many of the semi-professional groups springing up throughout Germany but they were adequate for the club and it made the renamed Cheetahs sound even better. The guitarist also had great contacts and was able to maintain the required supply of Preludin and pot for Adrian, Dave and Reg, while Jimmy preferred vast quantities of bier.

During the week Axel was able to cope, but at weekends he found it hard playing from five o'clock when the club opened until three or sometimes four o'clock in the morning, when understandably he flagged. But even then he still managed to keep the beat. His stamina was incredible; although he drank more bier than anyone else, he did sweat most of it out of his system while he was on stage.

Wherever they went Axel would find a space on the toilet wall to draw his favourite felt tip character, Dicky bird wank wank, a combination of a penis and testicles, with eyes and a smile. It was pathetic, but he thought it was hilarious.

The accommodation was basic; two dingy rooms furnished with single metal beds, a wafer thin mattress and a thin quilt. But the rooms were incredibly close to the stage, and near enough to allow them to prey on the female club goers, score, and be back on stage within the hour.

They were all happy except Jimmy, who missed Helga desperately and impatiently awaited her letters which arrived on a daily basis. He had also begun to turn his attention towards the impending birth and dreamt of being back in Hamburg. Unfortunately, he was the only one. Sex, morning, noon and night was the order of the day; it was non-stop, drip-fed.

Axel forced them to visit the local municipal baths once a week to shower or bath, and while Jimmy and Axel swam in the large pool the remaining three musicians, unable to swim, would spend time taking a leisurely shower.

Although Adrian preferred a bath, he agreed to shower with the rest of the group. Dave and Adrian showered on the opposite side of the room to Reg and Adrian, hardly able to contain his excitement, screamed encouragement across to Reg. 'Get yours over here, come on.'

'Come on Reg. Surely you're going to race, aren't you?' shouted Dave.

He ignored them, preferring to shampoo his hair.

The excitement was briefly interrupted when an unsuspecting middle aged German walked into the shower room. Faced by the shouting and cheering of the crazed longhaired English men, he grabbed at his clothes and ran out dripping, and shaking his head wildly as he sprinted out naked into the summer air.

Reg, totally confused but guided by Adrian, naïvely scratched the dark brown freckles that had mysteriously appeared amongst his pubic hair. They carefully identified and picked at a specific freckle and then laid the brown spot on the white ceramic tiled shelf and waited. When the freckle began to move, Reg was violently sick.

Adrian managed to coerce him to join the race and enter his personal crustacean, and much to Dave and Adrian's annoyance, Reg's visitor won by a claw. Whilst the two losers reluctantly congratulated him, Reg became angry when the three crabs tried to crawl away. He grabbed one of his boots and, with a burst of aggression and anger never seen before by his fellow musicians, brought the heel down several times onto the unsuspecting crabs, smashing the white tiles with the sheer force of the blows.

'You must be fucking crazy,' screamed Adrian.

'What?' asked Reg, desperately trying to catch his breath.

'You had the makings of a champion there,' smiled Adrian, as the grin slowly spread to the whole of his face.

They dried themselves, put on their clothes, and the triumphant Reg collected his winnings of twenty Deutsche marks.

His achievement soon turned to disgust when he realised how he had won the money. Nevertheless, although he found it hard to accept, when they all returned to the cafe he was pleased to buy everyone a celebratory bier.

That night he found it hard to sleep and in the early hours of the morning, feeling unclean and disgusted at the thought of having such repulsive creatures crawling around his penis and through his pubic hair, he took a drastic step. Using Adrian's razor, he stood alone in the half-light and carefully shaved his pubic hair. He smiled to himself when he touched the smooth, shaven area, and satisfied that he was once more in control of his body, took a deep breath and treated the area with Adrian's Max Factor aftershave. Seconds later, unaccustomed to shaving and using aftershave, he screamed out into the night as the sweet smelling liquid penetrated his freshly shaved tender skin.

The harsh treatment worked and the freckles miraculously vanished, his pubic hair regrew and he took great care to regularly inspect and remove any further visitors or uninvited guests before they had the opportunity to take refuge on his body.

Although Reg shared a room with Dave, he was taken by surprise when he walked in to see Dave sitting on the edge of his bed, wearing only a T-shirt, cupping his penis in his hands. 'We've got to try and control this sex thing, you know. Look at this,' he said. Dave removed his hands to reveal a hideous sight; his penis was raw, bleeding and swollen.

Reg couldn't help but smile and Dave reacted angrily. 'It's not funny, I'm in sodding agony,' he moaned.

Reg grimaced, appreciating the pain. 'I'm sure you are, but I've got a similar problem.' He paused, and a sharp intake of breath followed as he reluctantly took another look at Dave's glowing penis. 'Bloody hell that is bad, mine is nowhere near as bad as that, I thought it was only me.'

Reg subconsciously cupped his trousers at the crotch. 'All we can do is try and give it a rest for a while.' He stood and thought for a second. 'If we can.'

'I've got no option,' replied Dave, 'if I don't want my mate to drop off. What's the point of being in a group if this happens?'

Reg nodded in agreement.

With the decision made they helped each other, and rather than rush off with every fraulien they saw, they sat and had a drink instead. It went against the grain but they had no option. Within a few days they returned to their old ways but became much more selective in their choice.

There was little or no privacy in the rooms behind the stage and certain girls refused to visit them. Adrian had been showing an unusual amount of interest in Kerstin, a pretty long haired girl who came to the club nearly every night. Although she told him she wanted to sleep with him, she was too embarrassed to go to the room he shared with Jimmy. She suggested they go camping and she would bring her friend Pauline for Reg.

The girls arrived early and danced in front of the stage smiling at Reg and Adrian throughout the night. When they weren't on stage, they sat drinking with them. After finishing the last set Reg, Adrian and Pauline got into Kerstin's Mercedes saloon and drove off into the night. Within half an hour she pulled into a field beside a river. Kerstin and Pauline handed Reg and Adrian a bottle of korn and two glasses, rushed out of the car and into the darkness.

Adrian lit a joint and he and Reg took it in turns to smoke it while they stood watching in disbelief as the two girls fell over each other in the excitement and anticipation of what lay ahead. In less than fifteen minutes the white canvas tent was erected and, after laying blankets on the floor, the girls grabbed Reg and Adrian and pulled them inside. They stripped each other off in the darkness but no sooner were they naked than Reg had an attack. He scrambled around the floor of the tent, found his clothes and searched frantically for his tablets. He had forgotten to bring them. His breathing became more laboured and Adrian knew that he would have to do something.

'Help me,' wheezed Reg.

Adrian pleaded with Kerstin but she refused to help until he ran out of patience. 'Come on you silly bloody cow, you gotta take me back to the club,' he screamed.

In the tent Adrian's voice seemed extraordinarily loud and Kerstin finally took notice. 'What, now?' she cursed. 'You are fucking joking? Tell me you are?'

Before she'd put on her shoes, Adrian dragged her across the field to the car.

Pauline tried her best to calm Reg but it was too late, the only thing that could help him was a neo-epinine.

When Adrian returned, Reg lay fighting for breath. He grabbed at the bottle and forced a whole tablet under his tongue and waited for his recovery. After an immeasurable amount of time, he began to improve enough to be able to travel. Unable to hide their disappointment, Kerstin and Pauline took down the tent and drove them back to the club.

Adrian, sitting as always in the passenger seat, leaned over to Reg. 'Thanks a lot for screwing up tonight. I don't know why I bothered. I should have come without you,' he said.

Pauline and Kerstin never returned to the club and Reg and Adrian vowed not to go camping again.

Despite the disastrous experience, they all liked Bochum, and when Axel asked to join them permanently, they visited a number of clubs and were fortunate enough to sign a contract for the next month at a small club in the centre of town.

Chapter eighteen

Whatcha Gonna Do About It?

Without a drummer, the Contours made the decision to break up and go their separate ways. In no hurry to leave Bochum, they drove Axel and the rest of the Cheetahs to the new club; then on to their accommodation at the top floor of a three-storey building a few minutes walk away.

They were not surprised to find that the flat had three very basic furnished rooms, each with a wash hand basin, old beds, and a dilapidated bathroom situated down the long corridor. What really made this accommodation special was the small club in the basement where local German groups played every night, and a door next to the bar that linked the club to a lobby and staircase up to their rooms.

For the Cheaters, the month began and continued like a nightmare. Herr Braun owned the club but Billy Butz, a young go-ahead entrepreneur who unfortunately had no money, managed it. He certainly had the ideas and left alone would have made the small but atmospheric Angel club a place to be seen in, but the two men had differing ideas as to what type and style of music should be played.

Herr Braun made it quite clear that whenever he was in the club, he expected them to play at the volume he stipulated. In order to comply with the unusual request, Reg would sit himself inconspicuously behind an out of tune upright piano, which had stood neglected in a corner of the small stage for years. The rest of the group would play at the lowest volume possible and, rather than turning off the power completely, they would use practise volume settings on the amplifiers while Axel used brushes.

Everything changed when Billy was on duty; he wanted out and out Rock and Roll, and that was what he got. The Cheaters could now rock better than most groups on the circuit.

The difficulties started when the two of them were on duty. Herr Braun would go to his office deep in the cellar at the rear of the club and the group could play at a reasonable volume, but as soon as he reappeared behind the club bar, no matter how busy the club was, everything would change. It was impossible to please both of them at the same time.

Living in the city centre allowed them more time to explore but people didn't accept them in the same way they did in Hamburg. Wherever they went, in the bars, shops, even in the street, everyone stopped to stare as though they were from another planet. With Axel now a permanent member of the group, Dave arranged for a young photographer to take new publicity pictures and he sent them out to other agents and clubs for future work.

For the first time they felt they were part of a stable unit and, at last, things were improving.

As the days progressed, it was evident that something was going on that made some of the evenings in the club extremely quiet, then suddenly it would be full, transformed into a mass party and celebration. They soon became aware that the football World Cup was unfolding back in England. Although no one in the group, except Jimmy and Axel, had any real interest in any type of sport, let alone football, they were left with no option but to become involved. The tournament reached the semi finals and as it neared the cup final, pitting Germany and England against each other, the whole thing developed into what could easily have become World War Three.

The lead up to the final started to cause animosity between the two countries and the musicians knew no better. All they were aware of was the obvious difference between them; they were English. The group begrudgingly went to watch the final in the café near the Star Club. At first the bier flowed and all appeared to be good-natured but as the pressure began to build and England took the lead they divided into two groups.

Before the referee blew the final whistle, after extra time, it was clear that England could perhaps win. The English fans started to run onto the pitch as Geoff Hurst scored his hat trick sealing the score at 4 - 2, and as the final whistle blew the arguments over the validity of the decision regarding one of the goals started.

All hell let loose as the musicians were forced to run, leaving Axel in a very awkward position. Although he had done his best to break the tension between the two nationalities, there was little one man could do.

The group, although pleased to be English, had not realised the implications that victory against their hosts would have on them. That evening, bottles flew at the stage as the German fans drank and drank, leaving the group with no alternative but to desert the stage and take to the safety of their rooms for the rest of the evening while the disappointed Germans rampaged through the streets until well after dawn.

Although feelings gradually returned to normal, for the remainder of their stay in Bochum the Geoff Hurst goal was the talking point in every bar they dared to venture into.

Several days after the match, in early August, the relationship between the group and the club management progressively began to break down as Billy Butz and Herr Braun fought over what and how the group should play. The confusion began to affect the takings and came to a head at eleven o'clock on the following Saturday.

With less than a hundred people in the club, both the owner and his manager knew that the situation could continue no longer and two hours later they asked the group to stop playing. The club emptied and, with no more than three customers since midnight, the waiters and bar staff had been able to clean up earlier than usual and had already left.

As Adrian and Jimmy put their guitars into the cases, Herr Braun and Billy approached the stage. Herr Braun spoke first, addressing Axel in German, while the remainder of the group stood waiting for the drummer to translate. Adrian had already run out of patience and stood cockily looking at the two Germans. He was not prepared to wait any longer for the Krauts to speak to him. If they didn't want to speak in English, why should he be polite?

'Come on Axel, what the fuck did he say?' screamed Adrian.

Axel stood in silence while he mentally translated the exact words that Herr Braun had said to him.

'You must leave the club, your music is not good and you make no good business for us,' said Herr Braun. He could see that the musicians were shocked, but then Herr Braun continued in English. 'You will leave tonight,' he said firmly.

None of them could believe what he said. Dave screamed at them. 'Tonight, but we have a contract for a month. That's two more weeks.'

Billy Butz spoke in a clear raised voice. 'There is no negotiation. Tonight, you leave, and you will not receive any payment until you agree to sign this letter, then... we will pay you,' he said.

He pulled a neatly folded piece of white paper from his jacket pocket and passed it to Dave.

They all crowded around and read it. It didn't take them long.

'You can't do this. You've got to fuckin' pay us for the month,' shouted Adrian.

The Germans shook their heads at the same time. 'No, you are mistaken. If you do not sign, then you will receive not one Deutsche mark,' said Herr Braun.

Adrian's fingers started to twitch and, unable to control himself any longer, he lost his temper and ran directly at Herr Braun and Billy, knocking them onto the glass dance floor. His actions drew in everyone else and before they knew it all the musicians were punching and kicking the Germans.

Jimmy ran back, jumped onto the stage and picked up three spare guitar leads. With the adrenaline rising at the unexpected event, he jumped high in the air and onto the Germans. 'Come on let's tie up the bastards and then smash up this shit hole,' he screamed.

Dave grabbed two chairs from the nearest table and, with the coloured lights still flashing beneath the floor, placed the chairs back to back in the centre of the glass dance floor. Adrian pulled two lengths of filthy used gaffa tape from the stage floor, and now enjoying every minute pulled it forcefully across each of their abusive mouths.

Axel walked off into the darkness, locked the external door, and returned holding his trophy high in the air. Dave now took his turn. He walked across to the stage and returned to the glass dance floor with his microphone stand and held it menacingly high in the air. 'If you don't pay us we will smash the dance floor and then the rest of the club,' he said, a wide grin filling his face.

The bound Germans made a token struggle while their shaking heads confirmed that they had no intention of giving in.

Adrian walked over to the bar, switched on the jukebox and twisted the volume control full-up while Dave slammed the microphone stand into the flashing glass floor. His first blow did nothing, but the second, third and fourth blows shattered large pieces of the coloured glass panels and some of the flashing fluorescent lights below.

There was little reaction, although it was clear that the captives were getting worried as they began to sweat profusely. The combination of the flashing floor lights shining directly up into their eyes and the incessant thumping of the juke box caused the elderly Herr Braun to shake his head violently.

Jimmy, Reg, then Axel, began to systematically smash the tables and chairs, to the strained vocal chords of Stevie Marriott's *Whatcha Gonna Do About It?*

Seeing every chair and table smashed, Herr Braun began to nod. At first, no one noticed because they were enjoying the opportunity of releasing the frustration of the last two weeks.

The positive movement finally caught Jimmy's eye and he shouted for the demolition to stop. It took several minutes but it stopped as quickly as it had begun. Adrian now relished the opportunity of slowly and painfully pulling the gaffa tape from one angry mouth, then the other.

He stood back and waited.

'OK, we will pay you three and a half weeks,' said Herr Braun.

Dave walked towards them holding the microphone stand, ready to start all over again. 'OK, it is four weeks, yes,' said a deflated Herr Braun.

The whole group cheered loudly, briefly drowning out the music.

Still holding the chair leg menacingly in his right hand, Adrian released Herr Braun and walked with him to the office, where he ripped the telephone out of the wall.

Several minutes later he returned, victorious, holding a handful of money above his head. Dave scrambled around on the floor to find the letter, altered the amount, signed the bottom, passed it to Billy Butz for his signature, grabbed it back, ripped it in half and passed one half back to Herr Braun.

Axel reached forward, grabbed it, and wrote a few words on the bottom before handing it back for the last time. Herr Braun and Billy left for the relative safety of the office.

The musicians climbed back onto the stage, congratulated each other and finished packing up the equipment.

When he saw the equipment piled high on the stage Dave suddenly realised their problem. 'What are we going to do with that lot?' he asked.

They stood looking at it until Axel had a bright idea. 'We can take it to the 'bahnhof and put it in the luggage containers.'

'The left luggage?' said Adrian.

'Yeas, we can do it. I know this,' replied Axel.

A much relieved, Dave walked outside, hailed three taxis, and within ten minutes they were stowing it into two rows of left luggage lockers. As they walked along the platform, they suddenly felt hungry and piled into the all night 'bahnhof café for a well-earned meal and a few biers, drank far too much, staggering back to their rooms in the early morning sun, and into bed.

When they eventually woke, the realisation that they were miles from Hamburg and didn't have any way of travelling or transporting the equipment had now become a major problem.

With the sun streaming through the window and the noise of the German group's afternoon session blasting up from the cellar below, Dave lay in bed thinking. He knew the Cheaters could do well; they were certainly better than most of the groups on the German circuit, but what were they doing wrong?

He was suddenly aware of Jimmy screaming in the next room. Dave jumped out of bed to be met by the rest of the group, and joined him. 'Axel's gone. The German bastard's left us. What are we going to do now?' screamed Jimmy.

'What do mean he's gone?' asked Dave. 'He's probably gone for something to eat; you know he eats more than all of us put together.'

'He's bloody gone, I know he is. I went to the station to get my guitar and the larger lockers where he put his drums are all empty,' said Jimmy

'So what do we do now?' asked Reg.

Adrian looked at Jimmy as though it had been rehearsed. 'Me and Jimmy can go to Hamburg, borrow a van and come and get you and take the equipment back,' said Adrian smugly.

Jimmy nodded excitedly. He liked the idea; he could see his Helga.

'All right, but you'd better not forget we're here, I know what you two are like when you get together with the girls,' said Dave.

Adrian and Jimmy hurriedly packed their few clothes and belongings but Dave forced them to leave them in the lockers with the equipment.

As they boarded the train empty handed, there were mixed feelings as Reg and Dave stood watching the train pull away, neither of them knew how long it would be before Adrian and Jimmy would come back to fetch them.

Dave, sensing that Reg was terribly frightened, put his arm around him and gently guided him towards the 'bahnhof bar. 'Come on let's get drunk, they'll be back in a few days,' he said.

With no reason to get out of bed, they slept all day and then spent the night with any girls that were willing.

Early the next morning Reg was woken by horrendous banging. He looked out of the window and saw Herr Braun and Billy Butz standing at the entrance door below. He rushed in and shook Dave until he was conscious enough to hear him. 'Wake up, we've got a real problem,' stuttered Reg.

Dave struggled to open his eyes. 'What?' He paused. 'What the hell's going on?' he asked.

Reg ran back to the window. 'Shit, there are loads of people outside the door,' he said, beginning to panic. 'Dave, fucking hell, will you get out of that bed... come on, will you get up.'

Dave sat up and pushed Uschi, a young naked blonde, on to the floor as he tried to get out of bed. He climbed over her and rushed towards the door and, pushing his ear tight against it, listened as the men hammered at the entrance door below. The banging went on for several minutes until suddenly it stopped.

The three of them stood in silence, not even daring to breathe, until Dave moved towards the open window and carefully poked his head outside. He looked from side to side and, finally satisfied that the coast was clear, pulled himself in, hitting the side of his head in the excitement. 'They're gone.' He raised his voice. 'I said they've bloody well gone.' He ran over, hugged Reg and then Uschi.

They waited a while and then nervously followed each other down the long winding staircase. Reg turned the handle but the door wouldn't open. He tried the handle again, and then shook it violently, but it wouldn't budge. Dave impatiently pushed him aside and tried the same moves without success before charging at the door with his shoulder. 'The bastards have boarded us in, we're trapped. They're going to starve us out,' said Dave.

'It is not a problem; I have been here before but not through the door.'

Uschi hesitated and coyly looked at Dave before continuing. 'Please don't be angry at me,' she said.

Dave, now beginning to feel the pain in his shoulder, shook his head, failing to understand anything she was saying.

She reached out, took his hand and asked them to follow her up the stairs to the first half landing, where she effortlessly opened the window and climbed out onto a small flat roof. She smiled, gave a limp wave and disappeared over the side of the roof.

Dave shook his head. 'What a fucking mess? I can't believe how we got into such a bloody stupid situation.'

They lay on their beds and began to realise how serious it was and they had absolutely no idea how they would survive until Adrian and Jimmy returned, or if they ever would. There was only one reason for them to come back, to collect their guitars, assuming they hadn't done the same thing as Axel and already taken them with them.

As it began to get dark they heard a noise outside the door. Dave picked up a chair and Reg a bier bottle that he had used as a toilet during the night. The handle slowly turned and in walked Uschi with her girlfriend Marina. They each carried a large box crammed full of bier, schwein kotelet, bratwurst and bread. They shared a bed with their favourite musician and fed them before dragging them under the covers.

Reg, once again able to relax, shouted across the room to Dave. 'It's not so bad after all, is it mate?'

The next morning Reg was forced to think otherwise. He looked out onto the street and noticed Julian, the head waiter from the

Angel Club, standing on the other side of the road pretending to read a paper. It was quite obvious that he was keeping watch for Herr Braun and it made them realise that he had not forgotten what they had done to him and that he was looking to take revenge. Every six hours, someone else came and stood guard at the entrance. This continued twenty-four hours a day, every day, and it was clear that he was trying to wear them down.

Dave and Reg could never relax because they didn't know when Herr Braun would make his move and, throughout their enforced imprisonment, they lived in fear.

The two girls heard it first.

At dawn on the eleventh day, the hammering at the door grew louder and became more frantic; trying to speak in English was impossible as they shot out of bed and ran around the room looking for their clothes. The sound of splitting wood was followed by the sound of heavy footsteps rushing up the stairs towards them.

Unable to escape through the window, the four of them stood shaking, packed tightly together in the corner of the bedroom awaiting the inevitable. The footsteps finally reached their floor; they could hear the doors to the other rooms being kicked open without bothering to try the handles.

They were next.

Suddenly their door burst open. Adrian, Jimmy and Ricky, from one of the Scottish groups, stood looking at them.

Ricky spoke first. 'Come on then you's, what are we waiting for? Let's gae haim.'

Dave and Reg tried hard to hold back the tears of relief but when Uschi and Marina started to cry, they joined in, wiping the tears from their eyes while they packed their meagre belongings. 'When we see you again?' pleaded Uschi.

Dave was no longer interested. Like Reg, he wanted to get out of their prison as quickly as he could. He took a few minutes to try and console her as he carried his small suitcase down the stairs. 'I don't know when baby, but I will write to you when we get back to Hamburg and get sorted out, and then you can come and see us again.'

It worked and although the two girls continued to sob they accepted it. The girls were pushed and jostled by the early morning commuters making their way to their office while the two musicians, free at last, took in the fresh air and stared disbelievingly at the shiny van. They smiled to each other and congratulated Adrian, Jimmy and Ricky, in turn patting them on the back. It was then that they remembered Julian on the other side of the road. He stood looking at them unsure what he should do.

Adrian raised his hand to give him the V sign but Dave pulled at his arm. 'Let's just get out of here; I can't face any more crap from this lot. You've really got no fucking idea what it's been like for me and him.'

Reg nodded in agreement and climbed into the van. The others jumped in, Adrian immediately taking the front passenger seat, but for once Dave gave him a hard lingering stare. Without a word, Adrian slid across and sat on the engine casing between Dave and Ricky.

With the realisation beginning to sink in, Reg and Dave spoke at the same time. 'Come on let's get out of this shit hole.'

They drove to the bahnhof loaded the equipment and didn't look back.

For the first part of the journey Dave and Reg talked excitedly about the ordeal and how the girls had saved them, but then fell asleep exhausted.

Jimmy, not wanting to stop except to refill the van, was restless and desperate to get back to Hamburg. He hadn't wanted to travel down to Bochum with Adrian but had been blackmailed into coming with him. When he left Helga, he knew the baby was expected within a few days and he wanted to be there.

They arrived in Hamburg late in the evening and Ricky drove directly to Helga's flat in Altona. Renate, Helga's closest friend, greeted them. She was frantic. 'Zanc Gott you arrived.'

She pulled Jimmy from the van and they returned a few minutes later carrying a very hysterical Helga. They were surprised at the size of her; she looked ready to burst. She stood on the pavement and screamed continually while Jimmy tried to help her.

'Come on we've got to get my Helga to the hospital,' he screamed.

They all piled out of the van and helped her to climb inside, all the while she continued to scream and cry as the contractions came closer together. They laid her on the floor of the van amongst the equipment, on a pile of old torn blankets used to cushion the equipment. Renate climbed into the front and frantically tried to direct Ricky to the krankenhaus. Jimmy dutifully knelt beside Helga holding her hand and trying his utmost to console her.

Renate, in a state of sheer panic, shouted at Ricky. 'Schnell! Schnell! Schnell!'

Realising that everyone was relying on him, Ricky now screamed back at her. 'I'm doing me best, give me a break will yer woman,' he said.

It didn't matter. Every time Helga screamed, Renate shouted.

The van pulled up outside the large grey hospital building. Everyone jumped out and tried to support Helga as she tried to walk but when they realised it was impossible they lifted her shoulder height and carried her in. The nurses looked in amazement at the sight of the long haired entourage as it slowly made its way to casualty.

The tired musicians struggled to keep Helga in the air until she was placed on a stretcher and wheeled behind the curtains with Renate still holding her hand. Seconds later a baby cried. Jimmy rushed towards the curtains, pulled them apart and entered. He returned a few minutes later proudly holding the tiny newborn crumpled baby.

The rest of the group looked at each other, until Adrian broke the silence. 'Are you sure the father was a musician? It hardly looks human.'

Jimmy didn't hear a thing as the excitement took hold. 'It's a boy... a little boy,' he shouted excitedly.

He couldn't take his eyes off the tiny crying miracle. After showing the bundle to his friends he disappeared back behind the curtains to rejoin and congratulate Helga.

'He must be mad, you'd think it was his kid,' shrugged Adrian, as he walked off towards the exit, sickened by the sight of a musician holding a baby and being proud of it when ironically it wasn't even his. 'Come on, can we go now?' he asked.

Ricky was now totally confused. 'The wee bairn is nae his, are you's pulling me leg? Its nae his... the way he's carrying on, I thought that it...'

Adrian relished every word as he answered the question.

"Course it's not his, we think his father is another guitarist... maybe a drummer or an organist, who knows? Whoever it is, Jimmy's not all there, but it's his choice.'

As they drove back to the Reeperbahn, they agreed how sad it was that the little boy wasn't Jimmy's baby and they knew it wouldn't be long before the situation would hit him hard. They all felt for him, but they had better things to do.

Ricky drove directly to Mambo's where they were greeted like heroes. They spent what was left of the night recounting the story to anyone interested and whenever any latecomer bought them a bier, the story was retold.

Finally shattered by the events of the day Adrian took Dave and Reg to the Park where they slept until early the next evening.

Jimmy left the empty, silent flat, knowing that within a few short days it would be ringing with the cries of the new life, and the relationship between him and Helga would change forever. The euphoria of the last twenty-four hours gradually turned into fear of the unknown. 'Would Helga still feel the same towards him? Or would she change now that she had fulfilled her wish to start a family? Would she think of the real father whenever she looked at the baby? Perhaps she would pretend that it was Jimmy's child, and her heart would tell her otherwise?'

In Mambo's the depleted group were in a sombre mood; they had absolutely no idea what the next move would be. They couldn't perform in their present circumstances and Jimmy's position had still not been finalised. That night even the jukebox played to itself.

Jimmy walked into the bar and was immediately congratulated by Bernd. As soon as the other groups heard the news, congratulatory offers came thick and fast. 'Hello, dad, come and have a celebration drink with us,' they chanted, building to a crescendo. Jimmy grimaced at the remarks, not knowing how to take the complement when he wasn't the father.

They could clearly see his confused reaction and it was evident that he was having great difficulty in coming to terms with the situation, if indeed he could ever come to terms with it. He raised his glass in a thank you to Bernd and the groups and joined the Cheaters at their table.

'So what do we do now?' asked Adrian.

Jimmy looked at the three of them, a sense of loss and hopelessness written over his face. 'I don't know, I've got no idea... honestly, I don't know what I want.'

The bar began to fill and by two thirty it was buzzing; the jukebox pumped out *House of the Rising Sun*, the korn flowed, washed down with litres of bier, and the pills popped, like the old days.

Through the smoke, Dave saw Bruno walk in with three long haired young men who were obviously musicians. He was as loud as ever and the musicians were hanging on his every word. He turned, and seeing the Cheaters, walked over to their table and reverently made a show of shaking their hands. When he got to Jimmy, he shook his hand with energetic exaggeration. 'I hear Helga has her baby, I think it is a pity for you,' said Bruno.

'What's that supposed to mean?' asked Jimmy.

'Well, she is a mother, but the baby is a bastard,' said a smirking Bruno. He began to laugh loudly. 'You know what I mean?'

Without any warning Jimmy flew across the table and launched himself at Bruno. He was much too light but persevered punching him with as much force as he could; Bruno was too fat and much to slow to even hit out at Jimmy, and the heavy blows began to have an effect. He stumbled, lost his balance and crashed onto a table of drinks, soaking the tables' occupants. Without a word, they kicked out at the fat German as he rolled around on the floor amongst the glass.

Dave and Adrian finally intervened and Bruno crawled towards the door, pulled himself up and left. The German musicians standing at the bar shook their heads in disbelief, finished their drinks and followed close behind Bruno.

Bernd didn't waste a second; he turned up the jukebox even louder, picked up the table, brought over a tray of drinks for everyone sitting on it and then rushed off to tidy up.

'I've wanted to see that happen to him since the first day I met him... the fat bastard,' said Adrian.

The three breathed a sigh of relief; at least there was still a chance of getting back on the stage so Dave grabbed the initiative. 'I'll tell you what we can do. Reg and Adrian can have a few days on their own, we've still got some cash, and me and Jimmy will put out some feelers for a new drummer and a club for next month,' he said.

They spent what was left of the evening talking over old times, which amazingly rebuilt the camaraderie between them, and after a few more drinks they started to draw up a list of new songs that they could learn.

Dave used the few days to tidy up as many loose ends as possible and to occupy his time rather than waste it sitting in the many clubs, bars or Mambo's. He visited the garage with Jimmy, did a deal with the owner, on one hand paying for the long term garaging of the crippled van and then selling it to him, and eventually walking away with three hundred Deutsche marks and a smile.

Helga and her baby came out of hospital and at first things seemed to go well with the three of them. Gradually she spent more and more time with the baby, eventually ignoring Jimmy altogether except to order him to prepare either the evening meal or breakfast.

Chapter nineteen

The Price of Love

Dave wasted little time in spreading the word to everyone he met, telling them the group was looking for a replacement drummer. It paid off, and in a couple of days Mike Elliot arrived in Hamburg. His father was based with the British forces at Herford and the two of them made the journey, with the bass drum in its case, tied onto the roof rack, and the rest of the kit squeezed inside an immaculate, shiny, light blue Ford Anglia. The car drove up Grosse Freiheit in the summer sunshine and stopped outside the Kaiser Keller.

The depleted group were waiting outside the club and when they saw the English registration they inwardly felt home-sick but no one dared to show it.

While his father unloaded the car, Mike ran excitedly across the road to gaze open mouthed at the photographs and posters displayed on each side of the entrance to the famous club.

Mike was barely eighteen and had spent the last three years at an exclusive boarding school near Stevenage. It had been a difficult period in his life; cut off from his family, he had fended for himself in what was an atmosphere of academic plenty and a famine of friendship. His only friend Justin came from a wealthy family, which probably explained why he was a renegade at school. He knew full well that he would be found a position in his father's business and therefore saw no reason to attempt to learn any of the boring subjects that were persistently forced upon him throughout the week and even at weekends.

Justin and Mike, or Michael as Justin preferred to call him, would take every opportunity to escape the confines of the establishment. When he became bored Justin would pay the train fare for the two of them to travel to London, where they explored Carnaby Street and the Kings Road, inevitably coming back loaded with the new clothes that they had managed to steal.

Justin loved it. Mike found it exhilarating as they built up a wardrobe of the latest fashions they were not permitted to wear within the confines of the school grounds.

Towards the end of the summer term, on a rather adventurous trip, they were caught red handed at Lord John's in Carnaby Street, arrested, and taken back to school by the police. Justin's father, using his connections hushed up the matter, paid off the retailer and gave a financial inducement to the school, thus allowing Justin to continue his education.

Mike was more fortunate. He was expelled, and later that week he was collected by his father and taken to Germany, before being driven to Hamburg for the audition a few days later. Although his father hadn't seen him for several years, he was desperate to get his son out of his hair as quickly as possible. Joining a group based in Germany seemed the quickest and easiest way out.

Mike faultlessly played every song in the Cheaters repertoire and he was offered the job, which not surprisingly he accepted immediately. His father, pleased with his afternoon's work, bought them all a meal, gave Mike twenty pounds and fifty Deutsche marks, wished him good luck, and drove back to Herford.

Mike was good looking, five foot six tall with dark immaculately styled hair which he religiously backcombed and, when lacquer was available, used a short sharp spray to keep it in place. His earlier misdeamours now paid off, at last allowing him the opportunity to show off his ill-gotten gains. Posing in the latest stylish and expensive English mod clothes; colourful striped Madras cotton blazer, Italian styled trousers, Ben Sherman button down collared shirts in pastel shades, paisley shirts and white slip on shoes, he looked every inch a true mod.

The combination of style and good looks acted as a magnet to the young girls. He was in tune with what was happening back home and he soon settled into the glamorous life, fulfilling the first and second part of his dream simultaneously; that of becoming a member of a professional English group, and playing and living in Germany.

Mike and Reg soon became inseparable and overnight Reg was transformed. Mike used an old cut throat razor to layer his hair and then showed him how to backcomb it into an acceptable style. The transformation made Reg feel good and helped to mould him into the typically stylish and proud English mod that he had always wanted to be.

Dave was the next member to succumb to the *Mike* treatment; his hair was once more dyed blond and then layered in the same style as Reg and Mike. Jimmy stopped using the Brylcream, and after a certain amount of styling by Mike, and much to the disgust of Helga, he reluctantly met the change halfway. Adrian compromised and begrudgingly allowed Mike to trim a few inches off the length of his hair.

The Cheaters started to learn many of the songs from the pile of records that Mike had brought with him from England. He introduced them to an almost new set of material which was revamped to suit the five piece group.

Their new material brought the house down every time it was performed.

Overnight Dave rose to new heights of showmanship and the crowd loved it. He found and bought two sets of coloured T-shirts in a small clothes shop tucked away at the far end of Tal Strasse, for each member of the group. They were the first coloured T-shirts they'd ever seen.

The standard white US army issue was all they were previously aware of, and they had been presented to them by Wally as a farewell present back in Coburg.

Although Mike had several white T-shirts printed with coloured designs similar to those worn by the Who, Dave bought some black adhesive tape and they cut out pieces of the tape to make abstract designs on the front. From the dance floor it looked fantastic, but under close scrutiny it was obvious what they had done. No one had seen it before so they created a new fashion amongst the hardened Hamburg club regulars who always professed to have seen it all before.

The Cheaters rekindled the interest in their music and their appearance and this, coupled with the forthcoming spell at the Star Club, seemed to be just what they all needed. At last they sounded fresh, experienced, and more importantly looked like a professional group. Mike was good for them, very good.

The bier shop, with its pseudo Bavarian exterior and dimly lit interior, was only a few metres from the Star Club and it became their second home during their stay at the club. Most of their time would be spent in the bier shop, often drinking too much but sobering up long enough to play before returning for more drinks. It had built up a reputation and become part of history.

Everyone that played at the Star Club, from the days of the Beatles and the continual wave of groups from Liverpool, spent every spare minute there. It had become a meeting place for prostitutes who had more than a passing interest in the English musicians. The small entrance was deceiving but once inside, after walking past the full length bar, a few stairs led up to the much valued juke box and into a larger seating area. The seats near the window looking out onto Gross Freiheit were considered to be the prime position in the bar. Horst, a well built brown haired man was as much a friend as a waiter. He knew every girl that came in and, after a couple of visits, every musician. Like most German bars, it was customary for whoever ordered the drinks to pay for them, but not immediately. Horst would bring a tray of drinks and mark off the number of drinks on the bier mat of the person who ordered them. At the end of the night, each person would take his bier mat to the bar and pay. Horst appeared to trust everyone, but no one ever tried to leave without paying even if a huge bill had built up over the course of the evening. The atmosphere was always good and the Liverpool accents of the prostitutes was stronger there than anywhere else on the Reeperbahn. For the musicians it became the nearest thing to home.

The Star Club was unique in that it had a tie up with German television and, after appearing on Beat Club early on a Saturday evening, the top groups and artists would drive to Hamburg and make two appearances at the club.

For the first time the Cheaters were to share the stage with famous artists from England, to help their reputation to grow and their confidence to build. Mike's greatest hope was to share the stage of the Star Club with the Small Faces.

The group accommodation was at the Pacific Hotel in Neuer Pferdemarkt, a short walk from the club, where they shared the building with the other resident Star Club groups and a mixture of prostitutes and club employees.

They each had their own room and for the first time there was hot running water. It regularly ran out but at least they could now wash their hair and take a bath in the shared bathroom if the desire took them. The Pacific was different from anywhere they had stayed before, with clean sheets every week. The resident cleaner, who lived on the top floor, systematically worked her way through the building during the month

Music of all styles blasted out of the rooms from the record players, while guitarists and singers could be heard playing or singing along. For the first time Jimmy set up the record player in his room, although he still continued to spend some nights with Helga and the baby at her flat. It was heaven.

Mike had a room on the second floor amongst the young girls and waiters who all worked at clubs in Grosse Freiheit. The remainder of the group had rooms next to each other on the fourth floor, but Mike preferred to be away from the others. It gave him a feeling of independence and for the first time he was able to keep some distance between him and Reg. After playing his last set at three o'clock in the morning, he decided to go back to the Pacific. He didn't feel well, having mixed too many drinks too often that night, and for once did the sensible thing, sooner, rather than leaving it too late.

His room was next to Brigitte, a pretty nineteen-year-old girl that he had seen for the first time at the Kaiser Keller when he auditioned with the group. She had brought them all a bier and seemed to appreciate the music. He believed that her enjoyment of the music was the reason Dave had asked him to join the Cheaters. She seemed very friendly with the young barman and on several occasions, after ear splitting nights of rampant sex, he saw them leave together and go to work.

Mike had often watched the two of them together when they came to the Star Club for a late night drink and a dance. They made a perfect couple but it was clear that they were gradually being dragged down and poisoned by the very atmosphere of St Pauli.

The short walk from the Star Club was particularly exhilarating and he really began to appreciate his good fortune. As he stepped out of the lift and staggered down the corridor towards his room, he saw a light under Brigitte's door and could hear people talking.

He let himself into his room and turned on his most treasured possession, after his drum kit and clothes… a Bush transistor radio that his father had given him on his fifteenth birthday. At boarding school it had been his first introduction to music and had sown the seed for him to want to play the drums, and shaped the dream of some day joining a group.

Still fully clothed he lay on his bed and tried to relax but the room continuously spun around and around. A blood-curdling scream from the room next door brought him back to earth, and although at first he tried to ignore it, when he heard it for the second and third time he jumped off his bed and ran out into the corridor.

He pushed open the door to Brigitte's room and stood with one hand on the door handle, the fingers of his other hand supporting him on the architrave. What he saw was, at first, hard to comprehend. Brigitte was lying on her bed; her legs wide apart and her knees slightly bent, the sheet and her clothes were covered in bright red blood. She continued to scream as the well built shabby woman with long, greasy, dyed blonde hair stood over her with a face empty of all emotion, holding a long, pointed object in her right hand, covered with blood.

Brigitte continued to scream and cry at the same time. 'Hilfe, hilfe bitte Gott hilfe.'

Mike froze on the spot, his fingers digging painfully into the architrave as the long haired woman began to panic. She picked up her black leather bag, gathered up the various objects lying on the bed and rammed them inside. She stopped and stood still for a second, looking Mike up and down. Realising he wasn't a threat, she calmly dragged the long pointed instrument across the only clean piece of sheet. Without a word she grabbed her coat and ran out of the room, still holding the clean, shiny object in her hand. As she ran down the corridor, she slid the grotesque instrument of torture inside her bag.

Mike followed her, screaming as he ran. 'Come back, you can't leave her like that, come on, come back, you fucking bitch!'

She was very strong, in a hurry, and determined to get away. Mike grabbed at her but she easily pushed him away. He continued to plead with her in a raised voice, fast reaching fever pitch, but she continued to rush down the stairs. 'Come on you fucking cow, you've gotta come back, she needs help,' he pleaded. It was futile she was gone, disappearing into the night.

Mike ran back up the stairs and into Brigitte's room.

She spoke very little English and all she could do was scream. 'Doctor, Doctor, Gott hilfe mir!'

As she repeated the same words over and over, Mike could see that she was losing a lot of blood. He knelt beside her and tried to reassure her. 'Come on Brigitte, don't worry, you'll be alright.'

He could see that his words were having no effect and that she couldn't understand him. He straightened up and, seeing the full extent of the horrific sight around him, was violently sick.

She screamed out again. 'Hilfe, Doctor, hilfe!'

He looked at her and, as the colour continued to ebb from her, he leaned over and stroked her face. He spoke softly as he held her hand. 'I'm sorry Brigitte, I'm going to get help, and I'll be back as quick as I can.'

As he stood up he wiped his face with his sleeve, ran out of the room and along the corridor, banging on every door as he passed, down two flights of stairs and out into the street. A taxi pulled up to the kerbside and, seeing the hotel cleaner get out, Mike ran across to her. At first she ignored him, having been the victim of never ending practical jokes from the musicians over the years. He struggled to explain what had happened and when she realised that Mike was genuinely upset, she motioned to him to lead her.

She did well, running behind him trying to keep up with the crazed young musician. Surprisingly, no one had opened their doors, but then they were all probably working, or stoned. It was the middle of the night, still early for the residents.

When they reached the room, Brigitte had fallen into a coma and lay motionless in a contorted position on the bed. Mike could only stare at her and pray. The cleaner rushed back down the stairs and within a few minutes an ambulance arrived, followed close behind by two police cars.

Mike, now having had time to think, realised that Brigitte had had an illegal abortion, and it had gone terribly wrong.

The two ambulance men seemed unphased by the situation, first taking her pulse and then listening to her heart. After struggling for several minutes, they looked at each other and then at the cleaner. As they became more agitated, they took it in turns to stare across at Mike. Their disappointment was soon apparent and quietly they spoke to the nearest policemen now standing guard inside the door. They both shook their heads as the nearest ambulance man covered Brigitte's face with a new clean white sheet, contrasting with the now dark red.

Mike stood silently in the corner, eyes at first fixed on Brigitte's covered body, and then around her small cramped room which was identical to his. She had three large posters on the walls; two of German groups, the Lords and the Rattles, which some of the musicians had signed, and a poster from the Kaiser Keller advertising Rory Storm and the Hurricanes, and at the bottom in small print, the Beatles. On the top of a dilapidated chest of drawers stood a small rectangular mirror; and pushed into the corner was a curling strip of four black and white photo booth pictures of Brigitte with her boyfriend, pulling silly faces at each other.

Mike looked back towards the bed, and her covered body, and started to shake violently as he began to accept that Brigitte was really dead. He now felt useless as the realisation began to sink in that she probably took her last breath while he stood watching over her, unable to help.

He broke down and started to cry. Through the tears, he spoke softly. 'What a waste, she was so beautiful… Why her?'

No one understood a word he said.

While the police asked the cleaner a number of questions, they took it in turns to glance across at him. With the help of the cleaner's broken English he told the police all he knew and thankfully they seemed to accept his story. The ambulance men took Brigitte's body away on a stretcher; the cleaner locked her room and passed the key to the most senior policeman.

Mike returned to his room in a daze, lay back on his bed, and emptied the bottle of korn that the cleaner kindly gave to him. As the horror of the night took hold of him, he suddenly burst into tears until he eventually fell asleep, only to wake an hour later. He tried hard to force himself back to sleep but gave in and went off to look for Reg. He ran blindly in the heavy rain, across the wide cobbled road, oblivious to the potentially lethal slippery tram lines as he headed down Paul Roosen Strasse and back to the Blockhütte.

Mike found Reg, stoned and propped against the door, his eyes staring around but seeing very little. But even in that condition he couldn't help but notice the pitiful look on Mike's face. 'Are you all right? You look bloody awful. What's happened to you? You look like you've seen a ghost,' said Reg.

Mike replied in a quiet subdued voice. 'I have.'

He turned and started to walk in the direction of the Reeperbahn before turning back towards Reg. 'I've just been to hell... and back,' he said.

'Really!' said Reg, not fully understanding what he'd been told.

'She's dead.'

'Who is?' snapped Reg.

'Brigitte died a couple of hours ago, she was butchered.' As Mike spoke, he could see Brigitte's pained face and the spectacle that had unfolded in front of him. He shook his head, soaking Reg, but after composing himself, he slowly began to tell Reg what had happened.

Reg stood in silence as he tried to imagine what Brigitte had been through before speaking softly. 'The poor bitch.'

They wandered aimlessly until they found a quiet bar, and after a few biers agreed to look for Brigitte's boyfriend. It was nearly an hour before they saw him through the large window, in the imbiss on the corner of Grosse Freiheit, sitting alone at a long table eating curry wurst and chips. They walked in, ordered a couple of biers, and sat at his table.

Although he acknowledged them with a half smile as they sat down, it was clear that he was upset. Mike knew that he wouldn't have heard the news already and ordered him a drink, but before the waiter came back Brigitte's boyfriend spoke to them. 'I feel very bad about some things,' he said.

Mike nodded, and accepted a cigarette from him. He lit it and sat staring as the smoke rose into the air, disappearing into the already thick smoky atmosphere. Her boyfriend continued. 'Do you know that Brigitte told me she was pregnant? We had an argument; we are too young for a baby. Then I shouted at her. But now, I didn't think that it will be a bad thing to have a baby, we will still have much time to enjoy things when the baby is grown up. Yes?' he said, forcing a smile.

Reg looked across at Mike and they both drank from their bottles at the same time. Mike then swallowed hard and took another swig from the bottle, while Reg nervously got up and walked unnecessarily to the toilet.

Mike looked around at the other customers; a group of drunks, two bedraggled prostitutes and a long haired musician holding a guitar, all perhaps too tired to sleep, and dreading the new day. His attention returned to Brigitte's boyfriend and he coughed nervously. 'I'm sorry, but I don't know your name,' asked Mike.

He smiled. 'I am sorry, my friend, my name is Herbert. I know it's a terrible name but I did not choose it,' he said.

Mike put his arm around him. 'Herbert, I am very sorry, but I have very bad news for you.'

Herbert looked at him confused. 'Bad news? For me...?'

Mike took a deep breath and sighed before speaking. 'Earlier tonight, I was tired and I went back....' he paused before continuing, 'to the Pacific Hotel. Brigitte was in her room with another woman... a very strange woman,' said Mike. He choked, but forced himself to continue. 'The baby is dead.' He paused, but before he could get a reaction he continued. 'And so is Brigitte. I'm so very sorry.'

Herbert looked at him. 'What do you mean? It is a joke? Yes?' asked Herbert. He nodded, and smiled. 'I know,' Herbert sipped at his bier and continued, 'Brigitte asked you to make a joke with me.'

Mike shook his head as he clearly remembered what he had seen only a few hours earlier. 'No Herbert. Please believe me, Brigitte is dead,' said Mike. He suddenly lost control and talking at speed. *'She was killed by the fucking butcher,'* he screamed. Tears filled his eyes and he could hardly see. 'It is true. I am so dreadfully sorry,' whispered Mike.

Herbert jumped up from the table at the same time as Reg came out of the toilet thinking it would be safe. He pushed past Reg and ran out into Grosse Freiheit towards the Pacific Hotel, shouting his lovers name as he pushed his way through the staggering groups of drunks and desperate prostitutes.

Mike and Reg ordered another two biers and sat looking out onto the almost deserted streets. One of the prostitutes who had overheard the conversation walked over and sat at their table. They both looked at her pathetic face, her thick make-up smudged, as she spoke. 'You must not worry so much; it is common in St Pauli. Musicians like you, and pimps, all have sex without a Johnny. What do you expect? Of course, a baby is coming. No one has the time for baby, so of course there is a big business for that service, the abortion,' she said.

In disgust, the musicians pushed the half-full bottles across the table, got up and left.

The bier was not wasted.

The prostitute picked up the bottles and carried them across to the hopeless drunks.

Brigitte's funeral was held in the Chronik Der St Josephkirche, a small but beautiful church in Grosse Freiheit, next to the Star Club. The pathetic congregation of less than a dozen people was made up of Herbert, the Cheaters, the manager of the Kaiser Keller, and a few of Brigitte's girl friends.

Although the English musicians didn't understand the short service, they were deeply affected by the realisation that Brigitte was virtually the same age as Reg, Jimmy and Mike. When Herbert broke down, Mike tried desperately to console him, but blaming himself for ending the life of his Brigitte and their child, Herbert had too much guilt to bear.

Chapter twenty

Just One Look

Reg, now considered to be an old hand on the scene, was more than a little enthusiastic to show Mike the sights. After leaving the stage they had a few biers in the bier shop and made the short walk across the Reeperbahn to Herbert Strasse, or Herbie as the local girls affectionately referred to it, after the Walt Disney film.

As they entered the pedestrianised street between the high, offset, solid metal screens, Mike couldn't believe his eyes. The contrasting sizes, the different nationalities and shapes of the ladies who sat proudly in the windows, on view to anyone who dared to venture through the partition, enthralled him. He was finally looking at something that he had secretly seen so many times in the magazines and books at school. He had often wondered what the female body looked like in real life and, still a virgin, he was at last able to see it for himself in the flesh, in its entirety.

He stood in the shadows watching as the men approached the windows, which were quickly flung open, understanding that each party needed each other, but closed just as quickly if the potential client became abusive or antagonised the girls. Mike felt special and privileged, imagining what Julian and his other school friends would think and how envious they would be if they knew what he was doing and seeing. Still feeling terribly shy, he didn't dare look too closely, but what he saw excited him.

Reg elbowed Mike in the side as he stood drooling. 'If you fancy it, they're the safe ones. Checked regularly and they've all got a certificate to prove it,' he said.

Mike looked at him in disbelief. 'You must be sodding well joking,' he said.

Reg replied instantly. 'No I'm not, that's why it's always so crowded in here. If you walked outside you never know what you might catch.'

They continued walking while Mike continued to be mesmerised by the sheer choice of colour, age and size of the girls for sale. The two of them had only walked part way down Herbert Strasse when Reg heard his name being called from the opposite side of the narrow street. Nervously he turned and looked in that direction until, through the open window, he saw Astrid.

Apprehensively, he crossed the crowded street towards her, all the time being pushed and jostled by the masses of drunken and sober men, as they tried to make up their minds where they would finally spend their hard earned Deutsche marks.

Reg approached the window and Astrid leaned forward, her face smiling, probably for the first time in many months, truly happy to see him. She looked different, no longer the shy woman that he had last seen several months earlier in the police cell in Coburg. Her hair was expensively styled; she wore make-up and looked incredibly sexy as she stood under the red light wearing only matching white suspenders, stockings, and a half-cup brassiere.

He was dumbstruck as she leaned through the window and kissed him. The men nearest to him shouted and whistled as she put her arms around his neck squeezing the breath out of him. Reg could feel he was still blushing as she left him and walked back into the shadows of her small room. She quickly returned with a cream cake which she proceeded to feed to him.

He could take no more and he pulled away from her, cream around his mouth, cheeks and chin. He tried desperately to rub it off his face with his shirt sleeve, smudging it over his ears and collar.

'I love you Reg,' shouted Astrid, as he turned to walk away.

He turned back, realising that she had spoken in English.

He felt his penis harden but when he remembered what she had done with her children he lost all feeling. Although he still felt aroused he realised it was impossible to even consider going with her again.

She continued to shout after him but her voice was drowned out by the rising abuse from the drunken crowd as they excitedly bargained for the best deal with the streets residents.

Reg kept his head down as he walked between the metal barriers, pushed his way past the mixed groups of drunken sailors, tourists, voyeurs and businessmen, and out into the quiet darkness.

Realising that Mike had disappeared, he stopped. He then started to run back but, not wishing to go through any more humiliation, he slowed down and, emotionally drained, walked back towards the Star Club.

Unable to come to terms with what he'd just seen, he stopped at a small uninviting bar in Kastanien Allee. He pushed past a scrawny prostitute who propositioned him at the entrance, bought himself a bier and a korn, and trying to find a quiet spot to think, moved through the bar and sat in the darkest corner.

Reg contemplated what he had just experienced and for the first time realised that he was the reason Astrid had dumped her children. He felt ashamed of himself and was riddled with guilt. Did she really do it for him?

He lost all track of time as he sat alone in the semi-darkness and drank far too much. After struggling to focus on his watch and finally realising the time, he staggered off in the direction of the Star Club, reaching the stage as the curtains opened.

He was totally incapable and unable to play as he swayed on his stool, out of time with the music. Dave was immediately aware of the problem and turned off the power to his amplifier and waited until they finished the set. As the curtains closed and they walked across the stage, Dave went crazy.

Reg was too drunk to take any notice and he was too drunk to apologise. He stumbled off and fell asleep on the dressing room floor.

When the club closed several hours later, Adrian and Hazelle manhandled him back to his room and at the end of the week, Dave deducted a night's pay from his wages.

It was not uncommon for admirers or anyone impressed with a particular song or group member to send one of the waiters on to the stage carrying a silver tray containing a round of drinks for the whole group, or occasionally a korn and bier for a particular musician. The prostitutes often did it to tease fellow prostitutes or to steal them away from their monthly escort.

Despite Mike's bad experience with Brigitte, the whole atmosphere of the Reeperbahn and the Hamburg music scene quickly overawed and affected him. Sucked in, he soon began to act like a child who had the key to a sweet shop; they weren't sweets, but drugs and sex.

Well into the early hours of the morning, the Cheaters were playing their last set to an almost empty Star Club. Heike, a tall, curvaceous blonde, walked into the club, sat at the bar and within minutes took a real interest in Mike. She sent a tray of drinks on to the stage and, when he joined her at the bar, told him that she worked as a waitress at the Safari Club, across from the Star Club.

Discovering he was still a virgin gave her a terrific buzz and, after teasing him and buying him one bier after another, she took him to her flat where he gratefully and noisily lost his virginity.

The following day it was as though Mike had been reborn. Although worse for wear, he was ready and waiting for his next encounter. Heike didn't disappoint him and she became his regular late night escort, buying him expensive new clothes, introducing him to the experience of hashish and assorted drugs with unpronounceable names, and taking him for expensive dinners. Much to Reg's delight, Mike's old clothes found their way to him, while some of the more generous cuts went to Jimmy who, for some reason best known to himself, Helga and the long gone Tony, was beginning to look downright shabby.

Later in the week, while walking back from the bier shop, Mike crossed Gros Freiheit and studied the various windows of the Safari Club. Much to his surprise, he discovered that Heike was not a waitress, but a stripper, dancer and contortionist. She had been photographed on stage having sex with a dog, a donkey and a group of other girls. Although intrigued, it disgusted him so much that he found it hard to spend any more time with her.

By now he had found Ulli who, on the nights that he was able to avoid Heike, he took back to the Pacific for a session between sets at the Star Club.

By the end of the second week they were beginning to slip into the unreal world of non-stop sex, drugs and heavy drinking, which rendered them totally senseless.

Adrian and Reg both visited the doctor for yet another session of penicillin. But this time, and especially for Reg, it was proving extremely difficult to shift, and the doctor injected him in the arm and left buttock for the latest dose of particularly virulent VD. With the pain of the injections still clearly in their minds, the two of them treated themselves to steak and chips and a pot of tea at the Seaman's mission, and a quick glance at the English newspapers while they waited.

Succumbing to the beautiful warm summer afternoon they chose to walk and, passing the huge statue of Bismarck towering high above them and on past the overgrown wasteland, they heard the down-and-outs, tramps and drug addicts coughing and moaning in their makeshift homes, hastily constructed from cardboard boxes, tree branches, and pieces of polythene. This was where they all waited impatiently for the darkness when they could once again prey almost unnoticed on unsuspecting tourists or the better off drunks.

Enjoying the moment Adrian and Reg passed under the bridge, guarded on each side by giant effigies of the city fathers, and down to the docks for rollmops washed down with a Sinalco, although they would have much preferred a bottle of bier.

Being in the same predicament and feeling that at last they were both equal, Reg turned to asked Adrian. 'Do you mind if I ask you a question?'

Adrian stopped in his tracks. 'Course you can, but I may not know the answer.'

'I think you will.' Reg paused. 'What are you really doing this for, to play music, or for the girls and sex?' he asked.

Adrian smiled and took out a cigarette. He offered one to Reg but, remembering that he didn't smoke them, pulled the packet back and put it in his pocket.

Taking his time, he lit his cigarette and took a massive drag. He slowly exhaled, looked at the cigarette, and thought carefully before he answered. 'I reckon it's got to be the girls,' he said.

Reg smiled, pleased that Adrian thought the same as he had been thinking for a while. Adrian continued. 'The music doesn't improve but my technique gets better every night.'

Reg now opened up. 'I can't get enough, I think I'm hooked on sex,' he said, concerned.

Adrian nodded and smiled. 'I know. But didn't you ever ask yourself why so many groups are desperate to come to Germany? It's never been the music, and it probably never will be. It's a ticket to ride, nothing more, the music is only incidental and don't let anybody tell you different,' he said. Reg blushed and laughed.

'That wasn't supposed to be a joke. In Germany it only takes a smile, in England it can take all night, and then by the time you've packed the gear away, she's gone. A bloody lot of effort for nothing. At least here we get a fair crack of the whip; you get a month, and if you haven't sorted it by then, you probably never will,' said Adrian.

For once Adrian seemed to be enjoying himself. He grabbed Reg and pulled him on to a ferry that took them on a round trip across the hafen to Finkenwerder and back to Landungsbrücken.

On the return journey, much to their surprise, Jimmy got on at Altona. He was equally surprised to see Adrian and Reg out of bed at that time of day and, with time to spare, they did the whole trip a second time.

Margot was like so many of her fellow rock chicks who were almost inseparable from their musician for the month, and allowed a special but false bond to grow between them during that period. Following his long and tearful goodbye, James, the drummer from the Rebels, disappeared up the Reeperbahn to begin the long, cold and sad journey back to England. As soon as the van was out of sight Margot started to get impatient, knowing she would have to wait until later that evening when the Star Club reopened to display the new batch of resident groups for the next four weeks.

That night she paid even less interest in her clients as she fantasised about her imminent visit to see what her companion for the next month would be like. She was not disappointed and, once inside the Star Club, before the last note had time to fade she staked her claim on Richard, the drummer with the Legion

The Legion, a five piece close harmony group from London, was fantastic and brought the house down whenever they played their version of Good Vibrations. Their live sound was as good as the record and much better than anything the Beach Boys could expect to achieve live, thus confining the American groups live performances to sound much like a poor support group.

The crowd loved it and their reputation soon spread across Hamburg; and to prove it, the club aisles were jammed to capacity whenever they took to the stage.

For once, Margot, unable to claim her own seat at the bar, was relegated to the aisle and stood half way back looking proudly and adoringly up at Richard, her drummer, on stage. She felt a hand on her left shoulder but ignored it. When it continued, her sixth sense seemed to take over and, irritated by the intrusion, she turned angrily and saw James standing behind her.

'*Mein Gott,*' she screamed.

She faced the intruder full on and, lacking all emotion, pointed proudly towards the stage at her new companion, Richard. She pushed her face as close to James as she could, looked him in the eye and screamed into his face at the top of her voice. '*Fuck off... go on... don't embarrass yourself. Go back to England... he's **my** man.*'

James, now rendered speechless, lowered his head, turned, and with great difficulty, forced his way through the capacity crowd just as the Legion finished their epic rendition of the song. The whole club erupted around him cheering and clapping their newfound idols, further compounding the agony.

Tears filled his eyes as he fell out of the club, unconsciously turning left, away from the noisy drunken crowds that filled Grosse Freiheit. In the shadows, a few yards from the Chronik Der St Josephkirche, he was propositioned by an overweight middle-aged prostitute, and his sadness suddenly gave way to anger. Fortunately, realising that he might kill her, he forcefully pushed her away in disgust.

James had made the fatal mistake of falling in love with a prostitute and groupie, believing that the month's liaison with Margot was for real. Naively he returned to Hamburg to rejoin his true love, only to find that the events of the last month were for the sole purpose of her pleasure and for him to be paraded as her personal living trophy.

The Hamburg girls really knew how to have a good time and now in the middle of summer, every Sunday, sunshine permitting, as soon as the last group finished their set at the Star Club, any musicians and girls still awake would pile into every available van and make the journey to the beach at Travemünde. Starved of sleep they all relied heavily on any of the pills available, washed down with the obligatory bier, weinbrand or korn.

Typically, most of the musicians couldn't or didn't swim, and lay on the beach often fully clothed. After one pill too many Dave fell asleep on the beach and was ignored until they wanted him to drive them back to Hamburg for the first set of the afternoon.

The weekend playing rota at the Star Club was always the same. The group that finished at six o'clock on the Sunday morning was expected to start the four o'clock afternoon matinee session and it was usual for that group to stay up all night.

While Dave drove back to Hamburg everyone continued their party in the van.

Arriving with only a few minutes to spare, he had no option but to park the van outside the club. They sprinted through the teenage audience and on to the stage amid cheers and whistles, leaving an hour later to tumultuous applause.

The last thirty-six hours without sleep and the day at the beach began to take its toll and, now feeling famished, they made their way to the nearest imbiss for something to eat and more bier.

During the first song of the next set, Dave, his face now a bright scarlet and suffering from severe sunstroke, began to sway from side to side. As he turned to speak to Jimmy, he collapsed centre stage.

The stage manager helped to carry him off while the rest of the group struggled on by playing a mix of instrumentals and, much to Jimmy's delight, old rock and roll classics.

For the first time the Cheaters, playing without a lead singer, realised what a great job Dave had been doing.

Dave remained in bed for three days but for the whole period Adrian continued to push for a deduction from the singer's share of the week's fee. No one dared to back him up and his ludicrous suggestion was soon forgotten.

Dave had taken more than a passing interest in two beautiful young Swedish girls who looked absolutely perfect, with their long blonde hair, knee length white boots, white leather mini skirts and tightly fitting jumpers. Determined to enjoy their two week holiday they were noticed by every full blooded male wherever they went.

Although at first glance they looked like twins, on close examination and after numerous seemingly innocent chats, it was clear to Dave that there was an age difference of several years between them; Anita was nineteen and Ulrika barely sixteen.

Despite spending time with different girls, Reg also showed a great interest in them and fortunately for him the Swedish beauties seemed to like the idea of mixing with him and the other English musicians. But somehow they always managed to steer clear of the ultimate experience that Dave had in mind for the three of them.

They would often drink with Dave and Reg, followed by a visit to another club or sometimes to the Blockhütte, but never staying as late as their escorts, returning alone to the luxury of their hotel.

It wasn't long before they attracted the attention of the numerous go getting pimps on the look-out for fresh new girls.

At the beginning of the second week the two girls disappeared and, despite a thorough and futile search by Dave and Reg, they could not be found. They visited their hotel and, after a heated argument with the desk clerk, he reluctantly told them that the two girls had checked out of the hotel unexpectedly the night before with two large men.

Initially their disappearance was the talking point with the musicians but after a few days they were forgotten.

Chapter twenty-one

Candy Man

Although some prostitutes worked for themselves, many of the Hamburg pimps were split into specific groups. The young men who came to Hamburg with their girlfriends to seek their fame and fortune, overawed by the atmosphere and drug scene, were finally dragged into the dark world of heavy drugs and addiction. This forced the now desperate young men to drive their girlfriends into prostitution and then gradually add other vulnerable young girls to their stable to pay for their expensive ever-growing drug habit. The middle aged gamblers and alcoholics would pick up the older teenagers or vulnerable girls in their early twenties, forcing them into prostitution to work to pay for their frenzied gambling and the heavy bouts of drinking with their exceptionally overweight counterparts. These were the most dangerous men, and the girls lived in permanent fear of them because of their sheer size, mood swings, and the extended periods of drunkenness.

The seasoned pimps spent most of their life in local bars and even gambled with their girls' lives whenever they became short of cash. Strangely, the visiting English musicians were not seen as a threat to their livelihood and they were happy for their girls to spend what little spare time they had with them. The overweight drunken peddlers in human flesh paled into insignificance when they were compared to the calculating men who seldom drank or gambled but were driven on by greed, the thirst for power, and the dream of building an empire of brothels in and around Hamburg.

Marcel was without any doubt the master in these stakes - the leader of the pack. He had arrived in Hamburg from München in the late fifties and, after working in numerous bars and graduating into the lucrative club world, he saw there was a fortune to be made. He saved every pfennig and when the opportunity came to take a lease on a run down property near Herbert Strasse, his rise to riches began.

Marcel, in his late thirties, was a short man with jet-black hair which he greased and combed tightly to his scalp and finished off with symmetrically sculpted sideburns. With a slight physique, he did not appear to be a threat to the already thriving business of prostitution, but to conceal his vulnerability and protect himself he carefully handpicked two bodyguards. Despite their size they soon began to rely on him for everything, hooked for as long as he needed them.

Marcel had also noticed Ulrika and Anita.

Having already ensnared a young man with expensive designer drugs, he now directed him to follow the girls every minute of the day and night. Choosing the most opportune moment, he arranged for his henchmen to visit their hotel and torture the receptionist into immediate submission. He willingly let them into the room with his pass key and Ulrika and Anita were grabbed while they were still asleep. The young girls didn't have a chance. With their heads covered, they were carried out of their hotel room and taken to an insignificant building farther up the Reeperbahn.

Marcel's henchmen dragged them up flight after flight of never-ending stairs and threw them into an attic room which contained two old metal beds, dirty soiled mattresses, torn duvet covers, a wash hand basin and a bucket. The cracked panes of the two small windows, set high up in the roof slopes, had been painted out with black paint and the only light came from the peeling patches. The lathe and plastered walls were cracked and covered with thick blackened cobwebs that hung from the old timber beams.

During the day the searing heat from the high summer sun overpowered them as it penetrated the slates, making conditions in the confined space almost unbearable.

Ulrika and Anita cried and hammered on the door until they realised that their attempts were futile and, now exhausted and sweating profusely, they sat on the same bed, hugged each other, and sobbed.

'What can we do?' said Ulrika.

'Who are they? What do they want with us?' asked Anita.

They both felt that they knew the answer but were too petrified to admit it. Instead they sat staring at the door, waiting for it to open and for their unimaginable punishment and torture to begin.

The shock had begun to wear off and they were now feeling extremely hungry but as the sun began to go down and the attic room started to cool the door was unlocked and unbolted, and in walked Marcel's henchmen. While one giant of a man stood guard at the door, the other carried in a small tray of bratwurst, bread rolls and Coca-Cola. He placed the tray on the floor and without saying a word they both left.

The girls sat looking at the tray but as hunger finally got the better of them they raced for the tray, devouring and drinking everything on it.

Ulrika, being the youngest, broke down and mumbled. 'We will never escape from here will we? They will keep us prisoners forever.'

'We don't know that for sure, perhaps there is a another reason,' said Anita, as she tried to console her young friend.

There was no visit for the next two days but on the third the men came again, brought a similar tray of food and drinks, and left.

The starving girls immediately raced across and tore at the inadequate food before falling exhausted on the bed.

The following day the men came again but this time they didn't have any food. They left a tray with two bottles of Coca-Cola and a dozen white tablets in a saucer. One of them spoke shyly in broken English. 'Today, no food but...' He pointed at the saucer and smiled. 'Dis are very very good, no more hungry.'

The girls refused to touch the tablets but by the following evening they were starving and Ulrika finally gave in and, despite the attempted intervention of Anita, swallowed two tablets.

Within minutes the hunger had gone and, for the first time in days, she smiled. Anita saw the change in her but refused to be drawn into making the same mistake.

Ulrika woke early the next morning, tiptoed over to the saucer, swallowed two more tablets and went back to her bed.

Although she was disgusted with herself, it was mid-morning before Anita, unable to suffer the hunger pains any longer, reluctantly grabbed two of the tablets from the saucer and swallowed them.

They both sat on the edge of their beds, more alert than ever before, listening for the slightest sound. When the key turned in the lock the feeling of anticipation grew. They were not to be disappointed and the two giants brought in another tray with drinks and an identical saucer of pills.

But this time they teased the girls until they begged for the tray, handed it over and left.

As soon as they were on their own they rushed over to the tray, each grabbing at the saucer, swallowing three tablets and mechanically walking back to their respective beds where they lay smiling and gazing up at the ceiling.

This continued for a week and, although they were occasionally brought food, they now preferred the tablets.

At the beginning of the second week the key turned in the lock but this time there was no tray and no pills. They sat on their beds and stared at their jailers for a few minutes but, getting no response, became agitated.

Marcel pushed his way gently between the mountains of muscle and in a soft voice he spoke. 'Are you comfortable young ladies?' he asked.

They didn't know how to react and together they started to complain.

He listened for a few moments as though he was genuinely interested. 'I'm sorry but it is difficult to hear each of you when you speak together.'

He pointed at Ulrika. 'Would you like to come with me and I will hear what you have to tell me? Oh...' He paused and smiled at her. 'And I have something for you.'

In the palm between his delicate and well-manicured fingers he revealed a cluster of small white pills. Ulrika was hooked, any reluctance vanished, and she joined him at the door. He looked across at Anita. 'Don't worry, my friends will look after you,' he said.

But now more concerned for her own existence, she stopped worrying about what might befall her young friend, stiffened and froze on the bed.

Marcel took the sixteen-year-old virgin down the stairs and into a room on the floor below. It was a startling contrast to the room only a few stairs above.

The room was beautiful, mood lighting, modern décor, thick velvet curtains, a fully laid up dining table, two matching chairs, a three-piece leather suite, and through a beautiful ornate plaster arch, a huge bed took pride of place. Marcel courteously poured a glass of korn, passed it to her, and encouraged her to swallow the handful of tablets that he still held in his hand.

After she swallowed them, a young woman dressed in a crisp white uniform appeared from the bathroom and stood waiting reverently at the door.

Marcel, the consummate professional, spoke softly to Ulrika. 'Take as long as you wish young...?'

She looked at him and spoke nervously for the first time. 'Ulrika,' she said.

He smiled, handed her a beautiful purple crocheted see-through dress, a set of matching satin underwear, and continued. 'When you are ready my dear,' he paused, 'Ulrika, we will have a small dinner.'

The woman helped Ulrika to undress, threw her torn and dirty clothes into a plastic bag and tied it up. She asked Ulrika to choose a perfume, which she then poured from end to end of the steaming bath. At first she hesitated but the gentle reassurance from the German woman helped her to relax.

Marcel was talking on the telephone when Ulrika walked out, transformed into a beautiful young woman. He replaced the receiver and stood to greet her. He took his time to look her up and down and then with a wide smile he silently complimented himself, knowing that he had made the right choice and the long wait had been worthwhile. Ulrika tore into the hot meal of schwein kotelet and brat kartoffeln served by the silent attendant on a wooden platter, washed down with a mixture of korn, bier and wine.

When she finished the meal, Marcel passed her a freshly rolled joint. She inhaled several times and started to cough.

'You will soon enjoy this very much,' he said.

'I don't smoke before this time,' she said nervously.

'Trust me, you will enjoy it like many other things.'

She thought about it, took another hard drag, and began to fly.

'Do you know why I choose for you to be here with me?' he asked.

She looked at him blankly, not understanding the question.

'I would like you to work with me, and you will earn much money for us both. You enjoy that?' Marcel paused, 'and I know that you like the candy.'

She frowned and looked at him confused.

Marcel coughed. 'I am sorry, I mean the small white tablets,' he said.

She smiled and knowing that she was now well and truly hooked, he continued. 'Ok. Then you work for me and you can have as much candy as you wish.'

'Maybe I don't wish to work for you,' replied Ulrika, with a smile.

His voice and manner changed and he brought both of his fists down onto the table rattling the glasses and cutlery. 'There is no choice, you can only work for me, and if you do not work,' he screamed.

He thought before continuing. '*You... vill... not... wish... to... be... alive.*' He finished softly. 'Understand?'

She pushed herself back into the chair and gave a nervous cough. 'How do I work for you? What do I do for you?' she asked.

He began to relax. 'I will show you,' said Marcel.

He smiled and poured her another large drink. While he rolled a fresh joint, he continued. 'I have a very good friend and I know that he will like very much a beautiful young woman such as you are.'

'How does he know of me?' asked Ulrika.

He slowly nodded his head and smiled. 'He knows.'

Marcel left his leather armchair, walked towards the door, and as he closed it behind him he spoke in a soft voice. 'He knows.'

She couldn't remember what happened to her but one consolation was that Anita followed and went through exactly the same indoctrination in an identical room.

The process was repeated every day and each time the girls were given stronger drugs until by the end of the week they were addicted to substances that only Marcel could supply to them.

When he felt confident that they would not dare to run away, he took them to live and work in his luxury brothel near Herbert

Strasse, along with a wardrobe of designer clothes and all the drugs they needed.

They were the lucky ones; the less fortunate girls would be beaten into submission to live in permanent fear of their lives.

Like so many of the girls living and working on the Reeperbahn, they were trapped until they were either murdered or, as they aged and lost their value, were abandoned. Only then might they escape the squalor, distaste, sickness, VD, and the whole senseless life threatening existence of being a Hamburg prostitute.

They could find relief and freedom of sorts by spending time with the musicians and this was how and why so many of them enjoyed their company. At least the musicians were genuine, some of the time, if not overawed by the sheer number and choice of willing females.

Margot, Hazelle and Anita, like so many of the more mature girls, had always worked for themselves and were much better off not having to pay a pimp, but the risks were much greater without their protection.

Chapter twenty-two

Somebody Help Me

The month at the Star Club came to an end and for once the Cheaters were able to sit back at Mambo's on the last night knowing they only had to travel a few hundred yards down Grosse Freiheit and another hundred yards up the Reeperbahn to the Top Ten. This time the goodbyes took place all around them while they drank one farewell glass of bier after the other with the departing groups of musicians.

Because the Cheaters had such a short journey from the Star Club, they arrived first at the Top Ten and were able to choose where they stayed. By lunchtime they had already selected their rooms at the small hotel next to the club, relegating the other group to the spartan accommodation above the club.

Why shouldn't they?

It was much different than the Star Club. Instead of several resident groups and the weekend visitors, the Top Ten club booked only two groups for the month, playing one hour on and one off from six o'clock in the evening until three or four the next morning.

It was a much smaller, cleaner, and all round a much more professional club. The bright lights reflected off the metallic stage, wall and bulkhead, while the walls of the low open sided stage made the groups more accessible and visible to the whole audience.

Mike and Reg played on a raised podium behind the guitarists and singer, having to step over a small partition at the right hand side of the stage. The house P.A. and amplification ensured all groups played at the same volume, reducing the risk of playing too loud and upsetting anyone in the audience.

The sound was excellent, it was tight, and both groups sounded as though they were playing in a recording studio but, unlike the Star Club, there was no room for mistakes and they were all expected to wear smart clothes.

Dave wore a suit and much to the annoyance of Reg, Adrian, Mike and Jimmy, brought in a new regime of smart stage clothes for all of the members. No longer having suits, they settled for shirts and waistcoats.

The girls from the Star Club refused to set foot in the Top Ten, preferring the gritty, workmanlike feel of those groups, thus opening a whole new treasure trove of girls for Dave and the rest of the Cheaters.

Whilst the Liverpool groups had a rougher feel about them, the London groups seemed to approach the music in a calculating and trendy way. They generally looked more professional, wearing clothes that were modern and stylish.

The group sharing the playing times with them at the Top Ten was a group of seasoned musicians direct from London, with a brass section. To save time they brought their own supply of drugs with them; bottles of them, enough to last a month with a few spare either to sell or give to any girls that they shacked up with. It was the easy way up without the rolling or injecting, both of which needed peace, quiet and a certain amount of privacy. Black bombers were the speciality of the day and, after taking a handful of those, they partied all night and often into the next day.

When the Cheaters performed a block of instrumental tunes, Dave would sit at the bar and reflect on the way things had progressed. He still had serious reservations about how they looked on stage and knew that unless they had some direction they would never move up a notch.

As well as all now sporting sideburns, Jimmy had greased his hair recreating the styling of his idol, Gene Vincent. Adrian had let his hair grow down to his shoulders to look once again like an R and B musician. Reg had now randomly chopped at his hair to resemble a shaggy dog, whereas Mike looked cool.

The whole group played more confidently than ever before and it felt that at last they belonged in Germany.

Although they continued to visit the bier shop, to save time they visited the Paprika, next to the Top Ten.

Dave scrabbled through the dirty clothes, picking up and smelling one shirt after the other from the pile of different coloured shirts until he found one that didn't smell quite as bad as the others. He did up the buttons of a creased Ben Sherman, painfully tucked it in, and brushed his greasy hair, before making the short walk to the club.

The never-ending string of girls had left his penis raw and bleeding and every step caused him pain, forcing him to walk bow legged. Knowing he wouldn't get through the evening, he stopped off at the apotheke, bought a packet of painkillers and swallowed the whole packet with a large glass of bier before getting on stage.

He knew he would soon feel better.

In one way, playing at the Star Club and spending most of the time in the bier shop protected the musicians from the seedier side of St Pauli, but the Top Ten, situated on the main thoroughfare of the Reeperbahn, was different; everybody walked past it.

This month they really saw why Hamburg had the reputation of being the most violent city in Europe and, although stabbings, shootings and rapes took place day and night, the police, even if stretched, were able to deal with every eventuality.

The musicians had to pass the Sahara discotheque, a few metres from the Top Ten, on their way to either the Star Club or bier shop. It was the haunt of the coloured seamen who were regularly attacked, ending up bleeding on the wide pavement outside until they were either kicked to death or rescued by an ambulance or the police.

Late at night the prostitutes would start to gather around the raised bar of the Top Ten, overlooking the stage and the rest of the club. It would sometimes be half an hour before a particular musician took their fancy, and then a waiter carrying a tray of drinks would walk on to the stage, offer them first to the chosen musician and then the remainder of the group. It was then customary to toast the girl, who in turn would unashamedly hold her drink high in the air until she was acknowledged.

The musician was expected to join her at the bar and at the end of the evening, when the club closed, spend the rest of the night with her. This was how Reg came to visit the intimidating Sahara club. He was chosen by a pretty dark haired prostitute who coerced him into joining her on the raised dance floor in the centre of the club.

They were the only white people in the place and it hadn't gone unnoticed. When they tried to leave the club, a large group of drunken black seamen surrounded them. Fortunately Reg, now a familiar face around St Pauli, was recognised by several of the waiters as being a musician from the Top Ten, and the two of them left without so much as a scratch.

Reg, Adrian and Jimmy were obsessed by the sort of men who would pay for sex so, when they were bored during the week, their idea of fun was to walk across to Herbert Strasse and bet on how long the customers would stay with the prostitutes.

They were always wrong because the girls had an uncanny way of disposing of their customers within minutes, leaving the inquisitive musicians confused as to how they were able to satisfy anyone's sexual needs so quickly.

Trouble didn't just happen in the Top Ten unless it was planned. Unless there was an available seat, no one was allowed into the club and everyone was expected to have a drink. Because the waiters were regularly bored, they compensated for the long nights by making a sport of the clientele.

The quickest and easiest way to cause trouble was for the waiter to knock the drinks off the table and then immediately challenge the customer to buy another drink. Their unsuspecting prey would invariably refuse and that triggered a fight that he could never win. Every waiter was ready to pounce and, as well as the customer, anyone else who interfered would be beaten unconscious on the dance floor and carried out of the club; a warning to any other potential troublemaker.

From the stage Reg couldn't help but notice a tall bearded ginger-haired man wearing a trilby hat and a dark green full-length leather overcoat which, even in the intense heat of the club, he never took off.

Each night he would stand for as long as he could until he was offered a table near to the stage and every time Reg left the stage, the stranger would acknowledge him by touching his hat. On the fifth night, the man sent the waiter on stage with a tray of drinks and once again Reg politely thanked him and smiled.

The man returned the following night with a midget who handed Reg a huge bouquet of flowers as he left the stage. Reg began to shake and nervously looked around until he noticed that Dave and Adrian were smirking at him. Suddenly he snapped, gathered his thoughts, pushed the midget and his partner aside and rushed out of the club into the Paprika, where he downed several glasses of weinbrand and bier chasers.

When the Cheaters returned to play the next set, Adrian and Dave couldn't resist teasing him but now, high on drugs and alcohol, Reg ignored them and stumbled on to the stage. The bearded man stood close to his side of the stage and, still holding the flowers, continued to smile every time Reg looked up from the keyboard.

Without warning the midget climbed on to the stage, picked up the sticks from the other drummer's kit and began banging the drums and cymbals, while the bearded man stood smirking.

Reg finally losing his temper grabbed the midget and pushed him across the stage. The midget fell on to the front apron of the stage, slid between Jimmy's legs and onto the dance floor where the waiters began kicking him. Without any warning Reg ran off the stage and attacked the bearded man. The waiters took it from there and, after giving him a severe beating, the midget and his master were carried out of the club.

In the next break one of the waiters nudged Reg and winked. 'Do you like man?' he asked.

'What do you mean?' asked Reg, taken aback.

The waiter winked and replied. 'If you like to go with a man I can arrange this for you.'

Reg suddenly realised what had happened to him. The bearded man was a homo and he had fancied him. It was his first encounter; the more he thought about it the more repulsed he felt and the angrier he became.

Sunday nights were often crazy. It was a rest night for many of the girls and, following a busy weekend, they liked to let their hair down. The musicians were their way out, tolerated by their respective pimps; the musicians were wined, dined, and fucked, in that order.

It was two in the morning when Mike left the stage after playing their last set of the night, and he couldn't get out of the club quick enough. He rushed up to his room, cleaned his teeth, and poured a sachet of dry shampoo over his greasy hair. After rubbing it in, he spent the next ten minutes in front of the mirror, backcombing it methodically until he was totally satisfied. He changed his jacket, took one last look in the mirror, shot down the stairs past several club regulars and ran up Grosse Freiheit to the small bar opposite the Star Club. Mike couldn't wait to see Erna, his latest conquest - or that was what he believed - but as always it was the prostitute who chose her musician and called the tune.

Mike had already spent the last three nights with her; he thought he loved her and believed that this was how being in love should feel. He walked through the door and saw her sitting at the far end of the bar wearing dark glasses, unusual for the time of night and even more unusual for her. The bar was extremely narrow with the main counter running the whole length of the place, accommodating eighteen stools along it and nine tables of four against the wall. He picked his way carefully past the few occupied tables and bar stools but as he got nearer to Erna, he noticed that her face was badly bruised and her nose and mouth were bleeding.

'What the fuck has happened to you?' he asked.

He sat down opposite her, ordered a drink and reached across the table to give her a kiss when his arm was forcefully pulled back over his shoulder. Agitated, he turned to see who was interfering with him but the sheer strength of the perpetrator prevented him from moving out of his chair.

Two huge men, each weighing at least eighteen stone, wearing skin-tight pullovers that accentuated their arm muscles, biceps and shoulders, grabbed him and dragged him towards the bar. They signalled to the barman who, having understood their gestures, turned up the jukebox and scuttled away towards the end of the bar running mistakenly into the ladies toilet. The heavies each took one of Mike's arms and as they laid him over the bar, his head was pushed accidentally but painfully between the bier pumps. Ensuring each of his arms were held beneath his back by the weight of his own body, they spread-eagled his legs, each putting their full weight on a leg, pinning him down on the bar.

Erna began to protest but the volume of the jukebox drowned out her pained screams.

A third, much smaller well-dressed man in a powder blue lightweight suit, walked into the bar and silently acknowledged the two heavyweights. Marcel had decided to deal with this problem himself. He pulled out a flick knife from his inside pocket, and beginning at the middle button of Mike's favourite dark green paisley shirt, skilfully and without damaging the material, began to cut off each button, working in the direction of his captor's throat. Mike, now absolutely terrified, could hardly breathe. The top button was already undone but the knife still continued to move upwards and Mike knew that it was only a matter of time before his throat would be cut. He was too terrified to attempt a move in case the weapon slipped, but as the knife flew towards his throat he held his breath and screamed out with pain as he was struck hard under the chin.

Seconds later and much to his amazement he was still alive; he couldn't feel anything except a dull throbbing sensation in his throat. When he finally realised that it was Marcel's forefinger that had stuck him in the throat he slowly began to relax. But before he had time to fully catch his breath, the knife started to move down from the centre of his shirt until it reached his trousers.

It didn't stop; instead, it sliced through his belt and the elasticated waist of his underpants, exposing his penis and testicles. Once again he froze, not daring to attempt to give even the slightest resistance. The larger of the two men pulled out a large shiny metal cosh, nearly a foot long and shaped like a penis, with an intricately carved rosewood handle depicting a group of females performing sexual acts with animals. He kissed the handle, smiled and passed the cosh to Marcel, who began to tap each alternate rib until he reached Mike's penis. He lifted it on to the cosh, balanced it skilfully and moved it from side to side.

Mike, absolutely terrified, with his body contorted and stiff, waited for the inevitable.

Suddenly Marcel raised the cosh high in the air and brought it down heavily onto the bar between Mike's thighs. While Mike screamed louder than ever before, the two heavyweights shook so loudly with laughter that for a second they drowned out the jukebox.

They suddenly stopped, waited, and left Mike to sweat. The few people still sitting near the entrance door took the opportunity and left. The jukebox fell silent until, following a series of loud clicks, Wild Thing by the Troggs blasted across the bar.

As though they had performed their ritual so many times before, the giants flipped Mike over, laying him face down across the bar.

Marcel then redrew his knife and, with one stroke, sliced through the back of Mike's trousers, belt and underpants. Miraculously each trouser leg still hung on his stiff pale legs. They stretched his legs wide apart, allowing his penis and testicles to hang over the side of the bar. Marcel gently moved the cosh from side to side alternately between Mike's penis and anus.

Mike stiffened but was so frightened he was unable to scream. Marcel slowly inserted the end of the metal cosh into Mike's anus and paused as he relished the moment.

Although Erna had continued to scream throughout the attack she may as well have been invisible but, as Marcel was about to push the shiny cosh as far into Mike as he could, she raced up to him and grabbed at his arm. She continued to scream at him until finally the three men took notice. While Marcel's henchmen continued to exert their power over their pathetic victim, Marcel questioned Erna until he was satisfied with her explanation.

With their faces showing little remorse, they released their iron grip on Mike and let him drop heavily to the floor. He looked a pathetic sight as he lay in a heap, shaking and crying, trying to seek refuge against the bar. Marcel looked towards the jukebox and the larger of the two men screamed above the music until the barman nervously reappeared at the entrance of the ladies toilets.

Marcel looked down at Mike, said a few words to Erna, smiled, kissed her on the forehead, ordered an Asbach and a bier for Mike and Erna, adjusted his tie and suit and walked out, followed closely by the heavies.

Erna placed her leather jacket around Mike and helped him back to the table. He sat hyperventilating and shaking as she tried desperately to console him.

Finding it hard to speak in a full voice, he whispered. 'What was that all about? Has it got anything to do with your face?'

Erna nodded. 'I am so sorry Mike,' she said softly. She desperately wanted to kiss him but it hurt her. 'Yes, it has, my last customer did this to me. My pimp, Marcel, he thought that it was you. I really am so very sorry,' she murmured.

Mike smiled nervously. 'I'm bloody glad it wasn't me. Thanks anyway. But why should a client do that to you? I don't understand,' he said. He drank the Asbach in one large gulp, followed immediately by half of the bier.

'When we ask customers to buy us a drink, it is not brandy or whiskey, it is only cold tea. My client tasted it and then went crazy to me,' she said.

'But why bother to do that?' Mike asked.

'We all do it. It is more money for Marcel and a little more for the girls also,' she said.

'That's all well and good but what would they have done to me if you hadn't been here?' he asked.

She thought for a moment. 'I think kill you, or maybe damage you so very, very bad,' she paused and grabbed her Asbach, 'and maybe....'

She looked directly at him and, still obviously in pain, smiled. 'It's bad. You will not be able to go with a girl again.' Reaching across the table, she gently stroked his hand.

'Can we go?' he asked.

She lowered her eyes. 'If you still want to come with me?' she said. They finished their drinks and got up from the table.

While Mike waited inside the bar, Erna stood on the pavement until a taxi pulled in and she beckoned to Mike to join her. Nervously he stood at the door and looked across the street before he pulled her leather overcoat around him, ventured outside and joined her in the relative safety of the taxi.

On their last night, with the Top Ten already closed, everyone made for the Star Club. It was one big party; they took it in turns to join the groups and played on stage until dawn.

Following a drinking session with the obligatory glass stiefel in the bier shop, Reg swallowed a handful of innocent looking pills given to him by the organist from the London group, and left.

Minutes later he sat huddled, shaking and terrified in a shop doorway. Through the bright colours and flashing lights it seemed as though he would be eaten, by either an enormous three-headed snake, or a very large rabbit, who both fought each other to get hold of him.

Hours later, still shaking and screaming, Reg unknowingly but thankfully found himself being manhandled by Dave and Jimmy and dragged to his room. They didn't dare to risk leaving his side so they took it in turns to sit with him until he began to sleep soundly without hallucinatory effects.

At lunchtime, finding it too late to sleep, Dave decided to walk up the Reeperbahn to Music City with Jimmy to buy some new strings. On the opposite side of the road, Dave noticed two girls that looked very familiar. Dodging the cars, trams and buses, Dave and Jimmy ran across to them, but when the girls recognised the musicians, they tried to rush away.

Ulrika and Anita, now dressed in expensive clothes, their once innocent and naturally pretty faces replaced with heavy make-up and brightly painted manicured nails. Lacking all feeling, their hollow and sad eyes looked straight through him and nervously flitted in every direction.

Unusually, even Jimmy noticed they had changed; they were absolutely terrified and, refusing to say a word to either of the musicians, turned and walked off.

He knew they had been got at, corrupted forever and dragged forcibly into the sordid world of St Pauli to feed the unquenchable sexual appetite of the visitors who frequented the Reeperbahn.

Dave reluctantly made the decision they needed to get away from Hamburg or he knew that the group would disintegrate before his eyes. Taking the route of approaching an entertainment agency rather than the run of the mill agents, he negotiated a month at two American bases.

Chapter twenty-three

Help Me Make it Through the Night

As a direct result of Dave's shrewd housekeeping and the last two months of steady work, the group were at last able to buy a replacement van. There was little or no choice because everyone agreed that a second hand Volkswagen with a side-loading door was the best buy. Adrian loved the idea and couldn't wait to be driven down the English High Street in the German vehicle with the Hamburg number plates. And this time no one would dare argue that they hadn't just returned from Germany.

As they drew up at the main gates of Miesau army base, it was quite obvious that the next month, playing at two American bases, would be much different than any time since arriving in Germany. In fact, as soon as they were within fifty yards of the main gates, Dave was commanded to stop and they were all asked to show their papers.

They didn't have any but Adrian realised that passports were what were really needed. He collected them together and pushed them through the open window in the direction of the nearest military policeman armed to the teeth with a machine gun, side gun and baton.

It was the first time that any of them had any direct dealings with an American in uniform, except during the dark nights in distant Coburg. But this time they seemed more threatening than poor old Wally had been with them so many months earlier.

Dave reached into his pocket and passed the contract to the GI, who glanced at it for a few seconds. He walked into the small hut and, after making a brief telephone call, came out smiling. He pushed his head towards the van, gave a friendly salute of acknowledgment, described the complicated directions and waved them on.

'Have a nice day and I hope to catch up with you guys one evening,' said the MP. He motioned to the MP nearest to the barrier to raise it and then waved them through, directing them towards the club that was to be their musical home for the next two weeks.

'Bloody hell, are we doing the right thing?' asked Mike.

'It's spooky,' gushed Reg.

The van drove between a row of shops, past the school and church, and along the straight tree-lined tarmac roads, passing large American Cadillacs, brightly coloured Ford mustangs, pick-up trucks and huge civilian vehicles.

'This could be America. Perhaps we have made it after all,' joked Adrian.

The van pulled up outside the NCO club and not knowing what lay in store for them, they climbed out of the van. They walked past the photographs and posters of many suspect cabaret acts that had played before them and Dave could sense that all was not as it seemed and it certainly wasn't anything like they were expecting. 'At least they speak English. We've got to make the most of it and we can at least have a decent conversation with them.'

His words fell on deaf ears as they trooped into the club. It was small with a tiny stage in one corner. They knew they would be cramped but they were being paid well for the inconvenience.

As they searched desperately amongst several layers of thick velvet curtains for the power sockets, the club manager, a well-built black uniformed sergeant approached them. He climbed on to the stage and greeted them, flashing his perfect white teeth.

'Welcome to a little piece of the United States of America, Sergeant Benjamin Watson... Manager, at your service,' said the American.

He showed them into the dressing room and ordered coffee and doughnuts.

While they waited, they read the graffiti scrawled all over the walls and tried to come to terms with what was expected of them.

Sergeant Watson asked each of them their names, repeating them as Dave introduced them one by one. He took time to explain that they would be required to back visiting cabaret acts several nights of the week and they would also be expected to follow the many stringent rules of the club, which he promised to explain to them that evening. He then handed Dave the address of the accommodation.

After they set up the equipment Adrian tried to pull the curtains across the stage but as he pulled at the cord he realised they were so old that the stitching had rotted, exposing gaping holes all over them and releasing clouds of dust and the smell of stale cigarette smoke. He was soon to regret his actions and, with great difficulty, pulled them back and left them to hang unevenly at each side of the stage.

Reg walked excitedly over to the upright piano and lifted the lid. He played half a dozen notes and the rest of the group screamed at him to stop. It was so out of tune that whatever he was playing was unrecognisable.

From the stage, they now had the opportunity to take a good look at the club. The bar ran the length of the room and it appeared to contain every type of spirit and row upon row of flashing neon signs above it advertised Budweiser and Schlitz, and other meaningless names that were totally alien to them. The wall on the other side was taken up with large posters advertising the various specials of the day, while in the centre was a hatch where orders were taken for food. The other wall was given over to a row of one-armed bandits and, in pride of place, stood the largest shiniest jukebox they'd ever seen.

The group set up their equipment on a plinth at the rear of the stage placing the microphones on the apron in front of the highly polished dance floor. Adrian and Jimmy tuned up and they played several of the soul songs that Mike had been so keen for them to learn. As they put the guitars away they received an unexpected round of applause from the barman as he readied himself for the evening, and the small groups of GI's at the tables.

It was standard policy not to live on the base so as soon as they were happy with the stage set-up, they drove out of the camp along a quiet country road to the village of Bruchmühlbach, three kilometres away.

The owner, an elderly grey haired man, saw the van drive into the yard and shuffled slowly down the steps on to the large gravel parking and turning area in front of the house. He looked them all up and down as he shook their hands and led them to a small bungalow about fifty yards away from the main building. He unlocked the front door, handed each of them a key, and left.

Adrian was in the door and began his ritual of looking for the best room; unfortunately this time he was confused. They were all nice rooms, each with a wash hand basin and a window overlooking the surrounding fields. He chose the end room, farthest away from the front door and nearest to the toilet and bathroom, while the remaining musicians unloaded their cases from the van and filed into any room.

'This is a perfect spot but I don't think that we'll be having much contact with any girls for a while,' said Dave philosophically.

He was right. The only time they saw a female was in the village shop, on the camp walking with their children, or on a Saturday night when a busload of German women were brought into the camp from Frankfurt to entertain, or more often tease the American forces.

Saturday was a crazy night. It was fun and the evening was over before they knew it, but for a change the group played for their own pleasure and they improved beyond recognition. They had nothing else to do.

Two nights a week the cabaret shows visited the club and the assorted singers, dancers and strippers would cavort in front of a less than discerning but ecstatic audience. It was easy, providing the strippers received a good response from the sex starved GI's, but if the cat calls reached an unacceptable level, then for some reason Reg, sitting behind the organ, would bear the brunt of their vile tongues every time they turned their backs on the audience.

They gradually began to return to normality, drugs were almost none existent except for the odd piece of Hashish obtained from the visiting cabaret acts. But alcohol was cheaper than ever with the subsidised prices and they were able to drink as much as they wished, providing they were not seen to be drunk on stage.

Every evening from five until six o'clock it was Happy Hour. Anyone could buy two drinks for the price of one and, for the first time, they had to use American Dollars. They loved it and after buying a tray of drinks each they sat down to enjoy their dinner.

The food was something else, a huge T-bone steak for a US dollar on Tuesday, and assorted specials other nights of the week. They had never had it so good.

The crowning glory of playing on the base was one day off each week. They couldn't believe it. They would drive to Frankfurt, Saarbrucken or Kaiserslautern - K Town, as the Americans called it - to go shopping or listen to other groups, and visit the world that they were already badly missing.

Frankfurt was about an hour's drive from Miesau, a large city where they would explore the various clubs, all the while comparing them with Hamburg. It was very different; bright new office buildings, an impressive shopping centre with large stores, and long new roads. Although in every way a very modern German city, it still had a street to rival Herbert Strasse.

The nightclubs were very similar and it wasn't long before the English musicians were surrounded by frauleins of all ages. They were reluctant to take girls back with them but encouraged them to visit them on a Sunday when they would spend most of the day in bed.

Returning from Saarbrucken at the beginning of their second week, Reg felt sick and had dreadful stomach pains. Throughout the night the agony continued and, unable to make it down the corridor to the toilet, he was violently sick in his room. Despite his cries, Dave, Jimmy, Adrian and Mike refused to help him.

Left with no alternative, he struggled to dress himself then left the bungalow and began to walk down the road towards the centre of the village in search of a doctor. Reg reached the edge of the village but tripped and fell heavily on the partially made-up pavements. He lay motionless for a few minutes until he regained enough strength to pull himself up onto one knee. Blinded by the rising sun he rubbed his face as he tried to focus his watery eyes until he thought he saw a large glowing statue of the Virgin Mary directly in front of him. He tried to straighten his body but, unable to do so, dragged himself through the partially open metal gates along the short gravel drive and up towards the intricately carved wooden front doors.

Reg reached up, pulled on the extended bell cord at the right hand side of the door and collapsed on the steps. He awoke to find himself in a white room lying on a soft table and being stared at by three smiling nuns.

Miraculously the pain had gone but he was unable to move. 'Was ist los mit dir mein Kleiner?' asked the eldest nun.

Reg blinked and looked blankly at her, unable to understand what was happening to him.

The nun spoke again in English. 'What is the matter my little one?' she asked in a soft voice.

He pointed in the direction of his stomach. The nun leaned forward, gently pushed a thermometer into his mouth and moved a stethoscope around his chest and heart, listening intently. She carefully pulled up his shirt and lightly pushed her fingers into different parts of his stomach until Reg screamed with pain. She immediately removed her hand and spoke softly to the sisters.

'Ich denke, er hatte eine blinddarmentzündung,' she said.

Reg looked at her until she spoke to him in English.

'Please don't worry, we will help you,' she said reassuringly.

She left the room while the remaining nuns gently massaged his head and shoulders, taking care not to pull his long hair.

A few minutes later she returned and looked directly at Reg and smiled gently. 'Do not be afraid, we will make a small operation and you will be well again very soon. And...' She stroked his hair and continued. 'Mein kleiner Beatle, we will cut your hair when you are sleeping.'

When Reg came round he lay looking up at the ceiling before he was able to take in his surroundings. Was it for real?

A nun walked over to his bed, propped his head, and gave him a sip of water. 'You were in a very serious condition, the appendix was broken, you did not have very long to live, but you will be fine now, you must sleep,' she said.

The nurse gave Reg a small bag of sand to place directly onto the incision and tucked the covers in tightly around him. She gently touched his arm from outside the covers then glided towards the door.

Reg suddenly realised that the rest of the group would not know where he was and he called out to her. She turned and gracefully walked back to his bed. 'Could you please telephone the NCO club at Miesau and tell the group what has happened?' he asked.

She smiled at him understandingly, straightened his sheets once more and left. Reg, relieved and thankful that he was still alive, slipped into a deep sleep.

The remainder of the group got up well into the afternoon and sat impatiently in the van for several minutes waiting for Reg. Jimmy gave in to his hunger and stomped back into the bungalow and knocked on his door. Getting no response, and in sheer desperation, he charged the unlocked door. As he fell in to the darkened room the stench hit him but when he realised that Reg was not in the room, he ran out to the van.

'He's gone. Reg has gone,' he shouted.

Dave turned off the engine and they all piled out of the van, rushed back into the bungalow and into the bedroom.

'Bloody hell it stinks in here, he must have died,' joked Adrian.

'Sod off you bastard, that was uncalled for,' snarled Jimmy.

'Where is he?' quizzed Mike. 'You could see that he wasn't well last night.'

Adrian stood and thought for a second. 'Well, it's no good standing around here, we'll all be sick if we stay in here any longer. I'm starving, come on let's get to the base, perhaps he's already gone over there.'

With no better ideas, they climbed into the van and Dave started to pull away. He suddenly braked hard, throwing his human cargo all over the floor of the empty van, jumped out and ran up to the landlord's house. Dave took great pains to explain to him in broken English that he was worried about Reg and gave him the telephone number of the club in case Reg should return. He climbed back into the van and, while they each came up with their own far-fetched ideas of what they thought had happened to Reg, continued to drive to the camp.

At the club Dave immediately went in to see Benny to tell him what had happened.

Benny suggested that they should check the hospitals in the area but Dave felt that they should wait for a few hours before doing anything drastic.

They all ordered the special from the blackboard and sat down.

Jimmy was the first to think about the impending problem. 'If Reg doesn't turn up we'll have to play without him,' he said.

'We can't possibly…' interrupted Mike.

Adrian didn't even give Mike time to finish his sentence. 'This is the first time that I've played with an organist and it's never been a problem before,' he said.

Jimmy sat thinking. 'Mike's right, this isn't England. We're playing six sets here, we ought to at least look through the set lists and pick out the obvious songs before we leave it much longer, and then run through them.'

They began to eat their T-bone steaks, the special of the day, all thinking of songs that they could reasonably play without Reg but soon realising that it would not be that easy without him.

The problem affected each of them differently; Adrian ate quickly, Jimmy hardly touched his food, and Mike poked the food around and moved it from side to side on the plate. Dave was affected the least, he had to sing and whatever was going on behind him didn't really matter as long as they played the correct chords in the right order.

They tuned the guitars and slowly worked their way through the priority list of songs. It wasn't as easy as they thought; the sound was empty and missing the extra dimension that the organ gave it. As they were beginning to build *Tell Me What I Say*, the Ray Charles rocker, Benny came out of his office and rushed towards them. He reached the stage and stood directly in front of them. They stopped playing, unsure of what he was going to tell them.

'Reg has had an operation, he's in the Catholic hospital,' he said.

The group stood motionless and shocked.

'Operation?' said Mike

'Hospital?' asked Dave.

'Come on, tell us you're joking?' smirked Adrian.

'I promise you all that I'm not... but I can tell you one thing for sure.' Benny paused and they all stood staring at him, expecting the worst. 'He's going to be all right.' he said with a smile.

Realising that Benny was genuinely pleased and relieved at receiving the call, they all shouted together. 'Yeaaaas.'

'Come on you guys, let me buy you all a drink,' invited Sergeant Benny.

They followed him to the bar as if he was the pied piper, all the time bombarding him with one question after the other trying desperately to get more information that he didn't have.

'All I can tell you is that it was appendicitis, and it was serious, he's one hell of a lucky son of a bitch that one,' he said. Benny lifted his glass and gave a toast. 'Here's to yer, I really don't know any more, but you will be able to visit him in the morning.'

As he walked away, they talked excitedly over each other and drank, taking it in turns to buy a round, until they were summoned by Benny to start their evening's work. Fortunately for them it wasn't busy, the majority of the G.I.'s were out on exercise and they used the evening to continue to work through their much-depleted repertoire.

The next day they were up at lunch time as usual and made the short drive to the hospital. Dave drove the van through the gates and pulled the bell cord. As they stood on the steps of the large intimidating stone building, they suddenly felt nervous. The large heavy wooden doors were opened by a nun who smiled and led them down one long corridor after another until they reached the four-bedded ward where Reg lay looking aimlessly at the ceiling.

The musicians couldn't resist cracking jokes amongst themselves when they reached his ward.

'Are you ready for tonight then?' joked Jimmy.

'How did it go last night?' asked Reg, still finding it hard to speak in anything more than a whisper.

'Fine, I don't think we need an organist any more, it's a doddle with four of us and we've agreed to split your share of the money between us,' said Adrian defiantly.

'Don't listen to that silly sod, we'll be able to manage until you get out, just take it easy and don't worry,' Dave reassured him.

'I don't know how you keep your hands off the nurses,' teased Adrian.

'That was a bit below the belt that was, it was totally unnecessary' fumed Jimmy between his clenched teeth.

Dave handed Reg a pile of American magazines before they left for the base.

Although Reg found it impossible to converse with his elderly room mates, they made it abundantly clear that they disliked him because he was an Englander, and whenever they felt the urge they taunted him in broken English.

In an attempt to lift the intense depression, raise his spirits and relieve the boredom, he spent much of his time writing poetry drawing cartoons and writing letters to everyone that he could think of in England and Germany.

After finishing at the club and with nothing else to occupy them, the remaining group members would all visit the rastatte opposite the main gates where they would each buy a wafer thin pizza, the size of a dinner plate, at a cost of one US dollar a time. The pizza was then washed down with litre after litre of German bier to rekindle their taste buds. If they didn't finish the pizza, they would take any remaining pieces back to their room to finish off with a few more biers.

Each afternoon they reluctantly took it in turns to visit Reg although he never saw Adrian after his first visit. Dave took away the well-read magazines but to Reg's amazement, Jimmy brought them back again the next day.

He began to realise that they never really cared about him and he knew that he had no alternative but to accept things as they were. He was cheered up a little when Mike brought him in a Get Well card signed by many of the club regulars and Sergeant Benny, and while Reg painstakingly read every written word, Mike made no effort to cover his impatience of wanting to get back to the club.

Now suffering from acute boredom, he picked up the notebook that Reg had used to write some of his poems; he flicked through the pages until he stopped at the last page and slowly read it.

Alone on an island
That's me now
Perhaps that's hard to believe
With people all around me
I can hear them, see them, touch them
But little can I say
I lie here through the day
Waiting for the night
For when I sleep, I dream
Anything I wish
I can talk to who I want
Dream of what I want
There is no language barrier in a dream

He closed the book and handed it back to Reg.
'That's not bad. Have you ever tried to write a song?' he asked.
Reg shook his head, closed his eyes and went back to sleep.

He made a remarkable recovery and his scar healed without him suffering any ill effects. The nuns were genuinely sad to see him leave and he was extremely indebted to them for the way in which they had saved his life.

Much to his surprise, his clothes had been washed and ironed, and more importantly his Cuban heeled boots were polished to perfection, as well as being soled and heeled.

Dave came to fetch him and, as he cautiously climbed into the front seat of the van, they all stood on the steps waving, and gently raised their voices in unison.

'Auf weidersehen, kleiner Beatle, viel glück,' they said.

'Auf weidersehen,' stuttered Reg nervously in response.

As the van pulled away he felt a lump in his throat and for the first time realised how lucky he had been. He continued to wave until they were out of sight.

Only six days after the operation he was back on stage and very proud of the tiny scar and the fact that he had only three stitches, a third less than Dave and Adrian.

Because it was difficult and painful to sit up straight on his own drum stool, he decided to use a chair and a pile of blankets to raise him to the required height. He still had to take great care and was under strict instructions not to lift anything heavier than a glass of bier. As the two week stint came to an end, for the first and only time he escaped the stripping down and loading of the equipment.

They had a final drink with Sergeant Benny and in turn thanked him for the two weeks and his understanding. As they left he wished them luck and gave them a few parting words. 'If you think this was good, wait until you get to Ramstein,' he said.

Ramstein was huge; an American city in the centre of mainland Europe, the largest air base outside of America, and it had everything. Row after row of houses laid out in strangely named districts, a hospital, dentists and doctor's surgeries, several churches, shopping arcades, pizza and ice cream parlours, schools, car dealers, filling stations, garages, three cinemas, and several large clubs.

It was totally different to anything any of them had seen before and Jimmy seemed to enjoy the atmosphere more than anyone, feeling close to the roots of his American Rock and Roll idols. Their club for the remainder of the month was more like a theatre, with a large, wide stage, thick velvet curtains and several banks of coloured lights. The same posters they had seen at Miesau were displayed along the walls and several large notice boards advertised the same forthcoming attractions.

Once again they were accommodated off base but this time they wished that they weren't because the airmen had families, and in those families were young American girls.

The race was on.

This was an upmarket location, nothing was spared, the residents were the elite of the American forces and the sheer affluence left them in awe.

The first night was also cabaret night and they were required to play background music for a magician and a stripper. The magician came and went but the stripper was a different matter. Dave and Adrian caught her before she took to the stage. They discussed her requirements at great length, trying to impress her in the hope of spending time in the van with her. Throughout her act she smiled at the musicians, alternating between Adrian and Dave, who had taken it upon himself to play the tambourine on stage instead of drinking at the bar.

Once again, Reg unfortunately bore the brunt of her anger as she continually complained directly to him in the foulest language every time that she turned her back to the audience as she teased them. 'Come on you bastard it's too fast,' she seethed. The next time she turned. 'Sodding hell it's too slow,' she fumed.

Reg became more and more annoyed as he watched Dave and Adrian pandering to her every need. But hours later she had the last laugh, leaving the two of them to fight amongst themselves, when she left with the magician and the other acts in the tour bus.

During the day the group spent their spare time roaming round the base spending only American money, shopping at the huge PX store buying American goods that they had only previously seen on television or at the cinema back in England. Everything was subsidised and so cheap that they had their first taste of American cigarettes, cookies, sarsaparilla, more pizza, exotically flavoured ice cream and real Coca-Cola.

They made friends with many of the American airmen who were all keen to show them photographs of their girls back home and to swear to the musicians that their hair had been as long as theirs when they were back in America before joining the air force.

The photographs were nearly always cut from magazines and they never removed them from their wallet.

None of the musicians wasted an opportunity to sponge free drinks or cigarettes from their naïve prey and when they found a particularly vulnerable serviceman, they would go in for the kill, finding themselves proud owners of genuine American bomber jackets before the end of the first week.

Although they didn't leave until mid afternoon, Monday became Frankfurt day. A visit to some of the large stores was followed by a visit to as many clubs as they could before they were too drunk to care. It gave them the chance to find new girls for the weekend and it was easy, sometimes too easy. As a result, Mike soon found that the first visitors had invaded his pubic hair. Reg, now experienced at removing them, gave Mike instructions on how to evict them and burn them using an American Zippo lighter – much stronger and hotter than Dave's pathetic Ronson, and giving them a noisier death. By the time they were ready to leave the camp, his pubic hair had begun to grow again.

Jimmy had had a permanent toothache since arriving in Ramstein; despite constant nagging from Helga, he seldom cleaned his teeth. He loved peppermints, often sitting up in bed with the contents of several packets resting on the duvet between his legs. And then, in a fit of madness, he would fill the palms of his hands with the peppermints, lift them into the air and let them slip ecstatically through his fingers.

The young musicians found it hard to understand and come to terms with the American culture and the conflict between the black and white forces. When a black officer requested the Cheaters to play a country and western song, a fight broke out between the black and white crewmen leading to the man who had made the innocent request being ignored and cut off from the rest of his black friends for days.

The servicemen had their own team of dentists and medics and they would often visit the club after their shifts. Jimmy soon made friends with Roddy, a guitar playing dentist, who offered to give him free treatment in return for lessons. The group had finished rehearsing two new songs when Roddy arrived at the club to take

Jimmy to the surgery. The two of them left the club while Dave and Adrian stayed for another round of drinks.

Shortly after, another group of dentists and medics arrived and sat at the bar talking to Dave and Adrian. Dave told them that Jimmy was having treatment at the surgery. The dentists looked at each other and laughed. Adrian, not seeing the funny side, became agitated. 'What's so funny?' he asked.

The taller of the two dentists frowned. 'You say Jimmy's gone with Roddy?' he said.

'Yeah… for treatment?' replied Adrian.

'You must be kidding, he's not a dentist,' said the dentist.

Dave became agitated and shook his head wildly. 'The silly bastard. If he's not a dentist what the bloody hell is he?' screamed Dave.

'A surgery nurse,' replied the dentists.

'Surgery nurse? And he's been drinking,' screamed Dave.

They rushed out of the bar, into a Red Cross jeep, and drove in the direction of the military hospital. 'I hope that we're not too late, he could kill him.'

'He's a whacko, that one.'

They rushed through the entrance up two flights of stairs and into the dental unit to find Jimmy sitting in the dental chair. Roddy stood behind him holding a whirring drill and drunkenly swaying from side to side. When he saw them he dropped the drill, knocking the delicate instruments all over the floor. Dave grabbed him and threw a punch that landed on his jaw; he fell to the floor whimpering until he was dragged away by the camp's military police.

'What the hell do you think you're playing at?' shouted Jimmy. 'It was free.'

The dentists explained what had happened and Jimmy stood shaking his head as he imagined what might have been.

'Now you know why I don't trust dentists. Come on I need a drink,' said Jimmy.

A month inside America was long enough, finally realising that they preferred the mystery and excitement of Germany and the inability to understand everything said to them.

Now, proudly wearing matching dark green satin bomber jackets, they were pleased to be driving out of the Ramstein camp gates for the last time, bound for Berlin.

Chapter twenty-four

Strangers in the Night

They were extremely lucky having a free day at the end of the month and, after finishing on the thirtieth of August, they had almost two days to make the long journey to Berlin.

The drive through Hanover and along the RE30 autobahn proved boring and uneventful until they drove into East Germany. The change was startling and when they saw the East German farmers using horses to pull the archaic farm machinery working across the fields, the thought of arriving in West Berlin, an island in the sea of communist East Germany, sent a shiver up their spines. Getting through the various checkpoints was lengthy and intimidating but as Dave drove through an area of devastation, partially demolished buildings and ruins, it was mind blowing. This suddenly and dramatically gave way to newly made-up roads, modern buildings, flashing neon signs and high-class department stores in brightly lit streets. They easily found the Liverpool Hoop, their new home for the month. Dave parked the van as near to the entrance as he could and they all followed him inside.

The club, although very basic, was decorated in bright colours; a tastefully lit stage at one end, and a dance floor which was surrounded with brightly painted early post war tables and chairs spread throughout the club. An imaginatively lit bar, using strangely shaped flashing neon shapes, had pride of place in one corner.

After playing at so many clubs, they felt they were ready for anything. Herr Baumgart, the club manager in his mid-twenties, shook their hands, ordered them a drink, and asked his head waiter to take them to the accommodation, a few minutes drive from the club. Surprisingly, they had three rooms on the ground floor and as always the battle was on to find the best room. As though he could smell it, Adrian once again bagged the prime room with a large timber four-poster double bed.

Dave shared with Jimmy while Reg and Mike were relegated to the room with creaky bunk beds. On the first night, they made the short walk from the club to the flat, past the empty derelict bombed and shell-ridden buildings beneath the overhead S bahn that also passed through the veiled Eastern part of the city.

The S bahn, much of it supported on steel legs, cast long mysterious shadows across the road and pavement, giving them more than one reason to feel nervous. Their imagination ran riot with every step, fully expecting a spy or undercover agent to drag them into the dark underground world of the cold War.

On the second night, Dave and Reg noticed two pretty long haired girls sitting at the rear of the club. In the interval the musicians went in for the kill, turned off their respective amplifiers, dived towards the two girls and for once ordered and paid for drinks for their potential conquests. Dave asked the girls their names. The prettiest spoke first, introducing herself. 'My name is Tonia, and my friend is called Erina. What are your names?' she said.

Dave wasted no time and introduced himself first and then Reg.

The two girls laughed innocently and Erina spoke. 'They are nice names, and very English,' she said.

The two musicians felt relieved and very pleased the girls could at least speak English. They were getting carried away and didn't notice that Adrian, Mike and Jimmy were back on the stage until Jimmy started to play a slow blues riff.

Dave and Reg couldn't wait for the last set to finish and within twenty minutes they were back with the girls. Tonia towered above all of them and although Erina was shorter, she was still an inch taller than Reg. Undeterred, Dave asked the girls if they could all go to a bar for a few drinks to unwind.

Once inside the bar, Erina homed in on Reg and the matter was decided. Several drinks later the foursome found themselves standing outside a six-storey tenement block similar to the group accommodation.

Dave, never missing an opportunity, talked themselves inside, finding a small poorly furnished bedroom with one large double bed. Tonia and Erina told the musicians they were both seamstresses and worked in a factory on the outskirts of the city.

Somehow they all ended up drunk and naked in the same bed. Dave, oblivious to his bed mates, started to warm up Tonia. Reg, although keen to vent his frustration, stopped abruptly and crawled across the bed, felt around in his shoulder bag and removed a Durex. He opened the packet and she helped him to pull it over his penis. It ripped, springing with a crack, back across their hands. 'Bloody hell, that hurt,' he screamed.

'Be quiet Reg,' moaned Dave.

'How long have I been carrying that thing around?' asked Reg.

'Who cares?' replied the breathless singer.

Erina, finding it hard not to laugh out loud, pulled open the bedside drawer to reveal row upon row of different types and assorted coloured Durex. Reg ripped what was left of the shredded rubber from his penis. 'Sod it, what's the point?' he said.

To further embarrass him, Tonia pulled open the drawer on her side of the bed to reveal an equally diverse collection of contraceptives.

It was lunchtime before they left the apartment and they all agreed to meet later that night at the club.

The evening passed uneventfully but at two o'clock Tonia and Erina walked into the club wearing expensive clothes; the transformation was unbelievable.

As soon as they finished, Dave and Reg left the stage, and proudly walked up to the girls and kissed them. Adrian, Mike and Jimmy stood on the stage, looking on enviously, as the girls whisked them out the door. Tonia hailed a taxi and the four of them drove to a restaurant. The musicians were too embarrassed to order anything from the menu until Tonia reassured them that it was their treat.

As the night wore on, Dave and Reg seemed to grow in confidence, perhaps fulfilling their true expectations and savouring what success was really like.

The five-course dinner took nearly three hours, and throughout, Erina continued to send money, via the head waiter, to the trio ensuring they continued to play long enough for the two couples to dance between courses and again after the meal. At first Reg felt extremely awkward standing with his face nuzzling into Erina's breasts, but who cared?

Close to dawn, Erina paid the extortionate bill and they left.

Outside, on the pavement and much to their surprise, the girls each hailed a taxi.

Dave and Tonia took the first Mercedes, Erina and Reg took the second, driving away in opposite directions.

Reg felt extremely happy but wondered where they were going. Had he been set up or was he about to be kidnapped?

The taxi drove across Berlin in the early morning traffic and Erina held his hand as tight as she could, so tight in fact that Reg was worried that she might bruise his fingers, but she somehow she knew how hard she could squeeze without doing any damage.

They drove into the Tiergarten, pulled up to the gatehouse and stopped. Erina told him to get out; she paid the driver, reached out for Reg's hand and gently guided him towards the small but beautiful cottage at the entrance of the park.

She took his coat and then led him up the wooden spiral staircase to the bedroom where a huge bed covered in furs of various sizes and colours took pride of place in the centre of the room. Erina led him to the bed, undressed him and pulled him gently under the warm furs.

It was four o'clock in the afternoon before she brought Reg his breakfast of schwartz brot, ham and cheese, artistically arranged around a caffetiere. The naked Erina climbed back into bed and fed him. An hour later she led him to the bathroom where a steaming foam bath awaited him. He soaked for a long time in the deep water enjoying the luxury and taking the opportunity to use the talcum powder and deodorants.

She sat on the edge of the bed and watched him slowly dress. 'Reg, the taxi is coming in five minutes,' she said, smiling.

'Taxi? What? Now?' he said.

'Yes Reg, be quickly.'

She handed him a twenty Deutsche mark note. Reg looked back at her, finding it hard to believe that this was really happening to him. As the beam from the taxi's lights illuminated the room in the late grey autumn afternoon, he smiled back contentedly.

He spoke to her nervously, 'Danke schön.'

She kissed him several times, following him down the stairs kissing him again and again. For the first time, Reg felt his latest encounter was how sex should really be.

He arrived at the club the same time as Dave.

'Well, what did you think?' asked Reg.

'Don't ask. But I'll tell you this, if they're seamstresses, I'm Adolf bloody Hitler,' said Dave smiling.

The next day Erina took Reg shopping for the first of many trips to the numerous department stores and smaller fashionable boutiques. She chose him new trousers, an armful of shirts, the most expensive suede jacket in the shop, and she willingly paid for everything.

Reg had seen the more successful prostitutes buy clothes, and sometimes a new guitar, for their month-long sex machine in Hamburg; this was first time it had happened to him.

The couple met up with Tonia and Dave, who was overloaded with almost as many bags as Reg, in an exclusive restaurant in the Kaufhaus Des Westons - Ka De We - the Harrods of Berlin, overlooking the Kurfurstendam. While the two girls talked excitedly to each other, Reg and Dave sat almost shell shocked looking out over the city, finding it difficult to understand what had happened to them and how their fortunes had changed in just a few short days.

The new wardrobe of clothes felt great; at last Dave had clothes that he was once more proud to be seen in. Reg gave his old jacket to Jimmy, who loved and cherished it. But before either Dave or Reg could offer any of their clothes to Adrian, he laid into both of them. 'Don't you dare offer me any of your cast offs,' he said. He looked at Jimmy spitefully. 'I'm not a charity case yet.'

The late night dinners and extended sex sessions continued day after day and soon began to take its toll. Reg was finding it more and more difficult to keep awake and fell asleep, with his head resting on the lower keyboard, throughout the first verse of *Save the Last Dance For Me*. Adrian was livid and for once Jimmy and Mike took his side.

Reg told Erina what had happened to him and the following afternoon, as well as giving him a fifty Deutsche mark note, she handed him a small packet of blue tablets. At first one tablet kept him awake but gradually he needed a second to enable him to perform with Erina throughout the night. By the end of the first week he was taking two tablets twice a day and he was sometimes flying, not knowing who or where he was.

On Sunday evening the club and the streets of Berlin were unusually quiet and, at eleven o'clock, Erina and Tonia walked into the club. They smiled at Reg then Dave, sat down and ordered drinks. A few minutes later a drunk appeared through the door and, despite requests by the waiter to sit down at an empty table, he made a beeline for Erina. He hovered at the table, shouting and swearing at her. Reg guessed the drunk was probably her last customer, who after leaving her, had waited for her to change, then followed her to the club. He felt sick and strangely jealous; he jumped from the stage, ran at the drunk and punched him, knocking him to the floor. Reg followed that up by kicking out at the mumbling, pathetic heap until the drunk was almost unconscious.

The waiters pulled Reg away and immediately dragged the drunk out of the club, dumping him on the pavement outside.

Reg returned to the stage and continued to play as though nothing had happened but before they finished the next song the head waiter walked on to the stage carrying a tray of five schnapps and reverently passed them amongst the group. As Reg left the stage Adrian grabbed his arm and took him to one side. 'I know you don't need to worry about money but at least have a thought for the rest of us,' he said.

It was the first time that Reg had deliberately done anything to jeopardise the Cheaters, he felt ashamed and he didn't like it.

Although Dave said nothing, he knew that Reg was slowly getting out of control and it was the drugs that were changing him. That night, as Reg lay with Erina, he tried to come to terms with what had happened. He had already begun to lose interest in the never ending all night sessions and his whole body was beginning to suffer.

How Erina and Tonia could work night after night and then continue with him and Dave left him to wonder? Reg realised what he had thought for a long time, that sex was a drug to many of the prostitutes.

Having to spend so much time with a continuous stream of paying customers, they needed to have someone to love even if they had to pay for that love themselves. He accepted that he was no better than the prostitutes because night after night he was prostituting himself for the gifts, no longer the pleasure.

An hour later, spaced out by the effect of another three tablets, he walked through the mist in the Tiergarten. He felt as though he might have been on the set of Dr Zhivago, a film he had seen several times in Ramstein when he came out of hospital.

Surprisingly Erina woke Reg earlier the next afternoon and, following a short walk on the deserted sands at Zwansee, they sat in the autumn sun. Erina rested her head against Reg. 'Today it is so beautiful,' she sighed. Reg nodded in agreement and sat back. 'My father told me that the war came late to Berlin. Do you know that we did not have bombing in Berlin until 1942?' She pointed. 'Over the wall is where I was born with Tonia.'

Reg looked surprised. 'Yes, I come from Bernauer Strasse in East Berlin and I lived some houses from Tonia. She has been my friend since school; her father was always drinking with my father, we were like sisters, but then...' She paused and looked out across the lake and started to cry.

Reg pulled her towards him and tried to comfort her. She acknowledged him by touching his hand and then squeezing it gently. 'It was terrible, I will never forget it, in 1953 on the seventeenth of June, my birthday, the Russian tanks came to Potsdamer Platz. They killed many people. They killed Tonia's father and then the Russian soldiers made us prisoners in our part of the city. Reg we were so *very* hungry and when the horses died in the strasse, everyone is waiting in the line for the meat. It was very terrible my mother and father died. I found them in the bedroom; they were green because they eat the poison that we use to kill the rats.'

Reg could feel her whole body begin to shake. He pulled her even closer to him, kissed her on the forehead and ran his fingers down the full length of her long hair.

She gazed up at him. 'Tonia worked together with me and we managed to make clothes to earn enough money to live. The Government tried to break us and keep everything a secret, but it was impossible.' She smiled. 'They had no chance; we could hear the West German stations on the radio and we knew what was happening in the World.' She wiped her eyes. 'But in August 1961, everything changed, they came to all the blocks in our strasse and on the ground floor, they placed bricks into the doors and windows. We did not know what we should do.'

Reg stiffened, not knowing what to expect, but now it was Erina's turn to reassure him. 'Chatze, it is alright,' she said. She paused and gave a defiant smile in a way that he had not seen before. 'But then we jumped through the window in the flat above us and we were free at last, in West Berlin. Others were not lucky, they ran into the dangerous wire, screaming as they were trapped and bleeding, until they were shot and left to rot as a warning to others.'

'Is that the reason you told us you were seamstresses?' asked Reg.

She didn't answer him; instead she stood up and pulled Reg along with her. 'Come, I will show you how it was,' she said. Reg hesitated. 'Don't worry we will not go to there, it is safe now,' she said.

They took a taxi as far as the junction of Friedrichstrasse and Zimmestrasse and then walked along the road between the bombed and ruined buildings and climbed a wooden staircase.

Reg didn't know what to expect and as he looked down below him, Erina answered his question before he could ask it. 'Reg, this is Checkpoint Charlie and on the other side is my home in East Berlin.'

Erina began to cry as she looked at the heavily armed American soldiers patrolling their side of the border in front of the desolate area of no man's land.

The very thought and realisation that it was true and that everything Tonia had told him had happened and was still happening, sent a shiver up Reg's spine.

'Come on Reg, now I will take you to the real Berlin,' she said.

They looked a strange sight in the daylight as they walked arm in arm, under the Linden trees growing between the ruined buildings that had been left as a monument for all to see, and to remind them that life was still a long way from perfect.

Erina led Reg into a tiny dimly lit bar where she was instantly recognised by the barman and the few people sitting at the bar. They were immediately offered a secluded table but she declined, screaming at the barman and telling him, in no uncertain words, that Reg was not a client.

They were offered the stamm tisch - a very special table reserved for the regulars. Erina smiled to herself as she sat gracefully down and ordered two large glasses of Berliner Pilsner. She grabbed the dripping glasses from the tray, raised her glass high in the air and Reg proudly followed suit.

'Prost,' she said.

As they looked into each other's eyes and sipped at the frothy bier they knew it was a very precious moment.

Reg sat back in his chair and looked around the bar. Although it was dark, through the smoke he saw an antiquated jukebox that continually played obscure German records which the customers knew so well that they frequently sang along with the music.

It was a homely place and unlike any of the bars that Reg had frequented in Hamburg and other parts of Germany. The few customers seemed very happy and joked between themselves and the barman while two elderly ladies struggled to play cards in an even darker corner.

'Reg, these people are the same as me, from the East, and they are waiting for the day when they are free to go back home to their families,' she said sadly.

He thought that Erina was going to cry again but she took a long gulp of her bier and, after catching her breath, called the landlord and ordered two portions of Bouletten - traditional meatballs made from mince, onions and spices, and a plate of Schlüster jungen - small brown bread rolls.

It was served on wooden platters and as she fed Reg his first mouthful of the mysterious food, she smiled. 'This is how the Berliners eat; you will enjoy this very much. Yes?' she said.

Reg was so hungry that he ate everything on his plate and after a few more glasses of bier walked out into the last of the fading autumn sun.

Adrian surprised all of them. He had kept the secret of his relation living in East Berlin. The first they knew of it was when he took the S bahn into East Berlin. He entered at Friedrichstrasse station and, like all visitors to the East; he was expected to exchange West German Deutsche marks for East German notebank. It was treated as a type of entrance fee, although the East German currency was worthless outside of the country.

The rate of exchange was a rip-off, one East German mark for five West German Deutsche marks, but Adrian had no option. He handed over the money and walked past orderly lines of elderly people queuing to visit West Berlin, too old to be a problem and too old to want to start a new life away from their friends in the East.

As he walked further away from the station he was astounded at the difference between the two parts of the same city. The cobbled streets and the ancient trams rattled along the old rails past the neglected tenement blocks, a dark, grey hopeless place which gave him the feeling that the War had finished only a few months earlier.

Adrian returned later that afternoon with a stranger who he introduced as cousin Ralph. He was thin, extremely shy, and as well as looking a little like Adrian, was the same age.

He had been born to Adrian's aunt, an English nurse, who had met and married a German soldier from Dresden after the First World War. Ralph gave them a small present of local Tilsit cheese. No one dared to eat it and they left it on a chair in the café.

As a special treat, the musicians took him to one of the larger department stores for high tea. Mike continued to pump him for more and more information about the conditions in the East but Ralph, understandably, was reluctant to talk about his home.

In the early evening, after listening to them in the club for one set, he begrudgingly left them but, overawed by the decadence of the West, vowed one day to return, not only to West Berlin but to visit his relatives in England.

Dave, Reg, Erina and Tonia spent many wonderful afternoons together exploring what was left of the beautiful ever-changing city before returning to the large deserted beach at Zwansee or visiting the zoo, although they did feel a little threatened when they found that the underground station platform was crowded with heroin addicts and lazy Turks begging for their very existence.

Reg, still fascinated by Checkpoint Charlie, took Dave with him, and the two of them gazed in amazement at the two totally different worlds standing side by side. Strangely, tall weeds were permitted to grow freely amongst the rubble in such a heavily guarded strip of barren land between the separated city.

Reg and Dave found it difficult to understand why the surrounded West Berliners were so happy and the city was so vibrant, extolling a feeling of rebellion towards the Russians and the East German government, when they were an island in a communist sea of repression.

The reputation of the Cheaters was at last spreading and, after two weeks in Berlin, Dave had been left with the difficult choice of taking ten days in either Amsterdam or a week in Zurich. Wishing to persevere and learn the German language, they all agreed to go to Zurich. It was a very long journey but they had four days to get there.

Whilst the group shared a last drink with Herr Baumgart, Erina passed Reg passed an envelope. He took it from her and ripped it open, hoping that it was perhaps a few hundred Deutsche marks. But, to his horror, he pulled out a plane ticket to Zurich.

Having never flown, his first thought was to refuse, but not wanting to disappoint Erina he thanked her with a kiss and put it in his pocket.

Adrian led the resentment that was soon taken up by the others.

Tactful as always, Dave ushered them into the van and after a lengthy kiss with Tonia, closed the doors started the engine and, as he pulled away, Reg shouted after him. 'Make sure you pick me up on Wednesday at the airport.'

Dave's hand appeared through the window acknowledging Reg's plea and with that the organist finally breathed a sigh of relief.

While Erina tried to console Tonia, Reg began to feel very alone as the three of them stood waving as the van pulled away into the night. It was the first time for nearly a year that he had been separated from the group outside of Hamburg and he was very scared. He wanted to run after them but Erina suddenly pulled the three of them together, consciously making it impossible for any of them to move or follow the van.

She did have an ulterior motive, she wanted Reg to herself for two more days and nights and no one but no one would make her change her plans.

No one else commented as they drove back along the autobahn, they were too tired and pleased to be making the journey without any problems.

Zurich was not far over the German border and the group was more than a little relieved as the van drove into Switzerland then Zurich and along the Limmat River. The first impressions were that it was similar to Germany. The language was similar to that spoken in Germany but the accent made even the simplest words sound different.

Dave finally reached Hotel Hirschen in Niederdorf Strasse, their home and workplace for the next week. The hotel was situated in the heart of Zurich's oldest entertainment district. Adrian jumped out of the van as it pulled up outside the hotel but this time he was forced to wait for Dave before they could check in.

He stood on the narrow pavement looking around. 'It looks pretty tame to me, if this is where it happens, what the hell is the rest of Zurich like?' he asked.

Dave walked in and introduced himself to the elderly male receptionist while Adrian made more jokes asking where the nightlife and young people hung out.

Unusually this time the group were playing and staying in the same hotel and they were to share the playing times with another group.

The entrance to the hotel was also the entrance to the bar and the stage, which was inside the front doors facing the bar. Anyone that came into the bar had to walk between the stage and the bar to get to the seating in the large adjoining room. The strange laws did not permit dancing in many of the places where groups played and Hotel Hirschen was one of them.

On stage, The Lizards, a scruffy German group played to a few young girls and several older men who sat along the bar directly in front of the stage.

The Cheaters stood looking at the equipment already set up on the tiny stage. Adrian began to get agitated as he stared at the stage, refusing to take his eyes off it.

'Bloody hell. How are we expected to get on there as well? It's no bigger than a postage stamp. Perhaps we should have gone to Amsterdam after all.'

They all stood listening while the group finished their set and Helmut, the drummer, walked over and introduced himself to Dave. He smiled at them and before Adrian could upset him Dave introduced everyone, and the two of them agreed that they should use one set of equipment.

Dave's P.A. was more efficient and, because it was much smaller, could be hung from the ceiling, thus releasing enough space for Reg's organ.

Helmut went off with Dave to park the van several minutes walk away from the hotel.

The receptionist gave them their keys and directed them to their rooms. Not booked to play until the next day they spent the rest of the afternoon in bed.

It was mid evening before they got up and they were all surprised to find that the whole area had undergone a complete transformation. Buskers played on every corner, the bars and clubs pumped out music of all styles and volume, and the crowds filled the streets to saturation point. Strangely, at midnight, the whole area returned to total silence apart for the odd drunk.

Most of the first evening was spent discussing whether or not Reg would arrive in the morning. Adrian bet Mike a night's wages that he wouldn't turn up but Dave shared Mike's confidence that he would be on the morning plane from Berlin. Adrian, still sure that he would win the bet, got a tip off from Helmut and disappeared off to Platzspitz where he bought enough pot to last him, and anyone who wished to join him, for the two-week stay in Zurich.

Reg spent the final exhausting night with Erina before she took a taxi with him to Tempelhof airport. She waited with him until he finally pulled himself away, walked through passport control down the long corridor, disappeared through the boarding gate and on to the plane for his maiden flight.

Too nervous to enjoy the flight, he was also worried whether or not Dave would be at the airport to meet him or if the group were even in Switzerland. The Lufthansa plane touched down safely at Kloten airport on schedule. Reg, relieved to finally disembark, walked nervously out of the Arrivals area to meet the group, but they were nowhere to be seen. His fellow passengers soon disappeared, leaving him standing alone, frightened and lost in the large terminal building.

The rest of the group, paying no attention to the time, were all buying the most decadent postcards to send home to England to make their friends drool with envy.

Reg wandered around aimlessly and as he became more and more desperate, his breathing became laboured. Forced to sit down, he sucked at an unusually large piece of neo-epinine. He hadn't been waiting long when thankfully he saw Adrian walking towards the post box with a handful of postcards.

Reg was so pleased to see him he ran towards him and hugged him. Adrian seemed embarrassed at the unusual attention from Reg. 'Get off me will you, this isn't Germany, you'll get me arrested,' he said.

At the Hotel Hirschen the first group would start at midday and play for an hour before the other group would take to the stage, after which the groups would play alternately until midnight. And each day the playing order would be reversed.

Not used to the early start the Cheaters overslept and were woken by the hotel receptionist at five past twelve. They reluctantly jumped out of bed and ran down to the bar to play in their creased pyjamas.

The few people who sat at the bar thought that it was hilarious and from then on they made a point of playing the first set dressed that way - something that they would continue to do at the Kaiser Kellar in Hamburg later in the year.

The second day was extremely lucky for Mike and Adrian. As they started their first set, two immaculately dressed girls came and sat in front of the stage. They wore identical clothes and seemed to take to the drummer and bass player in a big way; it was to be the beginning of a confusing but very enjoyable two weeks for the four of them.

During the day Hotel Hirschen was a regular haunt for the go go dancers, strippers and prostitutes who would come and sit at the bar to drink coffee or liqueurs and listen to the music. At night the pimps who patrolled the area in their limousines would stop off for a drink before returning to cruise the area and protect their interests.

A few days after arriving in Zurich Dave once again realised that he had contracted VD, a legacy from Hamburg and no doubt unintentionally he had passed it on to Tonia. The cost of treatment, like everything else in Switzerland, was incredibly expensive and they all secretly hoped to go back to Germany where at least they could afford to live.

During the course of the first week they only managed to get up early enough to see one morning and it really was something to see. On a bright October morning, at the main station, a sea of men in dark suits made their way silently from the trains in a hurried procession to their banks and offices in Bahnhofstrasse.

The group made one trip down the world famous street to gaze in awe at the displays of clothes so expensive that Dave calculated he would need a month of the group earnings to be able to afford even the cheapest suit.

Crossing one of the numerous bridges to the other bank of the Limmat river, they visited some of the Mediterranean style pavement cafes and bars where they sat and dreamed what they would do if they had money secretly banked in one of the many Swiss banks.

They took a three-minute trip in the Poly-Bahn funicular railway up to the Polterrasse where they could look down onto Zurich nestling below them. It was something that they would never forget; yet despite Adrian's lengthy use of the telescope provided at the summit, he continued to curse under his breath.

'Even from up here, I still can't see the sodding gnomes,' he said, with a wry smile.

By the end of the week, having spent every Swiss franc they earned, they were all looking forward to travelling back into Germany for November and on to Hamburg in December.

Chapter twenty-five

Heroes and Villains

The drive from Zurich to Marburg took all night and most of the next day. They didn't care because in the VW van they knew they would complete the journey without too much trouble and even if they were unfortunate enough to break down they could easily get spares.

Jimmy, now the proud owner of a new provisional licence, was at last able to drive the van. He took long periods at the wheel, giving Dave a well earned rest. They were all looking forward to being back in Germany and the thought of spending Christmas in Hamburg kept their spirits high. Jimmy was looking forward to seeing Helga and the baby and spending their first Christmas together.

The Europa Tanz Bar was situated on the side of a hill in the old walled town of Marburg and although there were several clubs they appeared to have missed out on the ever-changing musical trends. The club was small with an unusually high stage, a tiny bar, and disproportionately, a large cloakroom which led out to the toilets. The club owner, Ricardo Tortelli, an Italian in his late forties, spoke very little English but fortunately his Italian head waiter did.

After setting up the equipment, Reg realised that he had left his drum seat in Zurich. Both groups had rushed to dismantle the two sets of equipment jammed onto one stage and it was inevitable that one or other of the groups would pick something up by accident or more likely on purpose. He rushed around the club looking for something to sit on but the only practical solution was an orange box softened by a folded blanket.

The accommodation was a short walk up the hill and down a narrow cobbled side street, through large double doors which led into a courtyard. They all shared one long dimly lit and sparsely furnished room on the lower floor beneath a row of small specialist shops.

Ignoring Ricardo's advice, within a few days Dave had made friends with Tigo the leader of the group of Zigeuner, a notorious group of violent, persecuted gypsies. They acted in much the same way as the Hells Angels and frequently terrorised not only the surrounding areas but most of Germany.

Tigo was vile and ugly, with his greasy shoulder length hair, scarred face, and few remaining teeth that were stained with nicotine. His overweight leather clad body was a complete contrast to Dave's attempt at a suave trendy image.

Whenever they came into the club Dave, perhaps deliberately blind to the bad vibes, encouraged their friendship and targeted him to participate. He coerced the group into playing a series of Rock and Roll songs that Tigo and his cronies loved; songs that Reg and Mike longed to forget.

At first it looked as though Dave would become yet another victim but his perseverance paid off and by the second week he was considered to be one of them.

The Zigeuner were feared wherever they went but strangely Dave had wound his way into their wretched world and for some sordid reason he enjoyed their company. Despite repeated warnings from Ricardo, Dave spent as much time as he could with them travelling in a trailer lashed to the back of Tigo's beat up and smoking two-stroke East German Trabant.

Dave was fascinated by their lifestyle. They lived for the minute and had absolutely no fear and, much to his delight, as an honoured guest, he visited their squalid enclave on the outskirts of Marburg. Perhaps it was the way he had always wanted to live his life.

There were several American bases in the area and it served as an overflow for troops who commuted to Frankfurt. The Zigeuner hated the Americans and authority in general and were a law unto themselves, living by threats, protection rackets and handouts from anyone that they asked to pay them, which were immediately divided amongst them, absorbed and spent.

The Tanz Bar was their regular haunt but on the nights they didn't come, the Americans did. Mike shrewdly suggested that whenever the Americans were in the club they play *Wooden Heart*, a German song made famous by Elvis Presley. It went down a storm and was requested several times a night followed by tray after tray of bier and schnapps.

There was trouble most nights, which was generally confined to the dance floor or outside of the club. But on an unusually quiet night, fighting broke out directly in front of the stage. Two drunken combatants fell against Reg's organ and, ignoring the consequences; he shot out from behind the organ and kicked out blindly. They stopped fighting and, after returning to their group and downing several more biers, came back to the front of the stage and began taunting him. Reg sat terrified behind the organ, dreading the next break and wanting to play forever. Fortunately for him, during the last song of the set, Tigo and a small group of the Zigeuner came into the club. Following some careful manipulation by Dave, the trouble makers left the club without daring to look back.

From the stage the musicians could look out into the foyer and cloakrooms, and Mike saw three Zigeuner gang members wrestling with Ricardo amongst the coats hanging on the pegs. Seconds later they left and Ricardo staggered out of the shadows into the club; he clutched at his throat with both hands to prevent the surge of blood as it gushed between his fingers and onto the dance floor.

Dave jumped from the stage, dragged him out of the club into the van and drove him to the hospital. It probably saved his life. His attackers had slashed his throat because he told them that he was no longer prepared to make the weekly mandatory protection payment.

Before midnight Dave and Ricardo were back in the club and, in an act of sheer defiance, Ricardo, now sporting nearly a dozen stitches in the almost fatal neck wound continued to wear the bloodstained roll neck jumper. After several days, the thick darkened blood stains drew attention to his previously disregarded lack of personal hygiene.

Ricardo appreciated Dave's help and after quietly paying the outstanding protection money, did all he could to make the month as enjoyable as possible. Luckily for the group, he owned another club in Alsfeld, a small town a few kilometres away where they would play on Tuesday, Wednesday and Thursday. Reluctantly they packed their equipment for the short journey to the nearby village before once again stripping it down and returning to Marburg on Friday morning.

As the van drove into the sleepy village of Alsfeld, Adrian slipped back into his old negative manner.

'I don't think we can get much lower than this bloody godforsaken place. Is there really anywhere smaller to play?' he moaned.

Once again he was proven to be wrong and by the time they'd set up and booked into the only gastatte in the centre of the town, he changed his mind realising that here in this tiny village they would at last be treated as famous pop stars from England. They all took full advantage of the situation and some nights, much to the disgust of the owner's wife, they each had sex with as many as three local frauleins in a session. That was until Dave invited her to the club and spent one night a week with her while her husband, a long distance lorry driver, drove to Hanover and on to Berlin.

There was a benefit of playing at the two clubs for Ricardo; he gave them every Monday night off. This allowed them to return to their old haunts in K town and Saarbrucken and revisit many of their old friends from Ramstein and Miesau. The result of their weekly visits was a never ending supply of female visitors who would travel to see them and spend one or two nights with them in either Marburg or Alsfeld.

Dave and Adrian both had their first encounters with black girls, who seemed to almost outnumber the white prostitutes and strippers in Frankfurt. According to Adrian, their role was to satisfy the insatiable sexual appetite of the thousands of American forces based in and around the area, but he bragged that they always held a little more in reserve for him.

On their third Monday night off, Amy, Adrian's diminutive black female partner, invited them all to a small club she visited regularly. They were extremely apprehensive, having seen the almost obligatory fights every night in the other clubs, but being English musicians and accepted by the waiters they at least had a certain amount of protection.

Egged on by Reg and Dave, they all agreed to accompany Adrian and Amy but they were immediately aware of the atmosphere and it made them all feel very uneasy. The crowd was split into two camps; the Germans and the Americans. When the German group took to the stage all hell let loose; fighting broke out on the dance floor and spilled in to the seated area. It was mayhem.

Mike walked into the toilets to escape the trouble but came face to face with a group of Americans violently thrusting and slashing at another American's face and neck with razor blades. His face, one mass of blood, thick layers of skin hanging from his forehead, cheeks and neck, he fell to the floor. Mike urged and threw up into the blood now surfing towards the gullies.

'He won't be doing that again,' said a GI as he made his way towards the door.

Mike wiped his mouth and looked at him. 'What did he do?'

'What's it to you fella?'

Mike wiped his mouth with his sleeve. 'I... I...I just wondered,' he mumbled incoherently.

'The bastard danced with my girl,' he paused, 'no one dances with my girl... right?'

He pushed past Mike, followed closely by his buddies.

Mike suffered nightmares for the next few evenings, often waking up in a cold sweat as he tried desperately to erase the horrific and vivid pictures from his mind.

The violence didn't end there and that weekend Henry Newman, an American GI living in Marburg, tore into the club, breathless and absolutely terrified. He rushed from empty table to empty table trying to lift the seat swabs, eventually winding up in front of the stage. At that moment a large group of Zigeuner led by Tigo appeared and as soon as they saw Henry, moved in to swamp him.

The American, his face strained and taut with panic, looked across at Reg, mouthed a few words, stretched out towards him and pushed something under his makeshift seat. Seconds later he was dragged to the ground and beaten unconscious. His attackers tore through his clothes, ripping his jacket and trouser pockets, but finding nothing they each gave him a kicking and dragged him out of the club to bleed into the gutter.

Reg found it hard to concentrate for the remainder of the evening as he tried to imagine what had caused Henry to take such a beating. It was not until the end of the evening, when the club was empty and the lights were low and subdued, that he stretched his hand inside the orange box and his fingers cautiously explored the emptiness until they touched a cold metal object. He began to shake and, after furtively looking around and choosing the moment, picked up a gun then nearly dropped it as he was taken by surprise at its weight.

Carefully he put it into his jacket pocket and rushed back to the flat and the privacy of his bed. Under the duvet he lay face down, lifted himself up onto his elbows, holding the gun in his right hand and balancing precariously, he cocked the hammer. Suddenly realising what he had done, he began to sweat and very slowly released the hammer. He buried his face deep into the pillow, breathing a huge sigh of relief as he relished the safety.

Now gaining in confidence he spun the chamber and, finding the clip, pushed it aside and let the bullets accidentally slide down the bed under his raised chest. He scrambled to retrieve them, carefully reloaded the empty chambers and lay in the darkness, gripping tightly onto the first real gun he had ever held. He made the decision not to tell the others and to keep the gun for himself.

After the latest trouble, Mike decided that he would prefer to spend their next day off with Reg writing songs. The basis of the material was the poems that Reg had written when he was in hospital, and within a few hours they were transformed into full-blown songs. The songs had a freshness and style about them and, as the duo grew in confidence, they approached the rest of the group to play them live. They both expected a problem but it didn't materialise.

Each musician worked out their part and the following night they played three new songs. The audience, unaware they were playing original material, continued to dance and even clapped when they finished.

That night they celebrated in style. Dave persuaded the owner's wife to arrange a party. The rest of the group rounded up nearly a dozen willing girls and they all made the short walk to the gastatte. Dave and Adrian rolled some of the dubious purchases they had made in Frankfurt; the weinbrand and bier flowed, compliments of the house, and for the rest of the night the girls and the owner's wife alternated between the five musicians in a mass orgy of non-stop rampant sex and debauchery.

The next afternoon, fuelled by the previous night and new found confidence in their new songs, they were working on more original songs when Ricardo walked in unexpectedly, as flamboyant as ever, with a tall well-dressed man in his early twenties. He proudly introduced his companion to Dave and the group. 'This isa my gooda friend Jochen Schmidt, he makesa musika.' They smiled politely, preferring to carry on with the rehearsal. Ricardo continued. 'I tell 'im you makea gooda musika, very gooda musika.'

Jochen smiled and took over. 'My dear friend Ricardo thinks very highly of your music and he has asked me to listen to you.'

He took out his wallet, removed a business card and handed it to Dave. Before he had time to read it, Mike reached forward for a second card. Jochen continued, 'I have a small recording studio in the next village and maybe I can record your music.' He paused and waited for their reaction, and seeing there was none, he continued. 'If you wish?'

Mike, having read the business card, realised Jochen was a record producer. 'Of course we're interested but you haven't heard us play,' he said.

Jochen smiled, 'Yes, I have heard you already and I like the sound.' Mike was as dumbstruck as the rest of the group and looked on open mouthed. Jochen continued, 'I understand that you have original music?' Before they could reply he sang the melody and chorus of two of the original songs. 'Please,' he paused, 'can you play them for me now?'

Ricardo smiled and nodded encouragement, feeling that at last he had been able to repay Dave.

They didn't play their best and for the first time since playing together at the Star Club in Hamburg they felt extremely nervous. When they finished, Ricardo clapped frantically, embarrassing them.

Jochen nodded to show his appreciation and walked towards the stage. 'We drink a bier?' he asked.

At that moment, they knew he liked what he heard.

Ricardo left and they joined Jochen in the bar at the gastatte. Excitedly they discussed other artists and what music Jochen had recorded at his studio. He explained he had recorded traditional

German and folk music but he now felt the time was right to become a little more adventurous.

It was agreed that they would record two songs at his studio the following Monday.

The result of the meeting was another party but this time it was to be only with the group. Bier flowed, substances were smoked, Preludin, Captagon and other assorted pills were swallowed by the handful. They were at last on their way.

The night before the recording session none of them could sleep. They had breakfast together, a rarity for any of them, and waited patiently for Jochen to come and guide them to his studio. They sat in the van outside the gastatte but it started to become uncomfortable as the autumn chill found its way through the almost empty van.

After waiting for more than an hour the excitement and nervous conversation gradually slowed down and Adrian had finally had enough. 'I'm going to get myself a drink. I'm freezing to death in here waiting for that Gerry bastard,' he said defiantly.

They all agreed with him but wanted to wait and give Jochen the benefit of the doubt. But after a few minutes Jimmy left to join Adrian in the bar.

It was another hour before Jochen arrived. He swept into the car park in his white Mercedes sports car looking every bit the record mogul although perhaps a little out of place in the middle of the German countryside. He wore a brown suede jacket, a white polo neck sweater, sharply pressed trousers and expensive Italian leather shoes. While he stood and apologised profusely to Reg and Mike, Dave ran into the bar to grab Adrian and Jimmy, only to find that they were stoned and well on the way to becoming very drunk indeed. For the first time in months he raised his voice and shouted at them as he guided the pair of them towards the van. 'You are a pair of total fucking wasters… it's our first and maybe only chance, and what do you do?' he paused and continued immediately, 'Get pissed.'

They both struggled as they were pushed into the back of the van but as they tried to sit down Dave accelerated hard and, with tyres screeching, they fell awkwardly on to the equipment.

Mike and Reg were also incredibly angry when they saw the state of the other two and, having already discussed the matter while Dave was fetching the drunks, they issued their first warning. 'If you two screw this up, we're both off,' said Mike and Reg simultaneously.

Adrian didn't flinch but Jimmy took the threat very seriously and tried to pull himself together by taking deep breaths through the open window.

The entourage came to a standstill a few kilometres up into the mountains. Falling over each other, they rushed to look inside their first recording studio.

The studio had been built into the side of the hill in what was effectively the basement of a large timber house. On first impressions, it seemed quite small but that didn't matter. They had a chance.

The studio was constructed in two parts; the control room which was Jochen's domain, and the studio area, which was then divided into booths for the drums and vocalist. Every inch of the walls was covered in posters of Bavarian 'oom pa' bands dressed in the traditional lëderhösen, proudly holding their brass instruments high in the air, and two posters of a middle aged German singer in different poses, advertising his latest LP. In pride of place were framed signed photographs of Jochen with many of the same musicians and singers.

The drums were squeezed into the largest soundproof booth; the skins were covered with assorted lengths of tape and the bass drum was filled with cushions, until they all sounded acceptable to Jochen. The amplifiers were placed behind padded screens and Dave stood in a semi-glazed booth which enabled him to look out on to the musicians in the studio.

Surrounded by microphones, metre upon metre of cable, and playing in such confined unfamiliar surroundings, it was nearly two hours before anyone played a note. When they eventually were asked to play together, the pressure of the day coupled with the alcohol and drugs was more than evident.

Jochen maintained his patience, plying them with endless cups of tea and coffee and giving them encouraging comments until Adrian and Jimmy were in a fit state to record.

The first song was recorded and Jochen asked them to join him in the tiny control room to listen to the results. After only a few bars Mike, swearing under his breath, pushed his way through the drooling musicians, who were congratulating each other on their efforts, and sat back behind his drums, thrashing around the kit.

Jochen was not happy with the recording and he joined them in the studio to discuss the mistakes. It was then that Mike took over and for the first time it was clear to all of them he knew what he wanted. He had spent most of his evenings under the bed covers in the boarding school dormitory listening to Radio Luxembourg and at every spare opportunity he listened repeatedly to his record collection until he knew how a hit record needed to sound.

With the combination of alcohol, drugs and nerves, it was quite obvious to him and Jochen that on this session they would not make a good enough job of the original songs.

Jochen persuaded them to take a break and he sat with them, rolling and smoking joint after joint until the mood mellowed. Their playing improved but, despite the outside influences, the end result of the recording of the first two songs was far from satisfactory. Mike then had a suggestion. He turned down the lights and they played a very slow bluesy version of *Summertime* and a slow jam that they called *The Last Train Blues*.

It worked so well and as the last note faded they all smiled for the first time. Jochen played the recording repeatedly through the large speakers in the main studio and while they dismantled their equipment they realised something had been salvaged from the potentially disastrous day

Jochen gave them a copy of the session in a boxed reel-to-reel tape on which he had written not only the name of the group but also the name of the songwriters, crediting the whole group with the instrumental.

Ricardo arrived at Alsfeld early the next evening and paid them the month's fee in full.

The remainder of the night was a combination of mixed emotions. All their recent conquests were out in force, even the gastatte owner's wife who, much to Dave's disgust, climbed on stage and had the last dance with him. Jochen came soon after with the remaining tapes, agreeing to contact them as soon as he had any feedback from his contacts. A photographer accompanied him and took film after film of them on and off stage, and several with Jochen in similar poses to the photographs already hanging at his studio.

There was however a major problem. Dave had tried hard but, despite a number of promises, the Cheaters had no work for the next month and they were going to begin their return journey to Hamburg on the first of December with nowhere to play.

Although they all knew it, they chose to ignore it.

Chapter twenty-six

It's too Late Now

As soon as Dave drove out of Alsfeld the musicians, feeling more optimistic than at any time since coming to Germany, started to get impatient. Every kilometre seemed to drag as they all eagerly shouted out the remaining distance to Hamburg on every road sign.

This journey was much different than the return from Coburg in February; this time Dave drove the VW with a confidence that he not had since leaving England, and being a German vehicle they would at least be able to afford to replace any spares if they were needed.

After passing Kassel, then Hanover, they began to feel more euphoric and as the remaining kilometres slowly reduced, they pushed Dave to race the last leg of the journey towards their adopted home of Hamburg.

The van slipped quietly and unnoticed into the city amongst the cars, trams and lorries and as it approached the Reeperbahn the last of the grey wintry daylight disappeared behind the buildings, allowing the clear December night sky to take its place.

The group was truly looking forward to the future and they seemed even more excited than nearly a year ago when they drove into Hamburg for the first time. As Dave drove past the Café Keese and down towards the Park Hotel, he silently worried if he would be able to keep the group together. They had all changed and he knew that once unleashed onto St Pauli, with most of their last three months earnings still intact, they would go crazy. It was almost Christmas, they all felt confident, and for the first time they were ready to celebrate it as a group. The fact that they had nowhere to play didn't seem to worry any of them, except him.

The van pulled up outside the Park Hotel but before Dave had time to turn off the engine Adrian leapt out and rushed towards the hotel to catch Helena before she left for work. While Reg and Mike raced each other to check-in, Dave opened the side door, took out his suitcase, then let Jimmy drive the van up to Altona to stay with Helga and the baby.

Reg and Mike booked a twin room whilst Dave, knowing that Tonia was due from Berlin to visit him in a few days time, and preferring more privacy, booked himself into a more expensive double room. The three of them took it in turns to have a bath and wash their hair and for the first time in nearly a month they looked, smelt and felt good.

They met Adrian late that night at the bier shop, and after a few drinks to celebrate their return they rushed off excitedly, arm in arm with several fraulcins they hardly knew, to a Bavarian restaurant near the top of the Reeperbahn for a rather expensive meal. Jimmy was missing but on this occasion they didn't let it deter them from enjoying every minute.

After repeated rounds of bier, weinbrand, korn and a meal that they all found hard to remember, they staggered, the worse for wear, down the Reeperbahn and back into the bier shop. Reg saw Margot walk in and now, after dozens of conquests, he felt confident enough to handle her. Oblivious to the fact that they were the only people dancing, they cavorted together between the tables for nearly an hour, to the differing styles of music as it was randomly delivered from the jukebox.

As the sun began to rise, Reg returned with Margot to her flat in Nobistor and they were soon standing naked in the shower. Although very drunk, he was pleased with himself at being able to come up with the hardness that would allow him to achieve another of his fantasies. Abruptly, she pulled her head back out of the line of the hot surging water and the pleasurable expression on her face vanished. 'You fucking bastard, I've waited nearly a year to get you,' she screeched, her guttural throaty voice piercing his eardrums. 'No one embarrasses me, especially a fucking musician. You should know that.' She forced her face into his, her intense eyes searing into his very soul. She continued to scream at him, her almost hysterical voice reverberating in the confined space of the shower cubicle. 'Try to get rid of that... '

She paused while a vile smirk spread slowly across her hard face. 'And this time...'

Miraculously he sobered up and, with his penis still throbbing inside her, he stared back at her. Margot started to laugh like a woman possessed and he could no longer remember the pleasure as she lowered her eyes towards his now shrunken penis and whispered in his ear. 'It will cost you much money.'

She laughed loudly. 'Maybe Trude will pay for you,' she snarled. 'Be lucky you bastard.' She posed erotically as her tongue slid sensually across her lips and whispered to him. 'You will need it... you fucking bastard.... Piss off!'

Her vile high pitched laugh deafened him as he stood trembling, unable to speak. He agonised over every word as he realised she had wreaked revenge on him because Trude had attacked her in Mambo Schankey's the previous winter.

Could anybody hold a grudge for that long?

He struggled to pull his clothes over his dripping body and in a state of shock rushed down the stairs, out into the freezing night and onto the crowded Reeperbahn. He pushed his way blindly through the crowds and made for the bier shop, all the while trying to remember and come to terms with everything that had just happened to him.

Dave and Mike were both holding court squeezed around a table with the newly arrived Scottish group who were hanging on Dave's every word and keen to learn about the girls and what they might expect. Pleased to see him, Mike introduced Reg to the new musicians, bought a stiefel of bier and they proceeded to tease each other until the residue finally gushed over Reg, who uncharacteristically lost his temper. He stormed out and raced back to the Park Hotel. Feeling dirty and uncertain as to what Margot had forced into his body, he ran a hot deep bath and, as he desperately tried to rid himself of the unknown, scrubbed his penis and testicles almost raw.

As he lay back in his warm bed he swallowed a handful of pills. They didn't help and he started to quiver with a mixture of frustration, helplessness and anger. In sheer desperation, he screamed across the empty bedroom into the darkness. 'You bloody bitch, what have you done to me?'

He didn't expect Mike to come back but nevertheless he waited, fighting the impending tiredness until he eventually fell asleep. Waking early in the morning and still alone in his room he took another bath, dressed and went to the imbiss and waited for the group.

It was late in the afternoon before Adrian crossed the road looking relaxed, happy and extremely pleased with his night's work. He took one look at Reg and pulled back. 'What the hell's up with you?' 'Do you really want to know? Are you really interested in me or anyone else?' grunted Reg.

'Come on, course I am.' He thought for a second and smiled to himself. 'What a great night...'

He noticed that Reg was getting annoyed. He swallowed hard and continued. 'Now come on then, what's the problem?' he asked.

While Reg slowly told him what had happened, Adrian smiled broadly.

Reg suddenly lost his temper. 'It's not bloody funny, I could have anything.' He paused and looked at Adrian with questioning eyes. 'Don't you care?'

Adrian finally realised how upset Reg was. 'Listen, it can't be that bad. Margot's been around for years and she's not that stupid.' He scratched his chin, 'I mean... think about it. Is she?'

Adrian smiled again as Reg shuffled nervously in his chair. 'I suppose not, but I'm fucked this time.' His voice wavered, and in almost a whisper he continued. 'Erina will be arriving in a few days, and whatever it is, there's no way,' he paused, 'I can't pass it on to her, can I?'

'That's not your problem. Do you know what you've got?' asked Adrian. Reg shook his head. 'Well don't worry about it. How many times have the fucking women given you a dose? And you've unknowingly passed it on to someone else.' Adrian shook his head and nudged him. 'Forget it. Why should you be different than anyone else?'

Although not totally satisfied with the outcome, Reg looked a little happier.

'Do you want a coffee then Reg?'

'No, let's go for a bier while we can,' replied Reg trying hard to force a smile.

They had a few drinks in the bier shop before moving on to the Star Club, paying no attention to the announcement as the curtains began to open. When they realised that it was Ronnie standing at the front of the stage with a new group, they were both struck speechless. She had grown and dyed her hair blonde, backcombing it into a bouffant, copying the beehive style of Dusty Springfield, singing many of her songs, and a mixture of new R and B and soul songs.

Adrian and Reg gazed at the stage open mouthed while the group played the first three songs and, as they started to play the introduction to the next song, they finally turned to each other.

A tight lipped Adrian nodded, impressed with what he saw and heard. 'What a fucking great group? She's got it right this time. She looks bloody fab.'

Reg nodded in agreement but his mind was on something else. 'Just wait until Dave finds out she's here, now *he's* fucked.'

Ronnie didn't see them. As soon as she finished her set and the curtains closed, they left for a small bar in Talstrasse, where they drank until dawn.

Adrian couldn't wait to tell Dave the news and rushed back to the Park and hammered on Dave's door. Dave eventually opened it. 'What the hell do you want this time of the day?'

'Guess who's at the Star Club this month?'

'Who gives a fuck? Does it matter?'

He closed the door. Adrian knocked again. 'What is wrong with you? Can't it wait?'

'You don't wanna know?'

'Well, if I don't wanna know, why the fuck are you here?'

Adrian smiled from ear to ear. 'If you could see yourself,' said Dave.

He could hold out no longer. 'It's... Ronnie... she's at the Star Club, with a new group.'

He waited in anticipation. 'Well?' questioned Dave

'Think about it.' He tapped excitedly on the door. 'You nicked her van.'

'She can have the wreck if she wants it. What's it worth? Fifty Deutsche marks?'

Adrian stood looking at him. 'Is that it?'

'I think so... Good night.' Dave slammed the door in Adrian's face and went back to bed.

Ronnie's band spent many hours with Dave and the Cheaters, smoking pot, popping pills and drinking together in the Blockhütte, reminiscing and discussing the last twelve months. The van was never mentioned. After all, it was great to meet someone from their hometown.

While Dave became more and more despondent, he knew it would almost certainly be the end of the Cheaters if he didn't find at least a few nights at any club. Mike didn't care. As well as alternating between Heike and Erna, he still found time to sleep with almost every other female that wanted his body.

Dave visited the Funny Crow, the Crazy Horse and dozens of the smaller clubs around the city until he heard that a German group had been involved in a road accident and was unable to fulfil the dates at the Kaiser Keller. He rushed around to see the manager and accepted a ten-day stretch beginning on the thirteenth of December.

The news was a great relief as they were now beginning to realise, much too late, that they had spent far too much money.

Carried away with the Christmas spirit, and shopping together like old times, they all bought extravagant and totally unsuitable presents and cards to send back home to their numerous relatives in England.

Surprisingly, Reg and Dave were looking forward to seeing and meeting Erina and Tonia and they took a bus to Fühlsbüttel airport, arriving nearly an hour before the flight from Berlin landed. It was not a problem; they sat in the bar and waited.

Tonia and Erina looked wonderful as they walked through Arrivals, each wheeling a trolley loaded with matching suitcases for what was only a short visit. Despite the luggage they all managed to squeeze into one taxi but rather than stay at the Park Hotel the girls had other ideas. Instead, the taxi took them to the magnificent Vier Jahrszeiten - the Four Seasons hotel, on the west side of the Binnenalster. The sheer size and luxury of the suite took the musicians' breath away.

While the porters struggled with the cases, delivering them several minutes later to the luxurious suite on the third floor, Reg and Dave stood on the balcony drinking Champagne, totally overawed and finding it difficult to come to terms with the fact that this was actually happening to them. It was a side of Hamburg they didn't know existed.

The suite had three bedrooms, each with a huge double bed; they used them all and, occasionally after drinking cocktails of pills and Weinbrand, while the Champagne flowed, they would all pile into one bed.

They visited the huge funfair at the top of the Reeperbahn and although the girls wanted to visit the clubs Reg and Dave successfully convinced them that it was better to spend their very special time together without the interference of the rest of the group members.

It was the beginning of a wonderful dream that would last for nearly five days and throughout that period Erina and Tonia spent a fortune on Reg and Dave in the most expensive boutiques in the city.

On the fourth afternoon, as they travelled the short journey back to the hotel by taxi, laden down with numerous bags of clothes and gifts, Reg whispered to Dave. 'The shops in Monkebergstrasse are even better this time of the year.'

Dave nodded and smiled. 'Especially when you don't have to pay for any of it.'

He pressed Tonia's hand, turned to Reg and gave an even broader smile. 'Well, what can I say? At last I've replaced all the suits stolen by the bastards down in Coburg. It's taken almost a year but I've done it.'

In the early evening, following several hours of steamy sex in as many positions as the four of them could manage, they made their way down to the restaurant. It was apparent that the other diners were disgusted at the thought of the long haired English musicians and their escorts invading their decadent world.

But after ordering and drinking several bottles of Champagne, which did not go unnoticed, the restaurant buzzed with animated conversation as the German diners tried to establish who Reg and Dave were. They finally left the restaurant to tumultuous applause as the confused diners agreed that the two long aired Englishmen must be famous musicians they just didn't recognise.

After dinner, with the applause still ringing in his ears, Reg stood with Erina on the balcony overlooking the Binnenalster while they both smoked marijuana and swallowed several Preludin washed down with more glasses of Champagne. As the riverbanks below came alive with crowds of people Erina grabbed at Reg's hand and dragged him out on to the street to join the ever-growing happy fun loving crowd.

They made their way into a huge bier tent that was full of people singing and dancing to the Bavarian oom pa band. Erina ordered two litre glasses of bier and four glasses of korn. The glasses were soon empty and Reg ordered the same again, swallowing another two Preludin with the first gulp of Korn.

With the effects of the drugs and drink finally taking effect, he was unable to comprehend why the crowd was enjoying the music so much. The response the band received was better than anything the Cheaters had ever achieved.

He suddenly felt depressed and quietly talked to himself. 'How is it that a group of overweight, bearded, old men in short leather trousers can get more response than a group like us?'

Reg realised that although he was enjoying his new found freedom and wealth, there was something missing - he was a real musician without anywhere to play, and it hurt him.

While he sat thinking, Erina leaned over and whispered in his ear. Reg looked back at her, his eyes wide open. She repeated it and, as everything around him went strangely silent, he heard every word. 'Reg, do you know that soon you will become a father?'

'No, it can't be. How do you know? Are you sure?' he responded loudly.

He dragged Erina away from the long wooden bench, knocking the glasses of bier across the table and onto the strangers, and staggered out into the cold December night oblivious to the damage he had caused.

Shadowed by Erina, he walked aimlessly along the side of the lake mesmerised by the bright reflections of the fairground rides as they rose into the night sky. Erina cuddled into him. 'Reg you do not want a baby with me?'

He stared at her with a look of indifference. 'The reason I left England was to get away from this thing with Julie. I've got years of playing before I settle down and when I do, I wouldn't think it would be with your sort...... *a prostitute!*' Reg spoke so fast and, with the drugs slurring his speech, Erina understood only a few words. She gave him an innocent smile and gently kissed his cold cheek.

He pulled at her and began to walk towards the hotel. 'Who gives a fuck? Come on let's have another bottle of Champagne.'

Most of the conversation and the remainder of the night was erased from his life forever as the drugs took complete control of his young mind and body.

The following evening before dinner, Dave and Reg had time to themselves in the hotel bar. Dave swallowed a glass of weinbrand and looked around at the wealthy people surrounding them.

'This is the life, I could settle for this,' he said with a smile.

Reg looked at him in disbelief. 'But it's not the same, when we're not playing is it?' Dave looked at him blankly. 'She's got to you hasn't she?' asked Reg, waiting nervously for Dave to argue, but when it failed to materialise he continued. 'And do you know that Erina told me she was pregnant?'

Now losing his temper, Reg raised his voice. 'What a load of fucking bollocks.'

As Erina and Tonia rejoined them, Dave spoke quickly so that they didn't understand him. 'You're the one who's talking bollocks. When they've gone you know full well that we start at the Kaiser Keller and before you know it, it'll be Christmas and then we can look forward to a decent New Year.'

The next afternoon everything came to an abrupt end when Erina and Tonia asked Reg and Dave to return to Berlin with them. The unquestionable refusal, seen as an insult, resulted in the four of them travelling to the airport in complete silence. Reg chose to wait outside of the departure lounge while Dave sat drinking with Tonia as they both attempted to console Erina.

Several days after Tonia and Erina returned to Berlin, the brief sexual encounter with Margot began to affect Reg. Large red spots appeared on his neck, face and back, followed a few days later by the deadly dark green poison, which oozed painfully out of the end of his penis.

He visited the doctor but was told he had a number of serious diseases and the cost to treat them would be extremely expensive. Depression set in and, although he tried desperately to maintain his enthusiasm while they played at the Kaiser Keller, the hours started to drag. The searing pain prevented him from sleeping and, unable to drink or sleep with girls, he jammed at the Star Club with Ronnie and her group on the late night sessions. Her group didn't have an organist and she really enjoyed singing some of her favourite songs, which only worked when Reg joined them.

She took to him and to avoid her German admirers, male and female, and the crude, lecherous English musicians, she chose to spend her breaks with him, discussing songs and records by mutually favourite artists.

In order to save money Reg chose to stay in one of the cramped hotel rooms provided by the club and, although Mike occasionally stayed with him for moral support, he preferred to spend as much time as he could with his ever-growing band of female followers.

The accommodation was dire and although it was verböten to cook in the room, to save money Reg chose to ignore it. Jimmy gave him an old portable electric cooker and two metal dinner plates that belonged to Helga. Reg bought eggs and bacon, which he would cook on the plates and eat directly off them.

It was easy and for the first few days no one took any notice. But at the beginning of the second week he became more adventurous, frying almost anything that was cheap. He bought a large Cod at the Fischmarkt but as it cooked the smell of fish spread throughout the hotel. This prompted the manager to systematically check all the rooms and, although Reg hid the sizzling frying pan in the wardrobe, when the manager entered he made straight for the wardrobe. As he pulled the doors open, the pan burst into flames.

They were able to put out the fire themselves but it was too late, the damage was done, and that night the Cheaters were thrown out of the hotel and the club.

The manager refused to pay them the full fee, withholding almost half of their money to pay for the superficial smoke damage.

It started to snow as they loaded the equipment into the van in silence. Once loaded and parked around the side of the club, they trouped off to the bier shop. Dave was the first to speak. 'We've just got to be patient. If we can just get into next year, then in a couple of weeks we'll put this year behind us and learn by our mistakes.'

Reg listened intently hoping to hear Dave say something more positive but, feeling totally disillusioned and unable to hold back his feelings of guilt, the frustration and fear took over. 'The only reason I cooked in the room was to save money. What am I going to do? There's no way I can afford the treatment and if I don't get it, who knows what will happen to me.'

'Your dick will probably drop off,' laughed Adrian loudly.

The rest of them tried not to laugh but none of them could resist a smirk. 'Come on Reg, don't give up, we'll try a different doctor tomorrow,' said Dave half-heartedly.

It didn't help and at that moment the situation seemed hopeless. They all felt desperately homesick, as though they were a million miles away from England, each wishing they could return home if only for the few days of Christmas.

They began to sink into differing depths of despair in the realisation that there was little any of them could do to improve their situation. Dave ordered a round of drinks and, surrounded by doting girls, they drank and smoked themselves silly, temporarily forgetting their problems. All except Reg who, after sipping at his bier, got up and left unnoticed.

When you've got the pox you don't dare to drink too much because it hurts so much to piss.

Chapter twenty-seven

Cryin' in the Rain

Jimmy, Helga and the baby made almost the perfect family. They were the envy of many of the girls while at the same time considered to be a joke to the musicians.

Early on the morning of the twenty third of December, leaving Helga sleeping heavily in bed, Jimmy hurriedly bathed and dressed the baby. He excitedly made the last long walk to the postampt before Christmas, to collect the cards and any presents that may have arrived for him and the rest of the group. He was surprised at how many letters and packages there were but, as the baby began to cry, he had no time to even attempt to open his own post. Although he was keen to see who had written to him and sent him cards, he piled them around the baby, fixed the waterproof cover over the pram and walked back down the darkening Reeperbahn.

With the baby asleep, he stopped at the first inviting bar, drank several korn and bier chasers in quick succession while he soaked up the atmosphere. Life was good.

By the time he had fed and changed the baby, it was mid afternoon when he arrived at the Park Hotel to deliver Adrian's post. He walked past the receptionist without acknowledging her and awkwardly dragged the pram up the two flights of stairs to Adrian's room. He knocked several times without any response so resorted to blindly kicking out at the door and waking the baby. He reached in to the pram and grabbed at the screaming infant. Balancing him precariously under one arm, he continued to hammer on the door with his other hand.

Not getting a response he rearranged the distressed baby in the pram and rushed down to reception. 'I need to get into room 213... **Now!**' he screamed.

'They are inside the room... I know this,' replied the receptionist.

Jimmy stormed back upstairs but, despite the incessant banging on the door, still didn't get any response. He kicked out at the pram, rushed down the stairs, and after screaming at the receptionist she agreed to follow him with the master key.

When she opened the door the neon lights flashed intermittently through the unlined curtains shedding an eerie light across the room. Jimmy carefully picked his way between the empty glasses, syringes, champagne and bier bottles, clothes strewn all over the carpet, and past the ashtrays piled high with partly smoked cigarettes.

Hazelle was stretched awkwardly across the bed, nude and looking a grotesque sight. Jimmy took a cursory glance at a small pile of cocaine on the dressing table and cleared an armchair before dropping the baby into it. He raced across to the bed, bent down and shook the prostitute violently until she stirred. Hazelle was still high and unable to speak coherently.

In disgust, Jimmy let her drop back onto the bed before picking his way gingerly through the debris towards the bathroom. Finding the door closed, he called out to Adrian.

There was no reply.

He knocked several times but there was still no answer.

Losing his patience, and beginning to panic, he screamed out. 'Adrian, come on, open the door will you.' He waited. 'Come on mate, I've still got to deliver the rest of the post.'

Jimmy turned the door handle; the door wasn't locked, but opened slightly though not enough for him to look inside. The receptionist helped him to push the door and it gradually opened to reveal Adrian lying naked on the bathroom floor.

She vomited and then ran screaming back into the bedroom, tripping on the bottles and falling across Hazelle on the bed.

As Jimmy knelt over Adrian, the baby started to scream, but he was too preoccupied to hear it. He tried in vain to find Adrian's pulse but, noticing that his naked body was cold, and given no other option, he slapped him around the face then pressed his chest hard.

He screamed at the receptionist who was now leaning against the door with the baby still crying in her arms.

'Can't you do something about that baby? Get a fucking ambulance.' Jimmy paused for breath and, realising that she didn't understand a word he was saying, screamed at her again. 'Go on.'

Still totally naked, Hazelle pushed past the receptionist and staggered blindly into the bathroom. She looked down at Adrian and started hitting Jimmy around the back of the head. 'What do you do to Adrian?' she asked.

Jimmy, now in tears, dragged one hand across his eyes and nose before ripping into her.

'Can't you see what you've done? You stupid fucking bitch, you've killed him.'

Hazelle looked at him blankly, her eyes grey and glazed as though Jimmy was a complete stranger. Still unaware that Adrian was dead, she tried to speak but her tired words were slurred and almost unintelligible. 'Why don't you leave us alone you Englischer bastard? Get us another drink won't you?'

Jimmy stood up and bundled her back into the bedroom but while he was helping the hysterical sobbing receptionist to console and feed the baby, Hazelle, unnoticed, staggered back into the bathroom carrying a bottle of bier and a handful of pills. She fell awkwardly onto the bathroom floor beside Adrian, dropping the pills all over the floor. Frantically, she scrambled around collecting the pills and, with her whole body trembling, she raised Adrian's head and forced the pills one at a time between his lips. It was not easy but, after forming a small gap between his lips, she pushed in nearly a dozen tablets before she forced the bier bottle between his lips. The frothing liquid poured back out of his mouth and ran down his chin onto his bare chest and stomach.

When Jimmy saw what she was doing, he flew at her and dragged her across the bathroom floor. 'You stupid fucking cow.... don't you ever know when enough is enough?'

There was no need for an ambulance except to take away Adrian's body. After talking to the police and reluctantly helping to sedate Hazelle, Jimmy left. He refused a lift in the police car, preferring to be alone to think, and in his own time push the baby back towards Altona.

Jimmy didn't remember the walk back in the steady drizzle, which soon turned into much heavier freezing rain, drenching his clothes and hair, and running down his neck. When he reached the flat he threw the post and parcels onto the table and broke down as he told Helga what had happened to Adrian. She poured him a large weinbrand and handed him the rest of the bottle, kissed him on the cheek and rubbed his dripping hair with a towel.

Subconsciously, he shook the glass and gazed into the pale liquid. 'Adrian didn't deserve something like that to happen to him.' He took a large gulp of weinbrand and coughed violently before continuing. 'Why?'

Slumped in the scratched wooden chair, he shook his head uncontrollably while Helga removed his saturated overcoat, hanging it on the back of the door to drip onto the rug. As he shivered, she tried to pacify him but the baby started to cry and she carried it screaming back into the bedroom.

Jimmy sat drawing his fingers through the deep red velvet table cover, sobbing and talking to himself. Still in shock, he looked around the flat at the unusually decorated Christmas tree with its white candles, cotton wool snowballs and silver thread, and the brightly wrapped presents that he had bought for Helga and the baby. On the wall, he gazed at the first photograph of the smiling Cheetahs taken outside the Funny Crow a few days after arriving in Hamburg. Next to it were several framed photographs of him with Helga at different stages of pregnancy. He took a long drink, put the glass down on to the table and opened the largest envelope. For a moment he smiled as he read it.

The card was from his grandmother, wishing him a Happy Christmas, and she had enclosed a five-pound note. He folded the note neatly, pushed it into his wet trouser pocket, and excitedly opened the envelope from his father, unfolded the letter inside the card and began to read it.

15th December 1966

Dear Jimmy

I am very sorry to have to tell you that your Nan passed away earlier today…

Jimmy couldn't read anymore. He screwed up the letter and threw it across the room, broke down and screamed as loud as he could. 'No, it can't be true, none of this is happening to me. Why is my life so fucked up? What have I done to deserve this shit?'

Helga rushed out of the bedroom empty handed. She now had a stern face and Jimmy, sensing the change in her mood, turned to look at her. Before he could tell her the bad news she snatched the bottle from him, poured herself a large glass of weinbrand, swallowed most of it and sat down opposite him. 'Jimmy, I have something to tell you.' He looked a sorry sight as he tried to focus through his tears. 'I have a baby.'

'I know.'

Helga shook her head. 'No Jimmy. I mean that I am having some other baby.' She paused and drank the remainder of the weinbrand before continuing. 'No... I don't think that you are understanding me?'

'Bloody hell that's fantastic, what a brilliant Christmas present. It's about time I had some good news.'

He sat up straight and wiped the tears from his eyes as a smile slowly crept across his face.

'Yes Jimmy, it is fantastic, but it is also bad.' She paused, took a deep breath, forced a smile and continued. 'Jimmy, I am sorry, it is not *your* baby.'

He lunged towards her and screamed into her face. 'How do you know that it's not mine?'

'Jimmy, my darlink, *I know.*'

'Are you sure?' He pleaded with her.

'Please don't make it difficult for me darlink.'

'How can you call me your darling?'

'You will always be my darlink.'

The baby began to scream and neither of them paid any attention to it.

'What about the bastard who fucked you and gave you that?' He poked hard at her pregnant belly. 'And that?'

He pointed to the bedroom and now, for the first time, they could both hear the baby crying.

'Please Jimmy, it is Christmas, our first Christmas. My darlink, please try to forget it for the holiday.'

'Forget it, I'll never forget it. How can you expect me to ignore ... forget that nothing has happened? I've been a laughing stock since I met you... What do you take me for?' He spat at her as he forced out the last sentence. 'A... a, a total fucking idiot?'

Carefully aiming his glass, he threw it across the room at the photographs of the two of them and stormed out of the flat, slamming the front door behind him.

Jimmy walked out into the freezing night, stood on the pavement for a moment, looked back towards the brightly lit window of the flat and the flowering plants on the window cills, and made several futile attempts before finally lighting a cigarette.

He staggered into the road and felt in his pockets for the van keys. He had no idea where he would go but he knew that he would feel safe in the sanctuary of the group's mobile home. Instead, his fingers found the flick knife that his father had given him. Realising that the keys were in his overcoat, he kicked out at the van door and then slowly removed the knife from his pocket. He pressed the button on the knife and, as the blade shot out in front of him, he slashed out viciously into the darkness at his imaginary victim. Losing all control he ran headlong across the road, oblivious to the cars bearing down on him as they flashed their lights and sounded their horns and struggled to avoid him, skidding on the now treacherous road surface. Having managed to cross to the safety of the pavement, he saw the flashing lights in the distance and wandered down towards the Reeperbahn. As the tears rolled down his cheeks, he was temporally unaware of the cold rain and sleet as it soaked through his already drenched jacket, trousers and boots.

The cold began to affect him and as he approached the Reeperbahn he could hear the drunken revellers. Trying desperately to avoid everyone, he made his way down a dark side street but wherever he walked there were more and more strangers having a good time. It was impossible to avoid the euphoria of the moment. He was frozen and the cold began to bite into his bones, causing pain in his fingers, feet and knees. He pulled at the thin narrow collar of his jacket and beat his arms randomly across his body, desperately trying to get warm. Feeling inside his pocket for a few Deutsche marks, he realised that he had nothing except the English five-pound note, which would be of no use to him in a German bar or café.

He passed the imbiss on the corner of Grosse Freiheit, looking for a face, any face he knew, or anyone who might recognise him. There was no one. He stumbled into the bier shop. It was empty apart from a few drunken tourists sitting at the bar who, when they realised that he was carrying a knife, stopped singing and sat staring at him apprehensively.

Jimmy glared at them, wavered, muttered a few angry words, and much to their relief staggered back out on to the street. He was sad, he couldn't find anyone he knew and he so desperately wanted to talk. Every minute his depression plummeted to new depths. Walking mindlessly up the Reeperbahn he turned the corner into Hein-Hoyer-Strasse and blindly walked down the long street towards number 65, subconsciously walked up the steps and stopped. It was locked and he didn't have a key to the front door. He had returned it at the end of January before the group left for Coburg, almost a year earlier.

Feeling light-headed, he fumbled in his pocket and took out the last cigarette. As he tried to light it, he lost all co-ordination and dropped it on to the rain soaked pavement. He leaned forward to pick it up, lost his balance, gave up in disgust and threw the empty packet into the air. The biting wind blew it back onto the pavement in front of him. He tried several times to kick it away but the cold wind had caused his eyes to stream and he was unable to focus. While the wind relentlessly continued to find and attack every vulnerable and exposed part of his face and wet body, he continued to rub at his eyes which by now were becoming extremely painful and sore. Feeling very tired, he started to walk back towards the bright lights but a few yards up the road he stumbled into an unlit alley and fell into a thick hedge growing wildly on a small area of wasteland. Exhausted and unable to stand, obscured from view amongst the branches and the accumulated rubbish, he pushed himself up against the building.

Hypothermia began to set in; he began to hallucinate as the cold bit deeper and deeper into his soaked, freezing and sad body. Finding it impossible to keep warm, and now shivering, he began to lose consciousness.

He saw himself pass his grandmother's cottage in a white Rolls Royce.

She leaned on the garden gate and, as she smiled to him, waved a five-pound note in her hand. He could see himself playing on a brightly lit stage in front of a huge audience; his father appeared through the crowd, in full battle dress, smiling and effortlessly holding his amplifier, echo chamber and the white Stratocaster high in the air above his head.

Jimmy smiled to himself as he remembered the glowing fire in the cottage where he had spent the previous Christmas Day with his father.

In the freezing night, as he sat with his head bowed and his body contorted into an unrecognisable shape, his voice slurred and teeth chattered as he talked to himself. 'I love you Dad, Happy Christmas.'

Last Christmas was the best Christmas he'd ever had.

Chapter twenty-eight

Town without Pity

Jimmy never woke up; freezing to death just a few yards from his first home in Hamburg, alone and only yards from the seasonal celebrations of the revellers in a distant country he had naively imagined would allow him to fulfil his dreams.

News of Adrian's death travelled fast. Babs broke it to Mike and Reg but they refused to believe her.

Why should they?

But when Hazelle appeared, drunk and stoned, accompanied by several of her cronies, it became clear that it was true.

Mike and Reg had no other option but to reluctantly accept it. They rushed to the Star Club and forced their way through the crowd to the front of the stage where Dave was now duetting with Ronnie on the Sonny and Cher song *I Got You Babe*.

They both stood in front of the stage staring up at Dave with expressionless looks on their faces, unaware of the music, lights and the crowd that surrounded them.

It was more than evident to Dave that something had gone seriously wrong. He finished the duet to a drunken standing ovation and joined them backstage in the changing room.

'You'd better be prepared for a shock,' mumbled Reg.

Mike nodded in agreement and passed Dave a bottle of bier. He pushed it aside, looked at them and waited, for once not knowing what to expect.

'Come on tell me. What the fuck has happened?' asked Dave impatiently.

'Adrian's dead,' said Reg.

'Is this his idea of a joke? How can he be dead? We were all with him last night. Whose idea is it?' He turned his back on them and punched at the wall. 'If I know Adrian, he put the two of you up to this.'

'No, it's true. Jimmy found him this afternoon at the Park, in the bathroom,' said Reg.

'He od'd on heroin,' continued Mike.

For a moment Dave stood staring at them and shaking his head until he eventually spoke, labouring over every word. 'Bloody... hell... the... poor... bastard...'

The three of them looked at each other as tears filled their eyes.

Dave was the first of them to uncontrollably burst into tears. They were all shaken, finding it impossible to accept or believe. The silence continued for several minutes while they each tried to take in what had happened.

Finally, Dave recovered a little. 'Where's Jimmy? This must have hit him pretty hard, especially if he found Adrian,' he said.

Mike and Reg looked at each other. 'We don't know.'

The three of them left the dressing room to search for Jimmy but well into the night, cold and exhausted, and unable to find him, they unanimously agreed that he must be with Helga and decided not to disturb him until the morning.

It was Helga who identified Jimmy's body late on Christmas Eve.

She found Mike, Heike, Reg and Dave on Christmas afternoon, in the deserted bier shop, staring at the pile of unopened presents.

A handful of assorted pills and korn had helped them get over the shock of the last twenty-four hours, and at last they were slowly beginning to accept the situation. She walked in carrying the baby in one arm and the post and parcels that Jimmy had left on the table in the other. The solemn look on her face gave them the feeling that she was about to tell them something that they wouldn't want to hear.

'Where's Jimmy?' asked Dave.

Speaking in German, she told them what had happened and then broke down in tears. They didn't understand every word but seemed to get the gist of what she was saying.

Helga stood up, placed the post on the table in front of them and walked out into the cold dark snowy afternoon, leaving Heike to reluctantly translate and confirm what they understood Helga to have said.

None of them could accept that Jimmy had frozen to death alone and so near to the Star Club when they were only a few hundred yards away enjoying themselves.

It was a beautiful, sunny, but cold afternoon on the thirty first of December, as the three remaining Cheaters made their way to the funeral of Adrian and Jimmy at the beautiful St Michaeliskirche.

The white, gold and grey interior of the enormous and magnificent building was almost filled to capacity by every musician in Hamburg, whatever the nationality, including strippers, prostitutes, pimps, waiters and most of the people from clubland in and around St. Pauli. They had collected more than three times the cost of the funeral and the excess was given to the seamen's mission.

Hazelle, Mike, Dave, Reg and Helga sat in the front row. Herr Langstein, Ria, Bruno, Pieter, the waiters and bar staff from the Funny Crow sat in the second row, followed by the Star and Top Ten club managers and staff.

Jimmy's father refused to attend, blaming the Germans for murdering his only son in retribution for the Nazis that he had killed during the War.

An English chaplain from the seamen's mission took the service and after two hymns, *The Lord Is My Shepherd* and *Morning Has Broken,* followed by a short address, Dave rose from his seat.

He climbed slowly up the marble steps beneath the large and ornate apse and, with his head and shoulders bent with grief, looked down at Adrian and Jimmy's coffins standing side by side beneath him in the knave.

On each of the coffins was a single wreath from the prostitutes of St Pauli. Adrian had a wreath in the shape of his bass guitar made up entirely of dark brown and deep red Chrysanthemums while Jimmy's wreath, also in the shape of a guitar, was made up of white and cream flowers to match his Fender Stratocaster.

Dave tried to focus his attention on to the sea of faces in front of him. He cleared his throat and, as tears filled his eyes, he spoke.

'A little over a year ago I had a dream but I needed other people to help me make it come true. Adrian and Jimmy were two of them. Since then we have slept, ate and got drunk. In fact...' He smiled and remembered. 'Like brothers, we did everything together. We tried to make all our dreams come true but perhaps they were only fantasies that deep down we all knew would never become a reality. The road was far from easy but with the premature passing of Adrian and Jimmy it has come to an abrupt end, and much too soon.' He wiped his eyes.

'Maybe we were never meant to grab even the tiniest piece of success, and perhaps the name was what we were truly about, *cheaters*, cheating ourselves into believing that we really had a chance.'

He attempted to dry his eyes, looked around the church and, as he recognised nearly all the solemn faces, in a few seconds he relived the previous year.

He slowly shook his head.

'Although the church is full today, a few days ago, Christmas, a time I always believed to be of love and goodwill to all men, Adrian and Jimmy died *alone*. Is this business really so... shallow?' He paused, swallowed hard and, with a whisper, he added. 'Who knows?'

He lowered his head and walked down the steps. After stopping briefly to look at the coffins, he ran his fingers through the flowers before he re-took his seat between Reg and Mike.

The following day Jimmy and Adrian were both cremated.

Mike, Dave, Reg, Helga and the baby, set out in a small boat from the Altona landing stage with the ashes, which they scattered onto the Elbe.

Hazelle an unwelcome passenger was left alone to drown her sorrows in a drunken stupor in a bar on the quayside.

The next day Mike received a telegram from Jochen. He had been able to get them a deal with a small record company in München. *Summertime* was to be the A side and *The Last Train Blues* the B side, and it was scheduled for release on 15th January 1967.

A few days later Dave arrived at the imbiss, bought himself a coffee, sat at one of the only two tables with chairs, looked out onto the wind ravaged Reeperbahn, and tried to imagine what different thoughts he would be having if Jimmy and Adrian were still alive.

Mike was the next to arrive. He acknowledged Dave, smiled, bought himself a coffee and sat down on the opposite side of the table.

Reg followed close behind but he looked terrible. Mike and Dave looked at him and then immediately glanced at each other. In the daylight, the lumps that had started on his neck had now spread. Rashes and sores now covered his face, which gave him a grotesque appearance. He was grey, gaunt and dreadfully thin.

Dave broke the silence. 'Shall we have something to eat?'

The offer was extremely welcome and he ordered a large plate of kartoffeln salat and frigadellas for each of them, and another drink. Reg finished his plate of food before Mike and Dave had hardly started theirs so Dave tactfully ordered the same again for Reg while he very slowly cleared his own plate.

Reg, his dead eyes hollow and strained, no longer hungry, sat looking at Dave apprehensively,

Dave continued to stir his coffee until Reg, now running out of patience, cleared his throat. After taking a deep breath, he spoke up. 'Dave have you decided what we are going to do?' he asked.

Uncharacteristically, Dave fidgeted in his chair, looked across at Mike and cleared his throat. 'Well, it's obvious we can't play anywhere, we're not a group any more.'

Unable to look at Reg, he looked across the table at Mike before he continued. 'And to be honest, I can't see how we will be able to start again as we are.'

Reg tried to stand but fell back into his chair exhausted. 'I can't believe you said that, I always thought you were a fighter, you've never given up before.' He took a deep breath and continued. 'Surely we can put something together by mid February?'

Dave shook his head. 'I'm sorry Reg but to be honest I'm worried about you, you look like shit.'

'No, I'm getting better, in a few days I'll be all right. I just need another couple of injections and then I'll be fine again,' gushed Reg, trying desperately to reassure the surviving members.

He looked at Mike for support but this time it wasn't forthcoming.

Instead Mike shook his head. 'I'm sorry Reg, I can't wait any longer.' Tears began to well up in his eyes. 'I need to play; I'm forming a new psychedelic group with some of the guys from the Package.'

Reg shook his head wildly and looked across at Dave. 'Did you know that? When did he decide to join them?'

Dave partly ignored the question and nodded. 'Yeah, I knew, and I'm leaving for Berlin in an hour. I've got a job in a new club. Tonia arranged it for me.'

'Tonia? Berlin? In a club? Doing what?' quizzed Reg, suddenly running short of breath.

'Playing records,' replied Dave quietly.

'What, no group?' gasped Reg.

Mike sat looking down at the table.

'No, they won't be booking any more groups, and I get the same money they would pay them.' Dave smiled and continued, 'All of them.'

'You bastard, you sold out. You never could sing, you're a fucking disgrace,' screamed Reg as he slumped back in his seat exhausted. With his mind now in overdrive, he looked down to the floor then out of the window, until he finally pushed himself uneasily up from his chair. 'OK, what about my equipment?'

Dave smiled. 'That's all taken care of, I...'

The anger caused Reg to stutter. 'I b...b... bet it sodding well is, just l... l... like everything else.'

Now that he had told Reg the bad news, Dave appeared to be unaffected by the outburst of anger and he continued. 'The organ, amp and speakers are in the store room at the Kaiser Keller. It's quite safe.'

'That's as maybe, but how am I supposed to move it?' asked Reg.

He stood shaking his head uncontrollably from side to side. He knew he was ill and, as he tried to straighten his body, he started to cough loudly. What frightened him was not his equipment, because he knew that until he could get his hands on enough money to pay for the expensive treatment, he would be in no fit state to play it anyway. 'I can't believe what I'm hearing, everything is conveniently sorted out and I knew nothing about it.'

Dave reached into his pocket, pulled out a bundle of Deutsche marks, counted out one hundred and fifty, and handed them to Reg.

As soon as Reg saw the money he flew into a rage and pushed Dave's hand away.

'I don't need your charity,' he screamed.

Mike knew that Reg had very little money left. 'It's not charity; it's your fare home. Dave can't take you, can he? He told you he's not going home.'

Reg stood looking out of the window and thought about it for a moment. 'All right, if you put it like that.' He reached across the table and begrudgingly took the money from Dave. 'Thanks for nothing.'

Mike smiled and then proudly passed Reg an envelope. 'And this is yours.'

A confused Reg sat down again and opened the envelope. As he pulled out the record he forced a smile, which split one of the many sores on his lips. 'Sod it.'

Mike and Dave looked at each other in disgust as Reg pulled a filthy, bloodstained handkerchief from his overcoat pocket and pressed it against the open sore with his right hand while, with the other hand, he held the record sleeve out in front of him. He sat mesmerised by the coloured photograph of the Cheaters, who, all except Adrian, in his well-rehearsed stance, smiled for the camera.

'Do you realise that when we had that taken none of us knew that it was going to be our last photograph together?' He glared at Dave. 'And we had no bloody idea what was coming next? Did we?'

His first reaction was to leave the record on the table but Dave and Mike both lit a cigarette and as they exhaled the smoke in his direction, he started coughing and urging as he fought for breath. He fingered both pockets of his waistcoat until he found a small dirty piece of neo-epinine and pushed it past the handkerchief and into his mouth. While he waited for the drug to take effect, he stared at the record knowing he would never see Adrian or Jimmy again.

Dave finished his cigarette, got up, and patted Reg patronisingly on the shoulder, paid the bill and left without saying another word. A few minutes later he drove the group van up the Reeperbahn heading towards West Berlin to begin his new life as a disc jockey, with Tonia.

Mike made an excuse and left.

Reg sat with a fixed expression on his face, his interest alternating between the record label and the sleeve, before he finally got up and walked out into the last of the afternoon sun. He knew that in his current condition he had no option but to return to England.

He took the tube to the 'bahnhof but as he walked towards the booking office two men in leather jackets approached him and bundled him into the toilets and forced him into a cubicle. While the punches rained down on him, the German Deutsche marks dropped out of his pocket; his attackers grabbed the money and kicked him several times before leaving him on the wet toilet floor.

As he lay bleeding, he felt no pain. He knew that he was hopelessly trapped in Hamburg and this time he had no way out.

Using his return ticket, he took the underground back to the Reeperbahn and staggered along Herbert Strasse looking for the only person that he knew would help him. His distress compounded even further when he saw that the curtain to Astrid's window was closed but as he turned into David Strasse he saw her walking arm in arm with a young, trendy musician.

He crossed the road and stood directly in front of her. 'Hello Astrid, please help me.'

In sheer disbelief she stared back at him but, after giving him a false smile of hope, spat directly into his face.

The musician pulled back and questioned her under his breath. 'Who the fuck is that?'

Glaring at Reg, she replied in almost perfect English. 'I have no idea my darlink, all the beggars look the same to me?'

She grabbed the musician's arm, pushed past Reg and walked off, laughing loudly.

Reg wiped the tears from his sore eyes and walked to the Kaiser Keller, asked the cleaner for the key to the cupboard, and taking care that no one was watching him removed the gun from inside the organ. He held it tightly in his hand and pretended to shoot into the darkness before pushing it into his overcoat pocket.

He locked the door and left.

Now virtually an outcast, Reg became weaker, almost unrecognisable and ignored by the prostitutes and musicians. Totally destitute and starving, he had no option but to start begging up and down the Reeperbahn. He started around Tal Strasse and David Strasse but as he grew weaker he had no choice but spend most of the night begging for a few pfennigs outside the St Pauli station.

Each morning, as it started to get light, he would make his way across the road to the wasteland and his home amongst the bushes. For the first few days he cried himself to sleep, knowing he had fallen into the world of pathetic drunks, drug addicts and down and outs he had passed with Adrian a few short months earlier. The poison began to spread throughout his body causing him to deteriorate rapidly until, towards the end of January, he found it almost impossible to move. However, he needed to beg long enough each day to collect enough money for a least one bowl of soup and, although it took him nearly two hours to get from his shelter to the tube station, he persevered knowing that his life depended on it.

Chapter twenty-nine

What a Difference a Day Makes

Mike joined a new Psychedelic group and remained in Hamburg until mid February. His experiments with acid meant he was almost permanently on a high or bombed out and, although he would often pass Reg at the underground station, he failed to even recognise him. He soon left Hamburg and returned to England where, within two weeks, he died from a drug overdose, homeless and penniless.

Reg was now alone and during the last few days of the month the weather turned incredibly cold, so cold that the few people who bothered to visit the Reeperbahn left early.

When he had eventually collected enough for a cup of soup he made his way to the nearest imbiss, paid them with a single Deutsche mark, made up of the smallest denominations possible, and after counting every coin, they handed him the soup dregs and a handful of stale bread.

Carrying the paper cup of luke-warm pea and ham soup and the bread, he walked slowly towards the crossing. As he turned his head to cross the wide road Reg noticed the two thugs who had robbed him at the 'bahnhof walking down from the tube station. As soon as they recognised him they ran towards their victim forcing him to drop his most precious, one and only, meal of the day. Punches reigned down on him indiscriminately and when he made a futile attempt to defend himself by raising his arms they smashed the stale crusty bread out of his hands, stamping it into the wet pavement.

Reg was in turmoil. He was starving, he had no more money for food and he had no idea what he could do to defend himself. Subconsciously he reached into his pocket, his quivering fingers felt the gun and his hand tightened around it. He pulled it out and nervously pointed it in their direction. In sheer defiance they jeered and shook their fists at him. Reg squeezed the trigger three times. The tallest attacker fell to the ground, blood pumping on to the pavement, while the other thug grabbed at his distorted shoulder and staggered up the Reeperbahn.

Reg sadistically found himself smiling with satisfaction. He bent down and snatched a handful of notes from the attacker's jacket pocket and, no longer feeling hungry, shuffled off into the dark world that he now knew so well.

Although they had once nearly ruined him, the thugs had now ironically saved his life.

Some of the notes were splattered with blood and he benevolently gave them to his fellow down and outs, to selfishly spread the blame and put the Politzei off his scent.

The remaining money allowed him to buy decent meals but, although he had enough money to keep himself alive, he had no alternative but to continue to beg at St Pauli station. He would sit for hours, periodically lowering his head to avoid recognition from anyone who might remotely know him. And when Klara walked up from the platform below, laughing and joking with her brother, he couldn't help but stare at her.

She looked so beautiful.

He felt a lump in his throat and as the tears rolled down his freezing cheeks, he knew he had made a serious mistake. Out of all his conquests, Klara was the only fraulien he truly loved. She looked in his direction for a split second and then turned to continue her happy animated conversation with her brother.

As soon as she was out of sight he scrambled to his feet and made his way back to his makeshift home where he cried himself to sleep.

A few days later Ronnie and Barry, her bass player, had taken the tube into Monkebergstrasse to buy a few belated Christmas presents for their families in England. Now well into their second month at the Star Club, and since the death of Adrian and Jimmy,

Hamburg was fast losing its glamour and they were all looking forward to returning home at the end of the month.

The two of them climbed the stairs and as they reached the last step, she saw the beggar. She turned to Barry. 'Look at that poor bastard.'

Reaching into her jeans she pulled out a handful of change and dropped it into the jar in front of him.

Barry looked down at him and then back at Ronnie. 'You're such a soft touch. He's probably loaded?'

Ronnie elbowed him in disgust and without looking up Reg thanked her.

'He spoke in English!' she said.

She waited at the top of the stairs while the impatient crowd jostled and pushed past her.

Barry, totally uninterested, preferring to get back to the warm Pacific Hotel, pulled at Ronnie. 'Come on, it's fucking freezing standing round here.'

'I'm telling you he spoke in English,' she said.

'So what?' he replied, lighting a cigarette.

Ronnie noticed the long coloured scarf, bent down and stared into the beggar's face. 'Fucking hell, Reg is that you?'

'Yeah it's me,' he whispered.

She tried to pick him up but the two of them fell onto the freezing pavement.

'Barry can you give me a hand, its Reg - the organist from the Cheaters. We can't leave the poor bastard here to die.'

They picked him up and, while Ronnie waved her arms frantically for a taxi, Barry reluctantly supported Reg against the wall, stared at by every passer-by who pushed past them.

At the Pacific hotel, they put him into the spare bed in Barry's room. Ronnie piled blankets and covers around him and managed to scrounge a hot water bottle from the housekeeper.

'This is our last night and tomorrow we're going home. We can take you back with us if you want?' She knew that Reg couldn't refuse, but she wondered if the next day might be too late.

Reg smiled up at her. 'Thank you,' he whispered.

He closed his eyes and fell asleep.

The next morning, after loading the van, Ronnie and Barry carried Reg down the stairs. The rest of the group refused to let him lay in the front with them and, after a heated argument that nearly came to blows, it was agreed that he could sleep in the back of the van on top of the equipment.

Throughout the journey Ronnie nursed Reg the best way she could and, much to the disgust of the rest of her group, at every stop she patiently fed him.

Two days after leaving Hamburg, on a bright morning winters morning, Reg arrived home.

The ambulance arrived and as they lifted him onto the stretcher, they removed the overcoat and scarf that had been his lifeline during his time in Hamburg.

As the ambulance pulled away Mrs Simms stood shivering on the pavement, watching the flashing light until it disappeared.

She returned to the front room and sat in silence gazing at the filthy overcoat before finally reaching across and snatching it towards her. She put it to her face and smelt it.

Retching violently, she pulled her head away before bending forward and smelling it again and pulling it tight to her confused face. The heavy lines etched deep into her forehead could no longer conceal her distress and disbelief. She felt blindly inside every pocket and much to her surprise found a small photograph of the three of them sitting in front of the Christmas tree, taken a few weeks before Reg left. In the deep inside pockets she discovered several of her most recent letters to him and a letter that he had written to her but failed to post. As she read it, she began to cry.

'Why didn't you post it? I could have helped you.'

Reg did have syphilis and during the weeks of treatment to fight the painful and potentially fatal effects of the debilitating disease, the doctor from the STD (Sexually Transmitted Diseases) Clinic visited him regularly.

'As soon as you have the opportunity, you should contact all of your close friends and tell them about your problem so, as a precaution, they can at least get treatment. You were one of the lucky ones, but if they don't get treatment, who knows what will happen to them.' He picked up Reg's apathy. 'You know who they are don't you? Can you still contact them?' pleaded the Doctor.

Reg flattened his bed sheets and smiled to himself.

'I know who they are, or should I say who she is, but I can't contact her.'

The doctor looked down at him, scratched his chin and moved on to his next patient.

Jenny and her mother stood impatiently with a group of strangers waiting for the ward to open at two o'clock. As soon as the nurse opened the door Jenny rushed excitedly towards the bed while Mrs Simms walked into the ward sister's office to get an update on her son's progress.

Reg looked forward to the daily visits but today even more than usual; it was the day when Jenny brought him the latest Melody Maker. But today, instead of passing the music paper to him, she excitedly whispered into his ear. 'Do you know who I saw this morning?'

Reg looked at her impatiently and waited for her to continue.

'Julie Summers. She's got a baby and guess who the father is?' she gushed with excitement.

Reg, now bored with the guessing games, wanted to get his hands on the papers to catch up on the latest music news, but Jenny was preventing him, although he did want to hear what she had to say next.

'Who?' he mumbled.

'You know him… in fact you used to play with him in a group,' shrieked Jenny excitedly.

Reg wondered who Julie had trapped as the alleged father. 'I've absolutely no idea,' he mused.

'Well try to guess,' teased Jenny.

'How do you expect me to know the answer to that? I've played with loads of people.'

Feigning disinterest, he opened the NME and pretended to read it.

She reached across the paper. 'All right I'll tell you.' She paused, '…well… it's…Tony.'

Reg dropped the paper and lay in the bed looking at her, his bottom jaw touching his chest. He wanted to tell her the truth but held himself back. 'Good for him,' he paused, '…clever girl.'

Surprised at his remark Jenny misunderstood his reply. 'I don't think it's very clever.'

Jenny may as well have not been there as he considered what Julie had done. He knew, as a last resort she had turned to Tony and he had jumped at the opportunity to get close to her; the naïve bastard.

'Oh, there is one more thing. This came from Germany this morning.' Jenny passed him a telegram.

With his face devoid of any feelings, he read it then folded and put it back into the envelope and smiled at his impatient sister.

'It's from Dave, the record's at number five in the German Hit Parade.'

She looked at him, confused. 'Aren't you going to say something? I mean it's what you always wanted.'

He thought for a minute and muttered to himself, 'So fucking what.'

Jenny found it hard to comprehend how her brother had dismissed something that he had dreamed of achieving for as long as she could remember.

He lay in bed pretending to read the papers, switching from one to the other, anxiously waiting for visiting time to come to an end; when he would be alone again and have the opportunity to take in what Jenny had told him about Tony and Julie, and to re-read Dave's unexpected telegram.

After they left, he turned on his transistor radio and pulled the blankets over his head. When the Rolling Stones' 1966 hit record, *The Last Time*, started to play it struck a nerve and when he heard Mick Jagger sing the end of the chorus, he couldn't help but sing it with him. 'Oh no...'

'No way was that going to be the last time,' he mumbled to himself as the record faded.

The End *Or is it?*

Graham Sclater

Top Ten Club Hamburg 1966

Interview with Graham Sclater
by Mike Stax - Ugly Things

1) Please tell me about the band (or bands) you played with in the 60s in Hamburg -- names, years, etc.? Did you make any records back then?

When I first went to Hamburg I played with a local band from my home town, here in Exeter called "The Wave." After about a year I joined a Birmingham band called "The Birds & Bees," two girl singers and a male singer. There were a lot of changes in the line-up but we did "Beat Club" the German equivalent of Top of the Pops.
The next band was a soul band from Manchester aptly called "The Manchester Playboys." We made a single, which was released on Barclay records and we also recorded a lot of the Woolworth's, six track E.P.'s of covers of chart songs. In 1967 we toured Sweden and that's where I jammed with Jimi Hendrix.

2) How much of the book was drawn from actual incidents that happened to you personally or people you knew? If possible please give examples of specific episodes and/or characters.

Everything in the book happened but not necessarily to me. I witnessed or was involved in much of what is in the book but over a longer period of time. The characters are made up of many musicians I knew and played with. I needed to work various events into the story, changing times and places to make it more effective. Artistic license if you like. There were many worse situations and times that I didn't feel I should write about.
Maybe in the next one?

3) As you were a Hammond organ player back then, is the character of Reg based on you to some extent?

Reg and I had similar backgrounds and some of his personality is loosely based on myself, but again, I am an author and therefore I am permitted to alter his thoughts and actions

Star Club Hamburg

4) What other research, other than your personal experiences, did you do for the book? Did you return to Germany and some of the old sites, for example?

Yes, I've returned to Hamburg a number of times, sometimes playing and more recently to research for the novel. I wanted to use the real street names and locations and to experience the whole ambience again. It has changed a great deal, many of our old haunts have disappeared, the Star Club has been demolished and the Top Ten Club is a disused and derelict disco. No doubt it will open again one day, hopefully as a live venue.
The people of Hamburg are fantastic and Hamburg will remain a very special city to me and any musician who has ever lived and played there will almost certainly feel the same.

5) Is *Ticket to Ride* your first novel?

Yes it was. I wrote it whilst working on several projects at the same time. I found it helped to come away and return to it, and of course I was continually editing sections and researching minute detail. In the end I became obsessed with the characters and found it difficult to keep away from my PC

6) So many books and movies today seem to have the same clichéd theme -- "follow your dreams" -- *Ticket to Ride* presents a more pessimistic outlook, almost the opposite in fact -- was that intentional? Was there a particular message that you wanted to deliver with the book?

It was intentional. So many films, plays and books portray the 60's with similar clichéd themes but most are not true to life or how it really was. Considering the number of groups in the mid sixties, probably no more than 1% had any success at all. In fact most groups had no thoughts of making a record, they wanted to play for a living and that was it. Playing in Germany and particularly Hamburg was the answer and only real option.

When I decided to write my novel I wanted it be factual and thought provoking. The idea was to let readers into what it was really like, warts and all and for them to experience how it was and be part of the journey. After all if they bought the book they had bought a ticket to ride, to experience the journey.

So far, judging by the feedback from anyone who has read it, I believe I have succeeded.

It would make a fantastic film, the opposite to "Back Beat," and other 60's music related films if it was not altered too much. But often filmmakers go for the well trodden easy option and end up with the same recycled 60's clichéd material.

Only time will tell

7) The book ends with some of the band members dead -- a pretty high body count that is quite shocking to the reader, because it's so unexpected. Was this a conscious decision for dramatic effect? Was the book tightly plotted from start to finish, or did you just let the characters and circumstances direct the story?

I wanted to dispel the myths that have been written and spoken about this subject - "The 60's." I carefully plotted each chapter of the book leading up to the break up of the group and demise of the musicians to bring the novel to a conclusion and tie up all loose ends.

You must remember it was tough in Hamburg and if you didn't learn fast you didn't make it home. Back then, England seemed a million miles away and at times it was a very lonely existence.

Being a musician and music publisher, I took a lot of time working out each and every chapter heading to fit the content. I use song titles for most things I write, I suppose it's a bit of a trademark.

8) At the end of the book you hint at a sequel. Any plans for this?

I decided to leave the reader guessing with regards to a follow up and the return ticket but there certainly is one although I don't have the time at the moment to write it. As well as producing music, I am working on a screenplay, television series and two more novels. Who knows, I might continue after that.

Graham Sclater 2012

Crash and Burn

A short story by Graham Sclater

When I woke up yesterday for once I felt great with absolutely no idea what the day had in store for me. If you had told me that I was going to be involved in a horrific car crash I would have said that you were crazy.

I'd never had an accident. Well, that's not totally true.

Is scraping the rear bumper considered to be an accident?

It depends who is driving. If it's a woman, then there is no doubt it would serious, but certainly not an accident. I wouldn't consider it serious if it was ever my fault. Thirty years without an accident. Not a bad record is it? When the published figures state, that on average, a driver will have an accident every 12,000 miles.

Well as I said, yesterday, I felt good and there was no indication that anything unusual would happen to me. The sun was shining, for once the music on the radio was good and I felt fine. But, by the time I reached the M5 things suddenly changed. The sun disappeared behind the blackest cloud and, before I knew it, the rain on the motorway was running like a river. Cars appeared from nowhere and skidded everywhere. The lane markings meant nothing and as a lorry and its trailer slewed across the three lanes I knew that it was time to worry.

Of course it was too late, it always is. Before I knew it, I was trapped, under the rear axle between the huge smoking tyres of the trailer and fighting for breath amongst a tangled mess of wrecked automobiles that would never be driven again.

The rain poured through the huge tear in the flattened car roof, ripped open like a tin, and the biting easterly wind forced the freezing spray and smoke into my face. There was an eerie silence for what seemed like hours of darkness until I heard the combination of moans and screams of helplessness from the drivers of some of the other cars, although the sudden and frequent moments of silence were much worse. I felt cold and numb until I became aware of the blood dripping onto my face before turning into a steady warm stream as it continued its journey down my chest and onto my shirt and neatly pressed suit trousers.

I waited patiently, there was nothing else I could do and after the paramedics loaded me onto the stretcher, I watched the ambulance pull away and race along the motorway, siren screaming, until it was out of sight.

That was yesterday.

Due for publication spring 2013

Too big to cry

by

Graham Sclater

Too Big to Cry

It is spring 2010 and over the past twelve months companies that had previously been extremely profitable succumbed to the recession that was spreading rampantly throughout the British Isles like some kind of uncontrollable disease or virus.

No area of business was safe.

Despite the deepening recession, Brian and Sylvia Chapman battled against the odds to keep their dream alive, to stay in business. Following major cash flow problems, the company's bankers decided to withdraw their financial support as they had done with so many companies during this period.

The liquidation of the company and the ensuing problems faced by them and their family, from employees, creditors, the Receivers, and the banks - in fact, from everyone - leads to a devastating and harrowing period resulting in disastrous consequences.

£

HATRED
IS THE
KEY

Graham Sclater

The early 1800's were a difficult time for England, already at war with France. The financial strain was further increased when it entered into a war with America.

The war of 1812, sometimes referred to as "the Second War of Independence" was fought between the United States and Great Britain from 1812 to 1814.

English ships instituted extensive maritime barricades of European ports to prevent American ships helping the French. The resulting seizure of American merchant shipping quickly brought demands for retaliation from the United States.

On June 18, 1812, the United States declared war on Great Britain. Almost immediately they called for an invasion of Canada. The initial   American successes turned to a number of defeats resulting in English ships effectively blockading the American coastline and subjecting it to a series of hit and run raids and the capture of numerous ships.

In 1814 with France collapsing, Great Britain launched a number of major attacks on American cities, resulting in the burning of the White House and other public buildings. With America facing bankruptcy morale was extremely low.

The majority of the crew captured from the American ships were transported to Plymouth in south west England to spend their time in the notorious Dartmoor depot, a prison constructed primarily to house three thousand French prisoners-of-war, which was soon filled with 10,000 Americans. The early 1800's was a difficult time for England. Already at war with France and Napoleon Bonaparte, the financial strain was further increased when it entered into a war with America. The War of 1812 sometimes referred to as "the Second War of Independence" was fought between the United States and Great Britain from 1812 to 1814.

The English instituted extensive maritime barricades of European ports to prevent American ships helping the French. The resulting seizures of American merchant shipping quickly brought demands for retaliation from the United States.

On June 18, 1812, the United States declared war on Great Britain. Almost immediately they called for an invasion of Canada. The initial American successes turned to a number of defeats resulting in English ships effectively blockading the American coastline and subjecting it to a series of hit and run raids and the capture of numerous ships.

In 1814 with France collapsing, Great Britain launched a number of major attacks on American cities, resulting in the burning of the White House and other public buildings. With America facing bankruptcy, morale was extremely low.

The majority of the crew captured from the American ships were transported to Plymouth in southwest England to spend their time in notorious Dartmoor prison, constructed primarily by French prisoners of War to house them and their countrymen. However, the rich French aristocracy were fortunate. Their money allowed the bribery of prison officers and paid for lodgings away from the prison in what could be considered to be luxurious accommodation with the local gentry and farms as far away as Plymouth and Tavistock.

Despite the signing of the Treaty of Ghent on 24 December 1914, several thousand American prisoners remained under lock and key in Dartmoor prison undergoing continued humiliation, near starvation and death in the cramped freezing conditions. The prison was infested with "creepers," as many as 1000 to every prisoner, and the severe overcrowding resulted in many of the prisoners sleeping uncomfortably on the roof trusses of the chapel roof.

The only respite was the opportunity for the prisoners to carve and sculptor animal bones and barter (at the barter gate) with the farmers for fresh local vegetables and produce. Uniquely, to Dartmoor prison, a daily market was eventually set up inside the prison, where the local people sold their fresh produce to the prisoners.

Despite the end of the war neither country could agree on who was responsible for repatriating the prisoners so they remained in jail. In April 1814 a drunken prison officer ordered a wanton and brutal massacre, the officers firing in all directions, on as many as 5000 prisoners in the yard, resulting in the death, it is alleged, of several hundred American seamen, although conflicting reports suggest the figure to be nearer seven deaths and numerous woundings.

The following day it was agreed to release all American prisoners and several years later a monument was erected for the dead prisoners who had been buried in unmarked graves on the moor outside of the prison walls.

Dartmoor Prison is still in use today for all to see.

$

We're gonna be famous

Young sisters Hannah and Abi are faced with a dilemma that would not be wished on anyone.

How do they help their seriously ill mother who is in desperate need of life saving and expensive treatment in America when all they have is their pocket money?

Perhaps their love of music will help them but can they do anything in time?

'I cried several times while I was reading this book... sometimes with happiness.'

'A feel-good story that will make everyone smile.'

Printed in Great Britain
by Amazon

78923502R00193